VINTAGE
INTERNATIONAL

ALSO BY JAMES JOYCE

Chamber Music

A Portrait of the Artist as a Young Man

Exiles

Ulysses

Pomes Penyeach

Finnegans Wake

Stephen Hero

DUBLINERS

JAMES JOYCE

Dubliners

EDITED BY

Hans Walter Gabler WITH *Walter Hettche*

Vintage International
Vintage Books
A Division of Random House, Inc.
New York

FIRST VINTAGE INTERNATIONAL EDITION, FEBRUARY 1993

Published in the United States by Vintage Books,
a division of Random House, Inc., New York,
and simultaneously in Canada by Random House
of Canada Limited, Toronto.

Library of Congress Cataloging-in-Publication Data
Joyce, James, 1882–1941.
Dubliners / James Joyce. — 1st Vintage international ed.
p. cm.
Includes bibliographical references (p.)
ISBN 0-679-73990-4 (pbk.)
1. Dublin (Ireland)—Fiction. I. Title.
PR6019.09D8 1992b
823'.912—dc20 91-50714
CIP

BOOK DESIGN BY CATHRYN S. AISON

Electronically typeset by Wolfhard Steppe for pagina GmbH, Tübingen
Printed and bound in the United States of America
79B8

CONTENTS

Dubliners

CONTENTS

DUBLINERS

The Sisters

There was no hope for him this time: it was the third stroke. Night after night I had passed the house (it was vacation time) and studied the lighted square of window: and night after night I had found it lighted in the same way, faintly and evenly. If he was dead, I thought, I would see the reflection of candles on the darkened blind for I knew that two candles must be set at the head of a corpse. He had often said to me: *I am not long for this world*, and I had thought his words idle. Now I knew they were true. Every night as I gazed up at the window I said softly to myself the word *paralysis*. It had always sounded strangely in my ears like the word *gnomon* in the Euclid and the word *simony* in the catechism. But now it sounded to me like the name of some maleficent and sinful being. It filled me with fear and yet I longed to be nearer to it and to look upon its deadly work.

Old Cotter was sitting at the fire, smoking, when I came downstairs to supper. While my aunt was ladling out my stirabout he said as if returning to some former remark of his:

—No, I wouldn't say he was exactly ...... but there was something queer ..... there was something uncanny about him. I'll tell you my opinion. ...

He began to puff at his pipe, no doubt arranging his opinion in his mind. Tiresome old fool! When we knew him first he used to be rather interesting, talking of faints and worms; but I soon grew tired of him and his endless stories about the distillery.

—I have my own theory about it, he said. I think it was one of those ... peculiar cases. ... But it's hard to say. ...

He began to puff again at his pipe without giving us his theory. My uncle saw me staring and said to me:

—Well, so your old friend is gone, you'll be sorry to hear.

—Who? said I.

—Father Flynn.

—Is he dead?

—Mr Cotter here has just told us. He was passing by the house.

I knew that I was under observation so I continued eating as if the news had not interested me. My uncle explained to old Cotter:

—The youngster and he were great friends. The old chap taught him a great deal, mind you; and they say he had a great wish for him.

—God have mercy on his soul, said my aunt piously.

Old Cotter looked at me for a while. I felt that his little beady black eyes were examining me but I would not satisfy him by looking up from my plate. He returned to his pipe and finally spat rudely into the grate.

—I wouldn't like children of mine, he said, to have too much to say to a man like that.

—How do you mean, Mr Cotter? asked my aunt.

—What I mean is, said old Cotter, it's bad for children. My idea is: let a young lad run about and play with young lads of his own age and not be. ... Am I right, Jack?

—That's my principle too, said my uncle. Let him learn to box his corner. That's what I'm always saying to that rosicrucian there: take exercise. Why, when I was a nipper every morning of my life I had a cold bath, winter and summer. And that's what stands to me now. Education is all very fine and large. .... Mr Cotter might take a pick of that leg of mutton, he added to my aunt.

—No, no, not for me, said old Cotter.

My aunt brought the dish from the safe and laid it on the table.

—But why do you think it's not good for children, Mr Cotter? she asked.

—It's bad for children, said old Cotter, because their minds are so impressionable. When children see things like that, you know, it has an effect. .....

I crammed my mouth with stirabout for fear I might give utterance to my anger. Tiresome old rednosed imbecile!

It was late when I fell asleep. Though I was angry with old Cotter for alluding to me as a child I puzzled my head to extract meaning from his unfinished sentences. In the dark of my room I imagined that I saw again the heavy grey face of the paralytic. I drew the blankets over my head and tried to think of Christmas. But the grey face still followed me. It murmured and I understood that it desired to confess something. I felt my soul receding into some pleasant and vicious region and there again I found it waiting for me. It began to confess to me in a murmuring voice and I wondered why it smiled continually and why the lips were so moist with spittle. But then I remembered that it had died of paralysis and I felt that I too was smiling feebly as if to absolve the simoniac of his sin.

The next morning after breakfast I went down to look at the little house in Great Britain Street. It was an unassuming shop, registered under the vague name of *Drapery*. The drapery consisted mainly of children's bootees and umbrellas and on ordinary days a notice used to hang in the window, saying *Umbrellas Recovered*. No notice was visible now for the shutters were up. A crape bouquet was tied to the doorknocker with ribbon. Two poor women and a telegram boy were reading the card pinned on the crape. I also approached and read:

July 1st 1895
The Rev. James Flynn (formerly of S. Catherine's
Church, Meath Street) aged sixty-five years.
R. I. P.

The reading of the card persuaded me that he was dead and I was disturbed to find myself at check. Had he not been dead I would have gone into the little dark room behind the shop to find him sitting in his armchair by the fire, nearly smothered in his greatcoat. Perhaps my aunt would have given me a packet of high toast for him and this present would have roused him from his stupefied doze. It was always I who emptied the packet into his black snuffbox for his hands trembled too much to allow him to do this without spilling half the snuff about the floor. Even as he raised his large trembling hand to his nose little clouds of smoke dribbled through his fingers over the front of his coat. It may have been these constant showers of snuff which gave his ancient priestly garments their green faded look for the red handkerchief, blackened as it always was with the snuffstains of a week, with which he tried to brush away the fallen grains was quite inefficacious.

I wished to go in and look at him but I had not the courage to knock. I walked away slowly along the sunny side of the street, reading all the theatrical advertisements in the shopwindows as I went. I found it strange that neither I nor the day seemed in a mourning mood and I felt even annoyed at discovering in myself a sensation of freedom as if I had been freed from something by his death. I wondered at this for, as my uncle had said the night before, he had taught me a great deal. He had studied in the Irish college in Rome and he had taught me to pronounce Latin properly. He had told me stories about the catacombs and about Napoleon Bonaparte and he had explained to me the meaning of the different ceremonies of the mass and of the different vestments worn by the priest. Sometimes he had amused himself by putting difficult questions to me, asking me what one should do in certain circumstances or whether such and such sins were mortal or venial or only imperfections. His questions showed me how complex and mysterious were certain institutions of the church which I had always regarded as the simplest acts. The duties of the priest towards the eucharist and towards the secrecy of the confessional seemed so grave to me that I wondered how anybody had ever found in himself the courage to undertake them: and I was not surprised when he told me that the fathers of the church had written books as thick as the post office directory and as closely printed as the law notices in the newspaper elucidating all these intricate questions. Often when I thought of this I could make no answer or only a very foolish and halting one upon which he used to smile and nod his head twice or thrice. Sometimes he used to put me through the responses of the mass which he had made me learn by heart: and as I pattered he used to smile pensively and nod his head, now and then pushing huge pinches of snuff up each nostril alternately. When he smiled he used to uncover his big discoloured teeth and let his tongue lie upon his lower lip—a habit which had made me feel uneasy in the beginning of our acquaintance before I knew him well.

As I walked along in the sun I remembered old Cotter's words and tried to remember what had happened afterwards in the dream. I remembered that I had noticed long velvet curtains and a swinging lamp of antique fashion. I felt that I had been very far away, in some land where the customs were strange, in Persia, I thought. ...... But I could not remember the end of the dream.

In the evening my aunt took me with her to visit the house of mourning. It was after sunset but the window panes of the houses that looked to the west reflected the tawny gold of a great bank of clouds. Nannie received us in the hall and, as it would have been unseemly to have shouted at her, my aunt shook hands with her for all. The old woman pointed upwards interrogatively and, on my aunt's nodding, proceeded to toil up the narrow staircase before us, her bowed head being scarcely above the level of the banister rail. At the first landing she stopped and beckoned us forward encouragingly towards the open door of the deadroom. My aunt went in and the old woman, seeing that I hesitated to enter, began to beckon to me again repeatedly with her hand.

I went in on tiptoe. The room through the lace end of the blind was suffused with dusky golden light amid which the candles looked like pale thin flames. He had been coffined. Nannie gave the lead and we three knelt down at the foot of the bed. I pretended to pray but I could not gather my thoughts because the old woman's mutterings distracted me. I noticed how clumsily her skirt was hooked at the back and how the heels of her cloth boots were trodden down all to one side. The fancy came to me that the old priest was smiling as he lay there in his coffin.

But no. When we rose and went up to the head of the bed I saw that he was not smiling. There he lay, solemn and copious, vested as for the altar, his large hands loosely retaining a chalice. His face was very truculent, grey and massive, with black cavernous nostrils and circled by a scanty white fur. There was a heavy odour in the room, the flowers.

We blessed ourselves and came away. In the little room downstairs we found Eliza seated in his armchair in state. I groped my way towards my usual chair in the corner while Nannie went to the sideboard and brought out a decanter of sherry and some wineglasses. She set these on the table and invited us to take a little glass of wine. Then, at her sister's bidding, she poured out the sherry into the glasses and passed them to us. She pressed me to take some cream crackers also but I declined because I thought I would make too much noise eating them. She seemed to be somewhat disappointed at my refusal and went over quietly to the sofa where she sat down behind her sister. No-one spoke: we all gazed at the empty fireplace.

My aunt waited until Eliza sighed and then said:

—Ah, well, he's gone to a better world.

Eliza sighed again and bowed her head in assent. My aunt fingered the stem of her wineglass before sipping a little.

—Did he ..... peacefully? she asked.

—O, quite peacefully, ma'am, said Eliza. You couldn't tell when the breath went out of him. He had a beautiful death, God be praised.

—And everything ....?

—Father O'Rourke was in with him a-Tuesday and anointed him and prepared him and all.

—He knew then?

—He was quite resigned.

—He looks quite resigned, said my aunt.

—That's what the woman we had in to wash him said. She said he just looked as if he was asleep, he looked that peaceful and resigned. No-one would think he'd make such a beautiful corpse.

—Yes, indeed, said my aunt.

She sipped a little more from her glass and said:

—Well, Miss Flynn, at any rate it must be a great comfort for you to know that you did all you could for him. You were both very kind to him, I must say.

Eliza smoothed her dress over her knees.

—Ah, poor James! she said. God knows we done all we could as poor as we are. We wouldn't see him want anything while he was in it.

Nannie had leaned her head against the sofa pillow and seemed about to fall asleep.

—There's poor Nannie, said Eliza looking at her, she's wore out. All the work we had, she and me, getting in the woman to wash him and then laying him out and then the coffin and then arranging about the mass in the chapel! Only for Father O'Rourke I don't know what we'd have done at all. It was him brought us all them flowers and them two candlesticks out of the chapel and wrote out the notice for the *Freeman's General* and took charge of all the papers for the cemetery and poor James's insurance.

—Wasn't that good of him? said my aunt.

Eliza closed her eyes and shook her head slowly.

—Ah, there's no friends like the old friends, she said, when all is said and done, no friends that a body can trust.

—Indeed, that's true, said my aunt. And I'm sure now that he's gone to his eternal reward he won't forget you and all your kindness to him.

—Ah, poor James! said Eliza. He was no great trouble to us. You wouldn't hear him in the house any more than now. Still, I know he's gone and all that. ....

—It's when it's all over that you'll miss him, said my aunt.

—I know that, said Eliza. I won't be bringing him in his cup of beeftea any more nor you, ma'am, sending him his snuff. Ah, poor James!

She stopped, as if she were communing with the past, and then said shrewdly:

—Mind you, I noticed there was something queer coming over him latterly. Whenever I'd bring in his soup to him there I'd find him with his breviary fallen on the floor, lying back in the chair and his mouth open.

She laid a finger against her nose and frowned: then she continued:

—But still and all he kept on saying that before the summer was over he'd go out for a drive one fine day just to see the old house again where we were all born down in Irishtown and take me and Nannie with him. If we could only get one of them newfangled carriages that makes no noise that Father O'Rourke told him about—them with the rheumatic wheels—for the day cheap, he said, at Johnny Rush's over the way there and drive out the three of us together of a Sunday evening. He had his mind set on that. ... Poor James!

—The Lord have mercy on his soul! said my aunt.

Eliza took out her handkerchief and wiped her eyes with it. Then she put it back again in her pocket and gazed into the empty grate for some time without speaking.

—He was too scrupulous always, she said. The duties of the

priesthood was too much for him. And then his life was, you might say, crossed.

—Yes, said my aunt, he was a disappointed man. You could see that.

A silence took possession of the little room and under cover of it I approached the table and tasted my sherry and then returned quietly to my chair in the corner. Eliza seemed to have fallen into a deep revery. We waited respectfully for her to break the silence: and after a long pause she said slowly:

—It was that chalice he broke. ... That was what was the beginning of it. Of course, they say it was all right, that it contained nothing, I mean. But still .... They say it was the boy's fault. But poor James was so nervous, God be merciful to him!

—And was that it? said my aunt. I heard something. ....

Eliza nodded.

—That affected his mind, she said. After that he began to mope by himself, talking to no-one and wandering about by himself. So one night he was wanted for to go on a call and they couldn't find him anywhere. They looked high up and low down and still they couldn't see a sight of him anywhere. So then the clerk suggested to try the chapel. So then they got the keys and opened the chapel and the clerk and Father O'Rourke and another priest that was there brought in a light for to look for him. .... And what do you think but there he was, sitting up by himself in the dark in his confession box, wideawake and laughing-like softly to himself?

She stopped suddenly as if to listen. I too listened but there was no sound in the house and I knew that the old priest was lying still in his coffin as we had seen him, solemn and truculent in death, an idle chalice on his breast.

Eliza resumed:

—Wideawake and laughing-like to himself. ... So then of course when they saw that that made them think that there was something gone wrong with him. ....

An Encounter

It was Joe Dillon who introduced the wild west to us. He had a little library made up of old numbers of *The Union Jack*, *Pluck* and *The Halfpenny Marvel*. Every evening after school we met in his back garden and arranged Indian battles. He and his fat young brother Leo, the idler, held the loft of the stable while we tried to carry it by storm; or we fought a pitched battle on the grass. But, however well we fought, we never won siege or battle and all our bouts ended with Joe Dillon's wardance of victory. His parents went to eight-o'clock mass every morning in Gardiner Street and the peaceful odour of Mrs Dillon was prevalent in the hall of the house. But he played too fiercely for us who were younger and more timid. He looked like some kind of an Indian when he capered round the garden, an old teacosy on his head, beating a tin with his fist and yelling:

—Ya! Yaka, yaka, yaka!

Everyone was incredulous when it was reported that he had a vocation for the priesthood. Nevertheless it was true.

A spirit of unruliness diffused itself among us and, under its influence, differences of culture and constitution were waived. We banded ourselves together, some boldly, some in jest and some almost in fear: and of the number of these latter, the reluctant Indians who were afraid to seem studious or lacking in robustness, I was one. The adventures related in the literature of the wild west were remote from my nature but, at least, they opened doors of escape. I liked better some American detective stories which were traversed from time to time by unkempt fierce and beautiful girls. Though there was nothing wrong in these stories and though their intention was sometimes literary they were circulated secretly at school. One day when Father Butler was hearing the four pages of Roman history clumsy Leo Dillon was discovered with a copy of *The Halfpenny Marvel*.

—This page or this page? This page? Now, Dillon, up! *Hardly had the day* .... Go on! What day? *Hardly had the day dawned* ..... Have you studied it? What have you there in your pocket?

Everyone's heart palpitated as Leo Dillon handed up the paper and everyone assumed an innocent face. Father Butler turned over the pages, frowning.

—What is this rubbish? he said. *The Apache Chief!* Is this what you read instead of studying your Roman history? Let me not find any more of this wretched stuff in this college. The man who wrote it, I suppose, was some wretched scribbler that writes these things for a drink. I'm surprised at boys like you, educated, reading such stuff. I could understand it if you were ..... national school boys. Now, Dillon, I advise you strongly, get at your work or .....

This rebuke during the sober hours of school paled much of the glory of the wild west for me and the confused puffy face of Leo Dillon awakened one of my consciences. But when the restraining influence of the school was at a distance I began to hunger again for wild sensations, for the escape which those chronicles of disorder alone seemed to offer me. The mimic warfare of the evening became at last as wearisome to me as the routine of school in the morning because I wanted real adventures to happen to myself. But real adventures, I reflected, do not happen to people who remain at home: they must be sought abroad.

The summer holidays were near at hand when I made up my mind to break out of the weariness of school life for one day at least. With Leo Dillon and a boy named Mahony I planned a day's miching. Each of us saved up sixpence. We were to meet at ten in the morning on the canal bridge. Mahony's big sister was to write an excuse for him and Leo Dillon was to tell his brother to say he was sick. We arranged to go along the Wharf Road until we came to the ships, then to cross in the ferryboat and walk out to see the Pigeon House. Leo Dillon was afraid we might meet Father Butler or someone out of the college, but Mahony asked, very sensibly, what would Father Butler be doing out at the Pigeon House. We were reassured: and I brought the first stage of the plot to an end by collecting sixpence from the other two, at the same time showing them my own sixpence. When we were making the last arrangements on the eve we were all vaguely excited. We shook hands, laughing, and Mahony said:

—Till tomorrow, mates!

That night I slept badly. In the morning I was firstcomer to the bridge as I lived nearest. I hid my books in the long grass near the ashpit at the end of the garden where nobody ever came and hurried along the canal bank. It was a mild sunny morning in the first week of June. I sat up on the coping of the bridge admiring my frail canvas shoes which I had diligently pipeclayed overnight and watching the docile horses pulling a tramload of business people up the hill. All the branches of the tall trees which lined the mall were gay with little light green leaves and the sunlight slanted through them on to the water. The granite stone of the bridge was beginning to be warm and I began to pat it with my hands in time to an air in my head. I was very happy.

When I had been sitting there for five or ten minutes I saw Mahony's grey suit approaching. He came up the hill, smiling, and clambered up beside me on the bridge. While we were waiting he brought out the catapult which bulged from his inner pocket and explained some improvements which he had made in it. I asked him why he had brought it and he told me he had brought it to have some gas with the birds. Mahony used slang freely and spoke of Father Butler as Bunsen Burner. We waited on for a quarter of an hour more but still there was no sign of Leo Dillon. Mahony, at last, jumped down and said:

—Come along. I knew Fatty'd funk it.

—And his sixpence ...? I said.

—That's forfeit, said Mahony. And so much the better for us –a bob and a tanner instead of a bob.

We walked along the North Strand Road till we came to the vitriol works and then turned to the right along the Wharf Road. Mahony began to play the Indian as soon as we were out of public sight. He chased a crowd of ragged girls, brandishing his unloaded catapult and, when two ragged boys began, out of chivalry, to fling stones at us, he proposed that we should charge them. I objected that the boys were too small and so we walked on, the ragged troop screaming after us *Swaddlers! Swaddlers!*, thinking that we were protestants because Mahony, who was dark complexioned, wore the silver badge of a cricket club in his cap. When we came to the Smoothing Iron we arranged a siege but it was a failure because you must have at least three. We revenged ourselves on Leo Dillon by saying what a funk he was and guessing how many he would get at three o'clock from Mr Ryan.

We came then near the river. We spent a long time walking about the noisy streets flanked by high stone walls, watching the working of cranes and engines and often being shouted at for our immobility by the drivers of groaning carts. It was noon when we reached the quays and, as all the labourers seemed to be eating their lunches, we bought two big currant buns and sat down to eat them on some metal piping beside the river. We pleased ourselves with the spectacle of Dublin's commerce—the barges signalled from far away by their curls of woolly smoke, the brown fishing fleet beyond Ringsend, the big white sailing-vessel which was being discharged on the opposite quay. Mahony said it would be right skit to run away to sea on one of those big ships and even I, looking at the high masts, saw or imagined the geography which had been scantily dosed to me at school gradually taking substance under my eyes. School and home seemed to recede from us and their influences upon us seemed to wane.

We crossed the Liffey in the ferryboat, paying our toll to be transported in the company of two labourers and a little Jew with a bag. We were serious to the point of solemnity but once during the short voyage our eyes met and we laughed. When we landed we watched the discharging of the graceful three-master which we had observed from the other quay. Some bystander said that she was a Norwegian vessel. I went to the stern and tried to decipher the legend upon it but, failing to do so, I came back and examined the foreign sailors to see had any of them green eyes for I had some confused notion .... The sailors' eyes were blue and grey and even black. The only sailor whose eyes could have been called green was a tall man who amused the crowd on the quay by calling out cheerfully every time the planks fell:

—All right! All right!

When we were tired of this sight we wandered slowly into Ringsend. The day had grown sultry and in the windows of the grocers' shops musty biscuits lay bleaching. We bought some biscuits and chocolate which we ate sedulously as we wandered through the squalid streets where the families of the fishermen live. We could find no dairy and so we went into a huckster's shop and bought a bottle of raspberry lemonade each. Refreshed by this Mahony chased a cat down a lane but the cat escaped into a wide field. We both felt rather tired and when we reached the field we made at once for a sloping bank over the ridge of which we could see the Dodder.

It was too late and we were too tired to carry out our project of visiting the Pigeon House. We had to be home before four o'clock lest our adventure should be discovered. Mahony looked regretfully at his catapult and I had to suggest going home by train before he regained any cheerfulness. The sun went in behind some clouds and left us to our jaded thoughts and the crumbs of our provisions.

There was nobody but ourselves in the field. When we had lain on the bank for some time without speaking I saw a man approaching from the far end of the field. I watched him lazily as I chewed one of those green stems on which girls tell fortunes. He came along by the bank slowly. He walked with one hand upon his hip and in the other hand he held a stick with which he tapped the turf lightly. He was shabbily dressed in a suit of greenish black and wore what we used to call a jerry hat with a very high crown. He seemed to be fairly old for his moustache was ashen grey. When he passed at our feet he glanced up at us quickly and then continued his way. We followed him with our eyes and saw that when he had gone on for perhaps fifty paces he turned about and began to retrace his steps. He walked towards us very slowly, always tapping the ground with his stick, so slowly that I thought he was looking for something in the grass.

He stopped when he came level with us and bade us good day. We answered him and he sat down beside us on the slope slowly and with great care. He began to talk of the weather, saying that it would be a very hot summer and adding that the seasons had changed greatly since he was a boy—a long time ago. He said that the happiest time of one's life was undoubtedly one's schoolboy days and that he would give anything to be young again. While he expressed these sentiments, which bored us a little, we kept silent. Then he began to talk of school and of books. He asked us whether we had read the poetry of Thomas Moore or the works of Sir Walter Scott and Lord Lytton. I pretended that I had read every book he mentioned so that in the end he said:

—Ah, I can see you are a bookworm like myself. Now, he added, pointing to Mahony who was regarding us with open eyes, he is different. He goes in for games.

He said he had all Sir Walter Scott's works and all Lord

Lytton's works at home and never tired of reading them. Of course, he said, there were some of Lord Lytton's works which boys couldn't read. Mahony asked why couldn't boys read them–a question which agitated and pained me because I was afraid the man would think I was as stupid as Mahony. The man, however, only smiled. I saw that he had great gaps in his mouth between his yellow teeth. Then he asked us which of us had the most sweethearts. Mahony mentioned lightly that he had three totties. The man asked me how many had I. I answered that I had none. He did not believe me and said he was sure I must have one. I was silent.

—Tell us, said Mahony pertly to the man, how many have you yourself?

The man smiled as before and said that when he was our age he had lots of sweethearts. Every boy, he said, has a little sweetheart.

His attitude on this point struck me as strangely liberal in a man of his age. In my heart I thought that what he said about boys and sweethearts was reasonable. But I disliked the words in his mouth and I wondered why he shivered once or twice as if he feared something or felt a sudden chill. As he proceeded I noticed that his accent was good. He began to speak to us about girls, saying what nice soft hair they had and how soft their hands were and how all girls were not so good as they seemed to be if one only knew. There was nothing he liked, he said, so much as looking at a nice young girl, at her nice white hands and her beautiful soft hair. He gave me the impression that he was repeating something which he had learned by heart or that, magnetised by some words of his own speech, his mind was slowly circling round and round in the same orbit. At times he spoke as if he were simply alluding to some fact that everybody knew and at times he lowered his voice and spoke mysteriously as if he were telling us something secret which he did not wish others to overhear. He repeated his phrases over and over again, varying them and surrounding them with his monotonous voice. I continued to gaze towards the foot of the slope, listening to him.

After a long while his monologue paused. He stood up slowly, saying that he had to leave us for a minute or so, a few minutes, and, without changing the direction of my gaze, I saw him walking slowly away from us towards the near end of the field. We remained silent when he had gone. After a silence of a few minutes I heard Mahony exclaim:

—I say! Look what he's doing!

As I neither answered nor raised my eyes Mahony exclaimed again:

—I say ..... He's a queer old josser!

—In case he asks us for our names, I said, let you be Murphy and I'll be Smith.

We said nothing further to each other. I was still considering whether I would go away or not when the man came back and sat down beside us again. Hardly had he sat down when Mahony, catching sight of the cat which had escaped him, sprang up and pursued her across the field. The man and I watched the chase. The cat escaped once more and Mahony began to throw stones at the wall she had escaladed. Desisting from this, he began to wander about the far end of the field, aimlessly.

After an interval the man spoke to me. He said that my friend was a very rough boy and asked did he get whipped often at school. I was going to reply indignantly that we were not national school boys to be *whipped*, as he called it; but I remained silent. He began to speak on the subject of chastising boys. His mind, as if magnetised again by his speech, seemed to circle slowly round and round its new centre. He said that when boys were that kind they ought to be whipped and well whipped. When a boy was rough and unruly there was nothing would do him any good but a good sound whipping. A slap on the hand or a box on the ear was no good: what he wanted was to get a nice warm whipping. I was surprised at this sentiment and involuntarily glanced up at his face. As I did so I met the gaze of a pair of bottlegreen eyes peering at me from under a twitching forehead. I turned my eyes away again.

The man continued his monologue. He seemed to have forgotten his recent liberalism. He said that if ever he found a boy talking to girls or having a girl for a sweetheart he would whip him and whip him: and that would teach him not to be talking to girls. And if a boy had a girl for a sweetheart and told lies about it then he would give him such a whipping as no boy ever got in this world. He said that there was nothing in this world he would like so well as that. He described to me how he would whip such a boy as if he were unfolding some elaborate mystery. He would love that, he said, better than anything in this world: and his voice, as he led me monotonously through the mystery, grew almost affectionate and seemed to plead with me that I should understand him.

I waited till his monologue paused again. Then I stood up abruptly. Lest I should betray my agitation I delayed a few moments pretending to fix my shoe properly and then, saying that I was obliged to go, I bade him good day. I went up the slope calmly but my heart was beating quickly with fear that he would seize me by the ankles. When I reached the top of the slope I turned round and, without looking at him, called loudly across the field:

—Murphy!

My voice had an accent of forced bravery in it and I was ashamed of my paltry stratagem. I had to call the name again before Mahony saw me and hallooed in answer. How my heart beat as he came running across the field to me! He ran as if to bring me aid. And I was penitent for in my heart I had always despised him a little.

Araby

North Richmond Street, being blind, was a quiet street except at the hour when the Christian Brothers' School set the boys free. An uninhabited house of two storeys stood at the blind end, detached from its neighbours in a square ground. The other houses of the street, conscious of decent lives within them, gazed at one another with brown imperturbable faces.

The former tenant of our house, a priest, had died in the back drawingroom. Air, musty from having been long enclosed, hung in all the rooms and the waste room behind the kitchen was littered with old useless papers. Among these I found a few papercovered books, the pages of which were curled and damp: *The Abbot* by Walter Scott, *The Devout Communicant* and *The Memoirs of Vidocq*. I liked the last best because its leaves were yellow. The wild garden behind the house contained a central apple tree and a few straggling bushes under one of which I found the late tenant's rusty bicycle pump. He had been a very charitable priest; in his will he had left all his money to institutions and the furniture of his house to his sister.

When the short days of winter came dusk fell before we had well eaten our dinners. When we met in the street the houses had grown sombre. The space of sky above us was the colour of everchanging violet and towards it the lamps of the street lifted their feeble lanterns. The cold air stung us and we played till our bodies glowed. Our shouts echoed in the silent street. The career of our play brought us through the dark muddy lanes behind the houses where we ran the gantlet of the rough tribes from the cottages, to the back doors of the dark dripping gardens where odours arose from the ashpits, to the dark odorous stables where a coachman smoothed and combed the horse or shook music from the buckled harness. When we returned to the street light from the kitchen windows had filled the areas. If my uncle was seen turning the corner we hid in the shadow until we had seen him safely housed. Or if Mangan's sister came out on the doorstep to call her brother in to his tea we watched her from our shadow peer up and down the street. We waited to see whether she would remain or go in and if she remained we left our shadow and walked up to Mangan's steps resignedly. She was waiting for us, her figure defined by the light from the half-opened door. Her brother always teased her before he obeyed and I stood by the railings looking at her. Her dress swung as she moved her body and the soft rope of her hair tossed from side to side.

Every morning I lay on the floor in the front parlour watching her door. The blind was pulled down to within an inch of the sash so that I could not be seen. When she came out on the doorstep my heart leaped. I ran to the hall, seized my books and followed her. I kept her brown figure always in my eye and when we came near the point at which our ways diverged I quickened my pace and passed her. This happened morning after morning. I had never spoken to her except for a few casual words and yet her name was like a summons to all my foolish blood.

Her image accompanied me even in places the most hostile to romance. On Saturday evenings when my aunt went marketing I had to go to carry some of the parcels. We walked through the flaring streets, jostled by drunken men and bargaining women, amid the curses of labourers, the shrill litanies of shop boys who stood on guard by the barrels of pigs' cheeks, the nasal chanting of street singers who sang a *come-all-you* about O'Donovan Rossa or a ballad about the troubles in our native land. These noises converged in a single sensation of life for me: I imagined that I bore my chalice safely through a throng of foes. Her name sprang to my lips at moments in strange prayers and praises which I myself did not understand. My eyes were often full of tears (I could not tell why) and at times a flood from my heart seemed to pour itself out into my bosom. I thought little of the future. I did not know whether I would ever speak to her or not or, if I spoke to her, how I could tell her of my confused adoration. But my body was like a harp and her words and gestures were like fingers running upon the wires.

One evening I went into the back drawingroom in which the priest had died. It was a dark rainy evening and there was no sound in the house. Through one of the broken panes I heard the rain impinge upon the earth, the fine incessant needles of water playing in the sodden beds. Some distant lamp or lighted window gleamed below me. I was thankful that I could see so little. All my senses seemed to desire to veil themselves and, feeling that I was about to slip from them, I pressed the palms of my hands together until they trembled, murmuring: *O love! O love!* many times.

At last she spoke to me. When she addressed the first words to me I was so confused that I did not know what to answer. She asked me was I going to *Araby*. I forget whether I answered yes or no. It would be a splendid bazaar, she said; she would love to go.

—And why can't you? I asked.

While she spoke she turned a silver bracelet round and round her wrist. She could not go, she said, because there would be a retreat that week in her convent. Her brother and two other boys were fighting for their caps and I was alone at the railings. She held one of the spikes, bowing her head towards me. The light from the lamp opposite our door caught the white curve of her neck, lit up the hair that rested there and, falling, lit up the hand upon the railing. It fell over one side of her dress and caught the white border of a petticoat, just visible as she stood at ease.

—It's well for you, she said.

—If I go, I said, I will bring you something.

What innumerable follies laid waste my waking and sleeping thoughts after that evening! I wished to annihilate the tedious intervening days. I chafed against the work of school. At night in my bedroom and by day in the classroom her image came between me and the page I strove to read. The syllables of the word *Araby* were called to me through the silence in which my soul luxuriated and cast an eastern enchantment over me. I asked for leave to go to the bazaar on Saturday night. My aunt was surprised and hoped it was not some freemason affair. I answered few questions in class. I watched my master's face pass from amiability to sternness; he hoped I was not beginning to idle. I could not call my wandering thoughts together. I had hardly any patience with the serious work of life which, now that it stood between me and my desire, seemed to me child's play, ugly monotonous child's play.

On Saturday morning I reminded my uncle that I wished to go to the bazaar in the evening. He was fussing at the hallstand, looking for the hatbrush, and answered me curtly:

—Yes, boy, I know.

As he was in the hall I could not go into the front parlour and lie at the window. I left the house in bad humour and walked slowly towards the school. The air was pitilessly raw and already my heart misgave me.

When I came home to dinner my uncle had not yet been home. Still it was early. I sat staring at the clock for some time and when its ticking began to irritate me I left the room. I mounted the staircase and gained the upper part of the house. The high cold empty gloomy rooms liberated me and I went from room to room singing. From the front window I saw my companions playing below in the street. Their cries reached me weakened and indistinct and, leaning my forehead against the cool glass, I looked over at the dark house where she lived. I may have stood there for an hour seeing nothing but the brownclad figure cast by my imagination, touched discreetly by the lamplight at the curved neck, at the hand upon the railings and at the border below the dress.

When I came downstairs again I found Mrs Mercer sitting at the fire. She was an old garrulous woman, a pawnbroker's widow who collected used stamps for some pious purpose. I had to endure the gossip of the teatable. The meal was prolonged beyond an hour and still my uncle did not come. Mrs Mercer stood up to go: she was sorry she couldn't wait any longer but it was after eight o'clock and she did not like to be out late as the night air was bad for her. When she had gone I began to walk up and down the room, clenching my fists. My aunt said:

—I'm afraid you may put off your bazaar for this night of Our Lord.

At nine o'clock I heard my uncle's latchkey in the halldoor. I heard him talking to himself and heard the hallstand rocking when it had received the weight of his overcoat. I could interpret these signs. When he was midway through his dinner I asked him to give me the money to go to the bazaar. He had forgotten.

—The people are in bed and after their first sleep now, he said.

I did not smile. My aunt said to him energetically:

—Can't you give him the money and let him go? You've kept him late enough as it is.

My uncle said he was very sorry he had forgotten. He said he believed in the old saying: *All work and no play makes Jack a dull boy*. He asked me where I was going and when I had told him a second time he asked me did I know *The Arab's Farewell to his Steed*. When I left the kitchen he was about to recite the opening lines of the piece to my aunt.

I held a florin tightly in my hand as I strode down Buckingham Street towards the station. The sight of the streets thronged with buyers and glaring with gas recalled to me the purpose of my journey. I took my seat in a third class carriage of a deserted train. After an intolerable delay the train moved out of the station slowly. It crept onward among ruinous houses and over the twinkling river. At Westland Row Station a crowd of people pressed at the carriage doors; but the porters moved them back, saying that it was a special train for the bazaar. I remained alone in the bare carriage. In a few minutes the train drew up beside an improvised wooden platform. I passed out on to the road and saw by the lighted dial of a clock that it was ten minutes to ten. In front of me was a large building which displayed the magical name.

I could not find any sixpenny entrance and, fearing that the bazaar would be closed, I passed in quickly through a turnstile, handing a shilling to a wearylooking man. I found myself in a big hall girdled at half its height by a gallery. Nearly all the stalls were closed and the greater part of the hall was in darkness. I recognised a silence like that which pervades a church after a service. I walked into the centre of the bazaar timidly. A few people were gathered about the stalls which were still open. Before a curtain over which the words *Café Chantant* were written in coloured lamps two men were counting money on a salver. I listened to the fall of the coins.

Remembering with difficulty why I had come I went over to one of the stalls and examined porcelain vases and flowered teasets. At the door of the stall a young lady was talking and laughing with two young gentlemen. I remarked their English accents and listened vaguely to their conversation.

—O, I never said such a thing!

—O, but you did!

—O, but I didn't!

—Didn't she say that?

—She did. I heard her.

—O, there's a ... fib!

Observing me the young lady came over and asked me did I

wish to buy anything. The tone of her voice was not encouraging: she seemed to have spoken to me out of a sense of duty. I looked humbly at the great jars that stood like eastern guards at either side of the dark entrance to her stall and murmured:

—No, thank you.

The young lady changed the position of one of the vases and went back to the two young men. They began to talk of the same subject. Once or twice the young lady glanced at me over her shoulder.

I lingered before her stall, though I knew my stay was useless, to make my interest in her wares seem the more real. Then I turned away slowly and walked down the middle of the bazaar. I allowed the two pennies to fall against the sixpence in my pocket. I heard a voice call from one end of the gallery that the light was out. The upper part of the hall was now completely dark.

Gazing up into the darkness I saw myself as a creature driven and derided by vanity: and my eyes burned with anguish and anger.

Eveline

She sat at the window watching the evening invade the avenue. Her head was leaned against the window curtains and in her nostrils was the odour of dusty cretonne. She was tired.

Few people passed. The man out of the last house passed on his way home; she heard his footsteps clacking along the concrete pavement and afterwards crunching on the cinder path before the new red houses. One time there used to be a field there in which they used to play every evening with other people's children. Then a man from Belfast bought the field and built houses in it—not like their little brown houses but bright brick houses with shining roofs. The children of the avenue used to play together in that field—the Devines, the Waters, the Dunns, little Keogh the cripple, she and her brothers and sisters. Ernest, however, never played: he was too grown up. Her father used often to hunt them in out of the field with his blackthorn stick but usually little Keogh used to keep nix and call out when he saw her father coming. Still they seemed to have been rather happy then. Her father was not so bad then, and besides her mother was alive. That was a long time ago; she and her brothers and sisters were all grown up; her mother was dead. Tizzie Dunn was dead, too, and the Waters had gone back to England. Everything changes. Now she was going to go away like the others, to leave her home.

Home! She looked round the room reviewing all its familiar objects which she had dusted once a week for so many years, wondering where on earth all the dust came from. Perhaps she would never see again those familiar objects from which she had never dreamed of being divided. And yet during all those years she had never found out the name of the priest whose yellowing photograph hung on the wall above the broken harmonium beside the coloured print of the promises made to Blessed Margaret Mary Alacoque. He had been a school friend of her father's. Whenever he showed the photograph to a visitor her father used to pass it with a casual word:

—He is in Melbourne now.

She had consented to go away, to leave her home. Was that wise? She tried to weigh each side of the question. In her home anyway she had shelter and food; she had those whom she had known all her life about her. Of course she had to work hard both in the house and at business. What would they say of her in the stores when they found out that she had run away with a fellow? Say she was a fool, perhaps; and her place would be filled up by advertisement. Miss Gavan would be glad. She had always had an edge on her, especially whenever there were people listening.

—Miss Hill, don't you see these ladies are waiting?

—Look lively, Miss Hill, please.

She would not cry many tears at leaving the stores.

But in her new home, in a distant unknown country, it would not be like that. Then she would be married—she, Eveline. People would treat her with respect then. She would not be treated as her mother had been. Even now, though she was over nineteen, she sometimes felt herself in danger of her father's violence. She knew it was that that had given her the palpitations. When they were growing up he had never gone for her, like he used to go for Harry and Ernest, because she was a girl; but latterly he had begun to threaten her and say what he would do to her only for her dead mother's sake. And now she had nobody to protect her. Ernest was dead and Harry, who was in the church decorating business, was nearly always down somewhere in the country. Besides, the invariable squabble for money on Saturday nights had begun to weary her unspeakably. She always gave her entire wages—seven shillings—and Harry always sent up what he could but the trouble was to get any money from her father. He said she used to squander the money, that she had no head, that he wasn't going to give her his hard earned money to throw about the streets and much more for he was usually fairly bad of a Saturday night. In the end he would give her the money and ask her had she any intention of buying Sunday's dinner. Then she had to rush out as quickly as she could and do her marketing, holding her black leather purse tightly in her hand as she elbowed her way through the crowds and returning home late under her load of provisions. She had hard work to keep the house together and to see that the two young children who had been left to her charge went to school regularly and got their meals regularly. It was hard work—a hard life—but now that she was about to leave it she did not find it a wholly undesirable life.

She was about to explore another life with Frank. Frank was very kind, manly, openhearted. She was to go away with him by the night boat to be his wife and to live with him in Buenos Ayres where he had a home waiting for her. How well she remembered the first time she had seen him; he was lodging in a house on the main road where she used to visit. It seemed a few weeks ago. He was standing at the gate, his peaked cap pushed back on his head and his hair tumbled forward over a face of bronze. Then they had come to know each other. He used to meet her outside the stores every evening and see her home. He took her to see the *Bohemian Girl* and she felt elated as she sat in an unaccustomed part of the theatre with him. He was awfully fond of music and sang a little. People knew that they were courting and when he sang about the lass that loves a sailor she always felt pleasantly confused. He used to call her Poppens out of fun. First of all it had been an excitement for her to have a fellow and then she had begun to like him. He had tales of distant countries. He had started as a deck boy at a pound a month on a ship of the Allan line going out to Canada. He told her the names of the ships he had been on and the names of the different services. He had sailed through the Straits of Magellan and he told her stories of the terrible Patagonians. He had fallen on his feet in Buenos Ayres, he said, and had come over to the old country just for a holiday. Of course, her father had found out the affair and had forbidden her to have anything to say to him:

—I know these sailor chaps, he said.

One day he had quarrelled with Frank and after that she had to meet her lover secretly.

The evening deepened in the avenue. The white of two letters in her lap grew indistinct. One was to Harry, the other was to her father. Ernest had been her favourite but she liked Harry too. Her father was becoming old lately, she noticed; he would miss her. Sometimes he could be very nice. Not long before, when she had been laid up for a day, he had read her out a ghost story and made toast for her at the fire. Another day, when their mother was alive, they had all gone for a picnic to the Hill of Howth. She remembered her father putting on her mother's bonnet to make the children laugh.

Her time was running out but she continued to sit by the window, leaning her head against the window curtain, inhaling the odour of dusty cretonne. Down far in the avenue she could hear a street organ playing. She knew the air. Strange that it should come that very night to remind her of the promise to her mother, her promise to keep the home together as long as she could. She remembered the last night of her mother's illness; she was again in the close dark room at the other side of the hall and outside she heard a melancholy air of Italy. The organ player had been ordered to go away and given sixpence. She remembered her father strutting back into the sickroom saying:

—Damned Italians! coming over here!

As she mused the pitiful vision of her mother's life laid its spell on the very quick of her being—that life of commonplace sacrifices closing in final craziness. She trembled as she heard again her mother's voice saying constantly with foolish insistence:

—Derevaun Seraun! Derevaun Seraun!

She stood up in a sudden impulse of terror. Escape! She must escape! Frank would save her. He would give her life, perhaps love too. But she wanted to live. Why should she be unhappy? She had a right to happiness. Frank would take her in his arms, fold her in his arms. He would save her.

◆ ◆ ◆

She stood among the swaying crowd in the station at the North Wall. He held her hand and she knew that he was speaking to her, saying something about the passage over and over again. The station was full of soldiers with brown baggages. Through the wide doors of the sheds she caught a glimpse of the black mass of the boat lying in beside the quay wall, with illumined portholes. She answered nothing. She felt her cheek pale and cold and out of a maze of distress she prayed to God to direct her, to show her what was her duty. The boat blew a long mournful whistle into the mist. If she went, tomorrow she would be on the sea with Frank, steaming towards Buenos Ayres. Their passage had been booked. Could she still draw back after all he had done for her? Her distress awoke a nausea in her body and she kept moving her lips in silent fervent prayer.

A bell clanged upon her heart. She felt him seize her hand:

—Come!

All the seas of the world tumbled about her heart. He was drawing her into them: he would drown her. She gripped with both hands at the iron railing.

—Come!

No! No! No! It was impossible. Her hands clutched the iron in frenzy. Amid the seas she sent a cry of anguish.

—Eveline! Evvy!

He rushed beyond the barrier and called to her to follow. He was shouted at to go on but he still called to her. She set her white face to him, passive, like a helpless animal. Her eyes gave him no sign of love or farewell or recognition.

After the Race

The cars came scudding in towards Dublin, running evenly like pellets in the groove of the Naas Road. At the crest of the hill at Inchicore sightseers had gathered in clumps to watch the cars careering homeward and through this channel of poverty and inaction the continent sped its wealth and industry. Now and again the clumps of people raised the cheer of the gratefully oppressed. Their sympathy, however, was for the blue cars—the cars of their friends, the French.

The French, moreover, were virtual victors. Their team had finished solidly; they had been placed second and third and the driver of the winning German car was reported a Belgian. Each blue car, therefore, received a double round of welcome as it topped the crest of the hill and each cheer of welcome was acknowledged with smiles and nods by those in the car. In one of these trimly built cars was a party of four young men whose spirits seemed to be at present well above the level of successful Gallicism: in fact, these four young men were almost hilarious. They were Charles Ségouin, the owner of the car; André Rivière, a young electrician of Canadian birth; a huge Hungarian named Villona and a neatly groomed young man named Doyle. Ségouin was in good humour because he had unexpectedly received some orders in advance (he was about to start a motor establishment in Paris) and Rivière was in good humour because he was to be appointed manager of the establishment; these two young men (who were cousins) were also in good humour because of the success of the French cars. Villona was in good humour because he had had a very satisfactory luncheon, and besides he was an optimist by nature. The fourth member of the party, however, was too excited to be genuinely happy.

He was about twenty-six years of age, with a soft, light brown moustache and rather innocent looking grey eyes. His father, who had begun life as an advanced nationalist, had modified his views early. He had made his money as a butcher in Kingstown and by opening shops in Dublin and in the suburbs he had made his money many times over. He had also been fortunate enough to secure some of the police contracts and in the end he had become rich enough to be alluded to in the Dublin newspapers as a merchant prince. He had sent his son to England to be educated in a big catholic college and had afterwards sent him to Dublin university to study law. Jimmy did not study very earnestly and took to bad courses for a while. He had money and he was popular and he divided his time curiously between musical and motoring circles. Then he had been sent for a term to Cambridge to see a little life. His father, remonstrative but covertly proud of the excess, had paid his bills and brought him home. It was at Cambridge that he had met Ségouin. They were not much more than acquaintances as yet but Jimmy found great pleasure in the society of one who had seen so much of the world and was reputed to own some of the biggest hotels in France. Such a person (as his father agreed) was well worth knowing, even if he had not been the charming companion he was. Villona was entertaining also —a brilliant pianist—but, unfortunately, very poor.

The car ran on merrily with its cargo of hilarious youth. The two cousins sat on the front seat; Jimmy and his Hungarian friend sat behind. Decidedly Villona was in excellent spirits; he kept up a deep bass hum of melody for miles of the road. The Frenchmen flung their laughter and light words over their shoulders and often Jimmy had to strain forward to catch the quick phrase. This was not altogether pleasant for him as he had nearly always to make a deft guess at the meaning and shout back a suitable answer in the teeth of a high wind. Besides, Villona's humming would confuse anybody: the noise of the car, too.

Rapid motion through space elates one; so does notoriety; so does the possession of money. These were three good reasons for Jimmy's excitement. He had been seen by many of his friends that day in the company of these continentals. At the control Ségouin had presented him to one of the French competitors and, in answer to his confused murmur of compliment, the swarthy face of the driver had disclosed a line of shining white teeth. It was pleasant after that honour to return to the profane world of spectators amid nudges and significant looks. Then as to money—he really had a great sum under his control. Ségouin, perhaps, would not think it a great sum but Jimmy who, in spite of temporary errors, was at heart the inheritor of solid instincts knew well with what difficulty it had been got together. This knowledge had previously kept his bills within the limits of reasonable recklessness and, if he had been so conscious of the labour latent in money when there had been question merely of some freak of the higher intelligence, how much more so now when he was about to stake the greater part of his substance! It was a serious thing for him.

Of course, the investment was a good one and Ségouin had managed to give the impression that it was by a favour of friendship the mite of Irish money was to be included in the capital of the concern. Jimmy had a respect for his father's shrewdness in business matters and in this case it had been his father who had first suggested the investment; money to be made in the motor business, pots of money. Moreover, Ségouin had the unmistakable air of wealth. Jimmy set out to translate into days' work that lordly car on which he sat. How smoothly it ran! In what style they had come careering along the country roads! The journey laid a magical finger on the genuine pulse of life and gallantly the machinery of human nerves strove to answer the bounding courses of the swift blue animal.

They drove down Dame Street. The street was busy with unusual traffic, loud with the horns of motorists and the gongs of impatient tramdrivers. Near the bank Ségouin drew up and Jimmy and his friend alighted. A little knot of people collected on the footpath to pay homage to the snorting motor. The party was to dine together that evening in Ségouin's hotel and meanwhile Jimmy and his friend, who was staying with him, were to go home to dress. The car steered out slowly for Grafton Street while the two young men pushed their way through the knot of gazers. They walked northward with a curious feeling of disappointment in the exercise while the city hung its pale globes of light above them in a haze of summer evening.

In Jimmy's house this dinner had been pronounced an occasion. A certain pride mingled with his parents' trepidation, a certain eagerness, also, to play fast and loose for the names of great foreign cities have at least this virtue. Jimmy, too, looked very well when he was dressed and, as he stood in the hall giving a last equation to the bows of his dress tie, his father may have felt even commercially satisfied at having secured for his son qualities often unpurchasable. His father, therefore, was unusually friendly with Villona and his manner expressed a real respect for foreign accomplishments but this subtlety of his host was probably lost upon the Hungarian who was beginning to have a sharp desire for his dinner.

The dinner was excellent, exquisite. Ségouin, Jimmy decided, had a very refined taste. The party was increased by a young Englishman named Routh whom Jimmy had seen with Ségouin at Cambridge. The young men supped in a snug room lit by electric candle lamps. They talked volubly and with little reserve. Jimmy, whose imagination was kindling, conceived the lively youth of the Frenchmen twined elegantly upon the firm framework of the Englishman's manner. A graceful image of his, he thought, and a just one. He admired the dexterity with which their host directed the conversation. The five young men had various tastes and their tongues had been loosened. Villona, with immense respect, began to discover to the mildly surprised Englishman the beauties of the English madrigal, deploring the loss of old instruments. Rivière, not wholly ingenuously, undertook to explain to Jimmy the triumph of the French mechanicians. The resonant voice of the Hungarian was about to prevail in ridicule of the spurious lutes of the romantic painters when Ségouin shepherded his party into politics. Here was congenial ground for all. Jimmy, under generous influences, felt the buried zeal of his father wake to life within him: he aroused the torpid Routh at last. The room grew doubly hot and Ségouin's task grew harder each moment: there was even danger of personal spite. The alert host at an opportunity lifted his glass to humanity and, when the toast had been drunk, he threw open a window significantly.

That night the city wore the mask of a capital. The five young men strolled along Stephen's Green in a faint cloud of aromatic smoke. They talked loudly and gaily and their cloaks dangled from their shoulders. The people made way for them. At the corner of Grafton Street a short fat man was putting two handsome ladies on a car in charge of another fat man. The car drove off and the short fat man caught sight of the party.

—André!

—It's Farley!

A torrent of talk followed. Farley was an American. No one knew very well what the talk was about. Villona and Rivière were the noisiest but all the men were excited. They got up on a car, squeezing themselves together amid much laughter. They drove by the crowd, blended now into soft colours, to a music of merry bells. They took the train at Westland Row and in a few seconds, as it seemed to Jimmy, they were walking out of

Kingstown station. The ticket collector saluted Jimmy; he was an old man.

—Fine night, sir!

It was a serene summer night; the harbour lay like a darkened mirror at their feet. They proceeded towards it with linked arms, singing *Cadet Roussel* in chorus, stamping their feet at every:

Ho! Ho! Hohé, vraiment!

They got into a rowboat at the slip and made out for the American's yacht. There was to be supper, music, cards. Villona said with conviction:

—It is beautiful!

There was a yacht piano in the cabin. Villona played a waltz for Farley and Rivière, Farley acting as cavalier and Rivière as lady. Then an impromptu square dance, the men devising original figures. What merriment! Jimmy took his part with a will; this was seeing life, at least. Then Farley got out of breath and cried *Stop!* A man brought in a light supper and the young men sat down to it for form' sake. They drank, however: it was bohemian. They drank Ireland, England, France, Hungary, the United States of America. Jimmy made a speech, a long speech, Villona saying: *Hear! hear!* whenever there was a pause. There was a great clapping of hands when he sat down. It must have been a good speech. Farley clapped him on the back and laughed loudly. What jovial fellows! What good company they were!

Cards! cards! The table was cleared. Villona returned quietly to his piano and played voluntaries for them. The other men played game after game, flinging themselves boldly into the adventure. They drank the health of the queen of hearts and of the queen of diamonds. Jimmy felt obscurely the lack of an audience: the wit was flashing. Play ran very high and paper began to pass. Jimmy did not know exactly who was winning but he knew that he was losing. But it was his own fault for he frequently mistook his cards and the other men had to calculate his I.O.U's for him. They were devils of fellows but he wished they would stop: it was getting late. Someone gave the toast of the yacht *The Belle of Newport* and then someone proposed one great game for a finish.

The piano had stopped; Villona must have gone up on deck. It was a terrible game. They stopped just before the end of it to drink for luck. Jimmy understood that the game lay between Routh and Ségouin. What excitement! Jimmy was excited too; he would lose, of course. How much had he written away? The men rose to their feet to play the last tricks, talking and gesticulating. Routh won. The cabin shook with the young men's cheering and the cards were bundled together. They began then to gather in what they had won. Farley and Jimmy were the heaviest losers.

He knew that he would regret in the morning but at present he was glad of the rest, glad of the dark stupor that would cover up his folly. He leaned his elbows on the table and rested his head between his hands, counting the beats of his temples. The cabin door opened and he saw the Hungarian standing in a shaft of grey light:

—Daybreak, gentlemen!

Two Gallants

The grey warm evening of August had descended upon the city and a mild warm air, a memory of summer, circulated in the streets. The streets, shuttered for the repose of Sunday, swarmed with a gaily coloured crowd. Like illumined pearls the lamps shone from the summits of their tall poles upon the living texture below which, changing shape and hue unceasingly, sent up into the warm grey evening air an unchanging unceasing murmur.

Two young men came down the hill of Rutland Square. One of them was just bringing a long monologue to a close. The other, who walked on the verge of the path and was at times obliged to step on to the road owing to his companion's rudeness, wore an amused listening face. He was squat and ruddy. A yachting cap was shoved far back from his forehead and the narrative to which he listened made constant waves of expression break forth over his face from the corners of his nose and eyes and mouth. Little jets of wheezing laughter followed one another out of his convulsed body. His eyes, twinkling with cunning enjoyment, glanced at every moment towards his companion's face. Once or twice he rearranged the light waterproof which he had slung over one shoulder in toreador fashion. His breeches, his white rubber shoes and his jauntily slung waterproof expressed youth. But his figure fell into rotundity at the waist, his hair was scant and grey and his face, when the waves of expression had passed over it, had a ravaged look.

When he was quite sure that the narrative had ended he laughed noiselessly for fully half a minute. Then he said:

—Well! ... That takes the biscuit!

His voice seemed winnowed of vigour; and to enforce his words he added with humour:

—That takes the solitary, unique and, if I may so call it, *recherché* biscuit!

He became serious and silent when he had said this. His tongue was tired for he had been talking all the afternoon in a publichouse in Dorset Street. Most people considered Lenehan a leech but in spite of this reputation his adroitness and eloquence had always prevented his friends from forming any general policy against him. He had a brave manner of coming up to a party of them in a bar and of holding himself nimbly at the borders of the company until he was included in a round. He was a sporting vagrant armed with a vast stock of stories, limericks and riddles. He was insensitive to all kinds of discourtesy. No-one knew how he achieved the stern task of living but his name was vaguely associated with racing tissues.

—And where did you pick her up, Corley? he asked.

Corley ran his tongue swiftly along his upper lip.

—One night, man, he said, I was going along Dame Street and I spotted a fine tart under Waterhouse's clock and said goodnight, you know. So we went for a walk round by the canal and she told me she was a slavey in a house in Baggot Street. I put my arm round her and squeezed her a bit that night. Then next Sunday, man, I met her by appointment. We went out to Donnybrook and I brought her into a field there. She told me she used to go with a dairyman. ... It was fine, man. Cigarettes every night she'd bring me and paying the tram out and back.

And one night she brought me two bloody fine cigars—O, the real cheese, you know, that the old fellow used to smoke. ... I was afraid, man, she'd get in the family way. But she's up to the dodge.

—Maybe she thinks you'll marry her, said Lenehan.

—I told her I was out of a job, said Corley. I told her I was in Pim's. She doesn't know my name. I was too hairy to tell her that. But she thinks I'm a bit of class, you know.

Lenehan laughed again noiselessly.

—Of all the good ones ever I heard, he said, that emphatically takes the biscuit.

Corley's stride acknowledged the compliment. The swing of his burly body made his friend execute a few light skips from the path to the roadway and back again. Corley was the son of an inspector of police and he had inherited his father's frame and gait. He walked with his hands by his sides, holding himself erect and swaying his head from side to side. His head was large, globular and oily, it sweated in all weathers and his large round hat, set upon it sideways, looked like a bulb which had grown out of another. He always stared straight before him as if he were on parade and when he wished to gaze after someone in the street it was necessary for him to move his body from the hips. At present he was about town. Whenever any job was vacant a friend was always ready to give him the hard word. He was often to be seen walking with policemen in plain clothes, talking earnestly. He knew the inner side of all affairs and was fond of delivering final judgments. He spoke without listening to the speech of his companions. His conversation was mainly about himself: what he had said to such a person and what such a person had said to him and what he had said to settle the matter. When he reported these dialogues he aspirated the first letter of his name after the manner of Florentines.

Lenehan offered his friend a cigarette. As the two young men walked on through the crowd Corley occasionally turned to smile at some of the passing girls but Lenehan's gaze was fixed on the large faint moon circled with a double halo. He watched earnestly the passing of the grey web of twilight across its face. At length he said:

—Well, ... tell me, Corley, I suppose you'll be able to pull it off all right, eh?

Corley closed one eye expressively as an answer.

—Is she game for that? asked Lenehan dubiously. You never can know women.

—She's all right, said Corley. I know the way to get around her, man. She's a bit gone on me.

—You're what I call a gay Lothario, said Lenehan. And the proper kind of a Lothario, too!

A shade of mockery relieved the servility of his manner. To save himself he had the habit of leaving his flattery open to the interpretation of raillery. But Corley had not a subtle mind.

—There's nothing to touch a good slavey, he affirmed. Take my tip for it.

—By one who has tried them all, said Lenehan.

—First I used to go with girls, you know, said Corley unbosoming, girls off the South Circular. I used to take them out, man, on the tram somewhere and pay the tram or take them to a band or a play at the theatre or buy them chocolate and sweets or something that way. I used to spend money on them right enough, he added in a convincing tone, as if he were conscious of being disbelieved.

But Lenehan could well believe it; he nodded gravely.

—I know that game, he said, and it's a mug's game.

—And damn the thing I ever got out of it, said Corley.

—Ditto here, said Lenehan.

—Only off of one of them, said Corley.

He moistened his upper lip by running his tongue along it. The recollection brightened his eyes. He too gazed at the pale disc of the moon, now nearly veiled, and seemed to meditate.

—She was ... a bit of all right, he said regretfully.

He was silent again. Then he added:

—She's on the turf now. I saw her driving down Earl Street one night with two fellows with her on a car.

—I suppose that's your doing, said Lenehan.

—There was others at her before me, said Corley philosophically.

This time Lenehan was inclined to disbelieve. He shook his head to and fro and smiled.

—You know you can't kid me, Corley, he said.

—Honest to God! said Corley. Didn't she tell me herself?

Lenehan made a tragic gesture.

—Base betrayer! he said.

As they passed along by the railings of Trinity College Lenehan skipped out into the road and peered up at the clock:

—Twenty after, he said.

—Time enough, said Corley. She'll be there all right. I always let her wait a bit.

Lenehan laughed quietly.

—Ecod, Corley, you know how to take them, he said.

—I'm up to all their little tricks, Corley confessed.

—But tell me, said Lenehan again, are you sure you can bring it off all right? You know it's a ticklish job. They're damn close on that point. Eh? ... What?

His bright small eyes searched his companion's face for reassurance. Corley swung his head to and fro as if to toss aside an insistent insect, and his brows gathered.

—I'll pull it off, he said. Leave it to me, can't you?

Lenehan said no more. He did not wish to ruffle his friend's temper, to be sent to the devil and told that his advice was not wanted. A little tact was necessary. But Corley's brow was soon smooth again. His thoughts were running another way.

—She's a fine decent tart, he said with appreciation, that's what she is.

They walked along Nassau Street and then turned into Kildare Street. Not far from the porch of the club a harpist stood in the roadway playing to a little ring of listeners. He plucked at the wires heedlessly, glancing quickly from time to time at the face of each newcomer and from time to time, wearily also, at the sky. His harp too, heedless that her coverings had fallen about her knees, seemed weary alike of the eyes of strangers and of her master's hands. One hand played in the bass the melody of *Silent, O Moyle* while the other hand careered in the treble after each group of notes. The notes of the air throbbed deep and full.

The two young men walked up the street without speaking, the mournful music following them. When they reached Stephen's Green they crossed the road. Here the noise of trams, the lights and the crowd released them from their silence.

—There she is! said Corley.

At the corner of Hume Street a young woman was standing. She wore a blue dress and a white sailor hat. She stood on the curbstone swinging a sunshade in one hand. Lenehan grew lively:

—Let's have a squint at her, Corley, he said.

Corley glanced sideways at his friend and an unpleasant grin appeared on his face.

—Are you trying to get inside me? he asked.

—Damn it! said Lenehan boldly, I don't want an introduction. All I want is to have a look at her. I'm not going to eat her.

—O ... A look at her? said Corley, more amiably. Well. ... I'll tell you what. I'll go over and talk to her and you can pass by.

—Right! said Lenehan.

Corley had already thrown one leg over the chains when Lenehan called out:

—And after? Where will we meet?

—Half ten, answered Corley, bringing over his other leg.

—Where?

—Corner of Merrion Street. We'll be coming back.

—Work it all right now, said Lenehan in farewell.

Corley did not answer. He sauntered across the road swaying his head from side to side. His bulk, his easy pace and the solid sound of his boots had something of the conqueror in them. He approached the young woman and, without saluting, began at once to converse with her. She swung her sunshade more quickly and executed half turns on her heels. Once or twice when he spoke to her at close quarters she laughed and bent her head.

Lenehan observed them for a few minutes. Then he walked rapidly along beside the chains to some distance and crossed the road obliquely. As he approached Hume Street corner he found the air heavily scented and his eyes made a swift anxious scrutiny of the young woman's appearance. She had her Sunday finery on. Her blue serge skirt was held at the waist by a belt of black leather. The great silver buckle of her belt seemed to depress the centre of her body, catching the light stuff of her white blouse like a clip. She wore a short black jacket with mother-of-pearl buttons and a ragged black boa. The ends of her tulle collarette had been carefully disordered and a big bunch of red flowers was pinned in her bosom, stems upwards. Lenehan's eyes noted approvingly her stout short muscular body. Frank rude health glowed in her face, on her fat red cheeks and in her unabashed blue eyes. Her features were blunt. She had broad nostrils, a straggling mouth which lay open in a contented leer and two projecting front teeth. As he passed Lenehan took off his cap and after about ten seconds Corley returned a salute to the air. This he did by raising his hand vaguely and pensively changing the angle of position of his hat.

Lenehan walked as far as the Shelbourne Hotel where he halted and waited. After waiting for a little time he saw them coming towards him and when they turned to the right he followed them, stepping lightly in his white shoes, down one side of Merrion Square. As he walked on slowly, timing his pace to theirs, he watched Corley's head which turned at every moment towards the young woman's face like a big ball revolving on a pivot. He kept the pair in view until he had seen them climbing the stairs of the Donnybrook tram; then he turned about and went back the way he had come.

Now that he was alone his face looked older. His gaiety seemed to forsake him and, as he came by the railings of the Duke's Lawn, he allowed his hand to run along them. The air which the harpist had played began to control his movements. His softly padded feet played the melody while his fingers swept a scale of variations idly along the railings after each group of notes.

He walked listlessly round Stephen's Green and then down Grafton Street. Though his eyes took note of many elements of the crowd through which he passed they did so morosely. He found trivial all that was meant to charm him and did not answer the glances which invited him to be bold. He knew that he would have to speak a great deal, to invent and to amuse, and his brain and throat were too dry for such a task. The problem of how he could pass the hours till he met Corley again troubled him a little. He could think of no way of passing them but to keep on walking. He turned to the left when he came to the corner of Rutland Square and felt more at ease in the dark quiet street, the sombre look of which suited his mood. He paused at last before the window of a poorlooking shop over which the words *Refreshment Bar* were printed in white letters. On the glass of the window were two flying inscriptions: *Ginger Beer* and *Ginger Ale*. A cut ham was exposed on a great blue dish while near it on a plate lay a segment of very light plumpudding. He eyed this food earnestly for some time and then, after glancing warily up and down the street, went into the shop quickly.

He was hungry for, except some biscuits which he had asked two grudging curates to bring him, he had eaten nothing since breakfast-time. He sat down at an uncovered wooden table opposite two work girls and a mechanic. A slatternly girl waited on him.

—How much is a plate of peas? he asked.

—Three halfpence, sir, said the girl.

—Bring me a plate of peas, he said, and a bottle of ginger beer.

He spoke roughly in order to belie his air of gentility for his entry had been followed by a pause of talk. His face was heated. To appear natural he pushed his cap back on his head and planted his elbows on the table. The mechanic and the two work girls examined him point by point before resuming their conversation in a subdued voice. The girl brought him a plate of hot grocer's peas seasoned with pepper and vinegar, a fork and his ginger beer. He ate his food greedily and found it so good that he made a note of the shop mentally. When he had eaten all the peas he sipped his ginger beer and sat for some time thinking of Corley's adventure. In his imagination he beheld the pair of lovers walking along some dark road, he heard Corley's voice in deep energetic gallantries and saw again the leer of the young woman's mouth. This vision made him feel keenly his own poverty of purse and spirit. He was tired of knocking about, of pulling the devil by the tail, of shifts and intrigues. He would be thirty-one in November. Would he never get a good job? Would he never have a home of his own? He thought how pleasant it would be to have a warm fire to sit by and a good dinner to sit down to. He had walked the streets long enough with friends and with girls. He knew what those friends were worth: he knew the girls too. Experience had embittered his heart against the world. But all hope had not left him. He felt better after having eaten than he had felt before, less weary of his life, less vanquished in spirit. He might yet be able to settle down in some snug corner and live happily if he could only come across some good simpleminded girl with a little of the ready.

He paid twopence halfpenny to the slatternly girl and went out of the shop to begin his wandering again. He went into Capel Street and walked along towards the City Hall. Then he turned into Dame Street. At the corner of George's Street he met two friends of his and stopped to converse with them. He was glad that he could rest from all his walking. His friends asked him had he seen Corley and what was the latest. He replied that he had spent the day with Corley. His friends talked very little. They looked vacantly after some figures in the crowd and sometimes made a critical remark. One said that he had seen Mac an hour before in Westmoreland Street. At this Lenehan said that he had been with Mac the night before in Egan's. The young man who had seen Mac in Westmoreland Street asked was it true that Mac had won a bit over a billiard match. Lenehan did not know: he said that Holohan had stood them drinks in Egan's.

He left his friends at a quarter to ten and went up George's Street. He turned to the left at the City Markets and walked on into Grafton Street. The crowd of girls and young men had thinned and on his way up the street he heard many groups and couples bidding one another goodnight. He went as far as the clock of the College of Surgeons: it was on the stroke of ten. He set off briskly along the northern side of the Green, hurrying for fear Corley should return too soon. When he reached the corner of Merrion Street he took his stand in the shadow of a lamp and brought out one of the cigarettes which he had reserved and lit it. He leaned against the lamppost and kept his gaze fixed on the part from which he expected to see Corley and the young woman return.

His mind became active again. He wondered had Corley managed it successfully. He wondered if he had asked her yet or if he would leave it to the last. He suffered all the pangs and thrills of his friend's situation as well as those of his own. But the memory of Corley's slowly revolving head calmed him somewhat: he was sure Corley would pull it off all right. All at once the idea struck him that perhaps Corley had seen her home by another way and given him the slip. His eyes searched the street: there was no sign of them. Yet it was surely half an hour since he had seen the clock of the College of Surgeons. Would Corley do a thing like that? He lit his last cigarette and began to smoke it nervously. He strained his eyes as each tram stopped at the far corner of the square. They must have gone home by another way. The paper of his cigarette broke and he flung it into the road with a curse.

Suddenly he saw them coming towards him. He started with delight and, keeping close to his lamppost, tried to read the result in their walk. They were walking quickly, the young woman taking quick short steps while Corley kept beside her with his long stride. They did not seem to be speaking. An intimation of the result pricked him like the point of a sharp instrument. He knew Corley would fail: he knew it was no go.

They turned down Baggot Street and he followed them at once, taking the other footpath. When they stopped he stopped too. They talked for a few moments and then the young woman went down the steps into the area of a house. Corley remained standing at the edge of the path, a little distance from the front steps. Some minutes passed. Then the halldoor was opened slowly and cautiously. A woman came running down the front steps and coughed. Corley turned and went towards her. His broad figure hid hers from view for a few seconds and then she reappeared running up the steps. The door closed on her and Corley began to walk swiftly towards Stephen's Green.

Lenehan hurried on in the same direction. Some drops of light rain fell. He took them as a warning and, glancing back towards the house which the young woman had entered to see that he was not observed, he ran eagerly across the road. Anxiety and his swift run made him pant. He called out:

—Hello, Corley!

Corley turned his head to see who had called him and then continued walking as before. Lenehan ran after him, settling the waterproof on his shoulders with one hand.

—Hello, Corley! he cried again.

He came level with his friend and looked keenly in his face. He could see nothing there.

—Well? he said. Did it come off?

They had reached the corner of Ely Place. Still without answering Corley swerved to the left and went up the side street. His features were composed in stern calm. Lenehan kept up with his friend, breathing uneasily. He was baffled and a note of menace pierced through his voice.

—Can't you tell us? he said. Did you try her?

Corley halted at the first lamp and stared grimly before him. Then with a grave gesture he extended a hand towards the light and, smiling, opened it slowly to the gaze of his disciple. A small gold coin shone in the palm.

The Boarding House

Mrs Mooney was a butcher's daughter. She was a woman who was quite able to keep things to herself: a determined woman. She had married her father's foreman and opened a butcher's shop near Spring Gardens. But as soon as his father-in-law was dead Mr Mooney began to go to the devil. He drank, plundered the till, ran headlong into debt. It was no use making him take the pledge: he was sure to break out again a few days after. By fighting his wife in the presence of customers and by buying bad meat he ruined his business. One night he went for his wife with the cleaver and she had to sleep in a neighbour's house.

After that they lived apart. She went to the priests and got a separation from him with care of the children. She would give him neither money nor food nor houseroom and so he was obliged to enlist himself as a sheriff's man. He was a shabby stooped little drunkard with a white face and a white moustache and white eyebrows, pencilled above his little eyes, which were pinkveined and raw; and all day long he sat in the bailiffs' room waiting to be put on a job. Mrs Mooney, who had taken what remained of her money out of the butcher business and set up a boarding house in Hardwicke Street, was a big imposing woman. Her house had a floating population made up of tourists from Liverpool and the Isle of Man and occasionally *artistes* from the musichalls. Its resident population was made up of clerks from the city. She governed her house cunningly and firmly, knew when to give credit, when to be stern and when to let things pass. All the resident young men spoke of her as *The Madam*.

Mrs Mooney's young men paid fifteen shillings a week for board and lodgings (beer or stout at dinner excluded). They shared in common tastes and occupations and for this reason they were very chummy with one another. They discussed with one another the chances of favourites and outsiders. Jack Mooney, the Madam's son, who was clerk to a commission agent in Fleet Street, had the reputation of being a hard case. He was fond of using soldiers' obscenities: usually he came home in the small hours. When he met his friends he had always a good one to tell them and he was always sure to be on to a good thing, that is to say, a likely horse or a likely *artiste*. He was also handy with the mits and sang comic songs. On Sunday nights there would often be a reunion in Mrs Mooney's front drawingroom. The musichall *artistes* would oblige; and Sheridan played waltzes and polkas and vamped accompaniments. Polly Mooney, the Madam's daughter, would also sing. She sang:

I'm a .... naughty girl.
You needn't sham:
You know I am.

Polly was a slim girl of nineteen; she had light soft hair and a small full mouth. Her eyes, which were grey with a shade of green through them, had a habit of glancing upwards when she spoke with anyone, which made her look like a little perverse madonna. Mrs Mooney had first sent her daughter to be a typewriter in a cornfactor's office but, as a disreputable sheriff's man used to come every other day to the office asking to be allowed to say a word to his daughter, she had taken her daughter home again and set her to do housework. As Polly was very lively the intention was to give her the run of the young men. Besides, young men like to feel that there is a young woman not very far away. Polly, of course, flirted with the young men but Mrs Mooney, who was a shrewd judge, knew that the young men were only passing the time away: none of them meant business. Things went on so for a long time and Mrs Mooney began to think of sending Polly back to typewriting when she noticed that something was going on between Polly and one of the young men. She watched the pair and kept her own counsel.

Polly knew that she was being watched but still her mother's persistent silence could not be misunderstood. There had been no open complicity between mother and daughter, no open understanding but, though people in the house began to talk of the affair, still Mrs Mooney did not intervene. Polly began to grow a little strange in her manner and the young man was evidently perturbed. At last, when she judged it to be the right moment, Mrs Mooney intervened. She dealt with moral problems as a cleaver deals with meat: and in this case she had made up her mind.

It was a bright Sunday morning of early summer, promising heat, but with a fresh breeze blowing. All the windows of the boarding house were open and the lace curtains ballooned gently towards the street beneath the raised sashes. The belfry of George's church sent out constant peals and worshippers, singly or in groups, traversed the little circus before the church, revealing their purpose by their self-contained demeanour no less than by the little volumes in their gloved hands. Breakfast was over in the boarding house and the table of the breakfast room was covered with plates on which lay yellow streaks of eggs with morsels of bacon fat and bacon rind. Mrs Mooney sat in the straw armchair and watched the servant, Mary, remove the breakfast things. She made Mary collect the crusts and pieces of broken bread to help to make Tuesday's bread pudding. When the table was cleared, the broken bread collected, the sugar and butter safe under lock and key, she began to reconstruct the interview which she had had the night before with Polly. Things were as she had suspected: she had been frank in her questions and Polly had been frank in her answers. Both had been somewhat awkward, of course. She had been made awkward by her not wishing to receive the news in too cavalier a fashion or to seem to have connived and Polly had been made awkward not merely because allusions of that kind always made her awkward but also because she did not wish it to be thought that in her wise innocence she had divined the intention behind her mother's tolerance.

Mrs Mooney glanced instinctively at the little gilt clock on the mantelpiece as soon as she had become aware through her revery that the bells of George's church had stopped ringing. It was seventeen minutes past eleven: she would have lots of time to have the matter out with Mr Doran and then catch short twelve at Marlborough Street. She was sure she would win. To begin with she had all the weight of social opinion on her side: she was an outraged mother. She had allowed him to live beneath her roof, assuming that he was a man of honour, and he had simply abused her hospitality. He was thirty-four or thirty-five years of age so that youth could not be pleaded as his excuse; nor could ignorance be his excuse since he was a man who had seen something of the world. He had simply taken advantage of Polly's youth and inexperience: that was evident. The question was: What reparation would he make?

There must be reparation made in such cases. It is all very well for the man: he can go his ways as if nothing had happened, having had his moment of pleasure, but the girl has to bear the brunt. Some mothers would be content to patch up such an affair for a sum of money: she had known cases of it. But she would not do so. For her only one reparation could make up for the loss of her daughter's honour: marriage.

She counted all her cards again before sending Mary up to

Mr Doran's room to say that she wished to speak with him. She felt sure she would win. He was a serious young man, not rakish or loudvoiced like the others. If it had been Mr Sheridan or Mr Meade or Bantam Lyons her task would have been much harder. She did not think he would face publicity. All the lodgers in the house knew something of the affair; details had been invented by some. Besides, he had been employed for thirteen years in a great catholic winemerchant's office and publicity would mean for him, perhaps, the loss of his sit. Whereas if he agreed all might be well. She knew he had a good screw for one thing and she suspected he had a bit of stuff put by.

Nearly the half-hour! She stood up and surveyed herself in the pierglass. The decisive expression of her great florid face satisfied her and she thought of some mothers she knew who could not get their daughters off their hands.

Mr Doran was very anxious indeed this Sunday morning. He had made two attempts to shave but his hand had been so unsteady that he had been obliged to desist. Three days' reddish beard fringed his jaws and every two or three minutes a mist gathered on his glasses so that he had to take them off and polish them with his pocket-handkerchief. The recollection of his confession of the night before was a cause of acute pain to him: the priest had drawn out every ridiculous detail of the affair and in the end had so magnified his sin that he was almost thankful at being afforded a loophole of reparation. The harm was done. What could he do now but marry her or run away? He could not brazen it out: the affair would be sure to be talked of. His employer would be certain to hear of it. Dublin is such a small city–everyone knows everyone else's business. He felt his heart leap warmly in his throat as he heard in his excited imagination old Mr Leonard calling out in his rasping voice *Send Mr Doran here, please.*

All his long years of service gone for nothing! All his industry and diligence thrown away! As a young man he had sown his wild oats, of course; he had boasted of his freethink=

ing and denied the existence of God to his companions in publichouses. But that was all past and done with .... nearly. He still bought a copy of *Reynolds's Newspaper* every week but he attended to his religious duties and for nine tenths of the year lived a regular life. He had money enough to settle down on: it was not that. But the family would look down on her. First of all there was her disreputable father and then her mother's boarding house was beginning to get a certain fame. He had a notion that he was being had. He could imagine his friends talking of the affair and laughing. She *was* a little vulgar; sometimes she said *I seen* and *If I had've known*. But what would grammar matter if he really loved her? He could not make up his mind whether to like her or despise her for what she had done. Of course, he had done it too. His instinct urged him to remain free, not to marry. Once you are married you are done for, it said.

While he was sitting helplessly on the side of the bed in shirt and trousers she tapped lightly at his door and entered. She told him all, that she had made a clean breast of it to her mother and that her mother would speak with him that morning. She cried and threw her arms round his neck, saying:

—O Bob! Bob! What am I to do? what am I to do at all?

She would put an end to herself, she said. He comforted her feebly, telling her not to cry, that it would be all right, never fear. He felt against his shirt the agitation of her bosom.

It was not altogether his fault that it had happened. He remembered well, with the curious patient memory of the celibate, the first casual caresses her dress, her breath, her fingers had given him. Then late one night as he was undressing for bed she had tapped at his door, timidly. She wanted to relight her candle at his for hers had been blown out by a gust. It was her bath night. She wore a loose open combing jacket of printed flannel. Her white instep shone in the opening of her furry slippers and the blood glowed warmly behind her perfumed skin. From her hands and wrists too as she lit and steadied her candle a faint perfume arose.

On nights when he came in very late it was she who warmed up his dinner. He scarcely knew what he was eating, feeling her beside him alone, at night, in the sleeping house. And her thoughtfulness! If the night was anyway cold or wet or windy there was sure to be a little tumbler of punch ready for him. Perhaps they could be happy together ......

They used to go upstairs together on tiptoe, each with a candle, and on the third landing exchange reluctant good-nights. They used to kiss. He remembered well her eyes, the touch of her hand and his delirium ....

But delirium passes. He echoed her phrase, applying it to himself: *What am I to do?* The instinct of the celibate warned him to hold back. But the sin was there: even his sense of honour told him that reparation must be made for such a sin.

While he was sitting with her on the side of the bed Mary came to the door and said that the missus wanted to see him in the parlour. He stood up to put on his coat and waistcoat, more helpless than ever. When he was dressed he went over to her to comfort her. It would be all right, never fear. He left her crying on the bed and moaning softly: *O my God!*

Going down the stairs his glasses became so dimmed with moisture that he had to take them off and polish them. He longed to ascend through the roof and fly away to another country where he would never hear again of his trouble and yet a force pushed him downstairs step by step. The implacable faces of his employer and of the Madam stared upon his discomfiture. On the last flight of stairs he passed Jack Mooney who was coming up from the pantry nursing two bottles of *Bass*. They saluted coldly and the lover's eyes rested for a second or two on a thick bulldog face and a pair of thick short arms. When he reached the foot of the stairs he glanced up and saw Jack regarding him from the door of the return room.

Suddenly he remembered the night when one of the music-hall *artistes*, a little blond Londoner, had made a rather free allusion to Polly. The reunion had been almost broken up on account of Jack's violence. Everyone tried to quieten him. The musichall *artiste*, a little paler than usual, kept smiling and saying that there was no harm meant but Jack kept shouting at him that if any fellow tried that sort of a game on with *his* sister he'd bloody well put his teeth down his throat, so he would.

◆ ◆ ◆

Polly sat for a little time on the side of the bed, crying. Then she dried her eyes and went over to the lookingglass. She dipped the end of the towel in the waterjug and refreshed her eyes with the cool water. She looked at herself in profile and readjusted a hairpin above her ear. Then she went back to the bed again and sat at the foot. She regarded the pillows for a long time and the sight of them awoke in her mind secret amiable memories. She rested the nape of her neck against the cool iron bedrail and fell into a revery. There was no longer any perturbation visible on her face.

She waited on patiently, almost cheerfully, without alarm, her memories gradually giving place to hopes and visions of the future. Her hopes and visions were so intricate that she no longer saw the white pillows on which her gaze was fixed or remembered that she was waiting for anything.

At last she heard her mother calling. She started to her feet and ran to the banisters.

—Polly! Polly!

—Yes, mamma?

—Come down, dear. Mr Doran wants to speak to you.

Then she remembered what she had been waiting for.

A Little Cloud

Eight years before he had seen his friend off at the North Wall and wished him godspeed. Gallaher had got on. You could tell that at once by his travelled air, his well-cut tweed suit and fearless accent. Few fellows had talents like his and fewer still could remain unspoiled by such success. Gallaher's heart was in the right place and he had deserved to win. It was something to have a friend like that.

Little Chandler's thoughts ever since lunchtime had been of his meeting with Gallaher, of Gallaher's invitation and of the great city London where Gallaher lived. He was called Little Chandler because, though he was but slightly under the average stature, he gave one the idea of being a little man. His hands were white and small, his frame was fragile, his voice was quiet and his manners were refined. He took the greatest care of his fair silken hair and moustache and used perfume discreetly on his handkerchief. The half moons of his nails were perfect and when he smiled you caught a glimpse of a row of childish white teeth.

As he sat at his desk in the King's Inns he thought what changes those eight years had brought. The friend whom he had known under a shabby and necessitous guise had become a brilliant figure on the London press. He turned often from his tiresome writing to gaze out of the office window. The glow of a late autumn sunset covered the grass plots and walks. It cast a shower of kindly golden dust on the untidy nurses and decrepit old men who drowsed on the benches; it flickered upon all the moving figures—on the children who ran screaming along the gravel paths and on everyone who passed through the gardens. He watched the scene and thought of life; and (as always happened when he thought of life) he became sad. A gentle melancholy took possession of him. He felt how useless it was to struggle against fortune, this being the burden of wisdom which the ages had bequeathed to him.

He remembered the books of poetry upon his shelves at home. He had bought them in his bachelor days and many an evening, as he sat in the little room off the hall, he had been tempted to take one down from the bookshelf and read out something to his wife. But shyness had always held him back, and so the books had remained on their shelves. At times he repeated lines to himself and this consoled him.

When his hour had struck he stood up and took leave of his desk and of his fellow clerks punctiliously. He emerged from under the feudal arch of the King's Inns, a neat modest figure, and walked swiftly down Henrietta Street. The golden sunset was waning and the air had grown sharp. A horde of grimy children populated the street. They stood or ran in the roadway or crawled up the steps before the gaping doors or squatted like mice upon the thresholds. Little Chandler gave them no thought. He picked his way deftly through all that minute verminlike life and under the shadow of the gaunt spectral mansions in which the old nobility of Dublin had roistered. No memory of the past touched him, for his mind was full of a present joy.

He had never been in Corless's but he knew the value of the name. He knew that people went there after the theatre to eat oysters and drink liqueurs; and he had heard that the waiters there spoke French and German. Walking swiftly by at night he had seen cabs drawn up before the door and richly dressed ladies, escorted by cavaliers, alight and enter quickly. They wore noisy dresses and many wraps. Their faces were powdered and they caught up their dresses, when they touched earth, like alarmed Atalantas. He had always passed without turning his head to look. It was his habit to walk swiftly in the street even by day and whenever he found himself in the city late at night he hurried on his way apprehensively and excitedly. Sometimes, however, he courted the causes of his fear. He chose the darkest and narrowest streets and, as he walked boldly forward, the silence that was spread about his footsteps troubled him, the wandering silent figures troubled him, and at times a sound of low fugitive laughter made him tremble like a leaf.

He turned to the right towards Capel Street. Ignatius Gallaher on the London press! Who would have thought it possible eight years before? Still, now that he reviewed the past, Little Chandler could remember many signs of future greatness in his friend. People used to say that Ignatius Gallaher was wild. Of course, he did mix with a rakish set of fellows at that time, drank freely and borrowed money on all sides. In the end he had got mixed up in some shady affair, some money transaction: at least, that was one version of his flight. But nobody denied him talent. There was always a certain ... something in Ignatius Gallaher that impressed you in spite of yourself. Even when he was out at elbows and at his wits' end for money he kept up a bold face. Little Chandler remembered (and the remembrance brought a slight flush of pride to his cheek) one of Ignatius Gallaher's sayings when he was in a tight corner:

—Half time now, boys, he used to say lightheartedly. Where's my considering cap?

That was Ignatius Gallaher all out; and, damn it, you couldn't but admire him for it.

Little Chandler quickened his pace. For the first time in his life he felt himself superior to the people he passed. For the first time his soul revolted against the dull inelegance of Capel Street. There was no doubt about it: if you wanted to succeed you had to go away. You could do nothing in Dublin. As he crossed Grattan Bridge he looked down the river towards the lower quays and pitied the poor stunted houses. They seemed to him a band of tramps huddled together along the river banks, their old coats covered with dust and soot, stupefied by the panorama of sunset and waiting for the first chill of night to bid them arise, shake themselves and begone. He wondered whether he could write a poem to express his idea. Perhaps Gallaher might be able to get it into some London paper for him. Could he write something original? He was not sure what idea he wished to express but the thought that a poetic moment had touched him took life within him like an infant hope. He stepped onward bravely.

Every step brought him nearer to London, farther from his own sober inartistic life. A light began to tremble on the horizon of his mind. He was not so old–thirty-two. His temperament might be said to be just at the point of maturity. There were so many different moods and impressions that he wished to express in verse. He felt them within him. He tried to weigh his soul to see if it was a poet's soul. Melancholy was the dominant note of his temperament, he thought, but it was a melancholy tempered by recurrences of faith and resignation and simple joy. If he could give expression to it in a book of poems perhaps men would listen. He would never be popular: he saw that. He could not sway the crowd but he might appeal to a little circle of kindred minds. The English critics perhaps would recognise him as one of the Celtic school by reason of the melancholy tone of his poems; besides that, he would put in allusions. He began to invent sentences and phrases from the notices which his book would get. *Mr Chandler has the gift of easy and graceful verse. ... A wistful sadness pervades these poems. ... The Celtic note.* It was a pity his name was not more Irish looking. Perhaps it would be better to insert his mother's name before the surname: Thomas Malone Chandler, or better still: T Malone Chandler. He would speak to Gallaher about it.

He pursued his revery so ardently that he passed his street and had to turn back. As he came near Corless's his former agitation began to overmaster him and he halted before the door in indecision. Finally he opened the door and entered.

The light and noise of the bar held him at the doorway for a few moments. He looked about him but his sight was confused by the shining of many red and green wineglasses. The bar seemed to him to be full of people and he felt that the people were observing him curiously. He glanced quickly to right and left (frowning slightly to make his errand appear serious) but when his sight cleared a little he saw that nobody had turned to look at him: and there, sure enough, was Ignatius Gallaher leaning with his back against the counter and his feet planted far apart.

—Hello, Tommy, old hero, here you are! What is it to be? What will you have? I'm taking whisky: better stuff than we get across the water. Soda? Lithia? No mineral? I'm the same. Spoils the flavour. ... Here, *garçon*, bring us two halves of malt whisky like a good fellow. ... Well, and how have you been pulling along ever since I saw you last? Dear God, how old we're getting! Do you see any signs of aging in me–eh, what? A little grey and thin on the top–what?

Ignatius Gallaher took off his hat and displayed a large closely cropped head. His face was heavy, pale and clean-shaven. His eyes, which were of bluish slate colour, relieved his unhealthy pallor and shone out plainly above the vivid orange tie he wore. Between these rival features the lips appeared very long and shapeless and colourless. He bent his head and felt with two sympathetic fingers the thin hair at the crown. Little Chandler shook his head as a denial. Ignatius Gallaher put on his hat again.

—It pulls you down, he said, press life. Always hurry and scurry, looking for copy and sometimes not finding it: and then always to have something new in your stuff. Damn proofs and printers, I say, for a few days. I'm deuced glad, I can tell you, to get back to the old country. Does a fellow good, a bit of a holiday. I feel a ton better since I landed again in dear dirty Dublin ... Here you are, Tommy. Water? Say when.

Little Chandler allowed his whisky to be very much diluted.

—You don't know what's good for you, my boy, said Ignatius Gallaher. I drink mine neat.

—I drink very little as a rule, said Little Chandler modestly. An odd half one or so when I meet any of the old crowd: that's all.

—Ah well, said Ignatius Gallaher cheerfully, here's to us and to old times and old acquaintance.

They clinked glasses and drank the toast.

—I met some of the old gang today, said Ignatius Gallaher. O'Hara seems to be in a bad way. What's he doing?

—Nothing, said Little Chandler. He's gone to the dogs.

—But Hogan has a good sit, hasn't he?

—Yes; he's in the Land Commission.

—I met him one night in London and he seemed to be very flush. ... Poor O'Hara! Boose, I suppose?

—Other things, too, said Little Chandler shortly.

Ignatius Gallaher laughed.

—Tommy, he said, I see you haven't changed an atom. You're the very same serious person that used to lecture me on Sunday mornings when I had a sore head and a fur on my tongue. You'd want to knock about a bit in the world. Have you never been anywhere, even for a trip?

—I've been to the Isle of Man, said Little Chandler.

Ignatius Gallaher laughed.

—The Isle of Man! he said. Go to London or Paris: Paris, for choice. That'd do you good.

—Have you seen Paris?

—I should think I have! I've knocked about there a little.

—And is it really so beautiful as they say? asked Little Chandler.

He sipped a little of his drink while Ignatius Gallaher finished his boldly.

—Beautiful? said Ignatius Gallaher, pausing on the word and on the flavour of his drink. It's not so beautiful, you know. Of course, it is beautiful. ... But it's the life of Paris: that's the thing. Ah, there's no city like Paris for gaiety, movement, excitement. ...

Little Chandler finished his whisky and after some trouble

succeeded in catching the barman's eye. He ordered the same again.

—I've been to the Moulin Rouge, Ignatius Gallaher continued when the barman had removed their glasses, and I've been to all the bohemian cafés. Hot stuff! Not for a pious chap like you, Tommy.

Little Chandler said nothing until the barman returned with the two glasses: then he touched his friend's glass lightly and reciprocated the former toast. He was beginning to feel somewhat disillusioned. Gallaher's accent and way of expressing himself did not please him. There was something vulgar in his friend which he had not observed before. But perhaps it was only the result of living in London amid the bustle and competition of the press. The old personal charm was still there under this new gaudy manner. And, after all, Gallaher had lived, he had seen the world. Little Chandler looked at his friend enviously.

—Everything in Paris is gay, said Ignatius Gallaher. They believe in enjoying life and don't you think they're right? If you want to enjoy yourself properly you must go to Paris. And, mind you, they've a great feeling for the Irish there. When they heard I was from Ireland they were ready to eat me, man.

Little Chandler took four or five sips from his glass.

—Tell me, he said, is it true that Paris is so ... immoral as they say?

Ignatius Gallaher made a catholic gesture with his right arm.

—Every place is immoral, he said. Of course you do find spicy bits in Paris. Go to one of the students' balls, for instance. That's lively, if you like, when the *cocottes* begin to let themselves loose. You know what they are, I suppose?

—I've heard of them, said Little Chandler.

Ignatius Gallaher drank off his whisky and shook his head.

—Ah, he said, you may say what you like. There's no woman like the Parisienne for style, for go.

—Then it is an immoral city, said Little Chandler with timid insistence, I mean, compared with London or Dublin?

—London! said Ignatius Gallaher. It's six of one and half a dozen of the other. You ask Hogan, my boy. I showed him a bit about London when he was over there. He'd open your eye. ... I say, Tommy, don't make punch of that whisky: liquor up.

—No, really. ...

—O, come on, another one won't do you any harm. What is it? The same again, I suppose?

—Well ... all right.

—*François*, the same again. ... Will you smoke, Tommy?

Ignatius Gallaher produced his cigar case. The two friends lit their cigars and puffed at them in silence until their drinks were served.

—I'll tell you my opinion, said Ignatius Gallaher, emerging after some time from the clouds of smoke in which he had taken refuge, it's a rum world. Talk of immorality! I've heard of cases–what am I saying–I've known them: cases of ... immorality ....

Ignatius Gallaher puffed thoughtfully at his cigar and then, in a calm historian's tone, he proceeded to sketch for his friend some pictures of the corruption which was rife abroad. He summarised the vices of many capitals and seemed inclined to award the palm to Berlin. Some things he could not vouch for (his friends had told him) but of others he had had personal experience. He spared neither rank nor caste. He revealed many of the secrets of religious houses on the continent and described some of the practices which were fashionable in high society: and ended by telling, with details, a story about an English duchess–a story which he knew to be true. Little Chandler was astonished.

—Ah, well, said Ignatius Gallaher, here we are in old jogalong Dublin where nothing is known of such things.

—How dull you must find it, said Little Chandler, after all the other places you've seen!

—Well, said Ignatius Gallaher, it's a relaxation to come over here, you know. And, after all, it's the old country, as they say, isn't it? You can't help having a certain feeling for it. That's human nature. ... But tell me something about yourself. Hogan told me you had ... tasted the joys of connubial bliss. Two years ago, wasn't it?

Little Chandler blushed and smiled.

—Yes, he said. I was married last May twelve months.

—I hope it's not too late in the day to offer my best wishes, said Ignatius Gallaher. I didn't know your address or I'd have done so at the time.

He extended his hand which Little Chandler took.

—Well, Tommy, he said, I wish you and yours every joy in life, old chap, and tons of money and may you never die till I shoot you. And that's the wish of a sincere friend, an old friend. You know that?

—I know that, said Little Chandler.

—Any youngsters? said Ignatius Gallaher.

Little Chandler blushed again.

—We have one child, he said.

—Son or daughter?

—A little boy.

Ignatius Gallaher slapped his friend sonorously on the back.

—Bravo, he said, I wouldn't doubt you, Tommy.

Little Chandler smiled, looked confusedly at his glass and bit his lower lip with three childishly white front teeth.

—I hope you'll spend an evening with us, he said, before you go back. My wife will be delighted to meet you. We can have a little music and ...

—Thanks awfully, old chap, said Ignatius Gallaher, I'm sorry we didn't meet earlier. But I must leave tomorrow night.

—Tonight, perhaps. ...

—I'm awfully sorry, old man. You see I'm over here with another fellow, clever young chap he is too, and we arranged to go to a little card party. Only for that ....

—O, in that case. ...

—But who knows? said Ignatius Gallaher considerately. Next year I may take a little skip over here now that I've broken the ice. It's only a pleasure deferred.

—Very well, said Little Chandler, the next time you come we must have an evening together. That's agreed now, isn't it?

—Yes, that's agreed, said Ignatius Gallaher. Next year if I come, *parole d'honneur*.

—And to clinch the bargain, said Little Chandler, we'll just have one more now.

Ignatius Gallaher took out a large gold watch and looked at it.

—Is it to be the last? he said. Because, you know, I have an a.p.

—O yes, positively, said Little Chandler.

—Very well then, said Ignatius Gallaher, let us have another one as a *deoc an doruis*—that's good vernacular for a small whisky, I believe.

Little Chandler ordered the drinks. The blush which had risen to his face a few moments before was establishing itself. A trifle made him blush at any time: and now he felt warm and excited. Three small whiskies had gone to his head and Gallaher's strong cigar had confused his mind for he was a delicate and abstinent person. The adventure of meeting Gallaher after eight years, of finding himself with Gallaher in Corless's surrounded by lights and noise, of listening to Gallaher's stories and of sharing for a brief space Gallaher's vagrant and triumphant life, upset the equipoise of his sensitive nature. He felt acutely the contrast between his own life and his friend's and it seemed to him unjust. Gallaher was his inferior in birth and education. He was sure that he could do something better than his friend had ever done, or could ever do, something higher than mere tawdry journalism if only he got the chance. What was it that stood in his way? His unfortunate timidity! He wished to vindicate himself in some way, to assert his manhood. He saw behind Gallaher's refusal of his invitation. Gallaher was only patronising him by his friendliness just as he was patronising Ireland by his visit.

The barman brought their drinks. Little Chandler pushed one glass towards his friend and took up the other boldly.

—Who knows? he said as they lifted their glasses. When you

come next year I may have the pleasure of wishing long life and happiness to Mr and Mrs Ignatius Gallaher.

Ignatius Gallaher in the act of drinking closed one eye expressively over the rim of his glass. When he had drunk he smacked his lips decisively, set down his glass and said:

—No blooming fear of that, my boy. I'm going to have my fling first and see a bit of life and the world before I put my head in the sack—if I ever do.

—Some day you will, said Little Chandler calmly.

Ignatius Gallaher turned his orange tie and slateblue eyes full upon his friend.

—You think so? he said.

—You'll put your head in the sack, repeated Little Chandler stoutly, like everyone else, if you can find the girl.

He had slightly emphasised his tone and he was aware that he had betrayed himself; but though the colour had heightened in his cheek he did not flinch from his friend's gaze. Ignatius Gallaher watched him for a few moments and then said:

—If ever it occurs you may bet your bottom dollar there'll be no mooning and spooning about it. I mean to marry money. She'll have a good fat account at the bank or she won't do for me.

Little Chandler shook his head.

—Why, man alive, said Ignatius Gallaher vehemently, do you know what it is? I've only to say the word and tomorrow I can have the woman and the cash. You don't believe it? Well, I know it. There are hundreds—what am I saying?—thousands of rich Germans and Jews, rotten with money, that'd only be too glad. ... You wait awhile, my boy. See if I don't play my cards properly. When I go about a thing I mean business, I tell you. You just wait.

He tossed his glass to his mouth, finished his drink and laughed loudly. Then he looked thoughtfully before him and said in a calmer tone:

—But I'm in no hurry. They can wait. I don't fancy tying myself up to one woman, you know.

He imitated with his mouth the act of tasting and made a wry face.

—Must get a bit stale, I should think, he said.

◆ ◆ ◆

Little Chandler sat in the room off the hall, holding a child in his arms. To save money they kept no servant but Annie's young sister Monica came for an hour or so in the morning and an hour or so in the evening to help. But Monica had gone home long ago. It was a quarter to nine. Little Chandler had come home late for tea and, moreover, he had forgotten to bring Annie home the parcel of coffee from Bewley's. Of course she was in a bad humour and gave him short answers. She said she would do without any tea but when it came near the time at which the shop at the corner closed she decided to go out herself for a quarter of a pound of tea and two pounds of sugar. She put the sleeping child deftly in his arms and said:

—Here. Don't waken him.

A little lamp with a white china shade stood upon the table and its light fell over a photograph which was enclosed in a frame of crumpled horn. It was Annie's photograph. Little Chandler looked at it, pausing at the thin tight lips. She wore the pale blue summer blouse which he had brought her home as a present one Saturday. It had cost him ten and elevenpence; but what an agony of nervousness it had cost him! How he had suffered that day, waiting at the shopdoor until the shop was empty, standing at the counter and trying to appear at his ease while the girl piled ladies' blouses before him, paying at the desk and forgetting to take up the odd penny of his change, being called back by the cashier and, finally, striving to hide his blushes as he left the shop by examining the parcel to see if it was securely tied. When he brought the blouse home Annie kissed him and said it was very pretty and stylish but when she heard the price she threw the blouse on the table and said it was a regular swindle to charge ten and elevenpence for that. At first she wanted to take it back but when she tried it on she was delighted with it, especially with the make of the sleeves, and kissed him and said he was very good to think of her.

Hm! ...

He looked coldly into the eyes of the photograph and they answered coldly. Certainly they were pretty and the face itself was pretty. But he found something mean in it. Why was it so unconscious and ladylike? The composure of the eyes irritated him. They repelled him and defied him: there was no passion in them, no rapture. He thought of what Gallaher had said about rich Jewesses. Those dark oriental eyes, he thought, how full they are of passion, of voluptuous longing! ... Why had he married the eyes in the photograph?

He caught himself up at the question and glanced nervously round the room. He found something mean in the pretty furniture which he had bought for his house on the hire system. Annie had chosen it herself and it reminded him of her. It too was prim and pretty. A dull resentment against his life awoke within him. Could he not escape from his little house? Was it too late for him to try to live bravely like Gallaher? Could he go to London? There was the furniture still to be paid for. If he could only write a book and get it published, that might open the way for him.

A volume of Byron's poems lay before him on the table. He opened it cautiously with his left hand lest he should waken the child and began to read the first poem in the book:

Hushed are the winds and still the evening gloom,
Not e'en a Zephyr wanders through the grove,
Whilst I return to view my Margaret's tomb
And scatter flowers on the dust I love.

He paused. He felt the rhythm of the verse about him in the room. How melancholy it was! Could he, too, write like that, express the melancholy of his soul in verse? There were so many things he wanted to describe: his sensation of a few hours before on Grattan Bridge, for example. If he could get back again into that mood. ...

The child awoke and began to cry. He turned from the page

and tried to hush it: but it would not be hushed. He began to rock it to and fro in his arms but its wailing cry grew keener. He rocked it faster while his eyes began to read the second stanza:

Within this narrow cell reclines her clay,
That clay where once ...

It was useless. He couldn't read. He couldn't do anything. The wailing of the child pierced the drum of his ear. It was useless, useless! He was a prisoner for life. His arms trembled with anger and suddenly bending to the child's face he shouted:

—Stop!

The child stopped for an instant, had a spasm of fright and began to scream. He jumped up from his chair and walked hastily up and down the room with the child in his arms. It began to sob piteously, losing its breath for four or five seconds and then bursting out anew. The thin walls of the room echoed the sound. He tried to soothe it but it sobbed more convulsively. He looked at the contracted and quivering face of the child and began to be alarmed. He counted seven sobs without a break between them and caught the child to his breast in fright. If it died! ...

The door was burst open and a young woman ran in, panting.

—What is it? What is it? she cried.

The child, hearing its mother's voice, broke out into a paroxysm of sobbing.

—It's nothing, Annie ... it's nothing. ... He began to cry. ...

She flung her parcels on the floor and snatched the child from him.

—What have you done to him? she cried, glaring into his face.

Little Chandler sustained for one moment the gaze of her eyes and his heart closed together as he met the hatred in them. He began to stammer:

—It's nothing. ... He ... he began to cry. ... I couldn't ... I didn't do anything. ... What?

Giving no heed to him she began to walk up and down the

room, clasping the child tightly in her arms and murmuring:

—My little man! My little mannie! Was 'ou frightened, love? ... There now, love! There now! ... Lambabaun! Mamma's little lamb of the world! ... There now!

Little Chandler felt his cheeks suffused with shame and he stood back out of the lamplight. He listened while the paroxysm of the child's sobbing grew less and less: and tears of remorse started to his eyes.

Counterparts

The bell rang furiously and, when Miss Parker went to the tube, a furious voice called out in a piercing north of Ireland accent:

—Send Farrington here!

Miss Parker returned to her machine, saying to a man who was writing at a desk:

—Mr Alleyne wants you upstairs.

The man muttered *Blast him!* under his breath and pushed back his chair to stand up. When he stood up he was tall and of great bulk. He had a hanging face, dark winecoloured with fair eyebrows and moustache; his eyes bulged forward slightly and the whites of them were dirty. He lifted up the counter and, passing by the clients, went out of the office with a heavy step.

He went heavily upstairs until he came to the second landing where a door bore a brass plate with the inscription *Mr Alleyne*. Here he halted puffing with labour and vexation and knocked. The shrill voice cried:

—Come in!

The man entered Mr Alleyne's room. Simultaneously Mr Alleyne, a little man wearing goldrimmed glasses on a clean=

shaven face, shot his head up over a pile of documents. The head itself was so pink and hairless that it seemed like a large egg reposing on the papers. Mr Alleyne did not lose a moment:

—Farrington! What is the meaning of this? Why have I always to complain of you? May I ask you why you haven't made a copy of that contract between Bodley and Kirwan? I told you it must be ready by four o'clock.

—But Mr Shelley said, sir, ...

—*Mr Shelley said, sir.* ..... Kindly attend to what I say and not to what *Mr Shelley says, sir.* You have always some excuse or another for shirking work. Let me tell you that if the contract is not copied before this evening I'll lay the matter before Mr Crosbie ... Do you hear me now?

—Yes, sir.

—Do you hear me now? .... Aye and another little matter! I might as well be talking to the wall as talking to you. Understand once for all that you get a half an hour for your lunch and not an hour and a half. How many courses do you want, I'd like to know? ... Do you mind me, now?

—Yes, sir.

Mr Alleyne bent his head again upon his pile of papers. The man stared fixedly at the polished skull which directed the affairs of Crosbie and Alleyne, gauging its fragility. A spasm of rage gripped his throat for a few moments and then passed, leaving after it a sharp sensation of thirst. The man recognised the sensation and felt that he must have a good night's drinking. The middle of the month was past and, if he could get the copy done in time, Mr Alleyne might give him an order on the cashier. He stood still, gazing fixedly at the head upon the pile of papers. Suddenly Mr Alleyne began to upset all the papers, searching for something. Then, as if he had been unaware of the man's presence till that moment, he shot up his head again, saying:

—Eh! Are you going to stand there all the day? Upon my word, Farrington, you take things easy!

—I was waiting to see. ....

—Very good, you needn't wait to see. Go downstairs and do your work.

The man walked heavily towards the door and as he went out of the room he heard Mr Alleyne cry after him that if the contract was not copied by evening Mr Crosbie would hear of the matter.

He returned to his desk in the lower office and counted the sheets which remained to be copied. He took up his pen and dipped it in the ink but he continued to stare stupidly at the last words he had written: *In no case shall the said Bernard Bodley be ......* The evening was falling and in a few minutes they would be lighting the gas: then he could write. He felt that he must slake the thirst in his throat. He stood up from his desk and, lifting the counter as before, passed out of the office. As he was passing out the chief clerk looked at him inquiringly.

—It's all right, Mr Shelley, said the man pointing with his finger to indicate the objective of his journey.

The chief clerk glanced at the hatrack but, seeing the row complete, offered no remark. As soon as he was on the landing the man pulled a shepherd's plaid cap out of his pocket, put it on his head and ran quickly down the rickety stairs. From the street door he walked on furtively on the inner side of the path towards the corner and all at once dived into a doorway. He was now safe in the dark snug of O'Neill's shop and, filling up the little window that looked into the bar with his inflamed face, the colour of dark wine or dark meat, he called out:

—Here, Pat, give us a g.p., like a good fellow!

The curate brought him a glass of plain porter. The man drank it at a gulp and asked for a caraway seed. He put his penny on the counter and, leaving the curate to grope for it in the gloom, retreated out of the snug as furtively as he had entered it.

Darkness, accompanied by a thick fog, was gaining upon the dusk of February and the lamps in Eustace Street had been lit. The man went up by the houses until he reached the door of the office, wondering whether he could finish his copy in time.

On the stairs a moist pungent odour of perfumes saluted his nose: evidently Miss Delacour had come while he was out in O'Neill's. He crammed his cap back again into his pocket and reentered the office, assuming an air of absentmindedness.

—Mr Alleyne has been calling for you, said the chief clerk severely. Where were you?

The man glanced at the two clients who were standing at the counter as if to intimate that their presence prevented him from answering. As the clients were both male the chief clerk allowed himself a laugh:

—I know that game, he said. Five times in one day is a little bit ..... Well, you better look sharp and get a copy of our correspondence in the Delacour case for Mr Alleyne.

This address in the presence of the public, his run upstairs and the porter he had gulped down so hastily confused the man and, as he sat down at his desk to get what was required, he realised how hopeless was the task of finishing his copy of the contract before half past five. The dark damp night was coming and he longed to spend it in the bars, drinking with his friends amid the glare of gas and the clatter of glasses. He got out the Delacour correspondence and passed out of the office. He hoped Mr Alleyne would not discover that the last two letters were missing.

The moist pungent perfume lay all the way up to Mr Alleyne's room. Miss Delacour was a middleaged woman of Jewish appearance. Mr Alleyne was said to be sweet on her or on her money. She came to the office often and stayed a long time when she came. She was sitting beside his desk now in an aroma of perfumes, smoothing the handle of her umbrella and nodding the great black feather in her hat. Mr Alleyne had swivelled his chair round to face her and thrown his right foot jauntily upon his left knee. The man put the correspondence on the desk and bowed respectfully but neither Mr Alleyne nor Miss Delacour took any notice of his bow. Mr Alleyne tapped a finger on the correspondence and then flicked it towards him as if to say *That's all right: you can go.*

The man returned to the lower office and sat down again at

his desk. He stared intently at the incomplete phrase *In no case shall the said Bernard Bodley be* .... and thought how strange it was that the last three words began with the same letter. The chief clerk began to harry Miss Parker, saying she would never have the letters typed in time for post. The man listened to the clicking of the machine for a few minutes and then set to work to finish his copy. But his head was not clear and his mind wandered away to the glare and rattle of the publichouse. It was a night for hot punches. He struggled on with his copy but when the clock struck five he had still fourteen pages to write. Blast it! He couldn't finish it in time. He longed to execrate aloud, to bring his fist down on something violently. He was so enraged that he wrote *Bernard Bernard* instead of *Bernard Bodley* and had to begin again on a clean sheet.

He felt strong enough to clear out the whole office singlehanded. His body ached to do something, to rush out and revel in violence. All the indignities of his life enraged him. ... Could he ask the cashier privately for an advance? No, the cashier was no good, no damn good: he wouldn't give an advance. ...... He knew where he would meet the boys: Leonard and O'Halloran and Nosey Flynn. The barometer of his emotional nature was set for a spell of riot.

His imagination had so abstracted him that his name was called twice before he answered. Mr Alleyne and Miss Delacour were standing outside the counter and all the clerks had turned round in anticipation of something. The man got up from his desk. Mr Alleyne began a tirade of abuse, saying that two letters were missing. The man answered that he knew nothing about them, that he had made a faithful copy. The tirade continued: it was so bitter and violent that the man could hardly restrain his fist from descending upon the head of the manikin before him:

—I know nothing about any other two letters, he said stupidly.

—*You – know – nothing*. Of course you know nothing, said Mr Alleyne. Tell me, he added, glancing first for approval to the lady beside him, do you take me for a fool? Do you think me an utter fool?

The man glanced from the lady's face to the little eggshaped head and back again: and almost before he was aware of it his tongue had found a felicitous moment:

—I don't think, sir, he said, that that's a fair question to put to me.

There was a pause in the very breathing of the clerks. Every=one was astounded (the author of the witticism no less than his neighbours) and Miss Delacour, who was a stout amiable per=son, began to smile broadly. Mr Alleyne flushed to the hue of a wild rose and his mouth twitched with a dwarf's passion. He shook his fist in the man's face till it seemed to vibrate like the knob of some electric machine:

—You impertinent ruffian! You impertinent ruffian! I'll make short work of you! Wait till you see! You'll apologise to me for your impertinence or you'll quit the office instanter! You'll quit this, I'm telling you, or you'll apologise to me!

◆ ◆ ◆

He stood in a doorway opposite the offices watching to see if the cashier would come out alone. All the clerks passed and finally the cashier came out with the chief clerk. It was no use trying to say a word to him when he was with the chief clerk. The man felt that his position was bad enough. He had been obliged to offer an abject apology to Mr Alleyne for his impertinence but he knew what a hornet's nest the office would be for him. He could remember the way in which Mr Alleyne had hounded little Peake out of the office in order to make room for his own nephew. He felt savage and thirsty and revengeful, annoyed with himself and with everyone else. Mr Alleyne would never give him an hour's rest: his life would be a hell to him. He had made a proper fool of himself this time. Could he not keep his tongue in his cheek? But they had never pulled together from the first, he and Mr Alleyne, ever since the day Mr Alleyne had overheard him mimicking his north of Ireland accent to amuse Higgins and Miss Parker: that had been the beginning of it. He might have tried Higgins for the money but sure Higgins never had anything for himself. A man with two establishments to keep up, of course he couldn't.

He felt his great body again aching for the comfort of the publichouse. The fog had begun to chill him and he wondered could he touch Pat in O'Neill's. He could not touch him for more than a bob–and a bob was no use. Yet he must get money somewhere or other: he had spent his last penny for the g.p. and soon it would be too late for getting money anywhere. Suddenly, as he was fingering his watchchain, he thought of Terry Kelly's pawnoffice in Fleet Street. That was the dart! Why didn't he think of it sooner?

He went through the narrow alley of Temple Bar quickly, muttering to himself that they could all go to hell because he was going to have a good night of it. The clerk in Terry Kelly's said *A crown!* but the consignor held out for six shillings and in the end the six shillings was allowed him literally. He came out of the pawnoffice joyfully, making a little cylinder of the coins between his thumb and fingers. In Westmoreland Street the footpaths were crowded with young men and women returning from business and ragged urchins ran here and there yelling out the names of the evening editions. The man passed through the crowd, looking on the spectacle generally with proud satisfaction and staring masterfully at the office girls. His head was full of the noises of tram gongs and swishing trolleys and his nose already sniffed the curling fumes of punch. As he walked on he preconsidered the terms in which he would narrate the incident to the boys:

—So, I just looked at him–coolly, you know–and looked at her. Then I looked back at him again–taking my time, you know. *I don't think that that's a fair question to put to me*, says I.

Nosey Flynn was sitting up in his usual corner of Davy Byrne's and when he heard the story he stood Farrington a half one, saying it was as smart a thing as ever he heard. Farrington stood a drink in his turn. After a while O'Halloran and Paddy Leonard came in and the story was repeated to them. O'Halloran stood tailors of malt, hot, all round and told the story of the retort he had made to the chief clerk when he was in Callan's of Fownes's Street; but, as the retort was after the manner of the liberal shepherds in the eclogues, he had to admit that it was not so clever as Farrington's retort. At this Farrington told the boys to polish off that and have another.

Just as they were naming their poisons who should come in but Higgins! Of course he had to join in with the others. The men asked him to give his version of it and he did so with great vivacity for the sight of five small hot whiskies was very exhilarating. Everyone roared laughing when he showed the way in which Mr Alleyne shook his fist in Farrington's face. Then he imitated Farrington, saying *And here was my nabs, as cool as you please*, while Farrington looked at the company out of his heavy dirty eyes, smiling and at times drawing forth stray drops of liquor from his moustache with the aid of his lower lip.

When that round was over there was a pause. O'Halloran had money but neither of the other two seemed to have any so the whole party left the shop somewhat regretfully. At the corner of Duke Street Higgins and Nosey Flynn bevelled off to the left while the other three turned back towards the city. Rain was drizzling down on the cold streets and when they reached the Ballast Office Farrington suggested the Scotch House. The bar was full of men and loud with the noise of tongues and glasses. The three men pushed past the whining matchsellers at the door and formed a little party at the corner of the counter. They began to exchange stories. Leonard introduced them to a young fellow named Weathers who was performing at the Tivoli as an acrobat and knockabout *artiste*. Farrington stood a drink all round. Weathers said he would take a small Irish and Apollinaris. Farrington, who had definite notions of what was what, asked the boys would they have an Apollinaris too: but the boys told Tim to make theirs hot. The talk became theatrical. O'Halloran stood a round and then Farrington stood another round, Weathers protesting that the hospitality was too Irish. He promised to get them in behind the scenes and introduce them to some nice girls. O'Halloran said that he and Leonard would go but that Farrington wouldn't go because he was a married man and Farrington's heavy dirty eyes leered at the company in token that he understood when he was being chaffed. Weathers made them all have just one little tincture at his expense and promised to meet them later on at Mulligan's in Poolbeg Street.

When the Scotch House closed they went round to Mulligan's. They went into the parlour at the back and O'Halloran ordered small hot specials all round. They were all beginning to feel mellow. Farrington was just standing another round when Weathers came back. Much to Farrington's relief he drank a glass of bitter this time. Funds were running low but they had enough to keep them going. Presently two young women with big hats and a young man in a check suit came in and sat at a table close by. Weathers saluted them and told the company that they were out of the Tivoli. Farrington's eyes wandered at every moment in the direction of one of the young women. There was something striking in her appearance. An immense scarf of peacockblue muslin was wound round her hat and knotted in a great bow under her chin; and she wore bright yellow gloves reaching to the elbow. Farrington gazed admiringly at the plump arm which she moved very often and with much grace; and, when after a little time she answered his gaze, he admired still more her large dark brown eyes. The oblique staring expression in them fascinated him. She glanced at him once or twice and, when the party was leaving the room, she brushed against his chair and said O, *pardon!* in a London accent. He watched her leave the room in the hope that she would look back at him but he was disappointed. He cursed his want of money and cursed all the rounds he had stood, particularly all the whiskies and Apollinaris which he had stood to Weathers. If there was one thing that he hated it was a sponge. He was so angry that he lost count of the conversation of his friends.

When Paddy Leonard called him he found that they were talking about feats of strength. Weathers was showing his biceps muscle to the company and boasting so much that the other two had called on Farrington to uphold the national honour. Farrington pulled up his sleeve accordingly and showed his biceps muscle to the company. The two arms were examined and compared and finally it was agreed to have a trial of strength. The table was cleared and the two men rested their elbows on it, clasping hands. When Paddy Leonard said *Go!* each was to try to bring down the other's hand on to the table. Farrington looked very serious and determined.

The trial began. After about thirty seconds Weathers brought his opponent's hand slowly down on to the table. Farrington's dark winecoloured face flushed darker still with anger and humiliation at having been defeated by such a stripling.

—You're not to put the weight of your body behind it. Play fair, he said.

—Who's not playing fair? said the other.

—Come on again. The two best out of three.

The trial began again. The veins stood out on Farrington's forehead and the pallor of Weathers' complexion changed to peony. Their hands and arms trembled under the stress. After a long struggle Weathers again brought his opponent's hand slowly on to the table. There was a murmur of applause from the spectators. The curate, who was standing beside the table, nodded his red head towards the victor and said with loutish familiarity:

—Ah! that's the knack!

—What the hell do you know about it? said Farrington fiercely, turning on the man. What do you put in your gab for?

—'Sh, 'sh! said O'Halloran, observing the violent expression of Farrington's face. Pony up, boys. We'll have just one little smahan more and then we'll be off!

A very sullenfaced man stood at the corner of O'Connell Bridge waiting for the little Sandymount tram to take him home. He was full of smouldering anger and revengefulness.

He felt humiliated and discontented: he did not even feel drunk and he had only twopence in his pocket. He cursed everything. He had done for himself in the office, pawned his watch, spent all his money; and he had not even got drunk. He began to feel thirsty again and he longed to be back again in the hot reeking publichouse. He had lost his reputation as a strong man, having been defeated twice by a mere boy. His heart swelled with fury and when he thought of the woman in the big hat who had brushed against him and said *Pardon!* his fury nearly choked him.

His tram let him down at Shelbourne Road and he steered his great body along in the shadow of the wall of the barracks. He loathed returning to his home. When he went in by the sidedoor he found the kitchen empty and the kitchen fire nearly out. He bawled upstairs:

—Ada! Ada!

His wife was a little sharpfaced woman who bullied her husband when he was sober and was bullied by him when he was drunk. They had five children. A little boy came running down the stairs.

—Who is that? said the man peering through the darkness.

—Me, pa.

—Who are you? Charlie?

—No, pa. Tom.

—Where's your mother?

—She's out at the chapel.

—That's right .... Did she think of leaving any dinner for me?

—Yes, pa. I ...

—Light the lamp. What do you mean by having the place in darkness? Are the other children in bed?

The man sat down heavily on one of the chairs while the little boy lit the lamp. He began to mimick his son's flat accent, saying half to himself: *At the chapel. At the chapel, if you please!* When the lamp was lit he banged his fist on the table and shouted:

—What's for my dinner?

—I'm ... going to cook it, pa, said the little boy.

The man jumped up furiously and pointed to the fire:

—On that fire! You let the fire out! By God, I'll teach you to do that again!

He took a step to the door and seized the walking stick which was standing behind it:

—I'll teach you to let the fire out! he said, rolling up his sleeve in order to give his arm free play.

The little boy cried *O, pa!* and ran whimpering round the table but the man followed him and caught him by the coat. The little boy looked about him wildly but, seeing no way of escape, fell upon his knees.

—Now, you'll let the fire out the next time! said the man, striking at him viciously with the stick. Take that, you little whelp!

The boy uttered a squeal of pain as the stick cut his thigh. He clasped his hands together in the air and his voice shook with fright.

—O, pa! he cried. Don't beat me, pa! And I'll ... I'll say a *Hail Mary* for you. ... I'll say a *Hail Mary* for you, pa, if you don't beat me. ... I'll say a *Hail Mary*. ...

Clay

The matron had given her leave to go out as soon as the women's tea was over and Maria looked forward to her evening out. The kitchen was spick and span: the cook said you could see yourself in the big copper boilers. The fire was nice and bright and on one of the sidetables were four very big barmbracks. These barmbracks seemed uncut but, if you went closer, you would see that they had been cut into long thick even slices and were ready to be handed round at tea. Maria had cut them herself.

Maria was a very, very small person indeed but she had a very long nose and a very long chin. She talked a little through her nose, always soothingly: *Yes, my dear*, and *No, my dear*. She was always sent for when the women quarrelled over their tubs and always succeeded in making peace. One day the matron had said to her:

—Maria, you are a veritable peacemaker!

And the submatron and two of the board ladies had heard the compliment. And Ginger Mooney was always saying what she wouldn't do to the dummy who had charge of the irons if it wasn't for Maria. Everyone was so fond of Maria.

The women would have their tea at six o'clock and she would be able to get away before seven. From Ballsbridge to the Pillar, twenty minutes; from the Pillar to Drumcondra, twenty minutes; and twenty minutes to buy the things. She would be there before eight. She took out her purse with the silver clasps and read again the words *A Present from Belfast*. She was very fond of that purse because Joe had brought it to her five years before when he and Alphy had gone to Belfast on a Whit Monday trip. In the purse were two half crowns and some coppers. She would have five shillings clear after paying tram fare. What a nice evening they would have, all the children singing! Only she hoped that Joe wouldn't come in drunk. He was so different when he took any drink.

Often he had wanted her to go and live with them; but she would have felt herself in the way (though Joe's wife was ever so nice with her) and she had become accustomed to the life of the laundry. Joe was a good fellow. She had nursed him and Alphy too; and Joe used often to say:

—Mamma is mamma but Maria is my proper mother.

After the breakup at home the boys had got her that position in the *Dublin by Lamplight* laundry and she liked it. She used to have such a bad opinion of protestants but now she thought they were very nice people, a little quiet and serious, but still very nice people to live with. Then she had her plants in the conservatory and she liked looking after them. She had lovely ferns and waxplants and whenever anyone came to visit her she always gave the visitor one or two slips from her conservatory. There was one thing she didn't like and that was the tracts on the walls; but the matron was such a nice person to deal with, so genteel.

When the cook told her everything was ready she went into the women's room and began to pull the big bell. In a few minutes the women began to come in by twos and threes, wiping their steaming hands in their petticoats and pulling down the sleeves of their blouses over their red steaming arms. They settled down before their huge mugs which the cook and the dummy filled up with hot tea, already mixed with milk and sugar in huge tin cans. Maria superintended the distribution of the barmbrack and saw that every woman got her four slices. There was a great deal of laughing and joking during the meal. Lizzie Fleming said Maria was sure to get the ring and, though Fleming had said that for so many Hallow Eves, Maria had to laugh and say she didn't want any ring or man either; and when she laughed her greygreen eyes sparkled with disappointed shyness and the tip of her nose nearly met the tip of her chin. Then Ginger Mooney lifted up her mug of tea and proposed Maria's health while all the other women clattered with their mugs on the table and said she was sorry she hadn't a sup of porter to drink it in. And Maria laughed again till the tip of her nose nearly met the tip of her chin and till her minute body nearly shook itself asunder because she knew that Mooney meant well though of course she had the notions of a common woman.

But wasn't Maria glad when the women had finished their tea and the cook and the dummy had begun to clear away the tea things? She went into her little bedroom and, remembering that the next morning was a mass morning, changed the hand of the alarm from seven to six. Then she took off her working skirt and her houseboots and laid her best skirt out on the bed and her tiny dressboots beside the foot of the bed. She changed her blouse too and, as she stood before the mirror, she thought of how she used to dress for mass on Sunday morning when she was a young girl; and she looked with quaint affection at the diminutive body which she had so often adorned. In spite of its years she found it a nice tidy little body.

When she got outside the streets were shining with rain and she was glad of her old brown raincloak. The tram was full and she had to sit on the little stool at the end of the car facing all the people, with her toes barely touching the floor. She arranged in her mind all she was going to do and thought how much better it was to be independent and to have your own money in your pocket. She hoped they would have a nice evening. She was sure they would but she could not help thinking what a pity it was Alphy and Joe were not speaking. They were always falling out now but when they were boys together they used to be the best of friends: but such was life.

She got out of her tram at the Pillar and ferreted her way quickly among the crowds. She went into Downes's cakeshop but the shop was so full of people that it was a long time before she could get herself attended to. She bought a dozen of mixed penny cakes and at last came out of the shop laden with a big bag. Then she thought what else would she buy: she wanted to buy something really nice. They would be sure to have plenty of apples and nuts. It was hard to know what to buy and all she could think of was cake. She decided to buy some plumcake but Downes's plumcake had not enough almond icing on top of it so she went over to a shop in Henry Street. Here she was a long time in suiting herself and the stylish young lady behind the counter, who was evidently a little annoyed by her, asked her was it weddingcake she wanted to buy. That made Maria blush and smile at the young lady but the young lady took it all very seriously and finally cut a thick slice of plumcake, parcelled it up and said:

—Two and four, please.

She thought she would have to stand in the Drumcondra tram because none of the young men seemed to notice her but an elderly gentleman made room for her. He was a stout gentleman and he wore a brown hard hat; he had a square red face and a greyish moustache. Maria thought he was a colonel-looking gentleman and she reflected how much more polite he was than the young men who simply stared straight before them. The gentleman began to chat with her about Hallow Eve and the rainy weather. He supposed the bag was full of good things for the little ones and said it was only right that the youngsters should enjoy themselves while they were young. Maria agreed with him and favoured him with demure nods and hems. He was very nice with her and when she was getting out at the Canal Bridge she thanked him and bowed and he bowed to her and raised his hat and smiled agreeably; and while she was going up along the terrace, bending her tiny head under the rain, she thought how easy it was to know a gentleman even when he has a drop taken.

Everybody said: *O, here's Maria!* when she came to Joe's house. Joe was there, having come home from business, and all the children had their Sunday dresses on. There were two big girls in from next door and games were going on. Maria gave the bag of cakes to the eldest boy, Alphy, to divide and Mrs Donnelly said it was too good of her to bring such a big bag of cakes and made all the children say:

—Thanks, Maria.

But Maria said she had brought something special for papa and mamma, something they would be sure to like, and she began to look for her plumcake. She tried in Downes's bag and then in the pockets of her raincloak and then on the hallstand but nowhere could she find it. Then she asked all the children had any of them eaten it—by mistake, of course—but the children all said no and looked as if they did not like to eat cakes if they were to be accused of stealing. Everybody had a solution for the mystery and Mrs Donnelly said it was plain that Maria had left it behind her in the tram. Maria, remembering how confused the gentleman with the greyish moustache had made her, coloured with shame and vexation and disappointment. At the thought of the failure of her little surprise and of the two and fourpence she had thrown away for nothing she nearly cried outright.

But Joe said it didn't matter and made her sit down by the fire. He was very nice with her. He told her all that went on in his office, repeating for her a smart answer which he had made to the manager. Maria did not understand why Joe laughed so much over the answer he had made but she said that the manager must have been a very overbearing person to deal with. Joe said he wasn't so bad when you knew how to take him, that he was a decent sort so long as you didn't rub him the wrong way. Mrs Donnelly played the piano for the children and they danced and sang. Then the two nextdoor girls handed round the nuts. Nobody could find the nutcracker and Joe was nearly getting cross over it and asked how did they expect Maria to crack nuts without a nutcracker. But Maria said she didn't like nuts and that they weren't to bother about her. Then Joe asked would she take a bottle of stout and Mrs Donnelly said there was port wine too in the house if she would prefer that. Maria said she would rather they didn't ask her to take anything: but Joe insisted.

So Maria let him have his way and they sat by the fire talking over old times and Maria thought she would put in a good word for Alphy. But Joe cried that God might strike him stone dead if ever he spoke a word to his brother again and Maria said she was sorry she had mentioned the matter. Mrs Donnelly told her husband it was a great shame for him to speak that way of his own flesh and blood but Joe said that Alphy was no brother of his and there was nearly being a row on the head of it. But Joe said he would not lose his temper on account of the night it was and asked his wife to open some more stout. The two nextdoor girls had arranged some Hallow Eve games and soon everything was merry again. Maria was delighted to see the children so merry and Joe and his wife in such good spirits. The nextdoor girls put some saucers on the table and then led the children up to the table, blindfold. One got the prayerbook and the other three got the water; and when one of the nextdoor girls got the ring Mrs Donnelly shook her finger at the blushing girl as much as to say: *O, I know all about it!* They insisted then on blindfolding Maria and leading her up to the table to see what she would get; and, while they were putting on the bandage, Maria laughed and laughed again till the tip of her nose nearly met the tip of her chin.

They led her up to the table amid laughing and joking and she put her hand out in the air as she was told to do. She moved her hand about here and there in the air and descended on one of the saucers. She felt a soft wet substance with her fingers and was surprised that nobody spoke or took off her bandage. There was a pause for a few seconds and then a great deal of scuffling and whispering. Somebody said something about the garden and at last Mrs Donnelly said something very cross to one of the nextdoor girls and told her to throw it out at once: that was no play. Maria understood that it was wrong that time and so she had to do it over again: and this time she got the prayerbook.

After that Mrs Donnelly played Miss McCloud's Reel for the children and Joe made Maria take a glass of wine. Soon they were all quite merry again and Mrs Donnelly said Maria would enter a convent before the year was out because she had got the prayerbook. Maria had never seen Joe so nice to her as he was that night, so full of pleasant talk and reminiscences. She said they were all very good to her.

At last the children grew tired and sleepy and Joe asked Maria would she not sing some little song before she went, one of the old songs. Mrs Donnelly said *Do, please, Maria!* and so Maria had to get up and stand beside the piano. Mrs Donnelly bade the children be quiet and listen to Maria's song. Then she played the prelude and said *Now, Maria!* and Maria, blushing very much, began to sing in a tiny quavering voice. She sang *I dreamt that I dwelt* and when she came to the second verse she sang again:

I dreamt that I dwelt in marble halls
  With vassals and serfs at my side
And of all who assembled within those walls
  That I was the hope and the pride.
I had riches too great to count, could boast
  Of a high ancestral name,
But I also dreamt, which pleased me most,
  That you loved me still the same.

But no one tried to show her her mistake and, when she had ended her song, Joe was very much moved. He said that there was no time like the long ago and no music for him like poor old Balfe, whatever other people might say; and his eyes filled up so much with tears that he could not find what he was looking for and in the end he had to ask his wife to tell him where the corkscrew was.

A Painful Case

Mr James Duffy lived in Chapelizod because he wished to live as far as possible from the city of which he was a citizen and because he found all the other suburbs of Dublin mean, modern and pretentious. He lived in an old sombre house and from his windows he could look into the disused distillery or upwards along the shallow river on which Dublin is built. The lofty walls of his uncarpeted room were free from pictures. He had himself bought every article of furniture in the room: a black iron bedstead, an iron washstand, four cane chairs, a clothesrack, a coalscuttle, a fender and irons and a square table on which lay a double desk. A bookcase had been made in an alcove by means of shelves of white wood. The bed was clothed with white bedclothes and a black and scarlet rug covered the foot. A little handmirror hung above the washstand and during the day a whiteshaded lamp stood as the sole ornament of the mantelpiece. The books on the white wooden shelves were arranged from below upwards according to bulk. A complete Wordsworth stood at one end of the lowest shelf and a copy of the Maynooth catechism, sewn into the cloth cover of a notebook, stood at one end of the top shelf. Writing materials were always on the desk. In the desk lay a manuscript translation of Hauptmann's *Michael Kramer*, the stage directions of which were written in purple ink, and a little sheaf of papers held together by a brass pin. In these sheets a sentence was inscribed from time to time and, in an ironical moment, the headline of an advertisement for bile beans had been pasted on to the first sheet. On lifting the lid of the desk a faint fragrance escaped–the fragrance of new cedarwood pencils or of a bottle of gum or of an overripe apple which might have been left there and forgotten.

Mr Duffy abhorred anything which betokened physical or mental disorder. A medieval doctor would have called him saturnine. His face, which carried the entire tale of his years, was of the brown tint of Dublin streets. On his long and rather large head grew dry black hair and a tawny moustache did not quite cover an unamiable mouth. His cheekbones also gave his face a harsh character but there was no harshness in the eyes which, looking at the world from under their tawny eyebrows, gave the impression of a man ever alert to greet a redeeming instinct in others but often disappointed. He lived at a little distance from his body, regarding his own acts with doubtful sideglances. He had an odd autobiographical habit which led him to compose in his mind from time to time a short sentence about himself containing a subject in the third person and a predicate in the past tense. He never gave alms to beggars and walked firmly, carrying a stout hazel.

He had been for many years cashier of a private bank in Baggot Street. Every morning he came in from Chapelizod by tram. At midday he went to Dan Burke's and took his lunch, a bottle of lager beer and a small trayful of arrowroot biscuits. At four o'clock he was set free. He dined in an eatinghouse in George's Street where he felt himself safe from the society of Dublin's gilded youth and where there was a certain plain honesty in the bill of fare. His evenings were spent either before his landlady's piano or roaming about the outskirts of the city.

His liking for Mozart's music brought him sometimes to an opera or a concert: these were the only dissipations of his life.

He had neither companions nor friends, church nor creed. He lived his spiritual life without any communion with others, visiting his relatives at Christmas and escorting them to the cemetery when they died. He performed these two social duties for old dignity' sake but conceded nothing further to the conventions which regulate the civic life. He allowed himself to think that in certain circumstances he would rob his bank but as these circumstances never arose his life rolled out evenly—an adventureless tale.

One evening he found himself sitting beside two ladies in the Rotunda. The house, thinly peopled and silent, gave distressing prophecy of failure. The lady who sat next him looked round at the deserted house once or twice and then said:

—What a pity there is such a poor house tonight! It's so hard on people to have to sing to empty benches.

He took the remark as an invitation to talk. He was surprised that she seemed so little awkward. While they talked he tried to fix her permanently in his memory. When he learned that the young girl beside her was her daughter he judged her to be a year or so younger than himself. Her face, which must have been handsome, had remained intelligent. It was an oval face with strongly marked features. The eyes were very dark blue and steady. Their gaze began with a defiant note but was confused by what seemed a deliberate swoon of the pupil into the iris, revealing for an instant a temperament of great sensibility. The pupil reasserted itself quickly, this half disclosed nature fell again under the reign of prudence, and her astrakhan jacket, moulding a bosom of a certain fulness, struck the note of defiance more definitely.

He met her again a few weeks afterwards at a concert in Earlsfort Terrace and seized the moments when her daughter's attention was diverted to become intimate. She alluded once or twice to her husband but her tone was not such as to make the allusion a warning. Her name was Mrs Sinico. Her husband's great-great-grandfather had come from Leghorn. Her husband was captain of a mercantile boat plying between Dublin and Holland: and they had one child.

Meeting her a third time by accident he found courage to make an appointment. She came. This was the first of many meetings; they met always in the evening and chose the most quiet quarters for their walks together. Mr Duffy, however, had a distaste for underhand ways and, finding that they were compelled to meet stealthily, he forced her to ask him to her house. Captain Sinico encouraged his visits, thinking that his daughter's hand was in question. He had dismissed his wife so sincerely from his gallery of pleasures that he did not suspect anyone else would take an interest in her. As the husband was often away and the daughter out giving music lessons Mr Duffy had many opportunities of enjoying the lady's society. Neither he nor she had had any such adventure before and neither was conscious of any incongruity. Little by little he entangled his thoughts with hers. He lent her books, provided her with ideas, shared his intellectual life with her. She listened to all.

Sometimes in return for his theories she gave out some fact of her own life. With almost maternal solicitude she urged him to let his nature open to the full; she became his confessor. He told her that for some time he had assisted at the meetings of an Irish Socialist Party where he had felt himself a unique figure amid a score of sober workmen in a garret lit by an inefficient oillamp. When the party had divided into three sections, each under its own leader and in its own garret, he had discontinued his attendances. The workmen's discussions, he said, were too timorous; the interest they took in the question of wages was inordinate. He felt that they were hardfeatured realists and that they resented an exactitude which was the product of a leisure not within their reach. No social revolution, he told her, would be likely to strike Dublin for some centuries.

She asked him why did he not write out his thoughts. For what? he asked her with careful scorn. To compete with phrasemongers, incapable of thinking consecutively for sixty seconds? To submit himself to the criticisms of an obtuse middle class which entrusted its morality to policemen and its fine arts to impresarios?

He went often to her little cottage outside Dublin: often they spent their evenings alone. Little by little as their thoughts entangled they spoke of subjects less remote. Her companionship was like a warm soil about an exotic. Many times she allowed the dark to fall upon them, refraining from lighting the lamp. The dark discreet room, their isolation, the music that still vibrated in their ears united them. This union exalted him, wore away the rough edges of his character, emotionalised his mental life. Sometimes he caught himself listening to the sound of his own voice. He thought that in her eyes he would ascend to an angelical stature; and as he attached the fervent nature of his companion more and more closely to him he heard the strange impersonal voice, which he recognised as his own, insisting on the soul's incurable loneliness. We cannot give ourselves, it said: we are our own. The end of these discourses was that one night, during which she had shown every sign of unusual excitement, Mrs Sinico caught up his hand passionately and pressed it to her cheek.

Mr Duffy was very much surprised. Her interpretation of his words disillusioned him. He did not visit her for a week; then he wrote to her asking her to meet him. As he did not wish their last interview to be troubled by the influence of their ruined confessional they met in a little cakeshop near the Parkgate. It was cold autumn weather but in spite of the cold they wandered up and down the roads of the Park for nearly three hours. They agreed to break off their intercourse: every bond, he said, is a bond to sorrow. When they came out of the Park they walked in silence towards the tram but here she began to tremble so violently that, fearing another collapse on her part, he bade her goodbye quickly and left her. A few days later he received a parcel containing his books and music.

Four years passed. Mr Duffy returned to his even way of life. His room still bore witness of the orderliness of his mind. Some new pieces of music encumbered the musicstand in the lower room and on his shelves stood two volumes by Nietzsche, *Thus Spake Zarathustra* and *The Gay Science*. He wrote seldom in the sheaf of papers which lay in his desk. One of his sentences, written two months after his last interview with Mrs Sinico, read: Love between man and man is impossible because there must not be sexual intercourse and friendship between man and woman is impossible because there must be sexual intercourse. He kept away from concerts lest he should meet her. His father died; the junior partner of the bank retired. And still every morning he went into the city by tram and every evening walked home from the city after having dined moderately in George's Street and read the evening paper for dessert.

One evening as he was about to put a morsel of corned beef and cabbage into his mouth his hand stopped. His eyes fixed themselves on a paragraph in the evening paper which he had propped against the watercroft. He replaced the morsel of food on his plate and read the paragraph attentively. Then he drank a glass of water, pushed his plate to one side, doubled the paper down before him between his elbows and read the paragraph over and over again. The cabbage began to deposit a cold white grease on his plate. The girl came over to him to ask was his dinner not properly cooked. He said it was very good and ate a few mouthfuls of it with difficulty. Then he paid his bill and went out.

He walked along quickly through the November twilight, his stout hazel stick striking the ground regularly, the fringe of the buff *Mail* peeping out of a sidepocket of his tight reefer overcoat. On the lonely road which leads from the Parkgate to Chapelizod he slackened his pace. His stick struck the ground less emphatically and his breath, issuing irregularly, almost with a sighing sound, condensed in the wintry air. When he reached his house he went up at once to his bedroom and, taking the paper from his pocket, read the paragraph again by the failing light of the window. He read it not aloud but moving his lips as a priest does when he reads the prayer *In Secretis*. This was the paragraph:

DEATH OF A LADY AT SYDNEY PARADE

A Painful Case

Today at the City of Dublin Hospital the Deputy Coroner (in the absence of Mr Leverett) held an inquest on the body of Mrs Emily Sinico, aged forty-three years, who was killed at Sydney Parade Station yesterday evening. The evidence showed that the deceased lady while attempting to cross the line was knocked down by the engine of the ten o'clock slow train from Kingstown, thereby sustaining injuries of the head and right side which led to her death.

James Lennon, driver of the engine, stated that he had been in the employment of the railway company for fifteen years. On hearing the guard's whistle he set the train in motion and a second or two afterwards brought it to rest in response to loud cries. The train was going slowly.

P. Dunne, railway porter, stated that as the train was about to start he observed a woman attempting to cross the lines. He ran towards her and shouted but before he could reach her she was caught by the buffer of the engine and fell to the ground.

A Juror – You saw the lady fall?

Witness – Yes.

Police Sergeant Croly deposed that when he arrived he found the deceased lying on the platform apparently dead. He had the body taken to the waitingroom pending the arrival of the ambulance.

Constable 57 E corroborated.

Dr Halpin, assistant house surgeon of the City of Dublin Hospital, stated that the deceased had two lower ribs fractured and had sustained severe contusions of the right shoulder. The right side of the head had been injured in the fall. The injuries were not sufficient to have caused death in a normal person. Death, in his opinion, had been probably due to shock and sudden failure of the heart's action.

Mr H. B. Patterson Finlay, on behalf of the railway company, expressed his deep regret at the accident. The company had always taken every precaution to prevent people crossing the lines except by the bridges, both by placing notices in every station and by the use of patent spring gates at level crossings. The deceased had been in the habit of crossing the lines late at night from platform to platform and, in view of certain other circumstances of the case, he did not think the railway officials were to blame.

Captain Sinico, of Leoville, Sydney Parade, husband of the deceased, also gave evidence. He stated that the deceased was his wife. He was not in Dublin at the time of the accident as he had arrived only that morning from Rotterdam. They had been married for twenty-two years and had lived happily until about two years ago when his wife began to be rather intemperate in her habits.

Miss Mary Sinico said that of late her mother had been in the habit of going out at night to buy spirits. She, witness, had often tried to reason with her mother and had induced her to join a league. She was not at home until an hour after the accident.

The jury returned a verdict in accordance with the medical evidence and exonerated Lennon from all blame.

The Deputy Coroner said it was a most painful case and expressed great sympathy with Captain Sinico and his daughter. He urged on the railway company to take strong measures to prevent the possibility of similar accidents in the future. No blame attached to anyone.

Mr Duffy raised his eyes from the paper and gazed out of his window on the cheerless evening landscape. The river lay quiet beside the empty distillery and from time to time a light appeared in some house on the Lucan road. What an end! The whole narrative of her death revolted him and it revolted him to think that he had ever spoken to her of what he held sacred. The threadbare phrases, the inane expressions of sympathy, the cautious words of a reporter won over to conceal the details of a commonplace vulgar death attacked his stomach. Not merely had she degraded herself; she had degraded him. He saw the squalid tract of her vice, miserable and malodorous. His soul's companion! He thought of the hobbling wretches whom he had seen carrying cans and bottles to be filled by the barman. Just God, what an end! Evidently she had been unfit to live, without any strength of purpose, an easy prey to habits, one of the wrecks on which civilisation has been reared. But that she could have sunk so low! Was it possible he had deceived himself so utterly about her? He remembered her outburst of that night and interpreted it in a harsher sense than he had ever done. He had no difficulty now in approving of the course he had taken.

As the light failed and his memory began to wander he thought her hand touched his. The shock which had first attacked his stomach was now attacking his nerves. He put on his overcoat and hat quickly and went out. The cold air met him on the threshold; it crept into the sleeves of his coat. When he came to the publichouse at Chapelizod Bridge he went in and ordered a hot punch.

The proprietor served him obsequiously but did not venture to talk. There were five or six workingmen in the shop discussing the value of a gentleman's estate in county Kildare. They drank at intervals from their huge pint tumblers and smoked, spitting often on the floor and sometimes dragging the sawdust over their spits with their heavy boots. Mr Duffy sat on his stool and gazed at them, without seeing or hearing them. After a while they went out and he called for another punch. He sat a long time over it. The shop was very quiet. The proprietor sprawled on the counter reading the *Herald* and yawning. Now and again a tram was heard swishing along the lonely road outside.

As he sat there, living over his life with her and evoking alternately the two images in which he now conceived her, he realised that she was dead, that she had ceased to exist, that she had become a memory. He began to feel ill at ease. He asked himself what else could he have done. He could not have carried on a comedy of deception with her; he could not have lived with her openly. He had done what seemed to him best. How was he to blame? Now that she was gone he understood how lonely her life must have been, sitting night after night alone in that room. His life would be lonely too until he, too, died, ceased to exist, became a memory – if anyone remembered him.

It was after nine o'clock when he left the shop. The night was cold and gloomy. He entered the Park by the first gate and walked along under the gaunt trees. He walked through the bleak alleys where they had walked four years before. She seemed to be near him in the darkness. At moments he seemed to feel her voice touch his ear, her hand touch his. He stood still to listen. Why had he withheld life from her? Why had he sentenced her to death? He felt his moral nature falling to pieces.

When he gained the crest of the Magazine Hill he halted and looked along the river towards Dublin, the lights of which burned redly and hospitably in the cold night. He looked down the slope and at the base, in the shadow of the wall of the Park, he saw some human figures lying. Those venal and furtive loves filled him with despair. He gnawed the rectitude of his life; he felt that he had been outcast from life's feast. One human being had seemed to love him and he had denied her life and happiness: he had sentenced her to ignominy, a death of shame. He knew that the prostrate creatures down by the wall were watching him and wished him gone. No-one wanted him; he was outcast from life's feast. He turned his eyes to the grey gleaming river, winding along towards Dublin. Beyond the river he saw a goods train winding out of Kingsbridge Station, like a worm with a fiery head winding through the darkness obstinately and laboriously. It passed slowly out of sight but still he heard in his ears the laborious drone of the engine reiterating the syllables of her name.

He turned back the way he had come, the rhythm of the engine pounding in his ears. He began to doubt the reality of what memory told him. He halted under a tree and allowed the rhythm to die away. He could not feel her near him in the darkness nor her voice touch his ear. He waited for some minutes, listening. He could hear nothing: the night was perfectly silent. He listened again: perfectly silent. He felt that he was alone.

Ivy Day in the Committee Room

Old Jack raked the cinders together with a piece of cardboard and spread them judiciously over the whitening dome of coals. When the dome was thinly covered his face lapsed into darkness but as he set himself to fan the fire again his crouching shadow ascended the opposite wall and his face slowly re-emerged into light. It was an old man's face, very bony and hairy. The moist blue eyes blinked at the fire and the moist mouth fell open at times, munching once or twice mechanically when it closed. When the cinders had caught he laid the piece of cardboard against the wall, sighed and said:

—That's better now, Mr. O'Connor.

Mr O'Connor, a greyhaired young man, whose face was disfigured by many blotches and pimples, had just brought the tobacco for a cigarette into a shapely cylinder but, when spoken to, he undid his handiwork meditatively. Then he began to roll the tobacco again meditatively and, after a moment's thought, decided to lick the paper.

—Did Mr Tierney say when he'd be back? he asked in a husky *falsetto*.

—He didn't say.

Mr O'Connor put his cigarette into his mouth and began to search his pockets. He took out a pack of thin pasteboard cards.

—I'll get you a match, said the old man.

—Never mind, this'll do, said Mr O'Connor.

He selected one of the cards and read what was printed on it:

Municipal Elections
Royal Exchange Ward
Mr Richard J Tierney P. L. G. respectfully solicits
the favour of your vote and influence at the coming
election in the Royal Exchange Ward.

Mr O'Connor had been engaged by Mr Tierney's agent to canvass one part of the ward but, as the weather was inclement and his boots let in the wet, he spent a great part of the day sitting by the fire in the Committee Room in Wicklow Street with Jack, the old caretaker. They had been sitting thus since the short day had grown dark. It was the sixth of October, dismal and cold out of doors.

Mr O'Connor tore off a strip of the card and, lighting it, lit his cigarette. As he did so the flame lit up a leaf of dark glossy ivy in the lapel of his coat. The old man watched him attentively and then, taking up the piece of cardboard again, began to fan the fire slowly while his companion smoked.

—Ah, yes, he said, continuing, it's hard to know what way to bring up children. Now who'd think he'd turn out like that. I sent him to the Christian Brothers and I done what I could for him and there he goes boosing about. I tried to make him someway decent.

He replaced the cardboard wearily.

—Only I'm an old man now I'd change his tune for him. I'd take the stick to his back and beat him while I could stand over him—as I done many a time before. The mother, you know, she cocks him up with this and that ....

—That's what ruins children, said Mr O'Connor.

—To be sure it is, said the old man. And little thanks you get for it, only impudence. He takes the upper hand of me whenever he sees I've a sup taken. What's the world coming to when sons speaks that way to their father?

—What age is he? said Mr O'Connor.

—Nineteen, said the old man.

—Why don't you put him to something?

—Sure, amn't I never done at the drunken bowsey ever since he left school. *I won't keep you*, I says. *You must get a job for yourself*. But, sure, it's worse whenever he gets a job: he drinks it all.

Mr O'Connor shook his head in sympathy and the old man fell silent, gazing into the fire. Someone opened the door of the room and called out:

—Hello! Is this a Freemasons' meeting?

—Who's that? said the old man.

—What are you doing in the dark? asked a voice.

—Is that you, Hynes? asked Mr O'Connor.

—Yes. What are you doing in the dark? said Mr Hynes advancing into the light of the fire.

He was a tall slender young man with a light brown moustache. Imminent little drops of rain hung at the brim of his hat and the collar of his jacket coat was turned up.

—Well, Mat, he said to Mr O'Connor, how goes it?

Mr O'Connor shook his head. The old man left the hearth and after stumbling about the room returned with two candlesticks which he thrust one after the other into the fire and carried to the table. A denuded room came into view and the fire lost all its cheerful colour. The walls of the room were bare except for a copy of an election address. In the middle of the room was a small table on which papers were heaped.

Mr Hynes leaned against the mantelpiece and asked:

—Has he paid you yet?

—Not yet, said Mr O'Connor. I hope to God he'll not leave us in the lurch tonight.

Mr Hynes laughed.

—O, he'll pay you. Never fear, he said.

—I hope he'll look smart about it if he means business, said Mr O'Connor.

—What do you think, Jack? said Mr Hynes satirically to the old man.

The old man returned to his seat by the fire, saying:

—It isn't but he has it, anyway. Not like the other tinker.

—What other tinker? said Mr Hynes.

—Colgan, said the old man scornfully.

—Is it because Colgan's a workingman you say that? What's the difference between a good honest bricklayer and a publican —eh? Hasn't the workingman as good a right to be in the Corporation as anyone else—aye, and a better right than those shoneens that are always hat in hand before any fellow with a handle to his name? Isn't that so, Mat? said Mr Hynes, addressing Mr O'Connor.

—I think you're right, said Mr O'Connor.

—One man is a plain honest man with no hunkersliding about him. He goes in to represent the labour classes. This fellow you're working for only wants to get some job or other.

—Of course, the working classes should be represented, said the old man.

—The workingman, said Mr Hynes, gets all kicks and no halfpence. But it's labour produces everything. The workingman is not looking for fat jobs for his sons and nephews and cousins. The workingman is not going to drag the honour of Dublin in the mud to please a German monarch.

—How's that? said the old man.

—Don't you know they want to present an address of welcome to Edward Rex if he comes here next year? What do we want kowtowing to a foreign king?

—Our man won't vote for the address, said Mr O'Connor. He goes in on the nationalist ticket.

—Won't he? said Mr Hynes. Wait till you see whether he will or not. I know him. Is it Tricky Dicky Tierney?

—By God! perhaps you're right, Joe, said Mr O'Connor. Anyway I wish he'd turn up with the spondulics.

The three men fell silent. The old man began to rake more cinders together. Mr Hynes took off his hat, shook it and then turned down the collar of his coat, displaying, as he did so, an ivy leaf in the lapel.

—If this man was alive, he said, pointing to the leaf, we'd have no talk of an address of welcome.

—That's true, said Mr O'Connor.

—Musha, God be with them times! said the old man. There was some life in it then.

The room was silent again. Then a bustling little man with a snuffling nose and very cold ears pushed in the door. He walked over quickly to the fire, rubbing his hands as if he intended to produce a spark from them.

—No money, boys, he said.

—Sit down here, Mr Henchy, said the old man, offering him his chair.

—O, don't stir, Jack, don't stir, said Mr Henchy.

He nodded curtly to Mr Hynes and sat down on the chair which the old man vacated.

—Did you serve Aungier Street? he asked Mr O'Connor.

—Yes, said Mr O'Connor, beginning to search his pockets for memoranda.

—Did you call on Grimes?

—I did.

—Well? How does he stand?

—He wouldn't promise. He said: *I won't tell anyone what way I'm going to vote*. But I think he'll be all right.

—Why so?

—He asked me who the nominators were and I told him. I mentioned Father Burke's name. I think it'll be all right.

Mr Henchy began to snuffle and to rub his hands over the fire at a terrific speed. Then he said:

—For the love of God, Jack, bring us in a bit of coal. There must be some left.

The old man went out of the room.

—It's no go, said Mr Henchy, shaking his head. I asked the little shoeboy but he said: O, *now, Mr Henchy, when I see the work going on properly I won't forget you, you may be sure*. Mean little tinker! 'Usha, how could he be anything else?

—What did I tell you, Mat? said Mr Hynes. Tricky Dicky Tierney.

—O, he's as tricky as they make 'em, said Mr Henchy. He hasn't got those little pig's eyes for nothing. Blast his soul! Couldn't he pay up like a man instead of: O, *now, Mr Henchy, I must speak to Mr Fanning ... I've spent a lot of money*? Mean little shoeboy of hell! I suppose he forgets the time his little old father kept the hand-me-down shop in Mary's Lane.

—But is that a fact? asked Mr O'Connor.

—God, yes! said Mr Henchy. Did you never hear that? And the men used to go in on Sunday morning before the houses were open to buy a waistcoat or a trousers—moya!—but Tricky Dicky's little old father always had a tricky little black bottle up in a corner. Do you mind now? That's that. That's where he first saw the light.

The old man returned with a few lumps of coal which he placed here and there on the fire.

—That's a nice how-do-you-do, said Mr O'Connor. How does he expect us to work for him if he won't stump up?

—I can't help it, said Mr Henchy. I expect to find the bailiffs in the hall when I go home.

Mr Hynes laughed and, shoving himself away from the mantelpiece with the aid of his shoulders, made ready to leave.

—It'll be all right when King Eddie comes, he said. Well, boys, I'm off for the present. See you later. 'Bye, 'bye.

He went out of the room slowly. Neither Mr Henchy nor the old man said anything but, just as the door was closing, Mr O'Connor, who had been staring moodily into the fire, called out suddenly:

—'Bye, Joe.

Mr Henchy waited a few moments and then nodded in the direction of the door.

—Tell me, he said across the fire, what brings our friend in here? What does he want?

—'Usha, poor Joe! said Mr O'Connor throwing the end of his cigarette into the fire. He's hard up like the rest of us.

Mr Henchy snuffled vigorously and spat so copiously that he nearly put out the fire which uttered a hissing protest.

—To tell you my private and candid opinion, he said, I think he's a man from the other camp. He's a spy of Colgan's, if you ask me. *Just go round and try and find out how they're getting on. They won't suspect you.* Do you twig?

—Ah, poor Joe is a decent skin, said Mr O'Connor.

—His father was a decent respectable man, Mr Henchy admitted. Poor old Larry Hynes! Many a good turn he did in his day! But I'm greatly afraid our friend is not nineteen carat. Damn it, I can understand a fellow being hard up but what I can't understand is a fellow sponging. Couldn't he have some spark of manhood about him?

—He doesn't get a warm welcome from me when he comes, said the old man. Let him work for his own side and not come spying around here.

—I don't know, said Mr O'Connor dubiously as he took out cigarette papers and tobacco. I think Joe Hynes is a straight man. He's a clever chap, too, with the pen. Do you remember that thing he wrote .....?

—Some of these lousy hillsiders and fenians are a bit too clever if you ask me, said Mr Henchy. Do you know what my private and candid opinion is about some of those little jokers? I believe half of them are in the pay of the Castle.

—There's no knowing, said the old man.

—O, but I know it for a fact, said Mr Henchy. They're Castle hacks ..... I don't say Hynes .... No, damn it, I think he's a stroke above that .... But there's a certain little nobleman with a cockeye–you know the patriot I'm alluding to?

Mr O'Connor nodded.

—There's a lineal descendant of Major Sirr for you if you like! O, the heart's blood of a patriot! That's a fellow now that'd sell his country for fourpence–aye!–and go down on his bended knees and thank the Almighty Christ he had a country to sell.

There was a knock at the door.

—Come in! said Mr Henchy.

A person resembling a poor clergyman or a poor actor appeared in the doorway. His black clothes were tightly buttoned on his short body and it was impossible to say whether he wore a clergyman's collar or a layman's because the collar of his shabby frock coat, the uncovered buttons of which reflected the candlelight, was turned up about his neck. He wore a round hat of hard black felt. His face, shining with raindrops, had the appearance of damp yellow cheese save where two rosy spots indicated the cheekbones. He opened his very long mouth suddenly to express disappointment and at the same time opened wide his very bright blue eyes to express pleasure and surprise.

—O, Father Keon! said Mr Henchy, jumping up from his chair. Is that you? Come in!

—O, no, no, no! said Father Keon quickly, pursing up his lips as if he were addressing a child.

—Won't you come in and sit down?

—No, no, no! said Father Keon, speaking in a discreet indulgent velvety voice, don't let me disturb you now! I'm just looking for Mr Fanning ...

—He's round at the *Black Eagle*, said Mr Henchy. But won't you come in and sit down a minute?

—No, no, thank you. It was just a little business matter, said Father Keon. Thank you, indeed.

He retreated from the doorway and Mr Henchy, seizing one of the candlesticks, went to the door to light him downstairs.

—O, don't trouble, I beg!

—No, but the stairs is so dark.

—No, no, I can see .... Thank you, indeed.

—Are you right now?

—All right, thanks ... Thanks.

Mr Henchy returned with the candlestick and put it on the table. He sat down again at the fire. There was silence for a few moments.

—Tell me, John, said Mr O'Connor, lighting his cigarette with another pasteboard card.

—Hm?

—What is he exactly?

—Ask me an easier one, said Mr Henchy.

—Fanning and himself seem to me very thick. They're often in Kavanagh's together. Is he a priest at all?

—'Mmmyes, I believe so ... I think he's what you call a black sheep. We haven't many of them, thank God, but we have a few ... He's an unfortunate man of some kind ....

—And how does he knock it out? asked Mr O'Connor.

—That's another mystery.

—Is he attached to any chapel or church or institution or ....?

—No, said Mr Henchy, I think he's travelling on his own account .... God forgive me, he added, I thought he was the dozen of stout.

—Is there any chance of a drink itself? asked Mr O'Connor.

—I'm dry too, said the old man.

—I asked that little shoeboy three times, said Mr Henchy, would he send up a dozen of stout. I asked him again now but he was leaning on the counter in his shirtsleeves having a deep goster with Alderman Cowley.

—Why didn't you remind him? said Mr O'Connor.

—Well, I couldn't go over while he was talking to Alderman Cowley. I just waited till I caught his eye and said: *About that little matter I was speaking to you about ... That'll be all right, Mr H.*, he said. Yerra, sure the little hop-o'-my-thumb has forgotten all about it.

—There's some deal on in that quarter, said Mr O'Connor thoughtfully. I saw the three of them hard at it yesterday at Suffolk Street corner.

—I think I know the little game they're at, said Mr Henchy. You must owe the City Fathers money nowadays if you want to be made Lord Mayor. Then they'll make you Lord Mayor. By God I'm thinking seriously of becoming a City Father myself. What do you think? Would I do for the job?

Mr O'Connor laughed.

—So far as owing money goes ....

—Driving out of the Mansion House, said Mr Henchy, in all my vermin, with Jack here standing up behind me in a powdered wig–eh?

—And make me your private secretary, John.

—Yes. And I'll make Father Keon my private chaplain. We'll have a family party.

—Faith, Mr Henchy, said the old man, you'd keep up better style than some of them. I was talking one day to old Keegan, the porter. *And how do you like your new master, Pat?* says I to him. *You haven't much entertaining now*, says I. *Entertaining!* says he. *He'd live on the smell of an oilrag*. And do you know what he told me? Now, I declare to God, I didn't believe him.

—What? said Mr Henchy and Mr O'Connor.

—He told me: *What do you think of a Lord Mayor of Dublin sending out for a pound of chops for his dinner? How's that for high living?* says he. *Wisha! wisha*, says I. *A pound of chops*, says he, *coming into the Mansion House*. *Wisha!* says I, *what kind of people is going at all now?*

At this point there was a knock at the door and a boy put in his head.

—What is it? said the old man.

—From the *Black Eagle*, said the boy, walking in sideways and depositing a basket on the floor with a noise of shaken bottles.

The old man helped the boy to transfer the bottles from the basket to the table and counted the full tally. After the transfer the boy put his basket on his arm and asked:

—Any bottles?

—What bottles? said the old man.

—Won't you let us drink them first? said Mr Henchy.

—I was told to ask for bottles.

—Come back tomorrow, said the old man.

—Here, boy! said Mr Henchy, will you run over to O'Farrell's and ask him to lend us a corkscrew—for Mr Henchy, say. Tell him we won't keep it a minute. Leave the basket there.

The boy went out and Mr Henchy began to rub his hands cheerfully, saying:

—Ah, well, he's not so bad after all. He's as good as his word, anyhow.

—There's no tumblers, said the old man.

—O, don't let that trouble you, Jack, said Mr Henchy. Many's the good man before now drank out of the bottle.

—Anyway it's better than nothing, said Mr O'Connor.

—He's not a bad sort, said Mr Henchy, only Fanning has such a loan of him. He means well, you know, in his own tinpot way.

The boy came back with the corkscrew. The old man opened three bottles and was handing back the corkscrew when Mr Henchy said to the boy:

—Would you like a drink, boy?

—If you please, sir, said the boy.

The old man opened another bottle grudgingly and handed it to the boy.

—What age are you? he asked.

—Seventeen, said the boy.

As the old man said nothing further the boy took the bottle, said: *Here's my best respects, sir!* to Mr Henchy, drank the contents, put the bottle back on the table and wiped his mouth with his sleeve. Then he took up the corkscrew and went out of the door sideways, muttering some form of salutation.

—That's the way it begins, said the old man.

—The thin end of the wedge, said Mr Henchy.

The old man distributed the three bottles which he had opened and the men drank from them simultaneously. After having drunk each placed his bottle on the mantelpiece within hand's reach and drew in a long breath of satisfaction.

—Well, I did a good day's work today, said Mr Henchy after a pause.

—That so, John?

—Yes. I got him one or two sure things in Dawson Street, Crofton and myself. Between ourselves, you know, Crofton (he's a decent chap, of course), but he's not worth a damn as a canvasser. He hasn't a word to throw to a dog. He stands and looks at the people while I do the talking.

Here two men entered the room. One of them was a very fat man, whose blue serge clothes seemed to be in danger of falling from his sloping figure. He had a big face which resembled a young ox's face in expression, staring blue eyes and a grizzled moustache. The other man, who was much younger and frailer, had a thin cleanshaven face. He wore a very high double collar and a widebrimmed bowler hat.

—Hello, Crofton! said Mr Henchy to the fat man. Talk of the devil .....

—Where did the boose come from? asked the young man. Did the cow calve?

—O, of course, Bantam spots the drink first thing! said Mr O'Connor laughing.

—Is that the way you chaps canvass, said Mr Lyons, and Crofton and I out in the cold and rain looking for votes?

—Why, blast your soul, said Mr Henchy. I'd get more votes in five minutes than you two'd get in a week.

—Open two bottles of stout, Jack, said Mr O'Connor.

—How can I? said the old man, when there's no corkscrew?

—Wait now, wait now! said Mr Henchy, getting up quickly. Did you ever see this little trick?

He took two bottles from the table and, carrying them to the fire, put them on the hob. Then he sat down again by the fire and took another drink from his bottle. Mr Lyons sat on the edge of the table, pushed his hat towards the nape of his neck and began to swing his legs.

—Which is my bottle? he asked.

—This lad, said Mr Henchy.

Mr Crofton sat down on a box and looked fixedly at the other bottle on the hob. He was silent for two reasons. The first reason, sufficient in itself, was that he had nothing to say;

the second reason was that he considered his companions beneath him. He had been a canvasser for Wilkins, the conservative, but, when the conservatives had withdrawn their man and, choosing the lesser of two evils, given their support to the nationalist candidate, he had been engaged to work for Mr Tierney.

In a few minutes an apologetic *Pok!* was heard as the cork flew out of Mr Lyons's bottle. Mr Lyons jumped off the table, went to the fire, took his bottle and carried it back to the table.

—I was just telling them, Crofton, said Mr Henchy, that we got a good few votes today.

—Who did you get? asked Mr Lyons.

—Well, I got Parkes for one and I got Atkinson for two and I got Ward of Dawson Street. Fine old chap he is, too—regular old toff, old conservative! *But isn't your candidate a nationalist?* said he. *He's a respectable man*, said I. *He's in favour of whatever will benefit this country. He's a big ratepayer*, I said. *He has extensive house property in the city and three places of business and isn't it to his own advantage to keep down the rates? He's a prominent and respected citizen*, said I, *and a Poor Law Guardian and he doesn't belong to any party, good bad or indifferent*. That's the way to talk to 'em.

—And what about the address to the King? said Mr Lyons, after drinking and smacking his lips.

—Listen to me, said Mr Henchy. What we want in this country, as I said to old Ward, is capital. The King's coming here will mean an influx of money into this country. The citizens of Dublin will benefit by it. Look at all the factories down by the quays there, idle! Look at all the money there is in the country if we only worked the old industries, the mills, the shipbuilding yards and factories. It's capital we want.

—But look here, John, said Mr O'Connor. Why should we welcome the King of England! Didn't Parnell himself ....

—Parnell, said Mr Henchy, is dead. Now, here's the way I look at it. Here's this chap come to the throne after his old mother keeping him out of it till the man was grey. He's a man of the world and he means well by us. He's a jolly fine decent fellow, if you ask me, and no damn nonsense about him. He just says to himself: *The old one never went to see these wild Irish. By Christ, I'll go myself and see what they're like.* And are we going to insult the man when he comes over here on a friendly visit? Eh? Isn't that right, Crofton?

Mr Crofton nodded his head.

—But after all now, said Mr Lyons argumentatively, King Edward's life, you know, is not the very .....

—Let bygones be bygones, said Mr Henchy. I admire the man personally. He's just an ordinary knockabout like you and me. He's fond of his glass of grog and he's a bit of a rake, perhaps, and he's a good sportsman. Damn it, can't we Irish play fair?

—That's all very fine, said Mr Lyons. But look at the case of Parnell now.

—In the name of God, said Mr Henchy, where's the analogy between the two cases?

—What I mean, said Mr Lyons, is we have our ideals. Why, now, would we welcome a man like that? Do you think now after what he did Parnell was a fit man to lead us? Do you think he was a man I'd like the lady who is now Mrs Lyons to know? And why, then, would we do it for Edward the Seventh?

—This is Parnell's anniversary, said Mr O'Connor, and don't let us stir up any bad blood. We all respect him now that he's dead and gone—even the conservatives, he added, turning to Mr Crofton.

Pok! The tardy cork flew out of Mr Crofton's bottle. Mr Crofton got up from his box and went to the fire. As he returned with his capture he said in a deep voice:

—Our side of the house respects him because he was a gentleman.

—Right you are, Crofton! said Mr Henchy fiercely. He was the only man that could keep that bag of cats in order. *Down, ye dogs! Lie down, ye curs!* That's the way he treated them. Come in, Joe! Come in! he called out, catching sight of Mr Hynes in the doorway.

Mr Hynes came in slowly.

—Open another bottle of stout, Jack, said Mr Henchy. O, I forgot there's no corkscrew! Here, show me one here and I'll put it at the fire.

The old man handed him another bottle and he placed it on the hob.

—Sit down, Joe, said Mr O'Connor, we're just talking about the Chief.

—Aye, aye! said Mr Henchy.

Mr Hynes sat on the side of the table near Mr Lyons but said nothing.

—There's one of them, anyhow, said Mr Henchy, that didn't renege him. By God, I'll say that for you, Joe! No, by God, you stuck to him like a man!

—O, Joe! said Mr O'Connor suddenly. Give us that thing you wrote—do you remember? Have you got it on you?

—O, aye! said Mr Henchy. Give us that. Did you ever hear that, Crofton? Listen to this now: splendid thing.

—Go on, said Mr O'Connor. Fire away, Joe.

Mr Hynes did not seem to remember at once the piece to which they were alluding but, after reflecting a while, he said:

—O, that thing is it .... Sure, that's old now.

—Out with it, man! said Mr O'Connor.

—'Sh 'sh, said Mr Henchy. Now, Joe!

Mr Hynes hesitated a little longer. Then amid the silence he took off his hat, laid it on the table and stood up. He seemed to be rehearsing the piece in his mind. After a rather long pause he announced:

The Death of Parnell
6th October 1891

He cleared his throat once or twice and then began to recite:

He is dead. Our Uncrowned King is dead.
O, Erin, mourn with grief and woe
For he lies dead whom the fell gang
Of modern hypocrites laid low.

He lies slain by the coward hounds
He raised to glory from the mire:
And Erin's hopes and Erin's dreams
Perish upon her monarch's pyre.

In palace, cabin or in cot
The Irish heart where'er it be
Is bowed with woe–for he is gone
Who would have wrought her destiny.

He would have had his Erin famed,
The green flag gloriously unfurled,
Her statesmen, bards and warriors raised
Before the nations of the world.

He dreamed (alas, 'twas but a dream!)
Of Liberty: but as he strove
To clutch that idol, treachery
Sundered him from the thing he loved.

Shame on the coward caitiff hands
That smote their Lord or with a kiss
Betrayed him to the rabble-rout
Of fawning priests–no friends of his!

May everlasting shame consume
The memory of those who tried
To befoul and smear th' exalted name
Of one who spurned them in his pride!

He fell, as fall the mighty ones,
Nobly undaunted to the last,
And Death has now united him
With Erin's heroes of the past.

No sound of strife disturb his sleep!
Calmly he rests: no human pain
Or high ambition spurs him now
The peaks of glory to attain.

They had their way: they laid him low.
But Erin, list, his spirit may
Rise, like the Phoenix from the flames,
When breaks the dawning of the day,

The day that brings us Freedom's reign.
And on that day may Erin well
Pledge in the cup she lifts to Joy
One grief–the memory of Parnell.

Mr Hynes sat down again on the table. When he had finished his recitation there was a silence and then a burst of clapping: even Mr Lyons clapped. The applause continued for a little time. When it had ceased all the auditors drank from their bottles in silence.

Pok! The cork flew out of Mr Hynes's bottle but Mr Hynes remained sitting, flushed and bareheaded on the table. He did not seem to have heard the invitation.

—Good man, Joe! said Mr O'Connor, taking out his cigarette papers and pouch the better to hide his emotion.

—What do you think of that, Crofton? cried Mr Henchy. Isn't that fine–what?

Mr Crofton said that it was a very fine piece of writing.

A Mother

Mr Holohan, assistant secretary of the *Eire Abu* Society, had been walking up and down Dublin for nearly a month, with his hands and pockets full of dirty pieces of paper, arranging about the series of concerts. He had a game leg and for this his friends called him Hoppy Holohan. He walked up and down constantly, stood by the hour at street corners arguing the point, and made notes: but in the end it was Mrs Kearney who arranged everything.

Miss Devlin had become Mrs Kearney out of spite. She had been educated in a high-class convent where she had learned French and music. As she was naturally pale and unbending in manner she made few friends at school. When she came to the age of marriage she was sent out to many houses where her playing and ivory manners were much admired. She sat amid the chilly circle of her accomplishments, waiting for some suitor to brave it and offer her a brilliant life. But the young men whom she met were ordinary and she gave them no encouragement, trying to console her romantic desires by eating a great deal of Turkish Delight in secret. However, when she drew near the limit and her friends began to loosen their tongues about her she silenced them by marrying Mr Kearney who was a bootmaker on Ormond Quay.

He was much older than she. His conversation, which was serious, took place at intervals in his great brown beard. After the first years of married life Mrs Kearney perceived that such a man would wear better than a romantic person but she never put her own romantic ideas away. He was sober, thrifty and pious: he went to the altar every first Friday, sometimes with her, oftener by himself. But she never weakened in her religion and was a good wife to him. At some party in a strange house when she lifted her eyebrow ever so slightly he stood up to take his leave and when his cough troubled him she put the eider-down quilt over his feet and made a strong rum punch. For his part he was a model father. By paying a small sum every week into a society he insured for both his daughters a dowry of one hundred pounds each when they came to the age of twenty-four. He sent the elder daughter, Kathleen, to a good convent where she learned French and music and afterwards paid her fees at the Academy. Every year in the month of July Mrs Kearney found occasion to say to some friend:

—My good man is packing us off to Skerries for a few weeks.

If it was not Skerries it was Howth or Greystones.

When the Irish Revival began to be appreciable Mrs Kearney determined to take advantage of her daughter's name and brought an Irish teacher to the house. Kathleen and her sister sent Irish picture postcards to their friends and these friends sent back other Irish picture postcards. On special Sundays when Mr Kearney went with his family to the pro-cathedral a little crowd of people would assemble after mass at the corner of Cathedral Street. They were all friends of the Kearneys, musical friends or nationalist friends: and when they had played every little counter of gossip they shook hands with one another all together, laughing at the crossing of so many hands, and said goodbye to one another in Irish. Soon the name of Miss Kathleen Kearney began to be heard often on people's lips. People said that she was very clever at music and a very nice girl and, moreover, that she was a believer in the language movement. Mrs Kearney was well content at this. Therefore she was not surprised when one day Mr Holohan came to her and proposed that her daughter should be the accompanist at a series of four grand concerts which his Society was going to give in the Antient Concert Rooms. She brought him into the drawingroom, made him sit down and brought out the decanter and the silver biscuit-barrel. She entered heart and soul into the details of the enterprise, advised and dissuaded; and finally a contract was drawn up by which Kathleen was to receive eight guineas for her services as accompanist at the four grand concerts.

As Mr Holohan was a novice in such delicate matters as the wording of bills and the disposing of items for a programme Mrs Kearney helped him. She had tact. She knew what *artistes* should go into capitals and what *artistes* should go into small type. She knew that the first tenor would not like to come on after Mr Meade's comic turn. To keep the audience continually diverted she slipped the doubtful items in between the old favourites. Mr Holohan called to see her every day to have her advice on some point. She was invariably friendly and advising: homely, in fact. She pushed the decanter towards him, saying:

—Now, help yourself, Mr Holohan!

And while he was helping himself she said:

—Don't be afraid! Don't be afraid of it!

Everything went on smoothly. Mrs Kearney bought some lovely blush-pink charmeuse in Brown Thomas's to let into the front of Kathleen's dress. It cost a pretty penny; but there are occasions when a little expense is justifiable. She took a dozen of two shilling tickets for the final concert and sent them to those friends who could not be trusted to come otherwise. She forgot nothing and, thanks to her, everything that was to be done was done.

The concerts were to be on Wednesday, Thursday, Friday and Saturday. When Mrs Kearney arrived with her daughter at the Antient Concert Rooms on Wednesday night she did not like the look of things. A few young men, wearing bright blue badges in their coats, stood idle in the vestibule: none of them wore evening dress. She passed by with her daughter and a quick glance through the open door of the hall showed her the cause of the stewards' idleness. At first she wondered had she mistaken the hour. No, it was twenty minutes to eight.

In the dressingroom behind the stage she was introduced to the secretary of the Society, Mr Fitzpatrick. She smiled and shook his hand. He was a little man with a white vacant face. She noticed that he wore his soft brown hat carelessly on the side of his head and that his accent was flat. He held a programme in his hand and while he was talking to her he chewed one end of it into a moist pulp. He seemed to bear disappointments lightly. Mr Holohan came into the dressingroom every few minutes with reports from the boxoffice. The *artistes* talked among themselves nervously, glanced from time to time at the mirror and rolled and unrolled their music. When it was nearly half past eight the few people in the hall began to express their desire to be entertained. Mr Fitzpatrick came in, smiled vacantly at the room and said:

—Well now, ladies and gentlemen, I suppose we'd better open the ball.

Mrs Kearney rewarded his very flat final syllable with a quick stare of contempt and then said to her daughter encouragingly:

—Are you ready, dear?

When she had an opportunity she called Mr Holohan aside and asked him to tell her what it meant. Mr Holohan did not know what it meant. He said that the committee had made a mistake in arranging for four concerts: four was too many.

—And the *artistes!* said Mrs Kearney. Of course they are doing their best but really they are no good.

Mr Holohan admitted that the *artistes* were no good but the committee, he said, had decided to let the first three concerts go as they pleased and reserve all the talent for Saturday night.

Mrs Kearney said nothing but, as the mediocre items followed one another on the platform and the few people in the hall grew fewer and fewer, she began to regret that she had put herself to any expense for such a concert. There was something she didn't like in the look of things and Mr Fitzpatrick's vacant smile irritated her very much. However she said nothing and waited to see how it would end. The concert expired shortly before ten and everyone went home quickly.

The concert on Thursday night was better attended but Mrs Kearney saw at once that the house was filled with paper. The audience behaved indecorously as if the concert were an informal dress rehearsal. Mr Fitzpatrick seemed to enjoy himself; he was quite unconscious that Mrs Kearney was taking angry note of his conduct. He stood at the edge of the screen, from time to time jutting out his head and exchanging a laugh with two friends in the corner of the balcony. In the course of the evening Mrs Kearney learned that the Friday concert was to be abandoned and that the committee was going to move heaven and earth to secure a bumper house on Saturday night. When she heard this she sought out Mr Holohan. She buttonholed him as he was limping out quickly with a glass of lemonade for a young lady and asked him was it true. Yes, it was true.

—But, of course, that doesn't alter the contract, she said. The contract was for four concerts. ...

Mr Holohan seemed to be in a hurry: he advised her to speak to Mr Fitzpatrick. Mrs Kearney was now beginning to be alarmed. She called Mr Fitzpatrick away from his screen and told him that her daughter had signed for four concerts and that, of course, according to the terms of the contract she should receive the sum originally stipulated for whether the Society gave the four concerts or not. Mr Fitzpatrick, who did not catch the point at issue very quickly, seemed unable to resolve the difficulty and said that he would bring the matter before the committee. Mrs Kearney's anger began to flutter in her cheek and she had all she could do to keep from asking:

—And who is the *cometty*, pray?

But she knew that it would not be ladylike to do that: so she was silent.

Little boys were sent out into the principal streets of Dublin early on Friday morning with bundles of handbills. Special puffs appeared in all the evening papers reminding the music-loving public of the treat which was in store for it on the following evening. Mrs Kearney was somewhat reassured but she thought well to tell her husband part of her suspicions. He listened carefully and said that perhaps it would be better if he went with her on Saturday night. She agreed. She respected her husband in the same way as she respected the General Post Office, as something large, secure and fixed; and though she knew the small number of his talents she appreciated his abstract value as a male. She was glad that he had suggested coming with her. She thought her plans over.

The night of the grand concert came. Mrs Kearney, with her husband and daughter, arrived at the Antient Concert Rooms three quarters of an hour before the time at which the concert was to begin. By ill luck it was a rainy evening. Mrs Kearney placed her daughter's clothes and music in charge of her husband and went all over the building looking for Mr Holohan or Mr Fitzpatrick. She could find neither. She asked the stewards was any member of the committee in the hall and, after a great deal of trouble, a steward brought out a little woman named Miss Beirne to whom Mrs Kearney explained that she wanted to see one of the secretaries. Miss Beirne expected them any minute and asked could she do anything. Mrs Kearney looked searchingly at the oldish face which was screwed into an expression of trustfulness and enthusiasm and answered:

—No, thank you!

The little woman hoped they would have a good house. She looked out at the rain until the melancholy of the wet street effaced all the trustfulness and enthusiasm from her twisted features. Then she gave a little sigh and said:

—Ah, well! We did our best, the dear knows.

Mrs Kearney had to go back to the dressingroom.

The *artistes* were arriving. The bass and the second tenor had already come. The bass, Mr Duggan, was a slender young man with a scattered black moustache. He was the son of a hall porter in an office in the city and, as a boy, he had sung prolonged bass notes in the resounding hall. From this humble state he had raised himself until he had become a first-rate *artiste*. He had appeared in grand opera. One night, when an operatic *artiste* had fallen ill, he had undertaken the part of the king in the opera of *Maritana* at the Queen's Theatre. He sang his music with great feeling and volume and was warmly welcomed by the gallery; but, unfortunately, he marred the good impression by wiping his nose in his gloved hand once or twice out of thoughtlessness. He was unassuming and spoke little. He said *yous* so softly that it passed unnoticed and he never drank anything stronger than milk for his voice' sake. Mr Bell, the second tenor, was a fairhaired little man who competed every year for prizes at the Feis Ceoil. On his fourth trial he had been awarded a bronze medal. He was extremely nervous and extremely jealous of other tenors and he covered his nervous jealousy with an ebullient friendliness. It was his humour to have people know what an ordeal a concert was to him. Therefore when he saw Mr Duggan he went over to him and asked:

—Are you in it too?

—Yes, said Mr Duggan.

Mr Bell laughed at his fellow sufferer, held out his hand and said:

—Shake!

Mrs Kearney passed by these two young men and went to the edge of the screen to view the house. The seats were being filled up rapidly and a pleasant noise circulated in the auditorium. She came back and spoke to her husband privately. Their conversation was evidently about Kathleen for they both glanced at her often as she stood chatting to one of her nationalist friends, Miss Healy, the contralto. An unknown solitary woman with a pale face walked through the room. The women followed with keen eyes the faded blue dress which was stretched upon a meagre body. Someone said that she was Madam Glynn, the soprano.

—I wonder where did they dig her up, said Kathleen to Miss Healy. I'm sure I never heard of her.

Miss Healy had to smile. Mr Holohan limped into the dressingroom at that moment and the two young ladies asked him who was the unknown woman. Mr Holohan said that she was Madam Glynn from London. Madam Glynn took her stand in a corner of the room, holding a roll of music stiffly before her and from time to time changing the direction of her startled gaze. The shadow took her faded dress into shelter but fell revengefully into the little cup behind her collarbone. The noise of the hall became more audible. The first tenor and the baritone arrived together. They were both well dressed, stout and complacent and they brought a breath of opulence among the company.

Mrs Kearney brought her daughter over to them and talked to them amiably. She wanted to be on good terms with them but, while she strove to be polite, her eyes followed Mr Holohan in his limping and devious courses. As soon as she could she excused herself and went out after him.

—Mr Holohan, I want to speak to you for a moment, she said.

They went down to a discreet part of the corridor. Mrs Kearney asked him when was her daughter going to be paid. Mr Holohan said that Mr Fitzpatrick had charge of that. Mrs Kearney said that she didn't know anything about Mr Fitzpatrick. Her daughter had signed a contract for eight guineas and she would have to be paid. Mr Holohan said that it wasn't his business.

—Why isn't it your business? asked Mrs Kearney. Didn't you yourself bring her the contract? Anyway, if it's not your business it's my business and I mean to see to it.

—You'd better speak to Mr Fitzpatrick, said Mr Holohan distantly.

—I don't know anything about Mr Fitzpatrick, repeated Mrs

Kearney. I have my contract and I intend to see that it is carried out.

When she came back to the dressingroom her cheeks were slightly suffused. The room was lively. Two men in outdoor dress had taken possession of the fireplace and were chatting familiarly with Miss Healy and the baritone. They were the *Freeman* man and Mr O'Madden Burke. The *Freeman* man had come in to say that he could not wait for the concert as he had to report the lecture which an American priest was giving in the Mansion House. He said they were to leave the report for him at the *Freeman* office and he would see that it went in. He was a greyhaired man with a plausible voice and careful manners. He held an extinguished cigar in his hand and the aroma of cigar smoke floated near him. He had not intended to stay a moment because concerts and *artistes* bored him considerably but he remained leaning against the mantelpiece. Miss Healy stood in front of him, talking and laughing. He was old enough to suspect one reason for her politeness but young enough in spirit to turn the moment to account. The warmth, fragrance and colour of her body appealed to his senses. He was pleasantly conscious that the bosom which he saw rise and fall slowly beneath him rose and fell at that moment for him, that the laughter and fragrance and wilful glances were his tribute. When he could stay no longer he took leave of her regretfully.

—O'Madden Burke will write the notice, he explained to Mr Holohan, and I'll see it in.

—Thank you very much, Mr Hendrick, said Mr Holohan. You'll see it in, I know. Now, won't you have a little something before you go?

—I don't mind, said Mr Hendrick.

The two men went along some tortuous passages and up a dark staircase and came to a secluded room where one of the stewards was uncorking bottles for a few gentlemen. One of these gentlemen was Mr O'Madden Burke who had found out the room by instinct. He was a suave elderly man who balanced his imposing body, when at rest, upon a large silk umbrella. His magniloquent western name was the moral umbrella upon which he balanced the fine problem of his finances. He was widely respected.

While Mr Holohan was entertaining the *Freeman* man Mrs Kearney was speaking so animatedly to her husband that he had to ask her to lower her voice. The conversation of the others in the dressingroom had become strained. Mr Bell, the first item, stood ready with his music but the accompanist made no sign. Evidently something was wrong. Mr Kearney looked straight before him, stroking his beard, while Mrs Kearney spoke into Kathleen's ear with subdued emphasis. From the hall came sounds of encouragement, clapping and stamping of feet. The first tenor and the baritone and Miss Healy stood together, waiting tranquilly, but Mr Bell's nerves were greatly agitated because he was afraid the audience would think that he had come late.

Mr Holohan and Mr O'Madden Burke came into the room. In a moment Mr Holohan perceived the hush. He went over to Mrs Kearney and spoke with her earnestly. While they were speaking the noise in the hall grew louder. Mr Holohan became very red and excited. He spoke volubly but Mrs Kearney said curtly at intervals:

—She won't go on. She must get her eight guineas.

Mr Holohan pointed desperately towards the hall where the audience was clapping and stamping. He appealed to Mr Kearney and to Kathleen. But Mr Kearney continued to stroke his beard and Kathleen looked down, moving the point of her new shoe: it was not her fault. Mrs Kearney repeated:

—She won't go on without her money.

After a swift struggle of tongues Mr Holohan hobbled out in haste. The room was silent. When the strain of the silence had become somewhat painful Miss Healy said to the baritone:

—Have you seen Mrs Pat Campbell this week?

The baritone had not seen her but he had been told that she was very fine. The conversation went no further. The first tenor bent his head and began to count the links of the gold chain which was extended across his waist, smiling and humming random notes to observe the effect on the frontal sinus. From time to time everyone glanced at Mrs Kearney.

The noise in the auditorium had risen to a clamour when Mr Fitzpatrick burst into the room, followed by Mr Holohan who was panting. The clapping and stamping in the hall were punctuated by whistling. Mr Fitzpatrick held a few bank notes in his hand. He counted out four into Mrs Kearney's hand and said she would get the other half at the interval. Mrs Kearney said:

—This is four shillings short.

But Kathleen gathered in her skirt and said *Now, Mr Bell*, to the first item who was shaking like an aspen. The singer and the accompanist went out together. The noise in the hall died away. There was a pause of a few seconds: and then the piano was heard.

The first part of the concert was very successful except for Madam Glynn's item. The poor lady sang *Killarney* in a bodiless gasping voice, with all the oldfashioned mannerisms of intonation and pronunciation which she believed lent elegance to her singing. She looked as if she had been resurrected from an old stage wardrobe and the cheaper parts of the hall made fun of her high wailing notes. The first tenor and the contralto, however, brought down the house. Kathleen played a selection of Irish airs which was generously applauded. The first part closed with a stirring patriotic recitation delivered by a young lady who arranged amateur theatricals. It was deservedly applauded; and when it was ended the men went out for the interval, content.

All this time the dressingroom was a hive of excitement. In one corner were Mr Holohan, Mr Fitzpatrick, Miss Beirne, two of the stewards, the baritone, the bass and Mr O'Madden Burke. Mr O'Madden Burke said it was the most scandalous exhibition he had ever witnessed. Miss Kathleen Kearney's musical career was ended in Dublin after that, he said. The baritone was asked what did he think of Mrs Kearney's conduct. He did not like to say anything. He had been paid his money and wished to be at peace with men. However, he said that Mrs Kearney might have taken the *artistes* into consideration. The stewards and the secretaries debated hotly as to what should be done when the interval came.

—I agree with Miss Beirne, said Mr O'Madden Burke. Pay her nothing.

In another corner of the room were Mrs Kearney and her husband, Mr Bell, Miss Healy and the young lady who had recited the patriotic piece. Mrs Kearney said that the committee had treated her scandalously. She had spared neither trouble nor expense and this was how she was repaid. They thought they had only a girl to deal with and that, therefore, they could ride roughshod over her. But she would show them their mistake. They wouldn't have dared to have treated her like that if she had been a man. But she would see that her daughter got her rights: she wouldn't be fooled. If they didn't pay her to the last farthing she would make Dublin ring. Of course she was sorry for the sake of the *artistes*. But what else could she do? She appealed to the second tenor who said he thought she had not been well treated. Then she appealed to Miss Healy. Miss Healy wanted to join the other group but she did not like to do so because she was a great friend of Kathleen's and the Kearneys had often invited her to their house.

As soon as the first part was ended Mr Fitzpatrick and Mr Holohan went over to Mrs Kearney and told her that the other four guineas would be paid after the committee meeting on the following Tuesday and that, in case her daughter did not play for the second part, the committee would consider the contract broken and would pay nothing.

—I haven't seen any committee, said Mrs Kearney angrily. My daughter has her contract. She will get four pounds eight into her hand or a foot she won't put on that platform.

—I'm surprised at you, Mrs Kearney, said Mr Holohan. I never thought you would treat us this way.

—And what way did you treat me? asked Mrs Kearney.

Her face was inundated with an angry colour and she looked as if she would attack someone with her hands.

—I'm asking for my rights, she said.

—You might have some sense of decency, said Mr Holohan.

—Might I indeed? ... And when I ask when my daughter is going to be paid I can't get a civil answer.

She tossed her head and assumed a haughty voice:

—You must speak to the secretary. It's not my business. I'm a great fellow fol-the-diddle-I-do.

—I thought you were a lady, said Mr Holohan, walking away from her abruptly.

After that Mrs Kearney's conduct was condemned on all hands: everyone approved of what the committee had done. She stood at the door, haggard with rage, arguing with her husband and daughter, gesticulating with them. She waited until it was time for the second part to begin in the hope that the secretaries would approach her. But Miss Healy had kindly consented to play one or two accompaniments. Mrs Kearney had to stand aside to allow the baritone and his accompanist to pass up to the platform. She stood still for an instant like an angry stone image and, when the first notes of the song struck her ear, she caught up her daughter's cloak and said to her husband:

—Get a cab!

He went out at once. Mrs Kearney wrapped the cloak round her daughter and followed him. As she passed through the doorway she stopped and glared into Mr Holohan's face:

—I'm not done with you yet, she said.

—But I'm done with you, said Mr Holohan.

Kathleen followed her mother meekly. Mr Holohan began to pace up and down the room in order to cool himself for he felt his skin on fire:

—That's a nice lady! he said. O, she's a nice lady!

—You did the proper thing, Holohan, said Mr O'Madden Burke, poised upon his umbrella in approval.

Grace

Two gentlemen who were in the lavatory at the time tried to lift him up: but he was quite helpless. He lay curled up at the foot of the stairs down which he had fallen. They succeeded in turning him over. His hat had rolled a few yards away and his clothes were smeared with the filth and ooze of the floor on which he had lain, face downwards. His eyes were closed and he breathed with a grunting noise. A thin stream of blood trickled from the corner of his mouth.

These two gentlemen and one of the curates carried him up the stairs and laid him down again on the floor of the bar. In two minutes he was surrounded by a ring of men. The manager of the bar asked everyone who he was and who was with him. No-one knew who he was but one of the curates said he had served the gentleman with a small rum.

—Was he by himself? asked the manager.

—No, sir. There was two gentlemen with him.

—And where are they?

No-one knew; a voice said:

—Give him air. He's fainted.

The ring of onlookers distended and closed again elastically. A dark medal of blood had formed itself near the man's head on the tessellated floor. The manager, alarmed by the grey pallor of the man's face, sent for a policeman.

His collar was unfastened and his necktie undone. He opened his eyes for an instant, sighed and closed them again. One of the gentlemen who had carried him upstairs held a dinged silk hat in his hand. The manager asked repeatedly did no-one know who the injured man was or where had his friends gone. The door of the bar opened and an immense constable entered. A crowd which had followed him down the laneway collected outside the door, struggling to look in through the glass panels.

The manager at once began to narrate what he knew. The constable, a young man with thick immobile features, listened. He moved his head slowly to right and left and from the manager to the person on the floor as if he feared to be the victim of some delusion. Then he drew off his glove, produced a small book from his waist, licked the lead of his pencil and made ready to indite. He asked in a suspicious provincial accent:

—Who is the man? What's his name and address?

A young man in a cycling suit cleared his way through the ring of bystanders. He knelt down promptly beside the injured man and called for water. The constable knelt down also to help. The young man washed the blood from the injured man's mouth and then called for some brandy. The constable repeated the order in an authoritative voice until a curate came running with the glass. The brandy was forced down the man's throat. In a few seconds he opened his eyes and looked about him. He looked at the circle of faces and then, understanding, strove to rise to his feet.

—You're all right now? asked the young man in the cycling suit.

—'Sha, 's nothing, said the injured man, trying to stand up.

He was helped to his feet. The manager said something

about a hospital and some of the bystanders gave advice. The battered silk hat was placed on the man's head. The constable asked:

—Where do you live?

The man, without answering, began to twirl the ends of his moustache. He made light of his accident. It was nothing, he said: only a little accident. He spoke very thickly.

—Where do you live? repeated the constable.

The man said they were to get a cab for him. While the point was being debated a tall agile gentleman of fair complexion, wearing a long yellow ulster, came from the far end of the bar. Seeing the spectacle he called out:

—Hallo, Tom, old man! What's the trouble?

—'Sha, 's nothing, said the man.

The newcomer surveyed the deplorable figure before him and then turned to the constable, saying:

—It's all right, constable. I'll see him home.

The constable touched his helmet and answered:

—All right, Mr Power!

—Come now, Tom, said Mr Power, taking his friend by the arm. No bones broken. What? Can you walk?

The young man in the cycling suit took the man by the other arm and the crowd divided.

—How did you get yourself into this mess? asked Mr Power.

—The gentleman fell down the stairs, said the young man.

—I' 'ery 'uch o'liged to you, sir, said the injured man.

—Not at all.

—'ant' we have a little ....?

—Not now. Not now.

The three men left the bar and the crowd sifted through the doors into the laneway. The manager brought the constable to the stairs to inspect the scene of the accident. They agreed that the gentleman must have missed his footing. The customers returned to the counter and a curate set about removing the traces of blood from the floor.

When they came out into Grafton Street Mr Power whistled for an outsider. The injured man said again as well as he could:

—I' 'ery 'uch o'liged to you, sir. I hope we'll 'eet again. 'y na'e is Kernan.

The shock and the incipient pain had partly sobered him.

—Don't mention it, said the young man.

They shook hands. Mr Kernan was hoisted on to the car and, while Mr Power was giving directions to the carman, he expressed his gratitude to the young man and regretted that they could not have a little drink together.

—Another time, said the young man.

The car drove off towards Westmoreland Street. As it passed the Ballast office the clock showed half past nine. A keen east wind hit them blowing from the mouth of the river. Mr Kernan was huddled together with cold. His friend asked him to tell how the accident had happened.

—I 'an't, 'an, he answered. 'y 'ongue is hurt.

—Show.

The other leaned over the well of the car and peered into Mr Kernan's mouth but he could not see. He struck a match and, sheltering it in the shell of his hands, peered again into the mouth which Mr Kernan opened obediently. The swaying movement of the car brought the match to and from the open mouth. The lower teeth and gums were covered with clotted blood and a minute piece of the tongue seemed to have been bitten off. The match was blown out.

—That's ugly, said Mr Power.

—'Sha, 's nothing, said Mr Kernan, closing his mouth and pulling the collar of his filthy frock coat across his neck.

Mr Kernan was a commercial traveller of the old school which believed in the dignity of its calling. He had never been seen in the city without a silk hat of some decency and a pair of gaiters. By grace of these two articles of clothing, he said, a man could always pass muster. He carried on the tradition of his Napoleon, the great Blackwhite, whose memory he evoked at times by legend and mimicry. Modern business methods had spared him only so far as to allow him a little office in Crowe Street on the window blind of which was written the name of his firm with the address—London, E. C. On the mantelpiece of this little office a little leaden battalion of canisters was drawn up and on the table before the window stood four or five china bowls which were usually half full of a black liquid. From these bowls Mr Kernan tasted tea. He took a mouthful, drew it up, saturated his palate with it and then spat it forth into the grate. Then he paused to judge.

Mr Power, a much younger man, was employed in the Royal Irish Constabulary Office in Dublin Castle. The arc of his social rise intersected the arc of his friend's decline but Mr Kernan's decline was mitigated by the fact that certain of those friends who had known him at his highest point of success still esteemed him as a character. Mr Power was one of these friends. His inexplicable debts were a byword in his circle; he was a debonair young man.

The car halted before a small house on the Glasnevin road and Mr Kernan was helped into the house. His wife put him to bed while Mr Power sat downstairs in the kitchen asking the children where they went to school and what book they were in. The children, two girls and a boy, conscious of their father's helplessness and of their mother's absence, began some horse-play with him. He was surprised at their manners and at their accents and his brow grew thoughtful. After a while Mrs Kernan entered the kitchen, exclaiming:

—Such a sight! O, he'll do for himself one day and that's the holy alls of it. He's been drinking since Friday.

Mr Power was careful to explain to her that he was not responsible, that he had come on the scene by the merest accident. Mrs Kernan, remembering Mr Power's good offices during domestic quarrels as well as many small but opportune loans, said:

—O, you needn't tell me that, Mr Power. I know you're a friend of his, not like some of those others he does be with. They're all right so long as he has money in his pocket to keep him out from his wife and family. Nice friends! Who was he with tonight, I'd like to know?

Mr Power shook his head but said nothing.

—I'm so sorry, she continued, that I've nothing in the house to offer you. But if you wait a minute I'll send round to Fogarty's at the corner.

Mr Power stood up.

—We were waiting for him to come home with the money. He never seems to think he has a home at all.

—O now, Mrs Kernan, said Mr Power, we'll make him turn over a new leaf. I'll talk to Martin. He's the man. We'll come here one of these nights and talk it over.

She saw him to the door. The carman was stamping up and down the footpath and swinging his arms to warm himself.

—It's very kind of you to bring him home, she said.

—Not at all, said Mr Power.

He got up on the car. As it drove off he raised his hat to her gaily.

—We'll make a new man of him, he said. Goodnight, Mrs Kernan.

◆ ◆ ◆

Mrs Kernan's puzzled eyes watched the car till it was out of sight. Then she withdrew them, went into the house and emptied her husband's pockets.

She was an active practical woman of middle age. Not long before she had celebrated her silver wedding and renewed her intimacy with her husband by valsing with him to Mr Power's accompaniment. In her days of courtship Mr Kernan had seemed to her a not ungallant figure: and she still hurried to the chapel door whenever a wedding was reported and, seeing the bridal pair, recalled with vivid pleasure how she had passed out of the Star of the Sea Church in Sandymount, leaning on the arm of a jovial wellfed man who was dressed smartly in a frock coat and lavender trousers and carried a silk hat gracefully balanced upon his other arm. After three weeks she had found a wife's life irksome and later on, when she was beginning to find it unbearable, she had become a mother. The part of mother presented to her no insuperable difficulties and for twenty-five years she had kept house shrewdly for her husband. Her two eldest sons were launched. One was in a draper's shop in Glasgow and the other was clerk to a tea merchant in Belfast. They were good sons, wrote regularly and sometimes sent home money. The other children were still at school.

Mr Kernan sent a letter to his office next day and remained in bed. She made beef tea for him and scolded him roundly. She accepted his frequent intemperance as part of the climate, healed him dutifully whenever he was sick and always tried to make him eat a breakfast. There were worse husbands. He had never been violent since the boys had grown up and she knew that he would walk to the end of Thomas Street and back again to book even a small order.

Two nights after his friends came to see him. She brought them up to his bedroom, the air of which was impregnated with a personal odour, and gave them chairs at the fire. Mr Kernan's tongue, the occasional stinging pain of which had made him somewhat irritable during the day, became more polite. He sat propped up in the bed by pillows and the little colour in his puffy cheeks made them resemble warm cinders. He apologised to his guests for the disorder of the room but at the same time looked at them a little proudly, with a veteran's pride.

He was quite unconscious that he was the victim of a plot which his friends Mr Cunningham, Mr M'Coy and Mr Power had disclosed to Mrs Kernan in the parlour. The idea had been Mr Power's but its development was entrusted to Mr Cunningham. Mr Kernan came of Protestant stock and, though he had been converted to the Catholic faith at the time of his marriage, he had not been in the pale of the Church for twenty years. He was fond, moreover, of giving side thrusts at Catholicism.

Mr Cunningham was the very man for such a case. He was an elder colleague of Mr Power's. His own domestic life was not very happy. People had great sympathy with him for it was known that he had married an unpresentable woman who was an incurable drunkard. He had set up house for her six times and each time she had pawned the furniture on him.

Everyone had respect for poor Martin Cunningham. He was a thoroughly sensible man, influential and intelligent. His blade of human knowledge, natural astuteness particularised by long association with cases in the police courts, had been tempered by brief immersions in the waters of general philosophy. He was well informed. His friends bowed to his opinions and considered that his face was like Shakespeare's.

When the plot had been disclosed to her Mrs Kernan had said:

—I leave it all in your hands, Mr Cunningham.

After a quarter of a century of married life she had very few illusions left. Religion for her was a habit and she suspected that a man of her husband's age would not change greatly before death. She was tempted to see a curious appropriateness in his accident and, but that she did not wish to seem bloody-minded, she would have told the gentleman that Mr Kernan's tongue would not suffer by being shortened. However Mr Cunningham was a capable man and religion was religion. The scheme might do good and, at least, it could do no harm. Her beliefs were not extravagant. She believed steadily in the Sacred Heart as the most generally useful of all Catholic devotions and approved of the sacraments. Her faith was bounded by her kitchen but, if she was put to it, she could believe also in the banshee and in the Holy Ghost.

The gentlemen began to talk of the accident. Mr Cunningham said that he had once known a similar case. A man of seventy had bitten off a piece of his tongue during an epileptic fit and the tongue had filled in again so that no-one could see a trace of the bite.

—Well, I'm not seventy, said the invalid.

—God forbid, said Mr Cunningham.

—It doesn't pain you now? asked Mr M'Coy.

Mr M'Coy had been at one time a tenor of some reputation. His wife, who had been a soprano, still taught young children to play the piano at low terms. His line of life had not been the shortest distance between two points and for short periods he had been driven to live by his wits. He had been a clerk in the

Midland Railway, a canvasser for advertisements for the *Irish Times* and for the *Freeman's Journal*, a town traveller for a coal firm on commission, a private enquiry agent, a clerk in the office of the Sub-Sheriff and he had recently become secretary to the City Coroner. His new office made him professionally interested in Mr Kernan's case.

—Pain? Not much, answered Mr Kernan. But it's so sickening: I feel as if I wanted to retch off.

—That's the boose, said Mr Cunningham firmly.

—No, said Mr Kernan. I think I caught a cold on the car. There's something keeps coming into my throat, phlegm or ......

—Mucus, said Mr M'Coy.

—It keeps coming like from down in my throat; sickening thing.

—Yes, yes, said Mr M'Coy, that's the thorax.

He looked at Mr Cunningham and Mr Power at the same time with an air of challenge. Mr Cunningham nodded his head rapidly and Mr Power said:

—Ah, well, all's well that ends well.

—I'm very much obliged to you, old man, said the invalid.

Mr Power waved his hand.

—Those other two fellows I was with .....

—Who were you with? asked Mr Cunningham.

—A chap—I don't know his name. Damn it now, what's his name? Little chap with sandy hair ...

—And who else?

—Harford.

—Hm, said Mr Cunningham.

When Mr Cunningham made that remark people were silent. It was known that the speaker had secret sources of information. In this case the monosyllable had a moral intention. Mr Harford sometimes formed one of a little detachment which left the city shortly after noon on Sunday with the purpose of arriving as soon as possible at some publichouse on the outskirts of the city where its members duly qualified themselves as *bonafide* travellers. But his fellow travellers had never consented to overlook his origin. He had begun life as an obscure financier by lending small sums of money to workmen at usurious interest. Later on he had become the partner of a very fat short gentleman, Mr Goldberg, in the Liffey Loan Bank. Though he had never embraced more than the jewish ethical code his fellow Catholics, whenever they had smarted in person or by proxy under his exactions, spoke of him bitterly as an Irish Jew and an illiterate and saw divine disapproval of usury made manifest through the person of his idiot son. At other times they remembered his good points.

—I wonder where did he go to, said Mr Kernan.

He wished the details of the incident to remain vague. He wished his friends to think there had been some mistake, that Mr Harford and he had missed each other. His friends, who knew quite well Mr Harford's manners in drinking, were silent. Mr Power said again:

—All's well that ends well.

Mr Kernan changed the subject at once.

—That was a decent young chap, that medical fellow, he said. Only for him ......

—O, only for him, said Mr Power, it might have been a case of seven days without the option of a fine.

—Yes, yes, said Mr Kernan, trying to remember. I remember now there was a policeman. Decent young fellow, he seemed. How did it happen at all?

—It happened that you were peloothered, Tom, said Mr Cunningham gravely.

—True bill, said Mr Kernan equally gravely.

—I suppose you squared the constable, Jack, said Mr M'Coy.

Mr Power did not relish the use of his Christian name. He was not straitlaced but he could not forget that Mr M'Coy had recently made a crusade in search of valises and portmanteaus to enable Mrs M'Coy to fulfil imaginary engagements in the country. More than he resented the fact that he had been victimised he resented such low playing of the game. He answered the question, therefore, as if Mr Kernan had asked it.

The narrative made Mr Kernan indignant. He was keenly

conscious of his citizenship, wished to live with his city on terms mutually honourable and resented any affront put upon him by those whom he called country bumpkins.

—Is this what we pay rates for? he asked. To feed and clothe these ignorant bostoons ... and they're nothing else.

Mr Cunningham laughed. He was a Castle official only during office hours.

—How could they be anything else, Tom? he said.

He assumed a thick provincial accent and said in a tone of command:

—65, catch your cabbage!

Everyone laughed. Mr M'Coy who wanted to enter the conversation by any door pretended that he had never heard the story. Mr Cunningham said:

—It is supposed—they say, you know—to take place in the depot where they get these thundering big country fellows, omadhauns, you know, to drill. The sergeant makes them stand in a row against the wall and hold up their plates.

He illustrated the story by grotesque gestures.

—At dinner, you know. Then he has a bloody big bowl of cabbage before him on the table and a bloody big spoon like a shovel. He takes up a wad of cabbage on the spoon and pegs it across the room and the poor devils have to try and catch it on their plates: *65, catch your cabbage.*

Everyone laughed again: but Mr Kernan was somewhat indignant still. He talked of writing a letter to the papers.

—These yahoos coming up here, he said, think they can boss the people. I needn't tell you, Martin, what kind of men they are.

Mr Cunningham gave a qualified assent.

—It's like everything else in this world, he said. You get some bad ones and you get some good ones.

—O yes, you get some good ones, I admit, said Mr Kernan, satisfied.

—It's better to have nothing to say to them, said Mr M'Coy. That's my opinion.

Mrs Kernan entered the room and, placing a tray on the table, said:

—Help yourselves, gentlemen.

Mr Power stood up to officiate, offering her his chair. She declined it, saying that she was ironing downstairs and, after having exchanged a nod with Mr Cunningham behind Mr Power's back, prepared to leave the room. Her husband called out to her:

—And have you nothing for me, duckie?

—O, you! The back of my hand to you! said Mrs Kernan tartly.

Her husband called after her:

—Nothing for poor little hubby!

He assumed such a comical face and voice that the distribution of the bottles of stout took place amid general merriment.

The gentlemen drank from their glasses, set the glasses again on the table and paused. Then Mr Cunningham turned towards Mr Power and said casually:

—On Thursday night, you said, Jack?

—Thursday, yes, said Mr Power.

—Righto! said Mr Cunningham promptly.

—We can meet in M'Auley's, said Mr M'Coy. That'll be the most convenient place.

—But we mustn't be late, said Mr Power earnestly, because it is sure to be crammed to the doors.

—We can meet at half seven, said Mr M'Coy.

—Righto! said Mr Cunningham. Half seven at M'Auley's be it!

There was a short silence. Mr Kernan waited to see whether he would be taken into his friends' confidence. Then he asked:

—What's in the wind?

—O, it's nothing, said Mr Cunningham. It's only a little matter that we're arranging about for Thursday.

—The opera, is it? said Mr Kernan.

—No, no, said Mr Cunningham in an evasive tone, it's just a little .... spiritual matter.

—O, said Mr Kernan.

There was silence again. Then Mr Power said point blank:

—To tell you the truth, Tom, we're going to make a retreat.

—Yes, that's it, said Mr Cunningham, Jack and I and M'Coy here—we're all going to wash the pot.

He uttered the metaphor with a certain homely energy and, encouraged by his own voice, proceeded:

—You see, we may as well all admit we're a nice collection of scoundrels, one and all. I say, one and all, he added with gruff charity and turning to Mr Power. Own up now!

—I own up, said Mr Power.

—And I own up, said Mr M'Coy.

—So we're going to wash the pot together, said Mr Cunningham.

A thought seemed to strike him. He turned suddenly to the invalid and said:

—Do you know what, Tom, has just occurred to me? You might join in and we'd have a fourhanded reel.

—Good idea, said Mr Power. The four of us together.

Mr Kernan was silent. The proposal conveyed very little meaning to his mind but, understanding that some spiritual agencies were about to concern themselves on his behalf, he thought he owed it to his dignity to show a stiff neck. He took no part in the conversation for a long while but listened, with an air of calm enmity, while his friends discussed the Jesuits.

—I haven't such a bad opinion of the Jesuits, he said, intervening at length. They're an educated order. I believe they mean well too.

—They're the grandest order in the Church, Tom, said Mr Cunningham with enthusiasm. The General of the Jesuits stands next to the Pope.

—There's no mistake about it, said Mr M'Coy, if you want a thing well done and no flies about it you go to a Jesuit. They're the boyos have influence. I'll tell you a case in point ....

—The Jesuits are a fine body of men, said Mr Power.

—It's a curious thing, said Mr Cunningham, about the Jesuit Order. Every other order of the Church had to be reformed at some time or other but the Jesuit Order was never once reformed. It never fell away.

—Is that so? asked Mr M'Coy.

—That's a fact, said Mr Cunningham. That's history.

—Look at their church too, said Mr Power. Look at the congregation they have.

—The Jesuits cater for the upper classes, said Mr M'Coy.

—Of course, said Mr Power.

—Yes, said Mr Kernan. That's why I have a feeling for them. It's some of those secular priests, ignorant, bumptious ......

—They're all good men, said Mr Cunningham, each in his own way. The Irish priesthood is honoured all the world over.

—O yes, said Mr Power.

—Not like some of the other priesthoods on the continent, said Mr M'Coy, unworthy of the name.

—Perhaps you're right, said Mr Kernan relenting.

—Of course I'm right, said Mr Cunningham. I haven't been in the world all this time and seen most sides of it without being a judge of character.

The gentlemen drank again, one following another's example. Mr Kernan seemed to be weighing something in his mind. He was impressed. He had a high opinion of Mr Cunningham as a judge of character and as a reader of faces. He asked for particulars.

—O, it's just a retreat, you know, said Mr Cunningham. Father Purdon is giving it. It's for business men, you know.

—He won't be too hard on us, Tom, said Mr Power persuasively.

—Father Purdon? Father Purdon? said the invalid.

—O, you must know him, Tom, said Mr Cunningham stoutly. Fine jolly fellow! He's a man of the world like ourselves.

—Ah ... yes. I think I know him. Rather red face; tall.

—That's the man.

—And tell me, Martin .... Is he a good preacher?

—Mmmno ..... It's not exactly a sermon, you know. It's just a kind of a friendly talk, you know, in a commonsense way.

Mr Kernan deliberated. Mr M'Coy said:

—Father Tom Burke, that was the boy!

—O, Father Tom Burke, said Mr Cunningham, that was a born orator. Did you ever hear him, Tom?

—Did I ever hear him! said the invalid, nettled. Rather! I heard him ......

—And yet they say he wasn't much of a theologian, said Mr Cunningham.

—Is that so? said Mr M'Coy.

—O, of course, nothing wrong, you know. Only sometimes, they say, he didn't preach what was quite orthodox.

—Ah! .. he was a splendid man, said Mr M'Coy.

—I heard him once, Mr Kernan continued. I forget the subject of his discourse now. Crofton and I were in the back of the .... pit, you know ... the ....

—The body, said Mr Cunningham.

—Yes, in the back near the door. I forget now what ...... O yes, it was on the Pope, the late Pope. I remember it well. Upon my word it was magnificent, the style of the oratory. And his voice! God! hadn't he a voice! *The Prisoner of the Vatican*, he called him. I remember Crofton saying to me when we came out .....

—But he's an Orangeman, Crofton, isn't he? said Mr Power.

—'Course he is, said Mr Kernan, and a damned decent Orangeman too. We went into Butler's in Moore Street–faith, I was genuinely moved, tell you the God's truth–and I remember well his very words. *Kernan*, he said, *we worship at different altars*, he said, *but our belief is the same*. Struck me as very well put.

—There's a good deal in that, said Mr Power. There used always be crowds of Protestants in the chapel when Father Tom was preaching.

—There's not much difference between us, said Mr M'Coy. We both believe in ....

He hesitated for a moment.

—... in the Redeemer. Only they don't believe in the Pope and in the mother of God.

—But, of course, said Mr Cunningham quietly and effectively, our religion is *the* religion, the old, original faith.

—Not a doubt of it, said Mr Kernan warmly.

Mrs Kernan came to the door of the bedroom and announced:

—Here's a visitor for you!

—Who is it?

—Mr Fogarty.

—O, come in! come in!

A pale oval face came forward into the light. The arch of its fair trailing moustache was repeated in the fair eyebrows looped above pleasantly astonished eyes. Mr Fogarty was a modest grocer. He had failed in business in a licensed house in the city because his financial condition had constrained him to tie himself to second class distillers and brewers. He had opened a small shop on the Glasnevin road where, he flattered himself, his manners would ingratiate him with the housewives of the district. He bore himself with a certain grace, complimented little children and spoke with a neat enunciation. He was not without culture.

Mr Fogarty brought a gift with him, a half pint of special whisky. He enquired politely for Mr Kernan, placed his gift on the table and sat down with the company on equal terms. Mr Kernan appreciated the gift all the more since he was aware that there was a small account for groceries unsettled between him and Mr Fogarty. He said:

—I wouldn't doubt you, old man. Open that, Jack, will you?

Mr Power again officiated. Glasses were rinsed and five small measures of whisky were poured out. This new influence enlivened the conversation. Mr Fogarty, sitting on a small area of the chair, was specially interested.

—Pope Leo XIII, said Mr Cunningham, was one of the lights of the age. His great idea, you know, was the union of the Latin and Greek Churches. That was the aim of his life.

—I often heard he was one of the most intellectual men in Europe, said Mr Power. I mean apart from his being Pope.

—So he was, said Mr Cunningham, if not *the* most so. His motto, you know, as Pope was *Lux upon Lux—Light upon Light*.

—No, no, said Mr Fogarty eagerly, I think you're wrong there. It was *Lux in Tenebris*, I think—*Light in Darkness*.

—O yes, said Mr M'Coy, *Tenebrae*.

—Allow me, said Mr Cunningham positively, it was *Lux upon Lux*. And Pius IX, his predecessor's motto was *Crux upon Crux*, that is, *Cross upon Cross*, to show the difference between their two pontificates.

The inference was allowed. Mr Cunningham continued:

—Pope Leo, you know, was a great scholar and a poet.

—He had a strong face, said Mr Kernan.

—Yes, said Mr Cunningham. He wrote Latin poetry.

—Is that so? said Mr Fogarty.

Mr M'Coy tasted his whisky contentedly and shook his head with a double intention, saying:

—That's no joke, I can tell you.

—We didn't learn that, Tom, said Mr Power, following Mr M'Coy's example, when we went to the penny-a-week school.

—There was many a good man went to the penny-a-week school with a sod of turf under his oxter, said Mr Kernan sententiously. The old system was the best: plain honest education. None of your modern trumpery ......

—Quite right, said Mr Power.

—No superfluities, said Mr Fogarty.

He enunciated the word and then drank gravely.

—I remember reading, said Mr Cunningham, that one of Pope Leo's poems was on the invention of the photograph—in Latin, of course.

—On the photograph! exclaimed Mr Kernan.

—Yes, said Mr Cunningham.

He also drank from his glass.

—Well, you know, said Mr M'Coy, isn't the photograph wonderful when you come to think of it?

—O, of course, said Mr Power, great minds can see things ....

—As the poet says: *Great minds are very near to madness*, said Mr Fogarty.

Mr Kernan seemed to be troubled in mind. He made an

effort to recall the Protestant theology on some thorny points and in the end addressed Mr Cunningham.

—Tell me, Martin, he said. Weren't some of the popes—of course, not our present man or his predecessor, but some of the old popes—not exactly .... you know .... up to the knocker?

There was a silence. Mr Cunningham said:

—O, of course, there were some bad lots .... But the astonishing thing is this. Not one of them, not the biggest drunkard, not the most ... out-and-out ruffian, not one of them ever preached *ex cathedra* a word of false doctrine. Now isn't that an astonishing thing?

—That is, said Mr Kernan.

—Yes, because when the Pope speaks *ex cathedra*, Mr Fogarty explained, he is infallible.

—Yes, said Mr Cunningham.

—O, I know about the infallibility of the Pope. I remember I was younger then ... Or was it that?

Mr Fogarty interrupted. He took up the bottle and helped the others to a little more. Mr M'Coy, seeing that there was not enough to go round, pleaded that he had not finished his first measure. The others accepted under protest. The light music of whisky falling into glasses made an agreeable interlude.

—What's that you were saying, Tom? asked Mr M'Coy.

—Papal infallibility, said Mr Cunningham, that was the greatest scene in the whole history of the Church.

—How was that, Martin? asked Mr Power.

Mr Cunningham held up two thick fingers.

—In the sacred college, you know, of cardinals and archbishops and bishops there were two men who held out against it while the others were all for it. The whole conclave except these two was unanimous. No! They wouldn't have it!

—Ha! said Mr M'Coy.

—And they were a German cardinal by the name of Dolling ... or Dowling ... or ...—

—Dowling was no German and that's a sure five, said Mr Power laughing.

—Well, this great German cardinal, whatever his name was, was one and the other was John MacHale.

—What? cried Mr Kernan. Is it John of Tuam?

—Are you sure of that now? asked Mr Fogarty dubiously. I thought it was some Italian or American ...

—John of Tuam, repeated Mr Cunningham, was the man.

He drank and the other gentlemen followed his lead. Then he resumed:

—There they were at it, all the cardinals and bishops and archbishops from all the ends of the earth and these two fighting dog and devil until at last the Pope himself stood up and declared infallibility a dogma of the Church *ex cathedra*. On the very moment John MacHale, who had been arguing and arguing against it, stood up and shouted out with the voice of a lion: *Credo!*

—*I believe!* said Mr Fogarty.

—*Credo!* said Mr Cunningham. That showed the faith he had. He submitted the moment the Pope spoke.

—And what about Dowling? asked Mr M'Coy.

—The German cardinal wouldn't submit. He left the Church.

Mr Cunningham's words had built up the vast image of the Church in the minds of his hearers. His deep raucous voice had thrilled them as it uttered the word of belief and submission. When Mrs Kernan came into the room drying her hands she came into a solemn company. She did not disturb the silence but leaned over the rail at the foot of the bed.

—I once saw John MacHale, said Mr Kernan, and I'll never forget it as long as I live.

He turned towards his wife to be confirmed.

—I often told you that?

Mrs Kernan nodded.

—It was at the unveiling of Sir John Gray's statue. Edmund Dwyer Gray was speaking, blathering away, and here was this old fellow, crabbed-looking old chap, looking at him from under his bushy eyebrows.

Mr Kernan knitted his brows and, lowering his head like an angry bull, glared at his wife.

—God! he exclaimed, reassuming his natural face, I never saw such an eye in a man's head. It was as much as to say: *I have you properly taped, my lad.* He had an eye like a hawk.

—None of the Grays was any good, said Mr Power.

There was a pause again. Mr Power turned to Mrs Kernan and said with abrupt joviality:

—Well, Mrs Kernan, we're going to make your man here a good holy pious and God-fearing Roman Catholic.

He swept his arm round the company inclusively.

—We're all going to make a retreat together and confess our sins—and God knows we want it badly.

—I don't mind, said Mr Kernan, smiling a little nervously.

Mrs Kernan thought it would be wiser to conceal her satisfaction. So she said:

—I pity the poor priest that has to listen to your tale.

Mr Kernan's expression changed.

—If he doesn't like it, he said bluntly, he can .... do the other thing. I'll just tell him my little tale of woe. I'm not such a bad fellow .....

Mr Cunningham intervened promptly.

—We'll all renounce the devil, he said, together, not forgetting his works and pomps.

—Get behind me, Satan! said Mr Fogarty, laughing and looking at the others.

Mr Power said nothing. He felt completely outgeneralled. But a pleased expression flickered across his face.

—All we have to do, said Mr Cunningham, is to stand up with lighted candles in our hands and renew our baptismal vows.

—O, don't forget the candle, Tom, said Mr M'Coy, whatever you do.

—What? said Mr Kernan. Must I have a candle?

—O yes, said Mr Cunningham.

—No, damn it all, said Mr Kernan sensibly, I draw the line there. I'll do the job right enough. I'll do the retreat business and confession and ... all that business. But ... no candles! No, damn it all, I bar the candles!

He shook his head with farcical gravity.

—Listen to that! said his wife.

—I bar the candles, said Mr Kernan, conscious of having created an effect on his audience and continuing to shake his head to and fro. I bar the magic lantern business.

Everyone laughed heartily.

—There's a nice Catholic for you! said his wife.

—No candles! repeated Mr Kernan obdurately. That's off!

◆ ◆ ◆

The transept of the Jesuit Church in Gardiner Street was almost full; and still at every moment gentlemen entered from the sidedoor and, directed by the lay brother, walked on tiptoe along the aisles until they found seating accommodation. The gentlemen were all well dressed and orderly. The light of the lamps of the church fell upon an assembly of black clothes and white collars, relieved here and there by tweeds, on dark mottled pillars of green marble and on lugubrious canvasses. The gentlemen sat in the benches, having hitched their trousers slightly above their knees and laid their hats in security. They sat well back and gazed formally at the distant speck of red light which was suspended before the high altar.

In one of the benches near the pulpit sat Mr Cunningham and Mr Kernan. In the bench behind sat Mr M'Coy alone: and in the bench behind him sat Mr Power and Mr Fogarty. Mr M'Coy had tried unsuccessfully to find a place in the bench with the others and, when the party had settled down in the form of a quincunx, he had tried unsuccessfully to make comic remarks. As these had not been well received he had desisted. Even he was sensible of the decorous atmosphere and even he began to respond to the religious stimulus. In a whisper Mr Cunningham drew Mr Kernan's attention to Mr Harford, the moneylender, who sat some distance off, and to Mr Fanning, the registration agent and mayormaker of the city, who was sitting immediately under the pulpit beside one of the newly elected councillors of the ward. To the right sat old Michael Grimes, the owner of three pawnbroker's shops, and Dan

Hogan's nephew who was up for the job in the Town Clerk's office. Farther in front sat Mr Hendrick, the chief reporter of the *Freeman's Journal*, and poor O'Carroll, an old friend of Mr Kernan's, who had been at one time a considerable commercial figure. Gradually, as he recognised familiar faces, Mr Kernan began to feel more at home. His hat, which had been rehabilitated by his wife, rested upon his knees. Once or twice he pulled down his cuffs with one hand while he held the brim of his hat lightly but firmly with the other hand.

A powerful-looking figure, the upper part of which was draped with a white surplice, was observed to be struggling up into the pulpit. Simultaneously the congregation unsettled, produced handkerchiefs and knelt upon them with care. Mr Kernan followed the general example. The priest's figure now stood upright in the pulpit, two-thirds of its bulk crowned by a massive red face appearing above the balustrade.

Father Purdon knelt down, turned towards the red speck of light and, covering his face with his hands, prayed. After an interval he uncovered his face and rose. The congregation rose also and settled again on its benches. Mr Kernan restored his hat to its original position on his knee and presented an attentive face to the preacher. The preacher turned back each wide sleeve of his surplice with an elaborate large gesture and slowly surveyed the array of faces. Then he said:

—*For the children of this world are wiser in their generation than the children of light. Wherefore make unto yourselves friends out of the Mammon of iniquity so that when you die they may receive you into everlasting dwellings.*

Father Purdon developed the text with resonant assurance. It was one of the most difficult texts in all the scriptures, he said, to interpret properly. It was a text which might seem to the casual observer at variance with the lofty morality elsewhere preached by Jesus Christ. But, he told his hearers, the text had seemed to him specially adapted for the guidance of those whose lot it was to lead the life of the world and who yet wished to lead that life not in the manner of worldlings. It was a text for business men and professional men. Jesus Christ, with His divine understanding of every cranny of our human nature, understood that all men were not called to the religious life, that by far the vast majority were forced to live in the world and, to a certain extent, for the world: and in this sentence He designed to give them a word of counsel, setting before them as exemplars in the religious life those very worshippers of Mammon who were of all men the least solicitous in matters religious.

He told his hearers that he was there that evening for no terrifying, no extravagant purpose, but as a man of the world speaking to his fellow men. He came to speak to business men and he would speak to them in a businesslike way. If he might use the metaphor, he said, he was their spiritual accountant and he wished each and every one of his hearers to open his books, the books of his spiritual life, and see if they tallied accurately with conscience.

Jesus Christ was not a hard taskmaster. He understood our little failings, understood the weakness of our poor fallen nature, understood the temptations of this life. We might have had, we all had from time to time, our temptations: we might have, we all had, our failings. But one thing only, he said, he would ask of his hearers. And that was: to be straight and manly with God. If their accounts tallied in every point to say:
—Well, I have verified my accounts. I find all well.

But if, as might happen, there were some discrepancies, to admit the truth, to be frank and say like a man:
—Well, I have looked into my accounts. I find this wrong and this wrong. But, with God's grace, I will rectify this and this. I will set right my accounts.

The Dead

Lily, the caretaker's daughter, was literally run off her feet. Hardly had she brought one gentleman into the little pantry behind the office on the groundfloor and helped him off with his overcoat when the wheezy halldoor bell clanged again and she had to scamper along the bare hallway to let in another guest. It was well for her she had not to attend to the ladies also. But Miss Kate and Miss Julia had thought of that and had converted the bathroom upstairs into a ladies' dressingroom. Miss Kate and Miss Julia were there, gossiping and laughing and fussing, walking after each other to the head of the stairs, peering down over the banisters and calling down to Lily to ask her who had come.

It was always a great affair, the Misses Morkan's annual dance. Everybody who knew them came to it, members of the family, old friends of the family, the members of Julia's choir, any of Kate's pupils that were grown up enough and even some of Mary Jane's pupils too. Never once had it fallen flat. For years and years it had gone off in splendid style as long as anyone could remember, ever since Kate and Julia, after the death of their brother Pat, had left the house in Stony Batter and taken Mary Jane, their only niece, to live with them in the dark gaunt house on Usher's Island, the upper part of which they had rented from Mr Fullam, the corn factor on the groundfloor. That was a good thirty years ago if it was a day. Mary Jane, who was then a little girl in short clothes, was now the main prop of the household for she had the organ in Haddington Road. She had been through the academy and gave a pupils' concert every year in the upper room of the Antient Concert Rooms. Many of her pupils belonged to better class families on the Kingstown and Dalkey line. Old as they were, her aunts also did their share. Julia, though she was quite grey, was still the leading soprano in Adam and Eve's and Kate, being too feeble to go about much, gave music lessons to beginners on the old square piano in the back room. Lily, the caretaker's daughter, did housemaid work for them. Though their life was modest they believed in eating well, the best of everything: diamond bone sirloins, three shilling tea and the best bottled stout. But Lily seldom made a mistake in the orders so that she got on well with her three mistresses. They were fussy, that was all. But the only thing they would not stand was back answers.

Of course they had good reason to be fussy on such a night. And then it was long after ten o'clock and yet there was no sign of Gabriel and his wife. Besides they were dreadfully afraid that Freddy Malins might turn up screwed. They would not wish for worlds that any of Mary Jane's pupils should see him under the influence: and when he was like that it was sometimes very hard to manage him. Freddy Malins always came late but they wondered what could be keeping Gabriel: and that was what brought them every two minutes to the banisters to ask Lily had Gabriel or Freddy come.

—O, Mr Conroy, said Lily to Gabriel when she opened the door for him, Miss Kate and Miss Julia thought you were never coming. Good night, Mrs Conroy.

—I'll engage they did, said Gabriel, but they forget that my wife here takes three mortal hours to dress herself.

He stood on the mat, scraping the snow from his goloshes, while Lily led his wife to the foot of the stairs and called out:

—Miss Kate, here's Mrs Conroy.

Kate and Julia came toddling down the dark stairs at once. Both of them kissed Gabriel's wife, said she must be perished alive and asked was Gabriel with her.

—Here I am as right as the mail, aunt Kate! Go on up. I'll follow, called out Gabriel from the dark.

He continued scraping his feet vigorously while the three women went upstairs, laughing, to the ladies' dressingroom. A light fringe of snow lay like a cape on the shoulders of his overcoat and like toecaps on the toes of his goloshes; and, as the buttons of his overcoat slipped with a squeaking noise through the snowstiffened frieze, a cold fragrant air from out of doors escaped from crevices and folds.

—Is it snowing again, Mr Conroy? asked Lily.

She had preceded him into the pantry to help him off with his overcoat. Gabriel smiled at the three syllables she had given his surname and glanced at her. She was a slim growing girl, pale in complexion and with haycoloured hair. The gas in the pantry made her look still paler. Gabriel had known her when she was a child and used to sit on the lowest step nursing a rag doll.

—Yes, Lily, he answered, and I think we're in for a night of it.

He looked up at the pantry ceiling which was shaking with the stamping and shuffling of feet on the floor above, listened for a moment to the piano and then glanced at the girl who was folding his overcoat carefully at the end of a shelf.

—Tell me, Lily, he said in a friendly tone, do you still go to school?

—O no, sir, she answered, I'm done schooling this year and more.

—O then, said Gabriel gaily, I suppose we'll be going to your wedding one of these fine days with your young man—eh?

The girl glanced back at him over her shoulder and said with great bitterness:

—The men that is now is only all palaver and what they can get out of you.

Gabriel coloured as if he felt he had made a mistake and, without looking at her, kicked off his goloshes and flicked actively with his muffler at his patent leather shoes.

He was a stout tallish young man. The high colour of his cheeks pushed upwards even to his forehead where it scattered itself in a few formless patches of pale red; and on his hairless face there scintillated restlessly the polished lenses and bright gilt rims of the glasses which screened his delicate and restless eyes. His glossy black hair was parted in the middle and brushed in a long curve behind his ears where it curled slightly beneath the groove left by his hat.

When he had flicked lustre into his shoes he stood up and pulled his waistcoat down more tightly on his plump body. Then he took a coin rapidly from his pocket.

—O Lily, he said, thrusting it into her hand, it's Christmas time, isn't it? Just .... here's a little ....

He walked rapidly towards the door.

—O no, sir! cried the girl, following him. Really, sir, I wouldn't take it.

—Christmas time! Christmas time! said Gabriel, almost trotting to the stairs and waving his hand to her in deprecation.

The girl, seeing that he had gained the stairs, called out after him:

—Well, thank you, sir.

He waited outside the drawingroom door until the waltz should finish, listening to the skirts that swept against it and to the shuffling of feet. He was still discomposed by the girl's bitter and sudden retort. It had cast a gloom over him which he tried to dispel by arranging his cuffs and the bows of his tie. Then he took from his waistcoat pocket a little paper and glanced at the headings he had made for his speech. He was undecided about the lines from Robert Browning for he feared they would be above the heads of his hearers. Some quotation that they could recognise from Shakespeare or from the mel=

odies would be better. The indelicate clacking of the men's heels and the shuffling of their soles reminded him that their grade of culture differed from his. He would only make himself ridiculous by quoting poetry to them which they could not understand. They would think that he was airing his superior education. He would fail with them just as he had failed with the girl in the pantry. He had taken up a wrong tone. His whole speech was a mistake from first to last, an utter failure.

Just then his aunts and his wife came out of the ladies' dressingroom. His aunts were two small plainly dressed old women. Aunt Julia was an inch or so the taller. Her hair, drawn low over the tops of her ears, was grey; and grey also, with darker shadows, was her large flaccid face. Though she was stout in build and stood erect her slow eyes and parted lips gave her the appearance of a woman who did not know where she was or where she was going. Aunt Kate was more vivacious. Her face, healthier than her sister's, was all puckers and creases like a shrivelled red apple and her hair, braided in the same oldfashioned way, had not lost its ripe nut colour.

They both kissed Gabriel frankly. He was their favourite nephew, the son of their dead elder sister Ellen who had married T J Conroy of the Port and Docks.

—Gretta tells me you're not going to take a cab back to Monkstown tonight, Gabriel, said Aunt Kate.

—No, said Gabriel, turning to his wife, we had quite enough of that last year, hadn't we? Don't you remember, Aunt Kate, what a cold Gretta got out of it? Cab windows rattling all the way and the east wind blowing in after we passed Merrion. Very jolly it was. Gretta caught a dreadful cold.

Aunt Kate frowned severely and nodded her head at every word.

—Quite right, Gabriel, quite right, she said. You can't be too careful.

—But as for Gretta there, said Gabriel, she'd walk home in the snow if she were let.

Mrs Conroy laughed.

—Don't mind him, aunt Kate, she said. He's really an awful bother, what with green shades for Tom's eyes at night and making him do the dumbbells and forcing Lottie to eat the stirabout. The poor child! And she simply hates the sight of it! .... O, but you'll never guess what he makes me wear now!

She broke out into a peal of laughter and glanced at her husband whose admiring and happy eyes had been wandering from her dress to her face and hair. The two aunts laughed heartily too for Gabriel's solicitude was a standing joke with them.

—Goloshes! said Mrs Conroy. That's the latest. Whenever it's wet underfoot I must put on my goloshes. Tonight even he wanted me to put them on but I wouldn't. The next thing he'll buy me will be a diving suit.

Gabriel laughed nervously and patted his tie reassuringly while aunt Kate nearly doubled herself so heartily did she enjoy the joke. The smile soon faded from aunt Julia's face and her mirthless eyes were directed towards her nephew's face. After a pause she asked:

—And what are goloshes, Gabriel?

—Goloshes, Julia! exclaimed her sister. Goodness me, don't you know what goloshes are? You wear them over your .... over your boots, Gretta, isn't it?

—Yes, said Mrs Conroy. Guttapercha things. We both have a pair now. Gabriel says everyone wears them on the continent.

—O, on the continent, murmured aunt Julia, nodding her head slowly.

Gabriel knitted his brows and said, as if he were slightly angered:

—It's nothing very wonderful but Gretta thinks it very funny because she says the word reminds her of christy minstrels.

—But tell me, Gabriel, said aunt Kate with brisk tact. Of course you've seen about the room. Gretta was saying ....

—O, the room is all right, replied Gabriel. I've taken one in the Gresham.

—To be sure, said aunt Kate, by far the best thing to do. And the children, Gretta, you're not anxious about them?

—O, for one night, said Mrs Conroy. Besides Bessie will look after them.

—To be sure, said aunt Kate again. What a comfort it is to have a girl like that, one you can depend on! There's that Lily, I'm sure I don't know what has come over her lately. She's not the girl she was at all.

Gabriel was about to ask his aunt some questions on this point but she broke off suddenly to gaze after her sister who had wandered down the stairs and was craning her neck over the banisters.

—Now, I ask you, she said almost testily, where is Julia going. Julia! Julia! Where are you going?

Julia who had gone half way down one flight came back and announced blandly:

—Here's Freddy!

At the same moment a clapping of hands and a final flourish of the pianist told that the waltz had ended. The drawingroom door was opened from within and some couples came out. Aunt Kate drew Gabriel aside hurriedly and whispered into his ear:

—Slip down, Gabriel, like a good fellow and see if he's all right and don't let him up if he's screwed. I'm sure he's screwed. I'm sure he is.

Gabriel went to the stairs and listened over the banisters. He could hear two persons talking in the pantry. Then he recognised Freddy Malins' laugh. He went down the stairs noisily.

—It's such a relief, said aunt Kate to Mrs Conroy, that Gabriel is here. I always feel easier in my mind when he's here ..... Julia, there's Miss Daly and Miss Power will take some refreshment. Thanks for your beautiful waltz, Miss Daly. It made lovely time.

A tall wizenfaced man with a stiff grizzled moustache and swarthy skin who was passing out with his partner said:

—And may we have some refreshment too, Miss Morkan?

—Julia, said aunt Kate summarily, and here's Mr Browne and Miss Furlong. Take them in, Julia, with Miss Daly and Miss Power.

—I'm the man for the ladies, said Mr Browne, pursing his lips until his moustache bristled and smiling in all his wrinkles. You know, Miss Morkan, the reason they are so fond of me is .....

He did not finish his sentence but, seeing that aunt Kate was out of earshot, at once led the three young ladies into the back room. The middle of the room was occupied by two square tables placed end to end and on these aunt Julia and the caretaker were straightening and smoothing a large cloth. On the sideboard were arrayed dishes and plates and glasses and bundles of knives and forks and spoons. The top of the closed square piano served also as a sideboard for viands and sweets. At a smaller sideboard in one corner two young men were standing, drinking hop bitters.

Mr Browne led his charges thither and invited them all, in jest, to some ladies' punch, hot, strong and sweet. As they said they never took anything strong he opened three bottles of lemonade for them. Then he asked one of the young men to move aside and, taking hold of the decanter, filled out for himself a goodly measure of whisky. The young men eyed him respectfully while he took a trial sip.

—God help me, he said smiling, it's the doctor's orders.

His wizened face broke into a broader smile and the three young ladies laughed in musical echo to his pleasantry, swaying their bodies to and fro, with nervous jerks of their shoulders. The boldest said:

—O, now, Mr Browne, I'm sure the doctor never ordered anything of the kind.

Mr Browne took another sip of his whisky and said, with sidling mimicry:

—Well, you see, I'm like the famous Mrs Cassidy who is reported to have said: *Now, Mary Grimes, if I don't take it make me take it for I feel I want it.*

His hot face had leaned forward a little too confidentially and he had assumed a very low Dublin accent so that the young ladies, with one instinct, received his speech in silence. Miss Furlong, who was one of Mary Jane's pupils, asked Miss Daly what was the name of the pretty waltz she had played; and Mr Browne, seeing that he was ignored, turned promptly to the two young men who were more appreciative.

A redfaced young woman, dressed in pansy, came into the room, excitedly clapping her hands and crying:

—Quadrilles! Quadrilles!

Close on her heels came aunt Kate, crying:

—Two gentlemen and three ladies, Mary Jane!

—O, here's Mr Bergin and Mr Kerrigan, said Mary Jane. Mr Kerrigan, will you take Miss Power. Miss Furlong, may I get you a partner, Mr Bergin. O, that'll just do now.

—Three ladies, Mary Jane, said aunt Kate.

The two young gentlemen asked the ladies if they might have the pleasure and Mary Jane turned to Miss Daly.

—O, Miss Daly, you're really awfully good after playing for the last two dances but really we're so short of ladies tonight.

—I don't mind in the least, Miss Morkan.

—But I've a nice partner for you, Mr Bartell D'Arcy, the tenor. I'll get him to sing later on. All Dublin is raving about him.

—Lovely voice, lovely voice! said aunt Kate.

As the piano had twice begun the prelude to the first figure Mary Jane led her recruits quickly from the room. They had hardly gone when aunt Julia wandered slowly into the room, looking behind her at something.

—What is the matter, Julia? asked aunt Kate anxiously. Who is it?

Julia, who was carrying in a column of table-napkins, turned to her sister and said simply, as if the question had surprised her:

—It's only Freddy, Kate, and Gabriel with him.

In fact right behind her Gabriel could be seen piloting Freddy Malins across the landing. The latter, a young man of about forty, was of Gabriel's size and build with very round shoulders. His face was fleshy and pallid, touched with colour only at the thick hanging lobes of his ears and at the wide wings of his nose. He had coarse features, a blunt nose, a convex and receding brow, tumid and protruded lips. His heavylidded eyes and the disorder of his scanty hair made him look sleepy. He was laughing heartily in a high key at a story which he had been telling Gabriel on the stairs and at the same time rubbing the knuckles of his left fist backwards and forwards into his left eye.

—Good evening, Freddy, said aunt Julia.

Freddy Malins bade the Misses Morkan good evening in what seemed an offhand fashion by reason of the habitual catch in his voice and then, seeing that Mr Browne was grinning at him from the sideboard, crossed the room on rather shaky legs and began to repeat in an undertone the story he had just told to Gabriel.

—He's not so bad, is he? said aunt Kate to Gabriel.

Gabriel's brows were dark but he raised them quickly and answered:

—O no, hardly noticeable.

—Now, isn't he a terrible fellow! she said. And his poor mother made him take the pledge on New Year's Eve. But come on, Gabriel, into the drawingroom.

Before leaving the room with Gabriel she signalled to Mr Browne by frowning and shaking her forefinger in warning to and fro. Mr Browne nodded in answer and, when she had gone, said to Freddy Malins:

—Now then, Teddy, I'm going to fill you out a good glass of lemonade just to buck you up.

Freddy Malins, who was nearing the climax of his story, waved the offer aside impatiently but Mr Browne, having first called Freddy Malins' attention to a disarray in his dress, filled out and handed him a full glass of lemonade. Freddy Malins' left hand accepted the glass mechanically, his right hand being engaged in the mechanical readjustment of his dress. Mr Browne, whose face was once more wrinkling with mirth, poured out for himself a glass of whisky while Freddy Malins exploded, before he had well reached the climax of his story, in a kink of highpitched bronchitic laughter and, setting down his untasted and overflowing glass, began to rub the knuckles of his left fist backwards and forwards into his left eye, repeating words of his last phrase as well as his fit of laughter would allow him.

◆ ◆ ◆

Gabriel could not listen while Mary Jane was playing her academy piece, full of runs and difficult passages, to the hushed drawingroom. He liked music but the piece she was playing had no melody for him and he doubted whether it had any melody for the other listeners though they had begged Mary Jane to play something. Four young men, who had come from the refreshment room to stand in the doorway at the sound of the piano, had gone away quietly in couples after a few minutes. The only persons who seemed to follow the music were Mary Jane herself, her hands racing along the keyboard or lifted from it at the pauses like those of a priestess in momentary imprecation, and aunt Kate standing at her elbow to turn the page.

Gabriel's eyes, irritated by the floor which glittered with beeswax under the heavy chandelier, wandered to the wall above the piano. A picture of the balcony scene in *Romeo and Juliet* hung there and beside it was a picture of the two murdered princes in the tower which aunt Julia had worked in red, blue and brown wools when she was a girl. Probably in the school they had gone to as girls that kind of work had been taught, for one year his mother had worked for him as a birthday present a waistcoat of purple tabinet with little foxes' heads upon it, lined with brown satin and having round mulberry buttons. It was strange that his mother had had no musical talent though aunt Kate used to call her the brains-carrier of the Morkan family. Both she and Julia had always seemed a little proud of their serious and matronly sister. Her photograph stood before the pierglass. She held an open book on her knees and was pointing out something in it to Constantine who, dressed in a man-o'-war suit, lay at her feet. It was she who had chosen the names for her sons for she was very sensible of the dignity of family life. Thanks to her, Constantine was now senior curate in Balbriggan and, thanks to her, Gabriel himself had taken his degree in the royal university. A shadow passed over his face as he remembered her sullen opposition to his marriage. Some slighting phrases she had used still rankled in his memory. She had once spoken of Gretta as being country cute and that was not true of Gretta at all. It was Gretta who had nursed her all during her last long illness in their house at Monkstown.

He knew that Mary Jane must be near the end of her piece for she was playing again the opening melody with runs of scales after every bar and while he waited for the end the resentment died down in his heart. The piece ended with a trill of octaves in the treble and a final deep octave in the bass. Great applause greeted Mary Jane as, blushing and rolling up her music nervously, she escaped from the room. The most vigorous clapping came from the four young men in the doorway who had gone away to the refreshment room at the beginning of the piece but had come back when the piano had stopped.

Lancers were arranged. Gabriel found himself partnered with Miss Ivors. She was a frankmannered talkative young lady with a freckled face and prominent brown eyes. She did not wear a lowcut bodice and the large brooch which was fixed in the front of her collar bore on it an Irish device.

When they had taken their places she said abruptly:

—I have a crow to pluck with you.

—With me? said Gabriel.

She nodded her head gravely.

—What is it? asked Gabriel, smiling at her solemn manner.

—Who is G. C.? answered Miss Ivors turning her eyes upon him.

Gabriel coloured and was about to knit his brows as if he did not understand when she said bluntly:

—O, innocent Amy! I have found out that you write for the *Daily Express*. Now aren't you ashamed of yourself?

—Why should I be ashamed of myself? asked Gabriel blinking his eyes and trying to smile.

—Well, I'm ashamed of you, said Miss Ivors frankly. To say you'd write for a rag like that. I didn't think you were a west Briton.

A look of perplexity appeared on Gabriel's face. It was true that he wrote a literary column every Wednesday in the *Daily Express* for which he was paid fifteen shillings. But that did not make him a west Briton surely. The books he received for review were almost more welcome than the paltry cheque. He loved to feel the covers and turn over the pages of newly printed books. Nearly every day when his teaching in the college was ended he used to wander down the quays to the secondhand booksellers, to Hickey's on Bachelor's Walk, to Webb's or Massey's on Aston's Quay or to Clohissey's in the bystreet. He did not know how to meet her charge. He wanted to say that literature was above politics. But they were friends of many years' standing and their careers had been parallel, first at the university and then as teachers: he could not risk a grandiose phrase with her. He continued blinking his eyes and trying to smile and murmured lamely that he saw nothing political in writing reviews of books.

When their turn to cross had come he was still perplexed and inattentive. Miss Ivors promptly took his hand in a warm grasp and said in a soft friendly tone:

—Of course, I was only joking. Come, we cross now.

When they were together again she spoke of the university question and Gabriel felt more at ease. A friend of hers had shown her his review of Browning's poems. That was how she had found out the secret: but she liked the review immensely. Then she said suddenly:

—O, Mr Conroy, will you come for an excursion to the Aran Isles this summer? We're going to stay there a whole month. It will be splendid out in the Atlantic. You ought to come. Mr Clancy is coming and Mr Kilkelly and Kathleen Kearney. It would be splendid for Gretta too if she'd come. She's from Connacht, isn't she?

—Her people are, said Gabriel shortly.

—But you will come, won't you? said Miss Ivors, laying her warm hand eagerly on his arm.

—The fact is, said Gabriel, I have already arranged to go ...

—Go where? asked Miss Ivors.

—Well, you know, every year I go for a cycling tour with some fellows and so ...

—But where? asked Miss Ivors.

—Well, we usually go to France or Belgium or perhaps Germany, said Gabriel awkwardly.

—And why do you go to France and Belgium, said Miss Ivors, instead of visiting your own land?

—Well, said Gabriel, it's partly to keep in touch with the languages and partly for a change.

—And haven't you your own language to keep in touch with, Irish? asked Miss Ivors.

—Well, said Gabriel, if it comes to that, you know, Irish is not my language.

Their neighbours had turned to listen to the crossexamination. Gabriel glanced right and left nervously and tried to keep his good humour under the ordeal which was making a blush invade his forehead.

—And haven't you your own land to visit, continued Miss Ivors, that you know nothing of, your own people and your own country?

—O, to tell you the truth, retorted Gabriel suddenly, I'm sick of my own country, sick of it!

—Why? asked Miss Ivors.

Gabriel did not answer for his retort had heated him.

—Why? repeated Miss Ivors.

They had to go visiting together and, as he had not answered her, Miss Ivors said warmly:

—Of course, you've no answer.

Gabriel tried to cover his agitation by taking part in the dance with great energy. He avoided her eyes for he had seen a sour expression on her face. But when they met in the long chain he was surprised to feel his hand firmly pressed. She looked at him from under her brows for a moment quizzically until he smiled. Then, just as the chain was about to start again, she stood on tiptoe and whispered into his ear:

—West Briton!

When the lancers were over Gabriel went away to a remote corner of the room where Freddy Malins' mother was sitting. She was a stout feeble old woman with white hair. Her voice had a catch in it like her son's and she stuttered slightly. She had been told that Freddy had come and that he was nearly all right. Gabriel asked her whether she had had a good crossing. She lived with her married daughter in Glasgow and came to Dublin on a visit once a year. She answered placidly that she had had a beautiful crossing and that the captain had been most attentive to her. She spoke also of the beautiful house her daughter kept in Glasgow and of the nice friends they had there. While her tongue rambled on Gabriel tried to banish from his mind all memory of the unpleasant incident with Miss Ivors. Of course the girl or woman or whatever she was was an enthusiast but there was a time for all things. Perhaps he ought not to have answered her like that. But she had no right to call him a west Briton before people, even in joke. She had tried to make him ridiculous before people, heckling him and staring at him with her rabbit's eyes.

He saw his wife making her way towards him through the waltzing couples. When she reached him she said into his ear:

—Gabriel, aunt Kate wants to know won't you carve the goose as usual. Miss Daly will carve the ham and I'll do the pudding.

—All right, said Gabriel.

—She's sending in the younger ones first as soon as this waltz is over so that we'll have the table to ourselves.

—Were you dancing? asked Gabriel.

—Of course I was. Didn't you see me? What words had you with Molly Ivors?

—No words. Why! Did she say so?

—Something like that. I'm trying to get that Mr D'Arcy to sing. He's full of conceit, I think.

—There were no words, said Gabriel moodily, only she

wanted me to go for a trip to the west of Ireland and I said I wouldn't.

His wife clasped her hands excitedly and gave a little jump.

—O, do go, Gabriel, she cried. I'd love to see Galway again.

—You can go if you like, said Gabriel coldly.

She looked at him for a moment, then turned to Mrs Malins and said:

—There's a nice husband for you, Mrs Malins.

While she was threading her way back across the room Mrs Malins, without adverting to the interruption, went on to tell Gabriel what beautiful places there were in Scotland and beautiful scenery. Her son-in-law brought them every year to the lakes and they used to go fishing. Her son-in-law was a splendid fisher. One day he caught a fish, a beautiful big big fish: and the man in the hotel boiled it for their dinner.

Gabriel hardly heard what she said. Now that supper was coming near he began to think again about his speech and about the quotation. When he saw Freddy Malins coming across the room to visit his mother Gabriel left the chair free for him and retired into the embrasure of the window. The room had already cleared and from the back room came the clatter of plates and knives. Those who still remained in the drawingroom seemed tired of dancing and were conversing quietly in little groups. Gabriel's warm trembling fingers tapped the cold pane of the window. How cool it must be outside! How pleasant it would be to walk out alone, first along by the river and then through the park! The snow would be lying on the branches of the trees and forming a bright cap on the top of the Wellington monument. How much more pleasant it would be there than at the supper table!

He ran over the headings of his speech: Irish hospitality, sad memories, the Three Graces, Paris, the quotation from Browning. He repeated to himself a phrase he had written in his review: *One feels that one is listening to a thoughttormented music.* Miss Ivors had praised the review. Was she sincere? Had she really any life of her own behind all her propagandism?

There had never been any ill feeling between them until that night. It unnerved him to think that she would be at the supper table, looking up at him while he spoke with her critical quizzing eyes. Perhaps she would not be sorry to see him fail in his speech. An idea came into his mind and gave him courage. He would say, alluding to aunt Kate and aunt Julia: *Ladies and gentlemen, the generation which is now on the wane among us may have had its faults but for my part I think it had certain qualities of hospitality, of humour, of humanity, which the new and very serious and hypereducated generation that is growing up around us seems to me to lack.* Very good: that was one for Miss Ivors. What did he care that his aunts were only two ignorant old women?

A murmur in the room attracted his attention. Mr Browne was advancing from the door, gallantly escorting aunt Julia who leaned upon his arm, smiling and hanging her head. An irregular musketry of applause escorted her also as far as the piano and then, as Mary Jane seated herself on the stool and aunt Julia, no longer smiling, half turned so as to pitch her voice fairly into the room, gradually ceased. Gabriel recognised the prelude. It was that of an old song of aunt Julia's, *Arrayed for the Bridal*. Her voice strong and clear in tone attacked with great spirit the runs which embellish the air and, though she sang very rapidly, she did not miss even the smallest of the grace notes. To follow the voice, without looking at the singer's face, was to feel and share the excitement of swift and secure flight. Gabriel applauded loudly with all the others at the close of the song and loud applause was borne in from the invisible supper table. It sounded so genuine that a little colour struggled into aunt Julia's face as she bent to replace in the music stand the old leatherbound songbook that had her initials on the cover. Freddy Malins, who had listened with his head perched sideways to hear the better, was still applauding when everyone else had ceased and talking animatedly to his mother who nodded her head gravely and slowly in acquiescence. At last, when he could clap no more, he stood up suddenly and hurried across the room to aunt Julia, whose hand he seized and held in both his hands, shaking it when words failed him or the catch in his voice proved too much for him.

—I was just telling my mother, he said, I never heard you sing so well, never. No, I never heard your voice so good as it is tonight. Now! Would you believe that now? That's the truth. Upon my word and honour that's the truth. I never heard your voice sound so fresh and so ... so clear and fresh, never.

Aunt Julia smiled broadly and murmured something about compliments as she released her hand from his grasp. Mr Browne extended his open hand towards her and said to those who were near him in the manner of a showman introducing a prodigy to an audience:

—Miss Julia Morkan, my latest discovery!

He was laughing very heartily at this himself when Freddy Malins turned to him and said:

—Well, Browne, if you're serious you might make a worse discovery. All I can say is I never heard her sing half so well as long as I am coming here. And that's the honest truth.

—Neither did I, said Mr Browne. I think her voice has greatly improved.

Aunt Julia shrugged her shoulders and said with meek pride:

—Thirty years ago I hadn't a bad voice as voices go.

—I often told Julia, said aunt Kate emphatically, that she was simply thrown away in that choir. But she never would be said by me.

She turned as if to appeal to the good sense of the others against a refractory child while aunt Julia gazed in front of her, a vague smile of reminiscence playing on her face.

—No, continued aunt Kate, she wouldn't be said or led by anyone, slaving there in that choir night and day, night and day. Six o'clock on Christmas morning! And all for what?

—Well, isn't it for the honour of God, aunt Kate? asked Mary Jane twisting round on the piano stool and smiling.

Aunt Kate turned fiercely on her niece and said:

—I know all about the honour of God, Mary Jane, but I think it's not at all honourable for the pope to turn out the women out of the choirs that have slaved there all their lives and put little whippersnappers of boys over their heads. I suppose it is for the good of the church if the pope does it. But it's not just, Mary Jane, and it's not right.

She had worked herself into a passion and would have continued in defence of her sister for it was a sore subject with her but Mary Jane, seeing that all the dancers had come back, intervened pacifically:

—Now, aunt Kate, you're giving scandal to Mr Browne who is of the other persuasion.

Aunt Kate turned to Mr Browne, who was grinning at this allusion to his religion, and said hastily:

—O, I don't question the pope's being right. I'm only a stupid old woman and I wouldn't presume to do such a thing. But there's such a thing as common everyday politeness and gratitude. And if I were in Julia's place I'd tell that Father Healy straight up to his face ...

—And besides, aunt Kate, said Mary Jane, we really are all hungry and when we are hungry we are all very quarrelsome.

—And when we are thirsty we are also quarrelsome, added Mr Browne.

—So that we had better go to supper, said Mary Jane, and finish the discussion afterwards.

On the landing outside the drawingroom Gabriel found his wife and Mary Jane trying to persuade Miss Ivors to stay for supper. But Miss Ivors, who had put on her hat and was buttoning her cloak, would not stay. She did not feel in the least hungry and she had already overstayed her time.

—But only for ten minutes, Molly, said Mrs Conroy. That won't delay you.

—To take a pick itself, said Mary Jane, after all your dancing.

—I really couldn't, said Miss Ivors.

—I am afraid you didn't enjoy yourself at all, said Mary Jane hopelessly.

—Ever so much, I assure you, said Miss Ivors, but you really must let me run off now.

—But how can you get home? asked Mrs Conroy.

—O, it's only two steps up the quay.

Gabriel hesitated a moment and said:

—If you will allow me, Miss Ivors, I'll see you home if you really are obliged to go.

But Miss Ivors broke away from them.

—I won't hear of it, she cried. For goodness' sake go in to your suppers and don't mind me. I'm quite well able to take care of myself.

—Well, you're the comical girl, Molly, said Mrs Conroy frankly.

—*Beannacht libh*, cried Miss Ivors with a laugh as she ran down the staircase.

Mary Jane gazed after her, a moody puzzled expression on her face, while Mrs Conroy leaned over the banisters to listen for the halldoor. Gabriel asked himself was he the cause of her abrupt departure. But she did not seem to be in ill humour: she had gone away laughing. He stared blankly down the staircase.

At that moment aunt Kate came toddling out of the supper room, almost wringing her hands in despair.

—Where is Gabriel? she cried. Where on earth is Gabriel? There's everyone waiting in there, stage to let, and nobody to carve the goose!

—Here I am, aunt Kate! cried Gabriel with sudden animation, ready to carve a flock of geese, if necessary.

A fat brown goose lay at one end of the table and at the other end, on a bed of creased paper strewn with sprigs of parsley, lay a great ham, stripped of its outer skin and peppered over with crust crumbs, a neat paper frill round its shin, and beside this was a round of spiced beef. Between these rival ends ran parallel lines of side dishes: two little minsters of jelly, red and yellow, a shallow dish full of blocks of blancmange and red jam, a large green leafshaped dish with a stalkshaped handle on which lay bunches of purple raisins and peeled almonds, a companion dish on which lay a solid rectangle of Smyrna figs, a dish of custard topped with grated nutmeg, a small bowl full of chocolates and sweets wrapped in gold and silver papers and a glass vase in which stood some tall celery stalks. In the centre of the table there stood, as sentries to a fruit stand which upheld a pyramid of oranges and American apples, two squat oldfashioned decanters of cut glass, one containing port and the other dark sherry. On the closed square piano a pudding in a huge yellow dish lay in waiting and behind it were three squads of bottles of stout and ale and minerals drawn up according to the colours of their uniforms, the first two black with brown and red labels, the third and smallest squad white, with transverse green sashes.

Gabriel took his seat boldly at the head of the table and, having looked to the edge of the carver, plunged his fork firmly into the goose. He felt quite at ease now for he was an expert carver and liked nothing better than to find himself at the head of a well laden table.

—Miss Furlong, what shall I send you? he asked. A wing or a slice of the breast?

—Just a small slice of the breast.

—Miss Higgins, what for you?

—O, anything at all, Mr Conroy.

While Gabriel and Miss Daly exchanged plates of goose and plates of ham and spiced beef Lily went from guest to guest with a dish of hot floury potatoes wrapped in a white napkin. This was Mary Jane's idea and she had also suggested apple sauce for the goose but aunt Kate had said that plain roast goose without any apple sauce had always been good enough for her and she hoped she might never eat worse. Mary Jane waited on her pupils and saw that they got the best slices and aunt Kate and aunt Julia opened and carried across from the piano bottles of stout and ale for the gentlemen and bottles of minerals for the ladies. There was a great deal of confusion and laughter and noise, the noise of orders and counterorders, of knives and forks, of corks and glass stoppers. Gabriel began to carve second helpings as soon as he had finished the first round without serving himself. Everyone protested loudly so that he compromised by taking a long draught of stout for he had found the carving hot work. Mary Jane settled down quietly to her supper but aunt Kate and aunt Julia were still toddling round the table, walking on each other's heels, getting in each other's way and giving each other unheeded orders. Mr Browne begged of them to sit down and eat their supper and so did Gabriel but they said they were time enough so that, at last, Freddy Malins stood up and, capturing aunt Kate, plumped her down on her chair amid general laughter.

When everyone had been well served Gabriel said smiling:

—Now if anyone wants a little more of what vulgar people call stuffing let him or her speak.

A chorus of voices invited him to begin his own supper and Lily came forward with three potatoes which she had reserved for him.

—Very well, said Gabriel amiably as he took another preparatory draught, kindly forget my existence, ladies and gentlemen, for a few minutes.

He set to his supper and took no part in the conversation with which the table covered Lily's removal of the plates. The subject of talk was the opera company which was then at the Theatre Royal. Mr Bartell D'Arcy, the tenor, a dark-complexioned young man with a smart moustache, praised very highly the leading contralto of the company but Miss Furlong thought she had a rather vulgar style of production. Freddy Malins said there was a negro chieftain singing in the second part of the Gaiety pantomime who had one of the finest tenor voices he had ever heard.

—Have you heard him? he asked Mr Bartell D'Arcy across the table.

—No, answered Mr Bartell D'Arcy carelessly.

—Because, Freddy Malins explained, now I'd be curious to hear your opinion of him. I think he has a grand voice.

—It takes Teddy to find out the really good things, said Mr Browne familiarly to the table.

—And why couldn't he have a voice too? asked Freddy Malins sharply. Is it because he's only a black?

Nobody answered this question and Mary Jane led the table back to the legitimate opera. One of her pupils had given her a pass for *Mignon*. Of course, it was very fine, she said, but it made her think of poor Georgina Burns. Mr Browne could go back farther still to the old Italian companies that used to come to Dublin, Tietjens, Trebelli, Ilma de Murzka, Campanini, the great Giuglini, Ravelli, Aramburo. Those were the days, he said, when there was something like singing to be heard in Dublin. He told too of how the top gallery of the old Royal used to be packed night after night, of how one night an Italian tenor had sung five encores to *Let Me Like a Soldier Fall*, introducing a high C every time, and of how the gallery boys would sometimes in their enthusiasm unyoke the horses from the carriage of some great *prima donna* and pull her themselves through the streets to her hotel. Why did they never play the grand old operas now, he asked. *Dinorah, Lucrezia Borgia?* Because they could not get the voices to sing them: that was why.

—O, well, said Mr Bartell D'Arcy, I presume there are as good singers today as there were then.

—Where are they? asked Mr Browne defiantly.

—In London, Paris, Milan, said Mr Bartell D'Arcy warmly. I suppose Caruso, for example, is quite as good, if not better than any of the men you have mentioned.

—Maybe so, said Mr Browne. But I may tell you I doubt it strongly.

—O, I'd give anything to hear Caruso sing, said Mary Jane.

—For me, said aunt Kate, who had been picking a bone, there was only one tenor. To please me, I mean. But I suppose none of you ever heard of him.

—Who was he, Miss Morkan? asked Mr Bartell D'Arcy politely.

—His name, said aunt Kate, was Parkinson. I heard him when he was in his prime and I think he had then the purest tenor voice that was ever put into a man's throat.

—Strange, said Mr Bartell D'Arcy. I never even heard of him.

—Yes, yes, Miss Morkan is right, said Mr Browne. I remember hearing of old Parkinson but he's too far back for me.

—A beautiful pure sweet mellow English tenor, said aunt Kate with enthusiasm.

Gabriel having finished, the huge pudding was transferred to the table. The clatter of forks and spoons began again. Gabriel's wife served out spoonfuls of the pudding and passed the plates down the table. Midway down they were held up by Mary Jane who replenished them with raspberry or orange jelly or with blancmange and jam. The pudding was of aunt Julia's making and she received praises for it from all quarters. She herself said that it was not quite brown enough.

—Well, I hope, Miss Morkan, said Mr Browne, that I'm brown enough for you because, you know, I'm all brown.

All the gentlemen, except Gabriel, ate some of the pudding out of compliment to aunt Julia. As Gabriel never ate sweets the celery had been left for him. Freddy Malins also took a stalk of celery and ate it with his pudding. He had been told that celery was a capital thing for the blood and he was just then under doctor's care. Mrs Malins, who had been silent all through the supper, said that her son was going down to Mount Melleray in a week or so. The table then spoke of Mount Melleray, how bracing the air was down there, how hospitable the monks were and how they never asked for a penny-piece from their guests.

—And do you mean to say, asked Mr Browne incredulously, that a chap can go down there and put up there as if it were a hotel and live on the fat of the land and then come away without paying a farthing?

—O, most people give some donation to the monastery when they leave, said Mary Jane.

—I wish we had an institution like that in our church, said Mr Browne candidly.

He was astonished to hear that the monks never spoke, got up at two in the morning and slept in their coffins. He asked what they did it for.

—That's the rule of the order, said aunt Kate firmly.

—Yes, but why? asked Mr Browne.

Aunt Kate repeated that it was the rule, that was all. Mr Browne still seemed not to understand. Freddy Malins explained to him, as best he could, that the monks were trying to make up for the sins committed by all the sinners in the outside world. The explanation was not very clear for Mr Browne grinned and said:

—I like that idea very much but wouldn't a comfortable spring bed do them as well as a coffin?

—The coffin, said Mary Jane, is to remind them of their last end.

As the subject had grown lugubrious it was buried in a silence of the table during which Mrs Malins could be heard saying to her neighbour in an indistinct undertone:

—They are very good men, the monks, very pious men.

The raisins and almonds and figs and apples and oranges and chocolates and sweets were now passed about the table and aunt Julia invited all the guests to have either port or sherry. At first Mr Bartell D'Arcy refused to take either but one of his neighbours nudged him and whispered something to him upon which he allowed his glass to be filled. Gradually as the last glasses were being filled the conversation ceased. A pause followed, broken only by the noise of the wine and by unsettlings of chairs. The Misses Morkan, all three, looked down at the tablecloth. Someone coughed once or twice and then a few gentlemen patted the table gently as a signal for silence. The silence came and Gabriel pushed back his chair and stood up.

The patting at once grew louder in encouragement and then ceased altogether. Gabriel leaned his ten trembling fingers on the tablecloth and smiled nervously at the company. Meeting a row of upturned faces he raised his eyes to the chandelier. The piano was playing a waltz tune and he could hear the skirts sweeping against the drawingroom door. People perhaps were standing in the snow on the quay outside, gazing up at the lighted windows and listening to the waltz music. The air was pure there. In the distance lay the park where the trees were weighted with snow. The Wellington monument wore a gleaming cap of snow that flashed westward over the white field of Fifteen Acres.

He began:

—Ladies and gentlemen.

It has fallen to my lot this evening as in years past to perform a very pleasing task, but a task for which I am afraid my poor powers as a speaker are all too inadequate.

—No, no, said Mr Browne.

—But, however that may be, I can only ask you tonight to take the will for the deed and to lend me your attention for a few moments while I endeavour to express to you in words what my feelings are on this occasion.

—Ladies and gentlemen. It is not the first time that we have gathered together under this hospitable roof, around this hospitable board. It is not the first time that we have been the recipients–or, perhaps I had better say, the victims–of the hospitality of certain good ladies.

He made a circle in the air with his arm and paused. Everyone laughed or smiled at aunt Kate and aunt Julia and Mary Jane who all turned crimson with pleasure. Gabriel went on more boldly:

—I feel more strongly with every recurring year that our country has no tradition which does it so much honour and which it should guard so jealously as that of its hospitality. It is a tradition that is unique so far as my experience goes (and I have visited not a few places abroad) among the modern nations. Some would say, perhaps, that with us it is rather a failing than anything to be boasted of. But granted even that, it is, to my mind, a princely failing and one that I trust will long be cultivated among us. Of one thing, at least, I am sure. As long as this one roof shelters the good ladies aforesaid–and I wish from my heart it may do so for many and many a long year to come–the tradition of genuine warmhearted courteous

Irish hospitality, which our forefathers have handed down to us and which we in turn must hand down to our descendants, is still alive among us.

A hearty murmur of assent ran round the table. It shot through Gabriel's mind that Miss Ivors was not there and that she had gone away discourteously: and he said with confidence in himself:

—Ladies and gentlemen.

A new generation is growing up in our midst, a generation actuated by new ideas and new principles. It is serious and enthusiastic for these new ideas and its enthusiasm, even when it is misdirected, is, I believe, in the main sincere. But we are living in a sceptical and, if I may use the phrase, a thoughttormented age: and sometimes I fear that this new generation, educated or hypereducated as it is, will lack those qualities of humanity, of hospitality, of kindly humour which belonged to an older day. Listening tonight to the names of all those great singers of the past it seemed to me, I must confess, that we were living in a less spacious age. Those days might without exaggeration be called spacious days: and if they are gone beyond recall let us hope, at least, that in gatherings such as this we shall still speak of them with pride and affection, still cherish in our hearts the memory of those dead and gone great ones whose fame the world will not willingly let die.

—Hear! hear! said Mr Browne loudly.

—But yet, continued Gabriel, his voice falling into a softer inflection, there are always in gatherings such as this sadder thoughts that will recur to our minds: thoughts of the past, of youth, of changes, of absent faces that we miss here tonight. Our path through life is strewn with many such sad memories: and were we to brood upon them always we could not find the heart to go on bravely with our work among the living. We have all of us living duties and living affections which claim, and rightly claim, our strenuous endeavours.

Therefore I will not linger on the past. I will not let any gloomy moralising intrude upon us here tonight. Here we are gathered together for a brief moment from the bustle and rush of our everyday routine. We are met here as friends, in the spirit of good fellowship, as colleagues also, to a certain extent, in the true spirit of *camaraderie*, and as the guests of–what shall I call them?–the three Graces of the Dublin musical world.

The table burst into applause and laughter at this sally. Aunt Julia vainly asked each of her neighbours in turn to tell her what Gabriel had said.

—He says we are the three Graces, aunt Julia, said Mary Jane.

Aunt Julia did not understand but she looked up, smiling, at Gabriel who continued in the same vein:

—Ladies and gentlemen.

I will not attempt to play tonight the part that Paris played on another occasion. I will not attempt to choose between them. The task would be an invidious one and one beyond my poor powers. For when I view them in turn, whether it be our chief hostess herself, whose good heart, whose too good heart, has become a byword with all who know her, or her sister, who seems to be gifted with perennial youth and whose singing must have been a surprise and a revelation to us all tonight, or, last but not least, when I consider our youngest hostess, talented, cheerful, hard-working and the best of nieces, I confess, ladies and gentlemen, that I do not know to which of them I should award the prize.

Gabriel glanced down at his aunts and, seeing the large smile on aunt Julia's face and the tears which had risen to aunt Kate's eyes, hastened to his close. He raised his glass of port gallantly while every member of the company fingered a glass expectantly and said loudly:

—Let us toast them all three together. Let us drink to their health, wealth, long life, happiness and prosperity and may they long continue to hold the proud and selfwon position which they hold in their profession and the position of honour and affection which they hold in our hearts.

All the guests stood up, glass in hand and, turning towards

the three seated ladies, sang in unison with Mr Browne as leader:

—For they are jolly gay fellows,
For they are jolly gay fellows,
For they are jolly gay fellows
Which nobody can deny.

Aunt Kate was making frank use of her handkerchief and even aunt Julia seemed moved. Freddy Malins beat time with his pudding fork and the singers turned towards one another as if in melodious conference, while they sang with emphasis:

—Unless he tells a lie,
Unless he tells a lie.

Then turning once more towards their hostesses they sang:

—For they are jolly gay fellows,
For they are jolly gay fellows,
For they are jolly gay fellows
Which nobody can deny.

The acclamation which followed was taken up beyond the door of the supper room by many of the other guests and renewed time after time, Freddy Malins acting as officer with his fork on high.

◆ ◆ ◆

The piercing morning air came into the hall where they were standing so that aunt Kate said:
—Close the door, somebody. Mrs Malins will get her death of cold.
—Browne is out there, aunt Kate, said Mary Jane.
—Browne is everywhere, said aunt Kate lowering her voice.
Mary Jane laughed at her tone.
—Really, she said archly, he is very attentive.
—He has been laid on here like the gas, said aunt Kate in the same tone, all during the Christmas.

She laughed herself this time good-humouredly and then added quickly:

—But tell him to come in, Mary Jane, and close the door. I hope to goodness he didn't hear me.

At that moment the halldoor was opened and Mr Browne came in from the doorstep, laughing as if his heart would break. He was dressed in a long green overcoat with mock astrakhan cuffs and collar and wore on his head an oval fur cap. He pointed down the snowcovered quay whence the sound of shrill prolonged whistling was borne in.

—Teddy will have all the cabs in Dublin out, he said.

Gabriel advanced from the little pantry behind the office, struggling into his overcoat and, looking round the hall, said:

—Gretta not down yet?

—She's getting on her things, Gabriel, said aunt Kate.

—Who's playing up there? asked Gabriel.

—Nobody. They're all gone.

—O no, aunt Kate, said Mary Jane. Bartell D'Arcy and Miss O'Callaghan aren't gone yet.

—Someone is strumming at the piano, anyhow, said Gabriel.

Mary Jane glanced at Gabriel and Mr Browne and said with a shiver:

—It makes me feel cold to look at you two gentlemen muffled up like that. I wouldn't like to face your journey home at this hour.

—I'd like nothing better this minute, said Mr Browne stoutly, than a rattling fine walk in the country or a fast drive with a good spanking goer between the shafts.

—We used to have a very good horse and trap at home, said aunt Julia sadly.

—The never-to-be-forgotten Johnny, said Mary Jane laughing.

Aunt Kate and Gabriel laughed too.

—Why, what was wonderful about Johnny? asked Mr Browne.

—The late lamented Patrick Morkan, our grandfather that is, explained Gabriel, commonly known in his later years as the old gentleman, was a glue boiler.

—O now, Gabriel, said aunt Kate laughing, he had a starch mill.

—Well, glue or starch, said Gabriel, the old gentleman had a horse by the name of Johnny. And Johnny used to work in the old gentleman's mill walking round and round in order to drive the mill. That was all very well; but now comes the tragic part about Johnny. One fine day the old gentleman thought he'd like to drive out with the quality to a military review in the park.

—The Lord have mercy on his soul, said aunt Kate compassionately.

—Amen, said Gabriel. So the old gentleman, as I said, harnessed Johnny and put on his very best tall hat and his very best stock collar and drove out in grand style from his ancestral mansion somewhere near Back Lane, I think.

Everyone laughed, even Mrs Malins, at Gabriel's manner and aunt Kate said:

—O now, Gabriel, he didn't live in Back Lane really. Only the mill was there.

—Out from the mansion of his forefathers, continued Gabriel, he drove with Johnny. And everything went on beautifully until Johnny came in sight of King Billy's statue: and whether he fell in love with the horse King Billy sits on or whether he thought he was back again in the mill, anyhow he began to walk round the statue.

Gabriel paced in a circle round the hall in his goloshes amid the laughter of the others.

—Round and round he went, said Gabriel, and the old gentleman, who was a very pompous old gentleman, was highly indignant. *Go on, sir! What do you mean, sir? Johnny! Johnny! Most extraordinary conduct! Can't understand the horse!*

The peals of laughter which followed Gabriel's imitation of the incident were interrupted by a resounding knock at the halldoor. Mary Jane ran to open it and let in Freddy Malins. Freddy Malins, with his hat well back on his head and his shoulders humped with cold, was puffing and steaming after his exertions.

—I could only get one cab, he said.

—O, we'll find another along the quay, said Gabriel.

—Yes, said aunt Kate. Better not keep Mrs Malins standing in the draught.

Mrs Malins was helped down the front steps by her son and Mr Browne and, after many manoeuvres, hoisted into the cab. Freddy Malins clambered in after her and spent a long time settling her on the seat, Mr Browne helping him with advice. At last she was settled comfortably and Freddy Malins invited Mr Browne into the cab. There was a good deal of confused talk, then Mr Browne got into the cab. The cabman settled his rug over his knees and bent down for the address. The confusion grew greater and the cabman was directed differently by Freddy Malins and Mr Browne, each of whom had his head out through a window of the cab. The difficulty was to know where to drop Mr Browne along the route and aunt Kate, aunt Julia and Mary Jane helped the discussion from the doorstep with cross-directions and contradictions and abundance of laughter. As for Freddy Malins he was speechless with laughter. He popped his head in and out of the window every moment, to the great danger of his hat, and told his mother how the discussion was progressing till at last Mr Browne shouted to the bewildered cabman above the din of everybody's laughter:

—Do you know Trinity College?

—Yes, sir, said the cabman.

—Well, drive bang up against Trinity College gates, said Mr Browne, and then we'll tell you where to go. You understand now?

—Yes, sir, said the cabman.

—Make like a bird for Trinity College.

—Right, sir, cried the cabman.

The horse was whipped up and the cab rattled off along the quay amid a chorus of laughter and adieus.

Gabriel had not gone to the door with the others. He was in a dark part of the hall gazing up the staircase. A woman was standing near the top of the first flight in the shadow also. He could not see her face but he could see the terracotta and salmonpink panels of her skirt which the shadow made appear black and white. It was his wife. She was leaning on the banisters listening to something. Gabriel was surprised at her stillness and strained his ear to listen also. But he could hear little save the noise of laughter and dispute on the front steps, a few chords struck on the piano and a few notes of a man's voice singing.

He stood still in the gloom of the hall, trying to catch the air that the voice was singing and gazing up at his wife. There was grace and mystery in her attitude as if she were a symbol of something. He asked himself what is a woman standing on the stairs in the shadow, listening to distant music, a symbol of. If he were a painter he would paint her in that attitude. Her blue felt hat would show off the bronze of her hair against the darkness and the dark panels of her skirt would show off the light ones. *Distant Music* he would call the picture if he were a painter.

The halldoor was closed and aunt Kate, aunt Julia and Mary Jane came down the hall, still laughing.

—Well, isn't Freddy terrible? said Mary Jane. He's really terrible.

Gabriel said nothing but pointed up the stairs towards where his wife was standing. Now that the halldoor was closed the voice and the piano could be heard more clearly. Gabriel held up his hand for them to be silent. The song seemed to be in the old Irish tonality and the singer seemed uncertain both of his words and of his voice. The voice made plaintive by the distance and by the singer's hoarseness faintly illuminated the cadence of the air with words expressing grief:

—O, *the rain falls on my heavy locks*
And the dew wets my skin,
My babe lies cold ...

—O, exclaimed Mary Jane. It's Bartell D'Arcy singing and he

wouldn't sing all the night. O, I'll get him to sing a song before he goes.

—O do, Mary Jane, said aunt Kate.

Mary Jane brushed past the others and ran to the staircase but before she reached it the singing stopped and the piano was closed abruptly.

—O, what a pity! she cried. Is he coming down, Gretta?

Gabriel heard his wife answer yes and saw her come down towards them. A few steps behind her were Mr Bartell D'Arcy and Miss O'Callaghan.

—O, Mr D'Arcy, cried Mary Jane, it's downright mean of you to break off like that when we were all in raptures listening to you.

—I have been at him all the evening, said Miss O'Callaghan, and Mrs Conroy too, and he told us he had a dreadful cold and couldn't sing.

—O, Mr D'Arcy, said aunt Kate, now that was a great fib to tell.

—Can't you see that I'm as hoarse as a crow? said Mr D'Arcy roughly.

He went into the pantry hastily and put on his overcoat. The others, taken aback by his rude speech, could find nothing to say. Aunt Kate wrinkled her brows and made signs to the others to drop the subject. Mr D'Arcy stood swathing his neck carefully and frowning.

—It's the weather, said aunt Julia after a pause.

—Yes, everybody has colds, said aunt Kate readily, everybody.

—They say, said Mary Jane, we haven't had snow like it for thirty years: and I read this morning in the newspaper that the snow is general all over Ireland.

—I love the look of snow, said aunt Julia sadly.

—So do I, said Miss O'Callaghan. I think Christmas is never really Christmas unless we have the snow on the ground.

—But poor Mr D'Arcy doesn't like the snow, said aunt Kate smiling.

Mr D'Arcy came from the pantry, fully swathed and buttoned, and in a repentant tone told them the history of his cold. Everyone gave him advice and said it was a great pity and urged him to be very careful of his throat in the night air. Gabriel watched his wife who did not join in the conversation. She was standing right under the dusty fanlight and the flame of the gas lit up the rich bronze of her hair which he had seen her drying at the fire a few days before. She was in the same attitude and seemed unaware of the talk about her. At last she turned towards them and Gabriel saw that there was colour on her cheeks and that her eyes were shining. A sudden tide of joy went leaping out of his heart.

—Mr D'Arcy, she said, what is the name of that song you were singing?

—It's called *The Lass of Aughrim*, said Mr D'Arcy, but I couldn't remember it properly. Why? Do you know it?

—*The Lass of Aughrim*, she repeated. I couldn't think of the name.

—It's a very nice air, said Mary Jane. I'm sorry you were not in voice tonight.

—Now, Mary Jane, said aunt Kate, don't annoy Mr D'Arcy. I won't have him annoyed.

Seeing that all were ready to start she shepherded them to the door where goodnight was said:

—Well, goodnight aunt Kate, and thanks for the pleasant evening.

—Goodnight, Gabriel. Goodnight, Gretta!

—Goodnight, aunt Kate, and thanks ever so much. Goodnight, aunt Julia.

—O, goodnight, Gretta, I didn't see you.

—Goodnight, Mr D'Arcy. Goodnight, Miss O'Callaghan.

—Goodnight, Miss Morkan.

—Goodnight again.

—Goodnight all. Safe home.

—Goodnight. Goodnight.

The morning was still dark. A dull yellow light brooded over the houses and the river and the sky seemed to be descending. It was slushy underfoot and only streaks and patches of snow lay on the roofs, on the parapets of the quay and on the area railings. The lamps were still burning redly in the murky air and, across the river, the palace of the Four Courts stood out menacingly against the heavy sky.

She was walking on before him with Mr Bartell D'Arcy, her shoes in a brown parcel tucked under one arm and her hands holding her skirt up from the slush. She had no longer any grace of attitude but Gabriel's eyes were still bright with happiness. The blood went bounding along his veins and the thoughts went rioting through his brain, proud, joyful, tender, valorous.

She was walking on before him so lightly and so erect that he longed to run after her noiselessly, catch her by the shoulders and say something foolish and affectionate into her ear. She seemed to him so frail that he longed to defend her against something and then to be alone with her. Moments of their secret life together burst like stars upon his memory. A heliotrope envelope was lying beside his breakfast cup and he was caressing it with his hand. Birds were twittering in the ivy and the sunny web of the curtain was shimmering along the floor: he could not eat for happiness. They were standing on the crowded platform and he was placing a ticket inside the warm palm of her glove. He was standing with her in the cold, looking in through a grated window at a man making bottles in a roaring furnace. It was very cold. Her face, fragrant in the cold air, was quite close to his and suddenly she called out to the man at the furnace:

—Is the fire hot, sir?

But the man could not hear her with the noise of the furnace. It was just as well. He might have answered rudely.

A wave of yet more tender joy escaped from his heart and went coursing in warm flood along his arteries. Like the tender fire of stars moments of their life together, that no one knew of or would ever know of, broke upon and illumined his memory. He longed to recall to her those moments, to make her forget the years of their dull existence together and remember only their moments of ecstasy. For the years, he felt, had not quenched his soul or hers. Their children, his writing, her household cares had not quenched all their souls' tender fire. In one letter that he had written to her then he had said: *Why is it that words like these seem to me so dull and cold? Is it because there is no word tender enough to be your name?*

Like distant music these words that he had written years before were borne towards him from the past. He longed to be alone with her. When the others had gone away, when he and she were in their room in the hotel, then they would be alone together. He would call her softly:

—Gretta!

Perhaps she would not hear at once: she would be undressing. Then something in his voice would strike her. She would turn and look at him ....

At the corner of Winetavern Street they met a cab. He was glad of its rattling noise as it saved him from conversation. She was looking out of the window and seemed tired. The others spoke only a few words, pointing out some building or street. The horse galloped along wearily under the murky morning sky, dragging his old rattling box after his heels, and Gabriel was again in a cab with her galloping to catch the boat, galloping to their honeymoon.

As the cab drove across O'Connell bridge Miss O'Callaghan said:

—They say you never cross O'Connell bridge without seeing a white horse.

—I see a white man this time, said Gabriel.

—Where? asked Mr Bartell D'Arcy.

Gabriel pointed to the statue on which lay patches of snow. Then he nodded familiarly to it and waved his hand.

—Goodnight, Dan, he said gaily.

When the cab drew up before the hotel Gabriel jumped out and, in spite of Mr Bartell D'Arcy's protest, paid the driver. He gave the man a shilling over his fare. The man saluted and said:

—A prosperous new year to you, sir.

—The same to you, said Gabriel cordially.

She leaned for a moment on his arm in getting out of the cab and while standing at the kerbstone bidding the others good-night. She leaned lightly on his arm, as lightly as when she had danced with him a few hours before. He had felt proud and happy then, happy that she was his, proud of her grace and wifely carriage. But now after the kindling again of so many memories, the first touch of her body, musical and strange and perfumed, sent through him a keen pang of lust. Under cover of her silence he pressed her arm closely to his side: and, as they stood at the hotel door, he felt that they had escaped from their lives and duties, escaped from home and friends and run away together with wild and radiant hearts to a new adventure.

An old man was dozing in a great hooded chair in the hall. He lit a candle in the office and went before them to the stairs. They followed him in silence, their feet falling in soft thuds on the thickly carpeted stairs. She mounted the stairs behind the porter, her head bowed in the ascent, her frail shoulders curved as with a burden, her skirt girt tightly about her. He could have flung his arms about her hips and held her still for his arms were trembling with desire to seize her and only the stress of his nails against the palms of his hands held the wild impulse of his body in check. The porter halted on the stairs to settle his guttering candle. They halted too on the steps below him. In the silence Gabriel could hear the falling of the molten wax into the tray and the thumping of his own heart against his ribs.

The porter led them along a corridor and opened a door. Then he set his unstable candle down on a toilet table and asked at what hour they were to be called in the morning.

—Eight, said Gabriel.

The porter pointed to the tap of the electric light and began a muttered apology but Gabriel cut him short.

—We don't want any light. We have light enough from the street. And, I say, he added pointing to the candle, you might remove that handsome article, like a good man.

The porter took up his candle again, but slowly, for he was surprised by such a novel idea. Then he mumbled goodnight and went out. Gabriel shot the lock to.

A ghostly light from the street lamp lay in a long shaft from one window to the door. Gabriel threw his overcoat and hat on a couch and crossed the room towards the window. He looked down into the street in order that his emotion might calm a little. Then he turned and leaned against a chest of drawers with his back to the light. She had taken off her hat and cloak and was standing before a large swinging mirror, unhooking her waist. Gabriel paused for a few moments, watching her, and then said:

—Gretta!

She turned away from the mirror slowly and walked along the shaft of light towards him. Her face looked so serious and weary that the words would not pass Gabriel's lips. No, it was not the moment yet.

—You look tired, he said.

—I am a little, she answered.

—You don't feel ill or weak?

—No, tired: that's all.

She went on to the window and stood there, looking out. Gabriel waited again and then, fearing that diffidence was about to conquer him, he said abruptly:

—By the way, Gretta!

—What is it?

—You know that poor fellow Malins? he said quickly.

—Yes, what about him?

—Well, poor fellow, he's a decent sort of chap after all, continued Gabriel in a false voice. He gave me back that sovereign I lent him and I didn't expect it really. It's a pity he wouldn't keep away from that Browne because he's not a bad fellow at heart.

He was trembling now with annoyance. Why did she seem so abstracted? He did not know how he could begin. Was she annoyed too about something? If she would only turn to him or come to him of her own accord! To take her as she was would be brutal. No, he must see some ardour in her eyes first. He longed to be master of her strange mood.

—When did you lend him the pound? she asked after a pause.

Gabriel strove to restrain himself from breaking out into brutal language about the sottish Malins and his pound. He longed to cry to her from his soul, to crush her body against his, to overmaster her. But he said:

—O, at Christmas, when he opened that little Christmas card shop in Henry Street.

He was in such a fever of rage and desire that he did not hear her come from the window. She stood before him for an instant looking at him strangely. Then, suddenly raising herself on tiptoe and resting her hands lightly on his shoulders, she kissed him.

—You are a very generous person, Gabriel, she said.

—Gabriel, trembling with delight at her sudden kiss and at the quaintness of her phrase, put his hands on her hair and began smoothing it back, scarcely touching it with his fingers. The washing had made it fine and brilliant. His heart was brimming over with happiness. Just when he was wishing for it she had come to him of her own accord. Perhaps her thoughts had been running with his. Perhaps she had felt the impetuous desire that was in him and then the yielding mood had come upon her. Now that she had fallen to him so easily he wondered why he had been so diffident.

He stood, holding her head between his hands. Then, slipping one arm swiftly about her body and drawing her towards him, he said softly:

—Gretta dear, what are you thinking about?

She did not answer nor yield wholly to his arm. He said again softly:

—Tell me what it is, Gretta. I think I know what is the matter. Do I know?

She did not answer at once. Then she said in an outburst of tears:

—O, I am thinking about that song, *The Lass of Aughrim*.

She broke loose from him and ran to the bed and, throwing her arms across the bedrail, hid her face. Gabriel stood stock-still for a moment in astonishment and then followed her. As he passed in the way of the cheval glass he caught sight of himself in full length, his broad, wellfilled shirtfront, the face whose expression always puzzled him when he saw it in a mirror and his glimmering giltrimmed eyeglasses. He halted a few paces from her and said:

—What about the song? Why does that make you cry?

She raised her head from her arms and dried her eyes with the back of her hand like a child. A kinder note than he had intended went into his voice.

—Why, Gretta? he asked.

—I am thinking about a person long ago who used to sing that song.

—And who was the person long ago? asked Gabriel smiling.

—It was a person I used to know in Galway when I was living with my grandmother, she said.

The smile passed away from Gabriel's face. A dull anger began to gather again at the back of his mind and the dull fires of his lust began to glow angrily in his veins.

—Someone you were in love with? he asked ironically.

—It was a young boy I used to know, she answered, named Michael Furey. He used to sing that song, *The Lass of Aughrim*. He was very delicate.

Gabriel was silent. He did not wish her to think that he was interested in this delicate boy.

—I can see him so plainly, she said after a moment. Such eyes as he had, big dark eyes! And such an expression in them—an expression! ...

—O, then you were in love with him? said Gabriel.

—I used to go out walking with him, she said, when I was in Galway.

A thought flew across Gabriel's mind.

—Perhaps that was why you wanted to go to Galway with that Ivors girl? he said coldly.

She looked at him and asked in surprise:

—What for?

Her eyes made Gabriel feel awkward. He shrugged his shoulders and said:

—How do I know? To see him, perhaps.

She looked away from him along the shaft of light towards the window in silence.

—He is dead, she said at length. He died when he was only seventeen. Isn't it a terrible thing to die so young as that?

—What was he? asked Gabriel, still ironically.

—He was in the gasworks, she said.

Gabriel felt humiliated by the failure of his irony and by the evocation of this figure from the dead, a boy in the gasworks. The irony of his mood soured into sarcasm. While he had been full of memories of their secret life together, full of tenderness and joy and desire, she had been comparing him in her mind with another. A shameful consciousness of his own person assailed him. He saw himself as a ludicrous figure, acting as a pennyboy for his aunts, a nervous wellmeaning sentimentalist, orating to vulgarians and idealising his own clownish lusts, the pitiable fatuous fellow he had caught a glimpse of in the mirror. Instinctively he turned his back more to the light lest she might see the shame that burned upon his forehead.

He tried to keep up his tone of cold interrogation but his voice when he spoke was humble and indifferent.

—I suppose you were in love with this Michael Furey, Gretta, he said.

—I was great with him at that time, she said.

Her voice was veiled and sad. Gabriel, feeling now how vain it would be to try to lead her whither he had purposed, caressed one of her hands and said also sadly:

—And what did he die of so young, Gretta? Consumption, was it?

—I think he died for me, she answered.

A vague terror seized Gabriel at this answer as if, at that hour when he had hoped to triumph, some impalpable and vindictive being was coming against him, gathering forces against him in its vague world. But he shook himself free of it with an effort of reason and continued to caress her hand. He did not question her again for he felt that she would tell him of herself. Her hand was warm and moist: it did not respond to his touch but he continued to caress it just as he had caressed her first letter to him that spring morning.

—It was in the winter, she said, about the beginning of the winter when I was going to leave my grandmother's and come up here to the convent. And he was ill at the time in his lodgings in Galway and wouldn't be let out and his people in Oughterard were written to. He was in decline, they said, or something like that. I never knew rightly.

She paused for a moment and sighed.

—Poor fellow, she said, he was very fond of me and he was such a gentle boy. We used to go out together walking, you know, Gabriel, like the way they do in the country. He was going to study singing only for his health. He had a very good voice, poor Michael Furey.

—Well, and then? asked Gabriel.

—And then when it came to the time for me to leave Galway and come up to the convent he was much worse and I wouldn't be let see him so I wrote him a letter saying I was going up to Dublin and would be back in the summer and hoping he would be better then.

She paused for a moment to get her voice under control and then went on:

—Then the night before I left I was in my grandmother's house in Nun's Island, packing up, and I heard gravel thrown up against the window. The window was so wet I couldn't see so I ran downstairs as I was and slipped out the back into the garden and there was the poor fellow at the end of the garden shivering.

—And did you not tell him to go back? asked Gabriel.

—I implored of him to go home at once and told him he would get his death in the rain. But he said he did not want to live. I can see his eyes as well as well! He was standing at the end of the wall where there was a tree.

—And did he go home? asked Gabriel.

—Yes, he went home. And when I was only a week in the convent he died and he was buried in Oughterard where his people came from. O, the day I heard that, that he was dead! ....

She stopped, choking with sobs and, overcome by emotion, flung herself face downward on the bed, sobbing in the quilt. Gabriel held her hand for a moment longer, irresolutely, and then, shy of intruding on her grief, let it fall gently and walked quietly to the window.

She was fast asleep.

Gabriel, leaning on his elbow, looked for a few moments unresentfully at her tangled hair and half open mouth, listening to her deep drawn breath. So she had had that romance in her life: a man had died for her sake. It hardly pained him now to think how poor a part he, her husband, had played in her life. He watched her while she slept as though he and she had never lived together as man and wife. His curious eyes rested long upon her face and on her hair: and as he thought of what she must have been then, in that time of her first girlish beauty, a strange friendly pity for her entered his soul. He did not like to say even to himself that her face was no longer beautiful but he knew that it was no longer the face for which Michael Furey had braved death.

Perhaps she had not told him all the story. His eyes moved to the chair over which she had thrown some of her clothes. A petticoat string dangled to the floor. One boot stood upright, its limp upper fallen down: the fellow of it lay upon its side. He wondered at his riot of emotions of an hour before. From what had it proceeded? From his aunts' supper, from his own foolish speech, from the wine and dancing, the merrymaking when saying goodnight in the hall, the pleasure of the walk along the river in the snow. Poor aunt Julia! She too would soon be a shade with the shade of Patrick Morkan and his horse. He had caught that haggard look upon her face for a moment when she was singing *Arrayed for the Bridal*. Soon perhaps he would be sitting in that same drawingroom, dressed in black, his silk hat on his knees. The blinds would be drawn down and aunt Kate would be sitting beside him, crying and blowing her nose and telling him how Julia had died. He would cast about in his mind for some words that might console her and would find only lame and useless ones. Yes, yes: that would happen very soon.

The air of the room chilled his shoulders. He stretched himself cautiously along under the sheets and lay down beside his wife. One by one they were all becoming shades. Better pass boldly into that other world, in the full glory of some passion, than fade and wither dismally with age. He thought of how she who lay beside him had locked in her heart for so many years that image of her lover's eyes when he had told her that he did not wish to live.

Generous tears filled Gabriel's eyes. He had never felt like that himself towards any woman but he knew that such a feeling must be love. The tears gathered more thickly in his eyes and in the partial darkness he imagined he saw the form of a young man standing under a dripping tree. Other forms were near. His soul had approached that region where dwell the vast hosts of the dead. He was conscious of, but could not apprehend, their wayward and flickering existence. His own identity was fading out into a grey impalpable world: the solid world itself which these dead had one time reared and lived in was dissolving and dwindling.

A few light taps upon the pane made him turn to the window. It had begun to snow again. He watched sleepily the flakes, silver and dark, falling obliquely against the lamplight. The time had come for him to set out on his journey westward. Yes, the newspapers were right: snow was general all over Ireland. It was falling on every part of the dark central plain, on the treeless hills, falling softly upon the Bog of Allen and, farther westward, softly falling into the dark mutinous Shannon waves. It was falling, too, upon every part of the lonely churchyard on the hill where Michael Furey lay buried. It lay thickly drifted on the crooked crosses and headstones, on the spears of the little gate, on the barren thorns. His soul swooned slowly as he heard the snow falling faintly through the universe and faintly falling, like the descent of their last end, upon all the living and the dead.

APPENDIX

A CURIOUS HISTORY

[In 1911, enraged at the imminent failure of his second attempt to get Dubliners *published, James Joyce wrote an open letter to the British and the Irish press. Two papers printed it. In late 1913, he refashioned the letter into a preface for the first edition of* Dubliners. *No doubt–and rightly–anticipating that Grant Richards would be less than enthusiastic about it, he simultaneously sent it to Ezra Pound, who printed it in his weekly column in* The Egoist *under the title* "A Curious History." *The present text is reprinted diplomatically from* The Egoist *of 15 January 1914, pp. 26–27, though augmented by the excerpt from* "Ivy Day in the Committee Room" *there omitted. As a text,* "A Curious History" *is strangely structured. At its center, it conjoins a letter from Buckingham Palace and a lacuna for the* "Ivy Day" *passage. (This has an exceptional publication status of its own.* The James Joyce Archive, *vol. [4], p. 269, reproduces an exemplar of the excerpt slips of the passage that Joyce had specially printed to illustrate his grievance, and from which we take the text for the present inclusion.) Letter and lacuna are boxed in Joyce's 1911 letter to the press as modified for the 1913/1914 occasion. This in turn is framed in and to its intended preface purpose, and the whole is framed finally in Pound's column commentary.]*

A Curious History.

THE following statement having been received by me from an author of known and notable talents, and the state of the case being now, so far as I know, precisely what it was at the date of his last letter (November 30th), I have thought it more appropriate to print his communication entire than to indulge in my usual biweekly comment upon books published during the fortnight.

Mr. Joyce's statement is as follows:–

The following letter, which gives the history of a book of stories, was sent by me to the Press of the United Kingdom two years ago. It was published by two newspapers so far as I know: "Sinn Fein" (Dublin) and the "Northern Whig" (Belfast).

Via della Barriera Vecchia 32 III.,
Trieste,
Austria.

SIR,

May I ask you to publish this letter, which throws some light on the present conditions of authorship in England and Ireland?

Nearly six years ago Mr. Grant Richards, publisher, of London, signed a contract with me for the publication of a book of stories written by me, entitled "Dubliners." Some ten months later he wrote asking me to omit one of the stories and passages in others which, as he said, his printer refused to set up. I declined to do either, and a correspondence began between Mr. Grant Richards and myself which lasted more than three months. I went to an international jurist in Rome (where I lived then) and was advised to omit. I declined to do so, and the MS. was returned to me, the publisher refusing to publish, notwithstanding his pledged printed word, the contract remaining in my possession.

Six months afterwards a Mr. Hone wrote to me from Marseilles to ask me to submit the MS. to Messrs. Maunsel, publishers, of Dublin. I did so; and after about a year, in July, 1909, Messrs. Maunsel signed a contract with me for the publication of the book on or before 1st September, 1910. In December, 1909, Messrs. Maunsel's manager begged me to alter a passage in one of the stories, "Ivy Day in the Committee Room," wherein some reference was made to Edward VII. I agreed to do so, much against my will, and altered one or two phrases. Messrs. Maunsel continually postponed the date of publication and in the end wrote, asking me to omit the passage or to change it radically. I declined to do either, pointing out that Mr. Grant Richards, of London, had raised no objection to the passage when Edward VII. was alive, and that I could not see why an Irish publisher should raise an objection to it when Edward VII. had passed into history. I suggested arbitration or a deletion of the passage with a prefatory note of explanation by me, but Messrs. Maunsel would agree to neither. As Mr. Hone (who had written to me in the first instance) disclaimed all responsibility in the matter and any connection with the firm I took the opinion of a solicitor in Dublin, who advised me to omit the passage, informing me that as I had no domicile in the United Kingdom I could not sue Messrs. Maunsel for breach of contract unless I paid £100 into court, and that even if I paid £100 into court and sued them, I should have no chance of getting a verdict in my favour from a Dublin jury if the passage in dispute could be taken as offensive in any way to the late King. I wrote then to the present King, George V., enclosing a printed proof of the story, with the passage therein marked, and begging him to inform me whether in his view the passage (certain allusions made by a person of the story in the idiom of his social class) should be withheld from publication as offensive to the memory of his father. His Majesty's private secretary sent me this reply:–

Buckingham Palace.

The private secretary is commanded to acknowledge the receipt of Mr. James Joyce's letter of the 1st instant, and to inform him that it is inconsistent with rule for his Majesty to express his opinion in such cases. The enclosures are returned herewith.

11th August, 1911.

Here is the passage in dispute:

– But look here, John, – said Mr O'Connor. – Why should we welcome the king of England? Didn't Parnell himself ...? –

– Parnell, – said Mr Henchy, – is dead. Now, here's the way I look at it. Here's this chap come to the throne after his old mother keeping him out of it till the man was grey. He's a man of the world and he means well by us. He's a jolly fine decent fellow, if you ask me, and no damn nonsense about him. He just says to himself: – *The old one never went to see these wild Irish. By Christ, I'll go myself and see what they're like.* – And are we going to insult the man when he comes over here on a friendly visit? Eh? Isn't that right, Crofton? –

Mr Crofton nodded his head.

– But after all now, – said Mr Lyons, argumentatively, – King Edward's life, you know, is not the very ... –

– Let bygones be bygones, – said Mr Henchy – I admire the man personally. He's just an ordinary knockabout like you and me. He's fond of his glass of grog and he's a bit of a rake, perhaps, and he's a good sportsman. Damn it, can't we Irish play fair? –

I wrote this book seven years ago and hold two contracts for its publication. I am not even allowed to explain my case in a prefatory note: wherefore, as I cannot see in any quarter a chance that my rights will be protected, I hereby give Messrs. Maunsel publicly permission to publish this story with what changes or deletions they may please to make, and shall hope that what they may publish may resemble that to the writing of which I gave thought and time. Their attitude as an Irish publishing firm may be judged by Irish public opinion. I, as a writer, protest against the systems (legal, social, and ceremonious) which have brought me to this pass.

Thanking you for your courtesy,

I am, Sir,

Your obedient servant,

JAMES JOYCE.

18th August, 1911.

I waited nine months after the publication of this letter. Then I went to Ireland and entered into negotiations with Messrs. Maunsel. They asked me to omit from the collection the story, "An Encounter," passages in "Two Gallants," the "Boarding House," "A Painful Case," and to change everywhere through the book the names of restaurants, cake-shops, railway stations, public-houses, laundries, bars, and other places of business. After having argued against their point of view day after day for six weeks and after having laid the matter before two solicitors (who, while they informed me that the publishing firm had made a breach of contract, refused to take up my case or to allow their names to be associated with it in any way), I consented in despair to all these changes on condition that the book were brought out without delay and the original text were restored in future editions, if such were called for. Then Messrs. Maunsel asked me to pay into their bank as security £1,000 or to find two sureties of £500 each. I declined to do either; and they then wrote to me, informing me that they would not publish the book, altered or unaltered, and that if I did not make them an offer to cover their losses on printing it they would sue me to recover same. I offered to pay sixty per cent. of the cost of printing the first edition of one thousand copies if the edition were made over to my order. This offer was accepted, and I arranged with my brother in Dublin to publish and sell the book for me. On the morning when the draft and agreement were to be signed the publishers informed me that the matter was at an end because the printer refused to hand over the copies. I took legal advice upon this, and was informed that the printer could not claim the money due to him by the publisher until he had handed over the copies. I then went to the printer. His foreman told me that the printer had decided to forego all claim to the money due to him. I asked whether the printer would hand over the complete edition to a London or Continental firm or to my brother or to me if he were fully indemnified. He said that the copies would never leave his printing-house, and added that the type had been broken up, and that the entire edition of one thousand copies would be burnt the next day. I left Ireland the next day, bringing with me a printed copy of the book which I had obtained from the publisher.

JAMES JOYCE.

Via Donato Bramante 4, II.,
Trieste,
30th November, 1913.

OUR WEEKLY STORY.

THE SISTERS.

BY STEPHEN DÆDALUS.

[*First published version which appeared in* The Irish Homestead *on 13 August 1904*]

Three nights in succession I had found myself in Great Britain-street at that hour, as if by Providence. Three nights I had raised my eyes to that lighted square of window and speculated. I seemed to understand that it would occur at night. But in spite of the Providence which had led my feet, and in spite of the reverent curiosity of my eyes, I had discovered nothing. Each night the square was lighted in the same way, faintly and evenly. It was not the light of candles, so far as I could see. Therefore, it had not yet occurred.

On the fourth night at that hour I was in another part of the city. It may have been the same Providence that led me there–a whimsical kind of Providence to take me at a disadvantage. As I went home I wondered was that square of window lighted as before, or did it reveal the ceremonious candles in whose light the Christian must take his last sleep. I was not surprised, then, when at supper I found myself a prophet. Old Cotter and my uncle were talking at the fire, smoking. Old Cotter is the old distiller who owns a batch of prize setters. He used to be very interesting when I knew him first, talking about "faints" and "worms." Now I find him tedious.

While I was eating my stirabout I heard him saying to my uncle:

"Without a doubt. Upper storey–(he tapped an unnecessary hand at his forehead)–gone."

"So they said. I never could see much of it. I thought he was sane enough."

"So he was, at times," said old Cotter.

I sniffed the "was" apprehensively, and gulped down some stirabout.

"Is he better, Uncle John?"

"He's dead."

"O ... he's dead?"

"Died a few hours ago."

"Who told you?"

"Mr. Cotter here brought us the news. He was passing there."

"Yes, I just happened to be passing, and I noticed the window ... you know."

"Do you think they will bring him to the chapel?" asked my aunt.

"Oh, no, ma'am. I wouldn't say so."

"Very unlikely," my uncle agreed.

So old Cotter had got the better of me for all my vigilance of three nights. It is often annoying the way people will blunder on what you have elaborately planned for. I was sure he would die at night.

The following morning after breakfast I went down to look at the little house in Great Britain-street. It was an unassuming shop registered under the vague name of "Drapery." The drapery was principally children's boots and umbrellas, and on ordinary days there used to be a notice hanging in the window, which said "Umbrellas recovered." There was no notice visible now, for the shop blinds were drawn down and a crape bouquet was tied to the knocker of the door with white ribbons. Three women of the people and a telegram boy were reading the card pinned on the crape. I also went over and read:– "July 2nd, 189- The Rev. James Flynn (formerly of St. Ita's Church), aged 65 years. R. I. P."

Only sixty-five! He looked much older than that. I often saw him sitting at the fire in the close dark room behind the shop, nearly smothered in his great coat. He seemed to have almost stupefied himself with heat, and the gesture of his large trembling hand to his nostrils had grown automatic. My aunt, who is what they call good-hearted, never went into the shop without bringing him some High Toast, and he used to take the packet of snuff from her hands, gravely inclining his head for sign of thanks. He used to sit in that stuffy room for the greater part of the day from early morning, while Nannie (who is almost stone deaf) read out the newspaper to him. His other sister, Eliza, used to mind the shop. These two old women used to look after him, feed him, and clothe him. The clothing was not difficult, for his ancient, priestly clothes were quite green with age, and his dogskin slippers were everlasting. When he was tired of hearing the news he used to rattle his snuff-box on the arm of his chair to avoid shouting at her, and then he used to make believe to read his Prayer Book. Make believe, because, when Eliza brought him a cup of soup from the kitchen, she had always to waken him.

As I stood looking up at the crape and the card that bore his name I could not realise that he was dead. He seemed like one who could go on living for ever if he only wanted to; his life was so methodical and uneventful. I think he said more to me than to anyone else. He had an egoistic contempt for all women-folk, and suffered all their services to him in polite silence. Of course, neither of his sisters was very intelligent. Nannie, for instance, had been reading out the newspaper to him every day for years, and could read tolerably well, and yet she always spoke of it as the *Freeman's General*. Perhaps he found me more intelligent, and honoured me with words for that reason. Nothing, practically nothing, ever occurred to remind him of his former life (I mean friends or visitors), and still he could remember every detail of it in his own fashion. He had studied at the college in Rome, and he taught me to speak Latin in the Italian way. He often put me through the responses of the Mass, smiling often and pushing huge pinches of snuff up each nostril alternately. When he smiled he used to uncover his big, discoloured teeth, and let his tongue lie on his lower lip. At first this habit of his used to make me feel uneasy. Then I grew used to it.

That evening my aunt visited the house of mourning and took me with her. It was an oppressive summer evening of faded gold. Nannie received us in the hall, and, as it was no use saying anything to her, my aunt shook hands with her for all. We followed the old woman upstairs and into the dead-room. The room, through the lace end of the blind, was suffused with dusky golden light, amid which the candles looked like pale, thin flames. He had been coffined. Nannie gave the lead, and we three knelt down at the foot of the bed. There was no sound in the room for some minutes except the sound of Nannie's mutterings—for she prays noisily. The fancy came to me that the old priest was smiling as he lay there in his coffin.

But, no. When we rose and went up to the head of the bed I saw that he was not smiling. There he lay solemn and copious in his brown habit, his large hands loosely retaining his rosary. His face was very grey and massive, with distended nostrils and circled with scanty white fur. There was a heavy odour in the room—the flowers.

We sat downstairs in the little room behind the shop, my aunt and I and the two sisters. Nannie sat in a corner and said nothing, but her lips moved from speaker to speaker with a painfully intelligent motion. I said nothing either, being too young, but my aunt spoke a great deal, for she is a bit of a gossip—harmless.

"Ah, well! he's gone!"

"To enjoy his eternal reward, Miss Flynn, I'm sure. He was a good and holy man."

"He was a good man, but, you see ... he was a disappointed man ... You see, his life was, you might say, crossed."

"Ah, yes! I know what you mean."

"Not that he was anyway mad, as you know yourself, but he was always a little queer. Even when we were all growing up together he was queer. One time he didn't speak hardly for a month. You know, he was that kind always."

"Perhaps he read too much, Miss Flynn?"

"O, he read a good deal, but not latterly. But it was his scrupulousness, I think, affected his mind. The duties of the priesthood were too much for him."

"Did he ... peacefully?"

"O, quite peacefully, ma'am. You couldn't tell when the breath went out of him. He had a beautiful death, God be praised."

"And everything ...?"

"Father O'Rourke was in with him yesterday and gave him the Last Sacrament."

"He knew then?"

"Yes; he was quite resigned."

Nannie gave a sleepy nod and looked ashamed.

"Poor Nannie," said her sister, "she's worn out. All the work we had, getting in a woman, and laying him out; and then the coffin and arranging about the funeral. God knows we did all we could, as poor as we are. We wouldn't see him want anything at the last."

"Indeed you were both very kind to him while he lived."

"Ah, poor James; he was no great trouble to us. You wouldn't hear him in the house no more than now. Still I know he's gone and all that. ... I won't be bringing him in his soup any more, nor Nannie reading him the paper, nor you, ma'am, bringing him his snuff. How he liked that snuff! Poor James!"

"O, yes, you'll miss him in a day or two more than you do now."

Silence invaded the room until memory reawakened it, Eliza speaking slowly–

"It was that chalice he broke. ... Of course, it was all right. I mean it contained nothing. But still ... They say it was the boy's fault. But poor James was so nervous, God be merciful to him."

"Yes, Miss Flynn, I heard that ... about the chalice. .. He ... his mind was a bit affected by that."

"He began to mope by himself, talking to no one, and wandering about. Often he couldn't be found. One night he was wanted, and they looked high up and low down and couldn't find him. Then the clerk suggested the chapel. So they opened the chapel (it was late at night), and brought in a light to look for him. .. And there, sure enough, he was, sitting in his confession-box in the dark, wide awake, and laughing like softly to himself. Then they knew something was wrong."

"God rest his soul!"

OUR WEEKLY STORY.

EVELINE.

BY STEPHEN DÆDALUS.

[*First published version which appeared in* The Irish Homestead *on 10 September 1904*]

She sat at the window watching the evening invade the avenue. Her head was leaned against the window-curtain, and in her nostrils was the odour of dusty cretonne. She was tired. Few people passed. The man out of the last house passed on his way home; she heard his footsteps clacking along the concrete pavement, and afterwards crunching on the cinder path before the new red houses. One time there used to be a field there, in which they used to play in the evening with other people's children. Then a man from Belfast bought the field and built houses in it—not like their little brown houses, but bright brick houses, with shining roofs. The children of the avenue used to play together in that field—the Devines, the Waters, the Dunns, little Keogh, the cripple, she and her brothers and sisters. Ernest, however, never played; he was too grown-up. Her father used often to hunt them in out of the field with his blackthorn stick, but usually little Keogh used to keep "nix," and call out when he saw her father coming. Still they seemed to have been rather happy then. Her father was not so bad then, and besides her mother was alive. That was a long time ago; she and her brothers and sisters were all grown up; her mother was dead; Mrs. Dunn was dead, too, and the Waters had gone back to England. Everything changes; now she was going to go away, to leave her home.

Home! She looked round the room, passing in review all its familiar objects. How many times she had dusted it, once a week at least. It was the "best" room, but it seemed to secrete dust everywhere. She had known the room for ten years–more –twelve years, and knew everything in it. Now she was going away. And yet during all those years she had never found out the name of the Australian priest whose yellowing photograph hung on the wall, just above the broken harmonium. He had been a friend of her father's–a school friend. When he showed the photograph to a friend, her father used to pass it with a casual word, "In Australia now–Melbourne."

She had consented to go away–to leave her home. Was it wise–was it honourable? She tried to weigh each side of the question in her mind. In her home at least she had shelter and food; she had those whom she had known all her life about her. She had to work of course both in the house and at business. What would they think of her in the Stores when they discovered she had gone away? Think her a fool, perhaps, and fill up her place by advertisement. Miss Gavan would probably be glad. She, too, would not be sorry to be out of Miss Gavan's clutches. Miss Gavan had an "edge" on her, and used her superior position mercilessly, particularly whenever there were people listening. It was–"Miss Hill, will you please attend to these ladies?" "A little bit smarter, Miss Hill, if you please." She would not cry many tears at leaving the Stores. In her new home in a distant, unknown country, surely she would be free from such indignities! She would then be a married woman–she, Eveline. She would be treated with respect. She would not be treated as her mother had been treated. Even now–at her age, she was over nineteen–she sometimes felt herself in danger of her father's violence. Latterly he had begun to threaten her, saying what he would do were it not for her dead mother's sake. And now she had nobody to protect her. Ernest was dead, and Harry, who was in the church-decorating business, was nearly always down somewhere in the country. Besides, the invariable squabble for money on Saturday night had begun to weary her unspeakably. She always gave her entire wages–seven shillings–and Harry always sent up what he could, but the trouble was to get any money from her father. He said she used to squander the money, that she had no head, that he wasn't going to give her his hard-earned money to throw about the streets, and much more, for he was usually fairly bad on Saturday night. In the end he would give her the money, and ask her had she any intention of buying Sunday's dinner. Then she had to rush out as quickly as she could and do her marketing, holding her black leather purse tightly in her hand as she elbowed her way through the crowds, and returning home late under her load of provisions. She had hard work to keep the house together, and to see that the two young children who had been left to her charge went to school regularly and got their meals regularly. It was hard work—a hard life—but now that she was about to leave it she did not find it a wholly undesirable life.

She was about to explore another life with Frank. Frank was very kind, manly, open-hearted. She was to go away with him by the night boat to be his wife, and to live with him in Buenos Ayres, where he had a home waiting for her. How well she remembered the first time she had seen him (he was lodging in a house on the main road where she used to visit). A few weeks ago it seemed. He was standing at the gate, his peaked cap pushed back on his head, and his hair tumbled forward over a face of bronze. Then they had come to know each other. He used to meet her outside the Stores every evening, and see her home. He took her to see the "Bohemian Girl," and she felt elated as she sat in an unaccustomed part of the theatre with him. He was very fond of music, and sang a little. People knew that they were courting, and when Frank sang about the lass that loves a sailor she always felt pleasantly confused. He used to call her "Poppens" out of fun. First it had been an excitement for her to have a young man, and then she had begun to like him. He had tales of distant countries. He had started as a deck boy at a pound a month on a ship of the Allan line going out to Canada. He told her the names of the ships he had been on, and the names of the different services. He had sailed through the Straits of Magellan, and he told her stories of the terrible Patagonians. He had fallen on his feet in Buenos Ayres, he said, and had come over to the old country just for a holiday. Of course, her father had found out the affair, and had forbidden her to have anything to do with him. "I know these sailor fellows," her father said. Frank and her father had quarrelled one day, and after that she had to meet her lover secretly.

The evening deepened in the avenue. The white of two letters lying in her lap grew indistinct. One was to Harry, the other was to her father. Ernest had been her favourite, but she liked Harry, too. Her father was becoming old lately, she noticed; he would miss her. Sometimes he could be very nice. Not long before, when she had been laid up for a day, he had read her out a ghost-story, and had made toast for her at the fire. Another day, when her mother was alive, they had all gone for a picnic to the Hill of Howth. She remembered her father putting on her mother's bonnet to make the children laugh.

Her time was running out, but she continued to sit by the window, leaning her head against the window-curtain, inhaling the odour of dusty cretonne. Down far in the avenue she could hear a street organ playing. She knew the air. Strange that it should come that very night to remind her of her promise to her mother, her promise to keep the home together as long as she could. She remembered the last night of her mother's illness; she was again in the close, dark room at the other side of the hall, and outside she heard a melancholy air of Italy. The organ-player had been ordered to go away, and given sixpence. She remembered her father strutting back into the sick room, saying: "Damned Italians! coming over here." As she mused, the pitiful vision of her mother's life laid its spell on the very quick of her being—that life of commonplace sacrifices closing in final craziness. She trembled as she heard again her mother's voice saying constantly with foolish insistence: "Derevaun Seraun," "Derevaun Seraun."

She stood up in a sudden impulse of terror. Escape? She

must escape! Frank would save her. He could give her life, perhaps love, too. But she wanted life. Why should she be unhappy? She had a right to happiness. Frank would take her in his arms, fold her in his arms. He would save her.

She stood among the swaying crowd in the station at the North Wall. He held her hand and she knew that he was speaking to her, saying something about the passage over and over again. The station was full of soldiers with brown baggages. Through the wide door she caught a glimpse of the black mass of the boat lying in beside the quay wall, with illumined portholes. She answered nothing. She felt her cheek pale and cold, and out of a maze of distress she prayed to God to direct her, to show her what was her duty. The boat blew a long, mournful whistle into the mist. If she went to-morrow she would be on the sea with Frank, steaming towards Buenos Ayres. Their passage had been booked. Could she still draw back, after all he had done for her? Her distress awoke a nausea in her body, and she kept moving her lips in silent, fervent prayer.

A bell clanged upon her heart. She felt him seize her hand.

"Come!"

All the seas of the world tumbled about her heart. He was drawing her into them; he would drown her. She gripped with both hands at the iron railing.

"Come!"

No! No! No! It was impossible. Her hands clutched the iron in frenzy. Amid the seas she sent a cry of anguish.

"Eveline! Evvy!"

He rushed beyond the barrier and called to her to follow. He was shouted at to go on, but he still called to her. She set her white face to him, passive, like a helpless animal. Her eyes gave him no sign of love, or farewell or recognition.

OUR WEEKLY STORY.

AFTER THE RACE.

BY STEPHEN DÆDALUS.

[*First published version which appeared in* The Irish Homestead *on 17 December 1904*]

The cars came scudding in towards Dublin, running evenly like pellets in the groove of the Naas-road. At the crest of the hill at Inchicore sightseers had gathered in clumps to watch the cars careering homeward, and through this channel of poverty and inaction the Continent sped its wealth and industry. Now and again the clumps of people raised the cheer of the gratefully oppressed. Their sympathy, however, was for the blue cars—the cars of their friends, the French.

The French, moreover, were virtual victors. Their team had finished solidly; they had been placed second and third, and the driver of the winning German car was reported a Belgian. Each blue car, therefore, received a double measure of welcome as it topped the crest of the hill, and each cheer of welcome was acknowledged with smiles and nods by those in the car. In one of these trimly built cars was a party of four young men, whose spirits seemed to be at present well above the level of successful Gallicism; in fact, these four young men were almost hilarious. They were:—Charles Segouin, the owner of the car; Andre Riviere, a young electrician of Canadian birth; a huge Hungarian named Villona, and a neatly-groomed young man named Doyle. Segouin was in good humour because he had unexpectedly received some orders in advance (he was about to start a motor establishment in Paris), and Riviere was in good humour because he was to be appointed manager of the establishment; these two young men (who were cousins) were also in good humour because of the success of the French cars. Villona was in good humour because he had had a very satisfactory luncheon, and besides he was an optimist by nature. The fourth member of the party, however, was too excited to be genuinely happy.

He was about twenty-six years of age, with a soft, light-brown moustache and rather innocent-looking grey eyes. His father, who had begun life as an advanced Nationalist, had modified his views early. He had made his money as a butcher in Kingstown, and by opening shops in Dublin and in the suburbs he had made his money many times over. He had also been fortunate enough to secure some of the police contracts, and in the end he had become rich enough to be alluded to in the Dublin newspapers as a "merchant prince." He had sent his son to England to be educated in a big Catholic college and had afterwards sent him to Dublin University to study law. Jimmy did not study very earnestly and took to bad courses for a while. He had money and he was popular and he divided his time curiously between musical and motoring circles. Then he had been sent for a term to Cambridge to see a little life. His father, remonstrative but covertly proud of the excess, had paid his bills and brought him home. It was at Cambridge that he had met Segouin. They were not much more than acquaintances as yet, but Jimmy found great pleasure in the society of one who had seen so much of the world and was reputed to own several of the biggest hotels in France. Such a person (as his father agreed) was well worth knowing, even if he had not been the charming companion he was. Villona was entertaining also—a brilliant pianist—but, unfortunately, very poor.

The car ran on merrily with its cargo of hilarious youth. The two cousins sat on the front seat; Jimmy and his Hungarian friend sat behind. Decidedly Villona was in excellent spirits; he kept up a deep bass hum of melody for miles of the road. The Frenchmen flung their laughter and light words over their shoulders, and often Jimmy had to strain forward to catch the quick phrase. This was not altogether pleasant for him as he had nearly always to make a deft guess at the meaning and shout back a suitable answer in the face of a high wind. Besides, Villona's humming would confuse anybody—the noise of the car, too.

Rapid motion through space elates one; so does notoriety; so does the possession of money. These were three good reasons for Jimmy's excitement. He had been seen by many of his friends that day in the company of these Continentals. At the control Segouin had presented him to one of the French competitors, and in answer to his confused murmur of compliment, the swarthy face of the driver had disclosed a line of shining white teeth. It was pleasant after that honour to return to the profane world of spectators amid nudges and significant looks. Then as to money–he really had a great sum under his control. Segouin, perhaps, would not think it a great sum, but Jimmy, who in spite of temporary errors was at heart the inheritor of solid instincts, knew well with what difficulty it had been got together. This knowledge had previously kept his bills within the limits of reasonable recklessness, and if he had been so conscious of the latent labour in money when there had been question merely of some freak of the higher intelligence, how much more so now when he was about to stake the greater part of his substance! It was a serious thing for him.

Of course the investment was a good one, and Segouin had managed to give the impression that it was by a favour of friendship his mite of Irish money was to be included in the capital of the concern. Jimmy had a respect for his father's shrewdness in business matters, and in this case it had been his father who had first suggested the investment; money to be made in the motoring business, pots of it. Moreover, Segouin had the unmistakable air of wealth. Jimmy set out to translate into days' work that lordly car in which he sat. How smoothly it ran! In what style they had come careering along the country roads! The journey laid a magical finger on the genuine pulse of life, and gallantly the machinery of human nerves strove to answer the bounding courses of the swift, blue animal.

They drove down Dame-street. The street was busy with unusual traffic, loud with the horns of motorists and the gongs of impatient tram drivers. Near the Bank Segouin drew up and Jimmy and his friend descended. A little knot of people collected on the footpath to pay homage to the snorting motor.

The party was to dine together that evening in Segouin's hotel, and meanwhile Jimmy and his friend who was staying with him, were to go home to dress. The car steered out slowly for Grafton-street while the two young men pushed their way through the knot of gazers. They walked northward with a curious feeling of disappointment in the exercise while the city hung its pale globes of light above them in a haze of summer evening.

In Jimmy's house this dinner had been pronounced an occasion. A certain pride mingled with his parents' trepidation, a certain eagerness, also, to play fast and loose, for the names of great foreign cities have at least this virtue. Jimmy, too, looked very well when he was dressed, and as he stood in the hall giving a last equation to the bows of his dress tie his father may have felt even commercially satisfied at having secured in his son unpurchasable qualities. His father, therefore, was unusually friendly with Villona, and his manner expressed a real respect for foreign accomplishments, but this subtlety of his host was probably lost upon the Hungarian, who was beginning to have a sharp desire for his dinner.

The dinner was excellent, exquisite. Segouin, Jimmy decided, had a very refined taste. The party was increased by a young Englishman named Routh, whom Jimmy had seen with Segouin in Cambridge. The five young men dined in a small comfortable room by candlelight. They talked a great deal, and with little reserve. Jimmy, whose imagination was kindling, conceived the lively youth of the Frenchmen twined elegantly upon the firm framework of the Englishman's manner. A graceful image of his, he thought, and a just one. He admired the dexterity with which their entertainer directed the conversation. The five young men had various tastes and their tongues had been loosened. Villona, with immense respect, began to discover to the mildly surprised Englishman the beauties of the English madrigal, deploring the loss of old instruments. Riviere, not wholly ingenuously, undertook to explain to Jimmy the triumph of the French mechanicians. The resonant voice of the Hungarian was about to prevail in ridicule of the spurious lutes of the romantic painters when Segouin shepherded his party into politics. Here was congenial ground for all. Jimmy, under generous influences, felt the ancient zeal of his father awake within him. He aroused the torpid Routh at last. The room grew doubly hot and Segouin's task grew harder each moment; there was even danger of personal spice. The alert host at an opportunity lifted his glass to Humanity, and when the toast had been drunk, he threw open a window significantly.

That night the city wore the air of a capital. The five young men strolled along Stephen's-green in a faint cloud of aromatic smoke. They talked loudly and gaily and their cloaks dangled from their shoulders. The people made way for them. At the corner of Grafton-street a short, fat man was putting two handsome ladies on a car in charge of another fat man. The car drove off and the short, fat man caught sight of the party.

"André!"

"It's Farley!"

A torrent of talk followed; Farley was an American. No one knew very well what the talk was about. Villona and Riviere were the noisiest, but all the men were excited. They got up on a car, squeezing themselves together amid much laughter. They drove by the crowd, blended now into soft colours, to a music of merry bells. They took the train at Westland-row, and in a few minutes, as it seemed to Jimmy, they were walking out of Kingstown Station. The ticket-collector saluted Jimmy; he was an old man.

"Fine night, sir!"

It was a serene summer night; the harbour lay like a darkened mirror at their feet. They proceeded towards it with linked arms, singing "Cadet Rouselle" in chorus, stamping their feet at every "Ho! Ho! Hobe! vraiment!" They got into a rowboat at the slip and made out for the American's yacht. There was to be supper, music, cards. Villona said with conviction, "It is delightful!"

There was a yacht-piano in the cabin. Villona played a waltz for Farley and Riviere, Farley acting as cavalier and Riviere as lady. Then an impromptu square dance, the men devising original figures. What merriment! Jimmy took his part with a will; this was life, at least. Then Farley got out of breath and they cried "Stop!" A man brought in a light supper and the young men sat down to it for form's sake. They drank, however; it was Bohemian. They drank Ireland, England, Hungary, France, the United States of America. Jimmy made a speech, a long speech, Villona saying "Hear! Hear!" whenever there was a pause. There was a great clapping when he sat down. It must have been a good speech. Farley clapped him on the shoulder and laughed loudly. What jovial fellows! What good company they were!

Cards! Cards! The table was cleared. Villona returned quietly to his piano and played voluntaries for them. The other young men played game after game, flinging themselves boldly into the adventure. They drank the health of the Queen of Hearts and of the Queen of Diamonds. Jimmy felt obscurely the lack of an audience; the wit was flashing. Play ran very high; paper began to pass. Jimmy did not know exactly who was winning: he knew that he was losing. But it was his own fault, for he frequently mistook his cards, and the other men had to calculate his I. O. U.'s for him. They were devils of fellows, but he wished they would stop; it was getting late. Some one gave the toast of the yacht, "The Belle of Newport." Someone proposed a great game for a finish. The piano had stopped; Villona must have gone up on deck. It was a terrible game; they stopped just before the end of it to drink for luck. Jimmy understood that the game was between Routh and Segouin. What excitement! Jimmy was excited too; he would lose of course. How much had he written away? The men rose to their feet to play the last tricks, talking and gesticulating. Routh won! The cabin shook with the young men's cheering, and the cards were bundled together. They began to gather in what they had won. Farley and Jimmy were the heaviest losers.

Jimmy knew that he would regret in the morning, but at present he was glad of the rest. He leaned his elbows on the table and rested his head on his hands, counting the beats of his temple. The cabin door opened and he saw the Hungarian standing in a shaft of grey light.

"Daybreak, gentlemen!"

A NOTE ON THE TEXT

AFTERWORD

SELECT BIBLIOGRAPHY

A NOTE ON THE TEXT

This edition is a copy-text edition of James Joyce's *Dubliners*. The copy-text is provided by fair copies in Joyce's hand, where such manuscripts exist. This is the case for eight stories—"The Sisters," "An Encounter," "The Boarding House," "Counterparts," "A Painful Case," "Ivy Day in the Committee Room," "A Mother" and "Grace"—and partly for a ninth, "The Dead." For the remaining stories—"Araby," "Eveline," "After the Race," "Two Gallants," "A Little Cloud," "Clay" and, again, for parts of "The Dead"—the copy-text is supplied by the nearest descendant of the autograph that once existed. This descendant is the typesetting of 1910 for a Dublin edition of *Dubliners* which, in the event, was never published. That typesetting survives in overlapping fragments as galleys, early page proofs and late page proofs. Galleys provide the copy-text for the sections of "The Dead" missing in that story's autograph. Late page proofs provide the copy-text for the six stories lacking a manuscript altogether.

Although a Dublin edition of *Dubliners* never appeared, it played a role in the transmission of the text. For the first edition of the collection, published in 1914 by Grant Richards in London (sheets were also taken over by B. W. Huebsch of New York for the first American issue in 1916), a set of the early page proofs served as printer's copy. This ensured the linear descent of the text from manuscript to first edition with only one intervening stage, namely the correction and revision of the 1910 galleys taking effect in the 1910 early page proofs. But it excluded from the transmission the further correction and revision of the 1910 early page proofs taking effect in the 1910 late page proofs. The first-editon text of 1914 became the collection's public text. However, it is a fact of the textual history that Joyce, in helping to see the first edition into print, did not prevail with the publisher and printers to the extent he wished; whereas the late page proofs of the abortive 1910 edition represent *Dubliners* as most closely and consistently under his control in print. Balancing this discrepancy in the transmission has been a main challenge of critically editing *Dubliners*.

The basis of the critically edited text is the wording, spelling and punctuation of the given copy-text. This means that the occasional original idiom has been confirmed against a normalizing change in the transmission (as when, for example, Mrs Mooney in "The Boarding House" sends her daughter Polly to be a "typewriter" [7.54], not a "typist"). By the rules of copy-text editing, however, Joyce's revisions are grafted onto the copy-text (so that—in the edited text as in the published text since the first edition—Gabriel Conroy's father was an employee of the "Port and Docks" [15.150], and not, as in the manuscript, of the "Post Office").

The same textual double standard of upholding the copy-text, though accepting for the edited text the author's revisions, extends to the punctuation and word forms. The manuscript copy-texts provide Joyce's original punctuation directly; and where the 1910 typesetting holds the edition's base text as much re-punctuated by the printers, Joyce's corrective effort was strong throughout to enforce the character of punctuation else evidenced in his originals. The Joycean mode of rhythmical lightness in punctuation is therefore upheld or restored in the edited text. But in the printed text as Joyce sought to control it, the restorative correction of punctuation went hand in hand with a revision of word forms. With great consistency, he unhyphenated compounds for the abortive 1910 edition, shaping the compounds into either two words or one. In this, he introduced for the first time a style of presentation, or properly indeed a linguistic feature, into his text in print which later, and more successfully (for in the case of *Dubliners*, the resetting for the first edition largely frustrated the earlier effort), he would insist upon again for *A Portrait of the Artist as a Young Man* and *Ulysses*.

The present edition is the text-only companion volume to the full critical edition of *Dubliners* simultaneously published by Garland Publishing, Inc. The established text may be assessed by the apparatus of the Garland edition. Typographically, the text of this edition broadly observes the standards and conventions of modern professional printing and publishing, yet endeavors at the same time to maintain the character of a scholarly edited text in preserving essential features of irregularity in the authorial writing. Word forms and word divisions, spellings, capitalization and punctuation have been neither normalized nor modernized, nor have typographical matters such as abbreviations or ellipses been standardized. To set out dialogue, the convention adopted is that of opening dialogue dashes only, placed flush left. It is the solution in print answering to Joyce's own strong views on the marking of dialogue which, at his forceful instigation, was realized in the third edition of *A Portrait of the Artist as a Young Man* (London: Jonathan Cape, 1924) and has now become the common feature of the critically edited texts of *Dubliners*, *A Portrait* and *Ulysses*. End-of-line hyphenation in the edited text (though not the "Appendix") occurs in two modes. The sign "=" marks a division for mere typographical reasons. Words so printed should always be cited as one undivided word. The regular hyphen indicates an authentic Joycean hyphen. The through line numbering for each story independent of the pagination is identical in the Vintage and Garland editions. ("7.54," cited above, means the 54th line in the seventh story, "The Boarding House"; and "15.150" the 150th line in the fifteenth story, "The Dead.")

The present text and that of Robert Scholes' Viking edition of 1967, while not concurring in every word, are close in their readings. Yet as a critical edition established afresh from the earliest sources of the writing and transmission, our edition encompasses, beyond the words of the text, the totality of its presentation in print. Reading *Dubliners* in the critically established patterns of Joyce's punctuation and word forms gives a different feel, subtly altering the shadings of the sense, for this early Joycean text.

Hans Walter Gabler

AFTERWORD

I

At the end of James Joyce's *A Portrait of the Artist as a Young Man* the hero, Stephen Dedalus, who has many affinities with the young Joyce, escapes from his circumscribed existence in Ireland with the cry: "Welcome, O Life! I go to encounter for the millionth time the reality of experience and to forge in the smithy of my soul the uncreated conscience of my race." This exuberant outburst articulates three themes that Joyce was to spend his life exploring, and which are central to *Dubliners*. The first is the desire for freedom, the impulse to welcome life, to escape the nets, whether they be of nationality, language, or religion, which seemed to Joyce to impede the full expression of human potentiality. Most of his Dubliners long for escape into a fuller and more meaningful existence (the word "life" occurs in every story and seventy-nine times in the book as a whole) but at the crucial moment they miss or surrender their chance and remain trapped in a condition that Joyce described in medical terms as paralysis and hemiplegia, but which has psychological, spiritual, and social, as well as physical, implications.

A second theme introduced in Stephen's cry is the relationship of reality to consciousness and artistic representation, the encounter with the "reality of experience," a reality so manifold and so mysterious that meeting it a million times is not enough. In *Dubliners*, Joyce's first attempt to register in language and fictive form the protean complexities of the "reality of experience," he learns the paradoxical lesson that only through the most rigorous economy, only by concentrating on the minutest of particulars, can he have any hope of engaging with the immensity of the world. His problem in *Dubliners* was to find a style and technique that would allow the venal commonplaces with which the book is ostensibly concerned to reverberate with wider significance. To this end he organized his stories around moments of illumination described as "epiphanies," resolved to render them in a style of "scrupulous meanness," and so orchestrated his allusions as to maximize their symbolic and mythical resonances.

Finally there is the relationship of the writer to his audience, or "race," which involves the relationship of his fiction to morality, to "conscience." In letters to his publishers, Joyce repeatedly insisted that his stories would have a moral and salutary effect on his audience, not in any obvious or didactic way, but in alerting them to the pettiness of their condition and attitudes. As he told Grant Richards, his "intention was to write a chapter of the moral history of my country and I chose Dublin for the scene because that city seemed to me the centre of paralysis." Yet, although saturated in the sights and sounds of Dublin, the stories are not mere exercises in local color. As modern city-dwellers, his characters encounter problems and conditions familiar elsewhere in the modern world. The specific Dublin orientation of those problems and conditions gives the stories a particularity which extends rather than limits their wider interest.

II

Who was this young man who had set himself such a challenging artistic agenda, and with what success did he pursue it? James Augustine Joyce was born in Dublin in February 1882, the eldest child of a then relatively well-off family. In September 1888 he was sent as a boarder to Clongowes Wood College, the leading Jesuit school in Ireland, but the rapidly increasing family (eventually there were four boys and six girls), together with his father's irresponsibility in financial matters, began to strain resources, and in June 1891 he was withdrawn from school. At the beginning of 1892, the family moved from the gracious seaside town of Bray to a less imposing house in Blackrock, a suburb in south Dublin, and they descended to even humbler quarters in the north of the city in 1893. Joyce was to turn this experience of the various strata of middle-class life, and the attendant preoccupation with money and its lack, to artistic effect when he came to write *Dubliners*. A chance meeting between his father and the ex-headmaster at Clongowes led to Joyce and his brother Stanislaus being given free places as day boys at another Jesuit school, Belvedere College.

Joyce enjoyed a distinguished academic career at Belvedere, but his school days were disturbed by sexual and religious perturbations and before he left he had rejected the possibility of becoming a priest. In 1899, he enrolled at University College, then part of the Royal University of Ireland, where he developed an enthusiasm for modern drama, particularly that of Ibsen. In the summer of 1900, he wrote a play, *A Brilliant Career*, strongly influenced by Ibsen but never published, and he had already begun to write poems in the manner of the so-called "Decadent" poets of the 1890s.

Soon after graduating in 1902, Joyce made the acquaintance of most of the leading Irish writers, including W. B. Yeats, who tried to further his literary ambitions, but in the autumn of that year he decided to pursue medical studies in France. Although his first visit to Paris only lasted two weeks, he returned in the middle of January, 1903, and settled down to writing reviews and reading Aristotle. In April 1903, he went back to Ireland to be near his dying mother (she died of cancer in August), and he remained in Dublin until October 1904, living a life of mild dissipation, mainly in the company of Oliver St. John Gogarty, a medical student and poet, and later the model for Malachi Mulligan in *Ulysses*. It was at this time that he began to write stories for *Dubliners*, and also the first version of *A Portrait of the Artist as a Young Man*. The latter was turned down by *Dana*, an Irish monthly, and he immediately began to recast it in a much expanded version, entitled *Stephen Hero*. In June 1904 he met and fell in love with a servant girl from Galway, Nora Barnacle, and in October eloped with her to the Continent. He taught English at the Berlitz School in Pola, where he continued writing *Stephen Hero* and further *Dubliners* stories. In March 1905 the Joyces moved to Trieste where, except for a brief residence in Rome, they were to remain for ten years and where, in July, their son, Giorgio, was born.

In October 1905, after unsuccessfully trying other firms, Joyce offered the London publisher Grant Richards "twelve short stories," to be called *Dubliners*. Although Richards thought "very highly" of the book as a work of fiction, he was less sanguine about its commercial success since it suffered under a double disadvantage: "it is about Ireland ... and it is a collection of short stories." Nevertheless, by 20 February 1906 the two had agreed to terms (a royalty of 10% on copies sold after the first hundred, 13 copies counting as 12), and Joyce promised to add a thirteenth story, "Two Gallants." But thirteen turned out to be particularly unlucky, for on receipt of the story in April, Richards sent part of it to his printers, who promptly declared it too obscene to print. Richards immediately asked Joyce to suppress or modify the story, to make changes in "Counterparts," and, now thoroughly alarmed, went carefully through the book, demanding the deletion of the expletive "bloody" and the omission not only of "Two Gallants" but also "An Encounter." Negotiations went on throughout the summer, with Joyce defending his artistic right to self-expression in a series of long and eloquent letters but promising to make what concessions he could. Grant Richards, who had recently gone bankrupt and was now trading under his wife's name, felt particularly vulnerable to possible public or legal attack, and, although he never wavered in his admiration for the book as a work of fiction, became less and less happy about the prospect of publishing it, urging Joyce to let him issue *Stephen Hero* instead. In early September Joyce submitted a revised manuscript of *Dubliners*, but after some delay, and despite further concessions, Richards returned the book on 26 October, assuring him that it was for the good of his own reputation as well as the firm's.

Although Joyce made strenuous attempts to place the book elsewhere (ten publishers had rejected it by 1913, and probably many more were approached) he was unsuccessful. Meanwhile, his brief and unhappy experience of Rome in 1906–7 caused him to revise his harsh memories of Dublin and led to the composition of "The Dead" in 1907, shortly before the publication of his volume of poetry, *Chamber Music*. While in hospital with rheumatic fever in the summer of that year, he decided to rewrite *Stephen Hero* as *A Portrait of the Artist as a Young Man*.

In 1909 the prospects for *Dubliners* seemed to grow more hopeful when he opened discussions with the Dublin firm of Maunsel, set up specifically to publish new Irish writing. All appeared to be going well until George Roberts, one of the firm's directors, took fright over certain passages, particularly the reference to Edward VII in "Ivy Day in the Committee Room." In an attempt to resolve this difficulty Joyce even wrote to Buckingham Palace, but matters dragged on interminably, and in 1911 he issued an open letter to the Irish press detailing his publishing vicissitudes (see "A Curious History," in the Appendix to this edition). Although the Maunsel edition of the book was actually set up in print, Roberts was now so terrified of possible legal action that in September 1912 he refused absolutely to issue it. The Dublin printer destroyed the type, and the publisher had kept merely a set of intermediate page proofs which Joyce, who was paying what turned out to be his last visit to Ireland, managed to rescue.

After this further disappointment, his affairs improved when, in January 1914, *The Egoist* began to serialize *A Portrait of the Artist as a Young Man*. Encouraged by this success, Joyce again approached Grant Richards about the publication of *Dubliners*, and, after careful enquiries about potential libel suits and possible alterations to the text (taken from the intermediate page proofs of the Maunsel edition), Richards agreed on 29 January 1914 to issue the book on the same terms as those of 1906, with the added stipulation that Joyce should take 120 copies himself at trade price. Despite quibbles about Joyce's unconventional punctuation, the printers losing part of "The Sisters," and Richards neglecting to make over 200 corrections that Joyce had sent him, the book finally appeared on 15 June 1914–to be greeted by an almost complete critical and public silence which the outbreak of the Great War a few weeks later did nothing to shatter. Joyce had been so sanguine about the book's success that in February 1914 he had negotiated an increased royalty of 15% after the first 8,000 copies, but in the year following publication sales amounted to only 379, a state of affairs that he described as "disastrous."

Nevertheless, he began to work on his play, *Exiles*, and embarked upon his most ambitious work to date, *Ulysses*, which in 1907 he had originally planned as a further story for *Dubliners*, though as such it never got beyond the title. After the entry of Italy into the First World War in 1915, the family moved to Zürich. The following year he published *A Portrait of the Artist* in book form (after Grant Richards had turned it down) and was awarded a grant of £100 from the Civil List. In 1920 the Joyces left Zürich for Paris, and *Ulysses* was published there in 1922. For the next seventeen years Joyce worked at his most revolutionary novel, *Finnegans Wake*, sections of which appeared in little magazines in the late 1920s and 1930s. The book was finally published in 1939, just before the declaration of the Second World War obliged him to move back to Zürich, where he died of a perforated ulcer in January 1941, at the age of fifty-nine.

III

It may seem a long way from the short stories of *Dubliners* to the highly textured linguistic complexities of *Finnegans Wake*, but with hindsight we can detect certain literary and artistic concerns running through Joyce's career. Central to those concerns is his continual interrogation of what constitutes the "reality of experience" and how the modern artist, heir to a sophisticated variety of techniques, genres, and linguistic possibilities, is authentically to render that experience. In *Dubliners* we see the beginning of the process through which his acute concern with realism transforms itself under the very pressure of its own economies and procedures into a form of symbolism.

"Realism" as an artistic movement emerged in the early nineteenth century and adopted the mirror, an apparently neutral reflecting instrument, as the metaphor for its artistic procedures, but pretensions to objectivity that this might seem to imply are disingenuous. The leading Realists–Balzac, George Eliot, and Tolstoy–cannot keep themselves from intervening directly in their text to air their views and guide their readers' responses. In this we detect a shaping ideology, a body of thought and opinion that colors their apprehension of the world. This is usually expressed and endorsed by a narrator whose point of view is indistinguishable from that of the author and who is deemed to be reliable and truthful in what he or she narrates.

Gustave Flaubert took Realism to another stage. He thought that authorial intervention destroyed the verisimilitude that was a contract of the Realist mode. He was therefore careful to excise the palpable presence of the novelist from his novels, arguing that the writer in his work should be like God in creation–everywhere apparent but nowhere seen. Joyce is in the Flaubertian tradition. He believes that the artist should remain outside his text, so disinterested, as he has Stephen Dedalus put it in *A Portrait of the Artist as a Young Man*, that he stands aside paring his fingernails while his novel proceeds. He will never let us know directly what he is thinking, but delegates this mode of authority in the text to the text itself, to structure, language, plot, allusion and to irony. Like Flaubert, he understood that this mode of writing made severe artistic demands on the author, and also that it put more responsibility on his audience: no longer having access to the author's would-be totalizing view of his fiction, the reader must pick up hints and allusions, he must, like the boy in "Araby," "interpret" the signs and fill in those aspects of the work that are left indeterminate or unspoken. Nor is the narrator as "reliable" as in earlier Realist novels. In *Dubliners* the narration frequently foregoes omniscience to take on the limited consciousness of the characters it is describing. Sometimes (as in "The Sisters") it is perplexed by not having access to the full facts.

Like other Realists, Joyce adopted the image of the mirror but he knew that the process of reflection is complicated by the choice of what is to be reflected (or omitted), by the consciousness of the author which shapes and interprets that material, and by questions (which became of more concern to him) about the extent to which language registers or actually creates that reality. He believed that it is the artist's task to approach truth, the "reality of experience," as nearly as possible, and he urged the reluctant Grant Richards to publish *Dubliners* because it offered the Irish "one good look at themselves" in his "nicely polished looking-glass." A scrupulous art took on value by its very scrupulousness: his art has polished the glass in an attempt to render a true account. This, he felt, was particularly important in Ireland where, because of the country's history, its religious and social complexion, literary mirrors were more likely to distort than to reflect accurately. In *Ulysses* Stephen Dedalus describes Irish art, asquint through colonialism and poverty, as "the cracked lookingglass of a servant," and in *Dubliners* – in "A Little Cloud," "A Mother," and "The Dead," for example – we find Irish pretensions to cultural or artistic expression twisted or thwarted by uncertainties and self-deceptions about identity and motivation.

The nice polish of Joyce's "lookingglass" is achieved by his style, and by the time he began to write *Dubliners* he understood that language was the key to style and to an accurate expression of reality or experience. He also knew that language revealed the world not in a series of simple denotative equations but through a series of complex relationships. With its puns, homonyms and homologies, acknowledged and unacknowledged figurativeness, it was an ambiguous, slippery, and unstable instrument. Language, crucial to negotiating the world, could also be used to evade the world, to disguise, to deceive, to idealize the ugly, and obfuscate motives and choices. Joyce told Grant Richards that he had written *Dubliners* in a style of "scrupulous meanness." In fact, his language in these stories (as in all his work) is never "mean" but always scrupulous. If art defines its value by its fidelity to the "reality of experience," so the author defines his morality through the precision and intelligence with which he deploys his language to articulate the expression of that reality. And that intelligence requires him to be aware that language is not a transparent medium, but already saturated in associations, nuances, and inflections, and governed by preexisting rules and protocols. It is this alertness to the possibilities and duplicities of language, not any meagerness or limitation, that constitutes the scrupulousness of Joyce's style.

IV

This scrupulousness is a crucial element both in Joyce's use of language, and in the form and structure of the stories. It is not just that Joyce extracts the maximum effect from the minimum words, but that the very economy of his procedures gives his work such concentration and resonance that it passes through realism into symbolism. The realism is securely rooted and part of George Roberts's and Grant Richards's hesitation in publishing the book was a reaction to this very accuracy. Joyce's characters use registers of language uncompromisingly appropriate to their social situations and psychological states; this shocked literary convention. They exhibit moral and social attitudes that are also an authentic expression of their position in society, and this too was found distasteful. They walk down named streets and enter named and known Dublin pubs and restaurants—and proprietors of real pubs and restaurants might well sue if they felt they or their establishments had been libeled.

But Joyce exacts more from his language than mere verisimilitude, as a few examples will show. Take, for instance, the mention of a "broken harmonium" among the household furniture in "Eveline." There is no apparent reason why this should not have been a fully working piano or any other musical instrument that would give texture to the naturalist background, but a "broken harmonium" is at once an authentic detail and also draws attention to the broken harmony of this household, with its long-suffering mother dead and its violent father growing more cantankerous and brutal by the week. If we wish to be even more ingenious we might also see it as a thematic counterpoint to the Italian organ that sounded as Eveline's mother lay dying. In the same story the domestically trapped and exploited Eveline meets an open-hearted man–aptly but not accidentally called Frank–who becomes her sweetheart and with whom she plans to elope. Joyce could have had them meet in almost any location in Dublin but in fact when they first see each other he is "standing at the gate" of his lodgings. The gate is an authentic detail, but it also combines realism and symbolism. Frank is Eveline's gateway to a new life, a way out of the dusty tired existence in which she is confined. But she will not take this exit: at the end of the story she remains trapped behind the iron railings at the North Wall docks, incapable of passing through.

Such examples demonstrate how Joyce's superbly alert and intelligent creativity could invest everyday objects with a deeper thematic and symbolic significance. The same alertness also enabled him to choose details which, while entirely realistic and unobtrusive in themselves, had preexisting associations that could extend the symbolic, historical and even mythical dimensions of his stories. This alertness had its cost, for Joyce took scholarly pains to get the facts he wanted. Writing to his brother from Trieste about "A Painful Case" he asked "Are the police at Sydney Parade of the *D* division? Would the city ambulance be called out to Sydney Parade for an accident? Would an accident at Sydney Parade be treated at Vincent's Hospital?" These questions seem prompted by a desire for exactitude for its own sake, to sustain the contract of verisimilitude upon which realism depends. But consider a further set of questions he poses about "Ivy Day in the Committee Room" in the same letter: "Are Aungier St and Wicklow in the Royal Exchange Ward? Can a municipal election take place in October?" It may appear that, once again, accuracy for the sake of accuracy is at issue. But why *should* he want Wicklow Street to be in the Royal Exchange Ward? And why is it important that a municipal election should take place in October? In answering these questions we see how Joyce selects his naturalistic details so as to exploit their symbolic significance. "Ivy Day in the Committee Room" is set in an Irish Party (i.e., nationalist) committee room during a local election in 1902, and it is dominated by the absent presence of the great Irish Parliamentary leader, the Wicklow-born Charles Stewart Parnell, known as the "Uncrowned King" of Ireland, who died in October 1891, a few months after the majority of his Party had rejected him (in a Westminster committee room) following a divorce action in which he was co-respondent. Joyce thought Parnell had been betrayed by his followers and that since then the Irish Party had declined into a time-serving gang of self-interested trimmers, represented in this story by the candidate "Tricky Dicky" Tierney who, it is suspected, will so compromise his nationalist principles as to support a loyal address to King Edward VII on the next royal visit. Thus in the Royal Exchange Ward is the Uncrowned King of Ireland, who was overthrown for one monogamous relationship, exchanged for the Crowned King of enemy England, who is notorious for his sexual promiscuity. By choosing Wicklow Street for the location of the Committee Room and by placing the election on 6 October, the very anniversary of Parnell's death, Joyce deftly keeps the memory of Parnell fresh throughout the story; by making the constituency the "Royal Exchange Ward" he ironically underlines the continuing betrayal of Parnell, and all he stood for, by his unworthy successors.

V

As we shall see, Joyce uses a similar technique by placing Mr Duffy in Chapelizod, so ironically associating him with Tristan and Iseult, in his reference to the Blessed Margaret Mary Alacoque in "Eveline," the description of the harp in "Two Gallants," and by organizing "Grace" as a parody of Dante's *Divine Comedy*. Such contrasts add another layer to the ironic texture of the stories, but Joyce did not intend the ironies to be infinitely regressive. If symbolism (as in "Two Gallants"), history (as in "Ivy Day"), or myth (as in "A Painful Case") are used to point up the inadequacies of the present, they also point up that present inadequacy *is* inadequate—that life provides better examples of how to live. The characters sense this too; all of them are looking for some larger fulfilment outside the dull, circumscribed limits of their everyday lives, for adventure, for excitement, for the sense of "life."

This point is sometimes overlooked by critics who see Joyce primarily as a destructive satirist, lacerating the obtuse and cowardly venalities of his fellow-citizens with sarcasm, irony, and parody. Joyce saw his mission as ultimately constructive. The letters he wrote at the time of composition echo in more sober language Stephen Dedalus's ambitions to constitute the "uncreated conscience of my race." If he chose Dublin as "the centre of paralysis" it was because, as we have seen, he wanted "to write a chapter of the moral history of my country."

Something of the spirit in which he approached what he saw as Dublin paralysis, and the implications it had for him, is conveyed in an incident in his contemporaneous novel *Stephen Hero*, in which Stephen watches three clerks playing billiards: "the hopeless pretence of those three lives before him, their unredeemable servility made the back of Stephen's eyes feel burning hot." Stephen's "burning eyes" are caused by mixed emotions, emotions close to those experienced by the boy at the end of "Araby," who on perceiving himself "a creature driven and derided by vanity," recalls that his "eyes burned with anguish and anger." Anguish and anger are recurring emotions in the stories and seem to be those that animated Joyce in writing them: anger at the waste of wasted lives; anguish at the servility which constrains the liberating act that is always a potential, and so keeps them wasted.

Joyce's artistic challenge in *Dubliners* is to excite sympathy for characters who appear hopeless, and to render significant lives that seem without significance, and to do this without falling into pathos. For his anguish has nothing sentimental about it. Joyce's keen sense of the false and meretricious, the sharp and probing exactitude of his ironies, will never allow complacent indulgence. His stories create a carefully wrought tension between a sympathetic anguish and a satire generated by anger. To exaggerate one at the expense of the other is to upset his taut balance.

He reveals enough about even the most unpleasant of his antiheroes to make their conduct comprehensible if not excusable. Mrs Mooney of "The Boarding House," who tricks one of her lodgers into marriage by pandering her daughter, has a husband who is a drunken wastrel, and from her point of view is attending to family affairs as best she can in these difficult circumstances. "Counterparts" closes sickeningly with Farrington's vicious assault on his small, defenseless son, but we have seen him trapped in a mind-numbing job, bullied by the diminutive tyrant, Alleyne, and humiliated throughout the afternoon and into the night. Even Eveline, perhaps the most inert example of passivity in *Dubliners*, is delivered from pathos by careful narrative strategies. Her choice does not reside in stark alternatives of fulfilment and stagnation. In choosing home rather than Buenos Ayres, she is consigning herself to a "life of commonplace sacrifices," but also honoring a promise to her dying mother. Moreover, the relationship with Frank is more ambiguous than it might have been: She is not entirely certain about the quality of his feelings towards her, reflecting that he "would give her life" and "perhaps love, too," and, although he has been in Dublin for some time, they are not to be married until they reach Argentina, so she must take on trust the word of a man who has already told her tall stories about the wild Patagonians.

VI

Joyce's favored narrative technique in *Dubliners* is the "free indirect style," in which the narrative takes on the language and sensibility of the person it is describing, and this also helps to hold the balance between sympathy and irony. The most sustained example of this method is in "Clay," where the narration throughout adopts the expressions and speech rhythms of the well-meaning and simple spinster Maria, but in all of the stories the narrative moves in and out of the character's consciousness, so that their point of view is unobtrusively smuggled into the text. This not only invites greater empathy but also makes possible a devastating deadpan irony, as apparently objective descriptions and observations disclose themselves to be expressions of the characters' bias and prejudice. At times (the three reveries at the end of "The Boarding House," for instance) this style develops into a "stream of consciousness" technique, through which we gain access not merely to the thoughts but also the thought processes of the characters. At other times the narrative may emphasize a thematic point about a character, as in "Counterparts" where the text stresses Farrington's anonymity and inconsequentiality as a mere cog in a large commercial world by constantly referring to him impersonally as "the man" rather than by name.

Through these techniques Joyce invites a sympathetic response to his flawed characters, but, as we have seen, he also wants to ascribe a moral and even spiritual aim to his enterprise. How, then, does he succeed in making his insignificant citizens significant and their trivial, and even shabby, actions important? This, again, is a matter of technique. By rigorous economy and selection he invests his texts with such a plurality of possible meanings that they set up symbolic and mythical reverberations which extend the reach and implications of the stories. Under the weight of such concentrated signification his characters and their actions take on a representative function without losing their particularity.

Joyce thought of this process in religious terms. One evening, as his brother Stanislaus was walking him to the National Library, he revealed what he had in mind:

> Don't you think there is a certain resemblance between the mystery of the Mass and what I am trying to do? I mean I am trying ... to give people some kind of intellectual pleasure or spiritual enjoyment by converting the bread of everyday life into something that has a permanent life of its own ... for their mental, moral, and spiritual uplift ...

And he spoke elsewhere of the "significance of trivial things."

As this analogy suggests, Joyce's symbolism is essentialist rather than transcendental; Aristotelian rather than Platonic. The Symbolist Movement, which flourished in the late nineteenth century, was Platonic or neo-Platonic in its underlying metaphysic. That is to say, it regarded the objects of the world as inferior representations of ideas which existed on a higher plane, in a transcendant realm. Joyce's symbolism owes more to Aristotle's idea of entelechy, that the soul is the form of all forms, that in and through particular examples one reaches the essential form. He did not at the time he was writing *Dubliners* describe this process in Aristotelian language, but, in a term borrowed from Christianity, as "epiphany." In *Stephen Hero* the epiphanic moment is conceived as the culminating apprehension of essential presence, the moment when "we recognise that it is *that* thing which it is. Its soul, its whatness leaps to us from the vestment of its appearance."

Epiphany means revelation, and is most familiar to Christians in the revelation of the Christ child to the Magi. What the Magi were ostensibly seeing was a realistic, even sordid sight, a newly born baby in the squalor of an animal house: what they were essentially seeing through and in this apparently trivial scene was the Logos, the Son of God, the Savior. So Joyce's art seeks to reveal essential truth in and through the everyday. He explained what he understood by an epiphany at some length in *Stephen Hero*. Passing by "one of those brown brick houses which seem the very incarnation of Irish paralysis," Stephen hears "the following fragment of colloquy out of which he received an impression keen enough to afflict his sensitiveness very severely":

> The Young Lady—(drawling discreetly) ... O, yes ... I was ... at the ... cha ... pel ...
>
> The Young Gentleman—(inaudibly) ... I ... (again inaudibly) ... I ...
>
> The Young Lady—(softly) ... O ... but you're ... ve ... ry ... wick ... ed ...
>
> This triviality made him think of collecting many such moments together in a book of epiphanies. By an epiphany he meant a sudden spiritual manifestation, whether in the vulgarity of speech or of gesture or in a memorable phase of the mind itself. He believed that it was for the man of letters to record these epiphanies with extreme care, seeing that they themselves are the most delicate and evanescent of moments. He told Cranly that the clock of the Ballast Office was capable of an epiphany ...

—... I will pass it time after time, allude to it, refer to it, catch a glimpse of it. It is only an item in the catalogue of Dublin's street furniture. Then all at once I see it and I know at once what it is: epiphany. ...

—Imagine my glimpses at that clock as the gropings of a spiritual eye which seeks to adjust its vision to an exact focus. The moment the focus is reached the object is epiphanised.

In *Dubliners* an epiphany may be an object correctly apprehended (as the coin at the end of "Two Gallants"), or a vulgarity of speech or of gesture (as at the last appearance of Mrs Kearney in "A Mother"), or a memorable phase of the mind itself (as at the end of "A Painful Case" or "The Dead"). In "Araby" a vulgarity of speech triggers an epiphany which is a memorable phase of the mind. Usually the epiphanies which depend upon vulgarity of speech or gesture–and by vulgarity Joyce does not necessarily mean grossness of expression, but that which, even if socially unobjectionable in manner, betrays a grossness of mind and feeling–reveal characters of limited sensibility and are experienced by the reader alone (as in "Counterparts," "The Boarding House" and "Grace"), whereas those which express a memorable phase of the mind are apprehended both by the reader and by characters of finer sensibility, such as Duffy and Gabriel Conroy. But in all cases these epiphanies are moments when the themes of the story find their exact focus, when the implications of the narrative suddenly manifest themselves.

VII

There have been many attempts to fit the individual stories of *Dubliners* into some larger pattern, especially since Joyce in his later works uses just such complex networks of mythological and symbolic allusions. Richard Levin and Charles Shattuck, taking their cue from the Homeric parallelism in *Ulysses*, try in their article "First Flight to Ithaca" to prove that *Dubliners* is also based on a Homeric pattern. Brewster Ghiselin argues in his "The Unity of *Dubliners*" that the stories are unified by repeated symbolic patterns, the chief of which are a desire by the trapped characters to escape to the East, and secular parodies of Christian sacraments, particularly the Eucharist. Perhaps the most energetic and ingenious of these attempts is Donald Torchiana's *Backgrounds for Joyce's "Dubliners"* which finds national, mythic, religious, and legendary references acting in the stories in a similar way to the paradigms in *Ulysses*. While these efforts often have splendid local successes in illuminating individual passages or references, most critics find that they fail in their larger claims. Too many elements in the stories have to be forced, twisted, or suppressed to achieve the supposed "unifying" pattern. Nor does the history of the stories confirm any such over-determined reading: they were written over an extended period when Joyce was feeling his way in fiction, and, although supremely precocious in his abilities, one detects a growing mastery and complexity in his texts as he proceeds.

Joyce himself offers a loose-knit general plan for the book, revealing that he had tried to present Dublin "under four of its aspects: childhood, adolescence, maturity and public life. The stories are arranged in this order." The stories of childhood are "The Sisters," "An Encounter," and "Araby"; those of adolescence, "Eveline," "After the Race," "Two Gallants," and "The Boarding House"; those of maturity, "A Little Cloud," "Counterparts," "Clay," and "A Painful Case"; and those of public life, "Ivy Day in the Committee Room," "A Mother," and "Grace." "The Dead" had not been composed when Joyce divulged this schema, and stands out in the collection by virtue of its late composition, its length, tone, and positioning.

The childhood tales differ from the others in being written in the first person and seem potentially more optimistic. This optimism is, however, illusory: the boy in "An Encounter" looks for adventure and excitement but finds only a sadistic pederast. The hero of "Araby" sublimates his erotic puppy love into a chivalric crusade, but discovers himself to be "a creature driven and derided by vanity." In these stories we see Dublin paralysis numbing childish wonder and hope as they come up against disappointment and disillusion. For the paralysis in *Dubliners* is progressive: the children learn disillusion and limitation; the adolescents are shown at a moment of entrapment or failure to escape; by maturity the characters are firmly fixed in an unsatisfying routine; and public life reveals that society at large is treacherous, mercenary, and inert.

Within this larger frame the theme of paralysis is expressed through a number of motifs or image clusters which disclose themselves in a series of oppositions: Death/Life ("The Sisters," "Clay," and "The Dead"); Past/Present ("Eveline," "A Little Cloud," "Ivy Day," and "The Dead"); Blindness/Sight ("Araby," "After the Race," "Eveline," "A Painful Case," "The Dead"); Dark/Light ("The Sisters," "An Encounter," "Two Gallants"); Cold/Warmth ("Araby," "Ivy Day," and "The Dead"); English superiority/Irish subservience ("Araby," "After the Race," "A Little Cloud," "Counterparts," "Ivy Day"). Green, the Irish national color, is constantly associated with frustration or perversion, and brown with Dublin paralysis. While there is not space to explore these motifs in full, nor to follow through all their allusive and symbolic possibilities, a brief account of the individual stories may help to indicate something of the book's richness and art.

VIII

"The Sisters" sets the tone for what follows and its two printed states afford us an insight into Joyce's fictional procedures. In the *Homestead* version the boy finds himself "by Providence" outside the priest's house for three nights, although on the fourth night, when the priest dies, "a whimsical kind of Providence" leads him to another part of the city. In the final version all references to Providence have disappeared, and we find instead three other terms:

> There was no hope for him this time: it was the third stroke. Night after night I had passed the house ... Every night as I gazed up at the window I said softly to myself the word *paralysis*. It had always sounded strangely in my ears like the word *gnomon* in the Euclid and the word *simony* in the catechism. But now it sounded to me like the name of some maleficent and sinful being. It filled me with fear and yet I longed to be nearer to it and to look upon its deadly work.

The whimsicality of a vague providence has given way to a far darker world of paralysis, sin, and maleficence. The boy picks out three words—*paralysis*, *simony*, and *gnomon*—which seem strange to him. On a realistic level this is perfectly feasible: two are from the Greek, the other derives from a proper name, and all fall exotically on ears used to English. But, as always in Joyce, the text is signalling more than a surface verisimilitude. Paralysis is not merely odd-sounding, nor only disturbing in the association it arouses; it is a term that infuses *Dubliners*. Thus the word, introduced and emphasized in the very first paragraph of the book, exerts a thematic pressure not merely upon this story, but upon the collection as a whole.

The term "simony" has a similar function. It is derived from the name of Simon Magus, who sold spiritual gifts for material gain. Perhaps the most obvious example of such a transaction occurs in "Grace" where, under the casuistic guidance of Father Purdon, theology is adapted to business interests, but if we define "spiritual" as all that Joyce understood by "life," a term that as we have seen occurs several times in each story, and which takes on associations of fulfilment, freedom, and self-expression, we realize that simony is at work in each story as these values are compromised or sacrificed to a morally bankrupt prudence.

Finally gnomon, an even more specialized term—but one which the boy would have encountered at school, where the geometry of the Greek mathematician Euclid was still standard. The gnomon in Euclid is the minimum part of a parallelogram—two sides and a common angle—needed to construct the whole figure. Some critics have seen in this a hint as to how Joyce structured his stories: he gives us as much as we need to know, but we as readers supply what the text omits. An example of this occurs in "Clay" when Maria makes the wrong choice among the Hallowe'en symbols. Since we read the story through her limited consciousness in the free indirect style, and since she is in any case blindfolded, her choice is not named, but the title and narrative directs us not merely to the saucer of clay, but to the associations of death that it signifies. We can therefore construct the larger meaning of this key incident, although the text leaves it indeterminate, and the protagonist remains ignorant of its implications.

"The Sisters" is in many ways the most puzzling story in the collection. It seems to be an account of a priest's inadequate vocation, or of his influence upon a young boy, but the title directs our attention not to him but to his two (literally) down-at-heel sisters, ostensibly attendant figures, peripheral to the action and themes. Moreover, the nature of the priest's inadequacy is left uncertain, and his relationship with the boy (or, rather, the boy's with him) vague. However, a comparison between the two versions of the story published in this edition helps to draw out some of the underlying themes.

In both versions the boy reads Father Flynn's death notice. In the *Homestead* this runs: July 2nd, 189- The Rev. James Flynn (formerly of St. Ita's Church), aged 65 years, R. I. P." In an interim draft Joyce provided an exact year, "July 2nd 1890," but named the church "S. Catherine's Church, Meath Street." He retained this in the final version, but altered the day and year of death to "July 1st, 1895." Why should he have made these apparently slight and capricious changes? Let us begin with the day. July 2nd is dedicated to the Visitation of the Blessed Virgin, an allusion that has little significance in this story, but July 1st is the Feast of the Most Precious Blood of Our Lord, a date that is ironically appropriate to a priest who has broken a chalice, the vessel consecrated to hold that Blood. Joyce again draws our attention to this accident in another emendation: in the *Homestead* the dead Father Flynn carries a rosary, but in the final version this has become an "idle" chalice.

By letting Flynn die in 1895 rather than 1890 Joyce makes his death coincide with the centenary of the founding of Maynooth, the most important Catholic seminary in Ireland. Moreover, since he died at the age of sixty-five, he stands an even chance of having been born in 1829, the year of Catholic Emancipation. His life is therefore coterminous with the revived Catholic Church in Ireland, and his paralysis, and the effect it has on others, symbolic of the influence on Ireland of the Church's influence.

Flynn's inadequacy as a priest and teacher is also ironically suggested in the two names given to his parish church, for both St Ita and St Catherine would have offered the contrast with Father Flynn that Joyce presumably sought. Whereas Flynn mystifies and alienates the boy (and himself) with his overawed account of Catholic dogma (so complicated it required books as thick as post office directories to elucidate it), St Ita was so convinced of her faith and so famous as a religious teacher of the young that she was called "the foster-mother of the saints of Ireland." Yet this is not to Joyce's purpose. "St. Ita's Church" was in fact a change introduced by the editor of the *Homestead* for the very reason that there is no St Ita's church in central Dublin. When Joyce was in a position to reaffirm his version of the text, he insisted on his chosen example of successful Christian teaching, and named St Catherine, who was the patron saint of an actual Dublin church, and who, among other examples of piety, is said to have refuted fifty pagan philosophers who tried to convince her of the errors of Christianity.

The *Homestead* version of "The Sisters" is roughly half as long as the final story, and is mainly a character sketch of the priest. There is little about his relationship with the boy and less about his sisters. One of the most significant of the later additions is the boy's dream, in which he imagines his and the priest's roles reversed, hears Flynn's confession, and absolves "the simoniac of his sin." The boy, who has picked up only hints and enigmatically unfinished sentences, has no real knowledge of what that sin constitutes, but his subconscious senses that something has been wrong, and that Flynn's "great wish" for his vocation will implicate him in the priest's spiritual paralysis. In elucidating this episode Donald Torchiana rightly directs our attention to the uncle's description of the boy as a "rosicrucian" and suggests that Joyce is offering in the paralyzed Flynn a pessimistic parallel to W. B. Yeats's essay "The Body of Father Christian Rosencrux." Yeats's essay proposes that another priest, the fifteenth-century sage Father Rosencrux, who according to legend lies in a state of suspended animation in his tomb, is about to reawaken, so symbolizing a hoped-for regeneration of imaginative energy in modern times. Joyce's Flynn, "truculent, grey and massive," presents a somber foil to Yeats's optimism, suggesting that the paralyzed weight of Irish Catholicism will stifle or pervert the country's imagination.

The title of the story directs our attention to Flynn's sisters. If the priest symbolizes the Catholic Church in Ireland, they represent the sacrifices the people of Ireland have made in serving that church. Ill-educated, ill-dressed, they hold their brother in a superstitious but puzzled awe, and if with him they have escaped through the Church's agency from the Dublin slum of Irishtown to Great Britain Street (the names suggesting a loss of roots, identity, and allegiance), that simoniac bargain has brought a niggardly reward. Their brother dies a "crossed" and "disappointed" man; they linger on poor and shabby.

Flynn's influence on the boy is more ambiguous. Some critics have argued that it blights his future life, and that there are affinities between him and Gabriel Conroy in "The Dead." It is possible to overstress this: even before the story begins he has learned to mistrust the priest's words (doubting his prognostication of death), adopts the Joycean resources of silence and cunning by studiously refusing to react when told of Flynn's death, and is well able to place Cotter as "Tiresome old fool!" Nevertheless, although he feels a sense of release at the priest's death, he cannot overcome his fascination with his "maleficent and sinful" paralysis and longs "to be nearer to it and to look upon its deadly work." His dream, in which his soul recedes into "some pleasant and vicious region," also suggests that he has been contaminated by Flynn's disappointed deviance.

"An Encounter," in its account of a failed quest by truant schoolboys, takes up the theme of the necessity for escape, for life, and the failure to find it. But interlinked with this theme is the suggestion that repression results in unnatural behavior, which leads in turn to an even more excessive repression. Thus the protagonist seeks out stories of the wild west *faute de mieux*, for although "remote from my nature ... at least, they opened doors of escape" and Joe Dillon, the most unruly of his companions, finally accepts the extreme discipline of the priesthood. Repression at school intensifies the "hunger ... for wild sensations," which, like the older Dubliners, he supposes "must be sought abroad."

But instead of finding adventure in their journey to the Pigeon House, an old fort and now a Dublin power station, the boys turn aside from their goal and encounter a green-eyed pederast whose perversion grows out of repression and whose conversation, "slowly circling round and round," is caught in the sadistic paralysis of its own obsessiveness. At the center of his rambling monologue is the insistence on total and violent repression: all that is "rough and unruly" must be chastised, any relationship between the sexes, even merely talking together, is to be punished by a whipping "such ... as no boy ever got in this world." The story ends with the boy's epiphany, the perception that his quest has failed, of the need for subterfuge, and the fear of the perversity that repression brings.

"Araby" also takes the form of a quest, not to a power station, but an exotic-sounding bazaar, modelled on an Eastern souk. A motif of the story is blindness and sight, and forms of the verbs "to see," "to gaze," "to watch," "to look," and "to imagine" permeate the story, as do the nouns "eye," "light," "lamp," and "blind." The sight of Mangan's sister, her brown dress artificially lit and romanticized by lamplight, with an erotic touch of petticoat, becomes transformed into an image of maidenhood that takes on chivalric and religious connotations. Thus the young protagonist imagines that "I bore my chalice safely through a throng of foes," and like a knight on a romantic quest sets out for the bazaar to bring her back some love token. He arrives to find the hall being plunged into darkness, and to overhear a flirtation shorn of any romantic or chivalric connotations in a banal exchange that recalls the conversation described by Stephen as epiphanic in *Stephen Hero*. It is a moment of epiphany for the boy. He has reached an empty chapel perilous; the lights go out but paradoxically darkness gives him a clearer image of himself than that produced by the sublimated gazings and artificial light of the previous weeks: "Gazing up into the darkness I saw myself as a creature driven and derided by vanity: and my eyes burned with anguish and anger."

IX

"Eveline," which we have already discussed briefly, opens the section dealing with adolescence. The short first paragraph reveals Eveline's state of mind: the verb "invade" suggests her defensive apprehension, the dustiness and tiredness her lack of energy. Joyce has moved from the first person narration to the third, but, as will frequently happen in subsequent stories, uses the free indirect style, whereby his narration imitates the language and thought processes of the protagonist rather than those of an omniscient narrator.

The victimized Eveline attempts to make the best out of meager childhood recollections, and her passivity and timidity make her still ready to find some value in her wretched existence: "now that she was about to leave it she did not find it a wholly undesirable life." The final version of "Eveline" differs from that in the *Homestead* (see Appendix) in adding to the "broken harmonium" and other household furniture a "coloured print of the promises made to Blessed Margaret Mary Alacoque." Why should Joyce have gone to the trouble of introducing this detail? To answer this we need to know that Margaret Mary Alacoque was a seventeenth-century French orphan who was treated harshly by her relatives. She joined a convent but was constantly berated for her clumsiness and slowness. Then, in December 1673, she experienced a divine visitation in which Christ told her that mankind had ignored His love; on a subsequent occasion He put her hand into His heart, and on another informed her that she would be a sacrificial victim for the lack of charity among the other nuns. As a result of these visions the veneration of the Sacred Heart became a worldwide Catholic practice.

There are clear parallels with Eveline. She has lost a mother and is harshly treated for supposed incompetence by her father (whose behavior gives her, in another addition to the final version, "palpitations" of the heart) and by the manageress of the shop where she works. She too has a vision—not of the open-hearted Christ, but of the "openhearted" Frank—although, unlike the Blessed Margaret Mary, she is unable to transform her life through this experience. Like Margaret Mary she will be a victim and scapegoat, but unlike her she cannot sustain herself in the experience of love. Whereas Margaret Mary put her hand into the burning heart of Christ, Eveline fears that Frank's love will extinguish her heart: "All the seas of the world tumbled about her heart. He was drawing her into them: he would drown her."

A central theme of "After the Race" appears in the first paragraph, where the "gratefully oppressed" Irish spectators make a "channel of poverty and inaction" while "the continent sped its wealth and industry." Jimmy Doyle, a *nouveau riche* young Irishman, seems to have escaped the poverty of the majority of his countrymen, but this escape is more apparent than real. Although glad to be seen in dashing international company, he takes a back seat and is obliged "to make a deft guess at the meaning" of the conversation in the car. While the others are in good spirits, for sound commercial or gastronomic reasons, he is "too excited to be genuinely happy."

Genuine is a word that recurs in the story, for Jimmy is an example of the difficulties of authenticity for the deracinated *nouveau riche*, particularly in an Irish context. Jimmy's crisis of identity is both social and national. His father, starting from humble beginnings and as "an advanced nationalist," has made his money by collaborating with the agents of British imperialism through police contracts. Jimmy has been educated in England and at Dublin University, which at that time had close links with the ruling Anglophile Protestant Ascendancy. Although this deracinating education involved a (controlled) extravagance, his father sees even this in materialist terms, and is "commercially satisfied at having secured for his son qualities often unpurchasable." Jimmy continues this mix of social climber and materialist. He cultivates Ségouin as a Continental sophisticate, but also hopes to make something out of him. Whether Jimmy makes "pots of money" from Ségouin or Ségouin from Jimmy remains outside the story, but the Frenchman's manipulation of him in the restaurant and the result of the card game augurs ill for the Irishman's investment.

Like Jimmy, Dublin is pretending to a position it can hardly maintain, and that night "wore the mask of a capital," but the Kingstown ticket collector automatically unmasks Jimmy by saluting him as the Irishman of the cosmopolitan party. On board Farley's yacht, Jimmy's eagerness for "genuine" excitement leads him to misconstrue a drunken dance as "seeing life," but characteristically he feels "obscurely the lack of an audience" to endorse his pretensions. The card game is fought out between Ségouin, the representative of Ireland's undependable ally, and Routh, representative of the exploitative colonizing power, while Jimmy, the "gratefully oppressed" representative Irishman, unable to compete in this company, collaborates asininely in his own heavy losses since "he frequently mistook his cards and the other men had to calculate his I. O. U's for him." His bitter epiphany occurs in the grey light of daybreak as he tries not to think about his folly and his debts.

"Two Gallants," the third story in the adolescent group, presents a case of arrested development, since Lenehan, although affecting the style and behavior of a gallant, is nearly thirty-one. He is introduced after an opening paragraph which with its deftly orchestrated assonance and bilabial and sibilant alliteration gives the lie to Joyce's assertion about the "meanness" of his style. Lenehan is a sponge, and Corley a police spy, and both are economically and deftly established. Lenehan's clothes express youth but he is balding, greying, falling "into rotundity," and has a "ravaged look." His fellow gallant preys upon servant girls and it becomes apparent that it is not the sexual conquest but the petty material gains that interest him: "Cigarettes every night she'd bring me and paying the tram out and back."

While Corley eyes passing girls, Lenehan fixes "on the large faint moon" and Joyce uses the moon in this story to establish a relationship between the gallants and women. Lenehan immediately asks Corley if he will "pull it off all right," although the narrative will not reveal what the "it" is until the final sentence. Shortly after Corley's account of a former conquest who is now a prostitute (a sordid affair which Lenehan affects to dramatize as a grand passion) they pass a street musician whose harp, "heedless that her coverings had fallen about her knees, seemed weary alike of the eyes of strangers and of her master's hands. One hand played in the bass the melody of *Silent, O Moyle* while the other hand careered in the treble after each group of notes." Harpists are common enough in Dublin, but Joyce is concerned with more than local detail. The harp, the national emblem of Ireland, is here personified as a naked girl worn out by her exploitation, and this association with the women exploited by the two gallants, one an unprincipled leech and the other a police informer, adds national as well as sexual betrayal to the theme of the story. The song, "Silent, O Moyle," telling of the woes of the sea god's daughter, Fionnuala, while Ireland lies paralyzed in pagan sleep, also contributes to this idea, as does the placing of the scene close to the ultra-Unionist and Ascendancy Kildare Street Club.

After Corley has departed with the girl, Lenehan circles back on himself to end up in Rutland Square, where the story began, his journey symbolizing his aimless existence. In the cheap refreshment bar he attains an insight into the inadequacy of this way of life: "He would be thirty-one in November. Would he never get a good job? ... all hope had not left him. He felt better after having eaten than he had felt before, less weary of his life, less vanquished in spirit. He might yet be able to settle down in some snug corner and live happily if he could only come across some good simpleminded girl with a little of the ready." Lenehan is perceptive enough to comprehend the poverty of his life, but too deeply conditioned by his parasitical assumptions to conceive any way out other than the ultimate sponge of a mercenary marriage with (and we note the adjectives) "some good simpleminded girl." This is Joyce's irony at its most deadpan.

As Lenehan walks back into town he begins to suspect that he has been double-crossed, for, as became clear when he asked to view the girl, there is no trust between these two gallant companions. Then he spots Corley but, convinced that he has failed, undergoes agonies of apprehension until the latter "with a grave gesture ... extended a hand towards the light and, smiling, opened it slowly to the gaze of his disciple. A small gold coin shone in the palm." This epiphany reveals that the whole evening's "gallantry" has been devoted to extracting the meager savings of an underpaid slavey.

"Two Gallants" told of the exploitation of a girl by two men but the narrative is oblique on this point until the end. "The Boarding House" tells of the exploitation of a man by two women, and the text itself becomes oblique and ambiguous. In his presentation of Mrs Mooney, "The Madam" of the boarding house in more senses than one, Joyce again exhibits his superb and unsentimental balance. After the breakdown of her unsatisfactory marriage to a drunken failure, Mrs Mooney has had to act decisively. Her concern is to see her daughter married and off her hands, and here the decisiveness of her character schools itself to a calculated indirection of language. Seeing that "Polly was very lively," she decides "to give her the run of the young men." The full implications of "lively" and "run" are not explored by the text, nor does Mrs Mooney spell them out even to herself. Polly, described as looking "like a little perverse madonna," understands this and acts her part—literally so at the Sunday night soirées, where she performs suggestive music hall songs. At last the bait is taken; Mrs Mooney, detecting "something" going on, "watched the pair and kept her own counsel." Polly knows she is being watched "but still her mother's persistent silence could not be misunderstood. There had been no open complicity between mother and daughter, no open understanding but ... still Mrs Mooney did not intervene."

The hinting at what is unspoken is constitutive of the text throughout the story. Even at the "frank" interview between Mrs Mooney and Polly both "had been made awkward by her not wishing to receive the news in too cavalier a fashion or to seem to have connived and Polly had been made awkward not merely because allusions of that kind always made her awkward but also because she did not wish it to be thought that in her wise innocence she had divined the intention behind her mother's tolerance." Even here Polly's seduction remains obliquely "the news" and "allusions of that kind."

The story ends with three reveries. Mrs Mooney's is one of calculating the odds. She does not suppose for a moment that Doran wants to marry her daughter, but she judges that she has public opinion on her side and that he will not dare risk the scandal and his job. Once more she automatically suppresses the fact of the seduction with a general circumlocution: she "would have lots of time to have the matter out with Mr Doran." The second reverie, that of the unfortunate Doran, shows that she has calculated correctly. Although he has "a notion that he was being had," transfers most of the guilt to Polly, and longs "to ascend through the roof and fly away to another country," he is "pushed ... downstairs step by step" by the fear of dismissal and an open disgrace. Once again a Dubliner balks the chance of escape and self-fulfilment by allowing lack of will and material considerations to ensnare him.

The story ends with Polly's reverie in which the unspoken indirections of the text find their most sublime expression. The recollection of her seduction of Doran leads to such intricate memories and future visions that she actually forgets what it has all been *for*, until she is wakened by her mother's call: "—Come down, dear. Mr Doran wants to speak to you. Then she remembered what she had been waiting for." Mrs Mooney, as she calculated, has executed her business in time to catch "the short twelve" mass at Marlborough Street Church, a church (as Joyce well knew) dedicated to the Immaculate Conception. With this hidden allusion Joyce sets up an ironic contrast between the

Blessed Virgin and the now deflowered "perverse madonna" of Hardwicke Street.

X

"A Little Cloud" is the first of the "adult life" stories, and contrasts two kinds of would-be writers, Little Chandler, who imagines himself writing melancholy and wistful "Celtic" poems for a select audience, and Ignatius Gallaher, a journalist whose success depends upon popularity. Both men's discourse is studded with clichés appropriate to their temperaments. Moreover, whereas Chandler vaguely idealizes or ignores the ugly (sunlight gilds the dust "on the untidy nurses and decrepit old men" and he shuts out the "verminlike" urchins in Henrietta Street), Gallaher dispassionately recounts the vices of all the European capitals "in a calm historian's tone." The over-delicate Chandler, consistently described in diminutive and even infantile terms, has not the passion to make himself a writer; Gallaher has not enough soul to make himself more than a popular and vulgar journalist.

Their meeting at Corless's is sharply observed social comedy. Little Chandler comes to resent Gallaher's patronizing manner, but has difficulty in catching the barman's eye, waters his whiskey, and flushes like a child, having "upset the equipoise of his delicate nature." He returns home to his prim, cold wife, haunted by Gallaher's account of sexual license and voluptuous Jewesses, reads one of Byron's earliest and most sentimental poems, and finally responds to real, unsentimentalized life by shouting at his crying son with disastrous results, for he cannot shut this child out of his consciousness as he has done to the children in Henrietta Street. Gallaher had fled Dublin amidst a financial scandal; Little Chandler, longing for escape, feels himself bound to remain since he is still paying for the domestic furniture he detests.

"A Little Cloud" ends with a weak father shouting at his small son; "Counterparts" ends with a strong father beating his small son mercilessly. We have already spoken of Farrington, and the ways in which Joyce manages to retain our sympathy even for so brutal a character. A man of strength and some spirit, he is trapped in an office presided over by the diminutive Alleyne, who has already bullied "little Peake" out of his job to make way for his nephew, and is out to get Farrington because he caught him mimicking him. The consciousness of entrapment, the impotent rage against it, and the hatred and self-hatred that it engenders, lead Farrington out on the spree in a desperate search for "life." Here a reckless generosity is an overcompensation for a day of indignities, but cannot save him from the final and greatest indignity when even his physical strength, the one source of pride left to him, is overcome by a younger Englishman. Like Little Chandler, he feels inadequate when confronted with English superiority; like him he is unhappily married, and, like him, the promise of all that life denies appears as sexual voluptousness and eastern promise, Miss Delacour, "a middleaged woman of Jewish appearance," and later the plump-armed London woman. Like Eveline, although in a different way, Farrington is conscious of the inadequacy of his life, but like her remains trapped in it, allowing his discontent no expression in meaningful action but in sterile violence that finally finds its target not in the dwarfish but powerful Alleyne, but his small and powerless son.

"Clay" consistently uses the free indirect style to portray Maria, the aging cook whose witch-like appearance on this Hallowe'en is belied by her good nature. Maria's tragedy is that with her maternal and domestic virtues she remains a spinster. She works in the "Dublin by Lamplight" laundry, a charitable Protestant institution for fallen women, although Maria with her tidy little body, her spick and span ways, her peace-keeping propensities, and her nice perception of social difference, is certainly not one of them. But if she is not sexually promiscuous she is sexually frustrated. When one of the girls makes her annual joke that Maria will get the ring, the symbol of marriage, from the Hallowe'en barmbrack, her reaction is unexpected. Although she "had to laugh and say she didn't want any ring or man either," when she laughed "her greygreen eyes sparkled with disappointed shyness." The "disappointed shyness" signals that though said "for so many Hallow Eves," the words still touch a sensitive spot.

This sensitivity reappears when, lingering over her purchase in the cake shop, a "stylish young lady" behind the counter asks her "was it weddingcake she wanted to buy." This reference to matrimony causes Maria to "blush and smile" and her perturbation is increased in the tram when a tipsy gentleman engages her in conversation. In favoring him "with demure nods and hems" she forgets her cake, and discovering its loss later, recalls "how confused the gentleman ... had made her" and colors "with shame and vexation and disappointment." Vexation and disappointment at losing the expensive cake we understand–but "shame" (apparently her first emotion) again suggests some suppressed sexual or matrimonial interest.

At Joe's house Maria's gifts as peace-maker fail to reconcile Joe to his brother Alphy. She has already worried about his drinking. Joe resembles a milder kind of Farrington–he has even given a smart answer to his manager–and he seems prone to anger (over nutcrackers, over his brother). The epiphany occurs when in the Hallowe'en game Maria chooses not the ring but a saucer of clay, a death symbol, the significance of which happily escapes her. After this she sings ("blushing very much") a romantic aria from Balfe's *The Bohemian Girl*, and in a Freudian slip for which we should now be prepared, repeats the first verse, a dream of fulfilled and reciprocal love. This is a moment of sentiment that could teeter into the sentimental, and the narrative brilliantly retains both possibilities by switching attention to the tippling and maudlin Joe, who is so overcome with tears "that he could not find what he was looking for and in the end he had to ask his wife to tell him where the corkscrew was."

If "Clay" tells of a reluctant spinster, "A Painful Case" is the story of an apparently confirmed bachelor, the fastidious and superior Mr Duffy, who rejects the love of a married woman and so drives her to drink and suicide. Scorning his fellow men, Duffy prefers to live away from the city and Joyce situates him in the village of Chapelizod, so associating him (the name is derived from "Chapel of Iseult") with Tristan and Iseult, whose passionate and adulterous love affair has been celebrated by medieval poets such as Béroul and Malory, and in more recent times by Wagner, Swinburne, Arnold, Bédier, and Binyon. By evoking this legend Joyce sets Mr Duffy's sterile restraint in ironic contrast to one of the most compelling love stories in world literature, and so underscores the poverty of his modern hero's emotional life.

The description of Duffy's room emphasizes his austere and contemptuous nature: overlooking a disused distillery, a place from which all spirit has departed, it is uncarpeted, pictureless, all iron or cane, angular and mainly in black and white. His books are arranged by size, and he has a complete edition of Wordsworth, a famous solitary. Although he retains a copy of the Maynooth Catechism, he is a man with "neither companions nor friends, church nor creed" and "his life rolled out evenly–an adventureless tale." Only his eyes, eager to greet a redeeming instinct in others, but "often disappointed," hint at a vulnerability in his character, and Mrs Sinico's eyes are also significant, "revealing for an instant a temperament of great sensibility." A relationship develops between them, her companionship acting like "a warm soil about an exotic," but he recoils when she catches up his hand passionately, and breaks off the affair.

Having turned down this chance to emotionalize his mental life, he begins to read Friedrich Nietzsche, a philosopher with an even more extreme scorn of the herd than his own, so that his initial reaction to the death of Mrs Sinico, and her evident inebriation, is one of disgust. But the apparently bald language of the newspaper report is susceptible to more than one interpretation. It reveals that she died of "shock and a sudden failure of the heart's action," but Duffy has cause to wonder whether the crucial shock to her heart was that administered by the locomotive or the one he delivered in breaking off the relationship four years before. Mrs Sinico was killed while going out "to buy spirits," an artificial stimulant to replace the emotional spirits provided by her affection for Duffy, who remains to contemplate "the empty distillery" from his window.

The story concludes with Duffy's epiphany. Too late, he realizes that Mrs Sinico could have enabled him to escape from the solitude of his over-determined and over-detached life, but he has let the moment pass. He "gnawed the rectitude of his life; he felt that he had been outcast from life's feast," and he is left in a condition he always supposed he wanted, but now no longer desires: "He felt that he was alone."

XI

With "Ivy Day in the Committee Room" we move to the stories of public life. As we have noted, this one takes place on 6 October 1902, eleven years to the day since Parnell's death, and far more is going on in it than the apparently desultory conversations between a group of cynical canvassers while they wait to be paid by "Tricky Dicky Tierney," the slippery candidate for municipal office. Each detail in the story contributes to a contrast between the soulless mediocrity of contemporary Ireland and the integrity of the Parnellite era. Although he has been dead for over a decade, Parnell's absence is more potent than the representatives of the present, his memory being silently evoked by the very title (recalling Committee Room 15), by the ivy leaves worn in his memory, by the location in Wicklow Street, and by the name of the electoral ward.

The themes find their fullest expression in a discussion over the royal visit. Henchy defends this on wholly materialistic grounds: what the country needs is capital and the "King's coming here will mean an influx of money into this country." When Lyons objects that Edward's life is immoral he is waved aside: "—This is Parnell's anniversary, said Mr O'Connor, and don't let us stir up any bad blood. We all respect him now that he's dead and gone." "Parnell ... is dead," and in that safe and fixed state can be paid lip-service while the betrayal of his policies goes on unabated. Old Jack, the caretaker, looks back to the days of Parnell as to a more vibrant age: "—Musha, God be with them times! ... There was some life in it then." Those were days when Parnell kept the backbiting transacting Irish politicians in control: "... He was the only man that could keep that bag of cats in order," recalls Mr Henchy, "*Down, ye dogs! Lie down, ye curs!* That's the way he treated them."

Without this discipline self-interest holds dreary sway. The canvassers are supporting Tricky Dicky for the money alone. Tierney himself is habitually described in diminutive terms a "little hop-o'-my-thumb" who is "as tricky as they make 'em," yet this physical and moral dwarf is the contemporary representative of Parnell's party. His *métier* is backroom intrigue with a strong implication of financial impropriety, and his nationalist sentiments are so feeble that the Conservative Unionists have no qualms about supporting him. Nor is this the most sinister of his alliances, for besides enlisting the influential Father Burke as his nominator, he has dealings with the dubious Father Keon, a spoiled priest of ambiguous manner, who hobnobs with notorious political fixers. Burke and Keon, the representatives of the priests who helped hound Parnell, are now hand in glove with his corrupt and unworthy successors.

If the politicians of the present generation are bad, there seems to be even less hope in future generations. Tierney himself is in appropriate succession as the son of a hand-me-down bootlegger. The son of Old Jack, the caretaker, is a drunken wastrel; Joe Hynes's father was a "decent respectable man" but Hynes himself "is not nineteen carat" and may be spying for the rival candidate or even the Castle, like another patriot who is "a lineal descendant of Major Sirr ... a fellow now that'd sell his country for fourpence –aye!–and go down on his bended knee and thank the Almighty Christ he had a country to sell."

The theme of betrayal permeates the elegy, "The Death of Parnell," that Hynes is persuaded to recite at the end of the story. This is a brilliant *tour-de-force* by Joyce, a doggerel poem in the vein of the effusions that filled the pages of the Parnellite press at the time of Parnell's death, but which is so exact that it transcends mere parody. Over half of the poem is devoted to a denunciation of Irish treachery and parallels Parnell with Christ, describing how his Judas-like followers "smote their Lord or with a kiss / Betrayed him ...." The last two stanzas make tentative gestures towards the future: "his spirit may / Rise, like the Phoenix from the flames, / When breaks the dawning of the day." It "may" (not "will") be that Parnell's spirit will rise Phoenix-like, but no-one reading this story would take any bets on that. The Phoenix flames (the image also glances at the Fenian tradition) have guttered down to Old Jack's inadequate fire, the dawning of the day of destiny seems very far away, while Tricky Dicky buys his way into power and the younger generation take discontentedly to drink. The "pok" of the stout cork is Joyce's ironic comment on these proceedings: the canvassers have been lifted for a moment out of their shabby, compromised world, but to no purpose.

"A Mother" is Joyce's hard look at the Irish revival. It is no accident that Miss Kearney's name is Kathleen (Kathleen ni Houlihan is a symbol of Ireland) and the lame organizer of the concert is called Holohan. Kathleen is the vehicle for her mother's thwarted romanticism and social pretensions, and the road to success lies in the exploitation of the Irish-Ireland movement—a contemporary initiative to restore the Irish language and culture. Significantly the Kearneys' commitment to the movement goes no further than sending brief postcards and the mouthing of a few Gaelic clichés, for all Mrs Kearney's social and cultural pretensions, and all her planning for the concert, are grounded in a precise calculation of the financial outlay and returns. She dockets every item: Kathleen's dress, the sum she is to receive for playing, the dozen two-shilling complimentary tickets sent to friends. When the concert is a disaster, it is the expense she has been put to that first worries her, and her agitation feeds on the suspicion that Kathleen is not to be paid in full.

The account of the artistes' gathering on Saturday night is Joyce's social and psychological observation at its sharpest, and he brilliantly orchestrates the growing tension beneath the surface as Mrs Kearney's insistence upon her bond becomes more strident and embarrassing. In the final epiphany her carefully cultivated ivory manner shatters as she vulgarly abuses Holohan and is left impotently at the door "haggard with rage, arguing with her husband and daughter, gesticulating with them."

According to Joyce's brother "Grace," which begins in an underground lavatory, moves to a stale bedroom and ends in a church, is a parody of Dante's *Divine Comedy*. Certainly its irony, as it concerns the businessmen, seems more good-humoredly parodic than in many of the earlier stories; anger and anguish have given way to a wry depiction of things as they are. The theme of the story is the simoniac exchange of spiritual values for those of commerce, and the satire in the story is aimed at Father Purdon's populist perversion of the doctrine of grace.

The drunken tea-taster, Kernan, is one of the few Dubliners to take a pride in his work, although as "a commercial traveller of the old school" he relies more upon the dignity of his calling than on modern business methods, and the humor of the story derives as much from ineffectual pomposity as venal materialism. Kernan's pretensions are signified by his clothes; although in frequent financial embarrassment, he is never seen "without a silk hat of some decency and a pair of gaiters. By grace of these two articles of clothing, he said, a man could always pass muster." As this quotation illustrates, the narrative itself takes on an appropriately pompous tone: the pub manager begins, for instance, to "narrate" the facts of Kernan's fall to the plodding provincial policeman, who makes "ready to indite" them in his notebook.

This self-importance continues splendidly in the bedroom scene. Kernan is fallen man, literally in his accident in the pub, financially in his declining business, theologically in his absence from the Church for twenty years. His friends conspire to "make a new man of him," by inveigling him into a religious retreat. Their discussion of Catholic history and doctrine is however so full of error, hearsay, and half-truths that to "wash the pot" may be more difficult than Cunningham thinks. Nevertheless, his imposing misinformation has the desired effect of building up "the vast image of the Church in the minds of his hearers," and Kernan agrees to join "the retreat business."

His qualms are quickly soothed on entering the Jesuit Church in Gardiner Street, for he feels at home among the pawnbrokers and money-lenders. Nor is the sermon, preaching of worldliness, Mammon, and spiritual accountancy, likely to shake him out of his former paths. High above the altar is a "distant speck of red light," the lamp which signifies the presence of the Blessed Sacrament. Closer to hand shines the red face of Father Purdon, named after the most notorious street in Dublin's red-light district. Prostitution can take many forms.

XII

"The Dead" holds a special place in the collection, not merely by virtue of its concluding position, but because it was written later than the other stories, when Joyce's attitude to Dublin and his fellow countrymen seemed to have softened. For these reasons the story has been seen as a test case for the tone and meaning of the book as a whole. Does Gabriel Conroy's vision of a universal snowstorm at the end of the story represent his and the other Dubliners' ultimate inconsequentiality, or is it the occasion of an epiphany that will help him to reinterpret and reconstruct his life? Our answer to this will depend upon our view of Conroy, and the way in which Joyce has shaped his material.

The story pivots on a series of oppositions: outside/inside; cold snow/party warmth; past/present; Gabriel's mother/Gabriel's wife; town/country; Europe/Ireland; statues/the living, and is pervaded with references to death. Conroy enters "fringed" with snow, like the statues with which he will be associated. It immediately becomes evident that this is a man who is acutely and painfully self-aware, and who finds it difficult to act with emotional spontaneity. If Mr Duffy lives "at a little distance from his body," Gabriel lives at a little distance from his feelings, and this lack of ultimate authenticity results in a recurrent desire to escape into the snow outside, and an habitual tendency to overreact in social and emotional situations. A characteristic pattern of behavior divulges itself in his awkward reaction to Lily the caretaker's daughter, and repeats itself in his response to Gretta's teasing about galoshes, to the imagined reception of his speech, to Miss Ivors' criticism, and finally to his wife's revelation about her youthful admirer. His uncertainty manifests itself in his physical behavior—he is constantly blushing, reddening, patting his tie, and adjusting his clothes—and also in the text which registers his hesitancy in conditional syntactical structures.

His opening encounter with Lily is characteristic. Her retort to his affable if conventional and condescending inquiry about her love life, that the "men that is now is only all palaver and what they can get out of you," causes a curious reaction: "Gabriel coloured as if he felt he had made a mistake." Most people realize they have made a mistake, and blush accordingly; Gabriel's reactions are so self-conscious that he cannot make this direct response. The syntax registers conditionally the uncertain response to his unintentional gaffe, and we shall find the "as if" construction repeated several times in the course of the story. The rawness of Lily's experience has broken through the conventional phrases with which Gabriel insulates himself against reality, and his solution to his ensuing discomfort is to resort to money. He overreacts by over-tipping Lily, as later he will over-tip the cab driver and, at a crucial moment in his bedroom conversation with Gretta, turn aside to tell her "in a false voice" of his loan to Freddy Malins. "You are a very generous person" she tells him on that occasion, but the end of the story will reveal that truly "generous tears" can only come with a larger generosity of spirit.

Just as T. S. Eliot's Prufrock uses clothes as a defense, so does Gabriel: "Still discomposed by the girl's bitter and sudden retort," he tries to dispel the gloom it causes "by arranging his cuffs and the bows of his tie." His glasses are most significant in this respect; scintillating restlessly, "the polished lenses and the bright gilt rims ... screened his delicate and restless eyes." Gabriel's life is a continually defeated attempt to screen his delicate restlessness: by glasses, by galoshes, by phrase-making, by over-tipping. For if his nervousness is caused by a lack of center and self-confidence, this arises not merely from emotional diffidence, but also from a sense of social and cultural displacement. Later he will tell of his grandfather, a "very pompous old gentleman" who rode out to a military review only to find his social pretensions confounded when his horse, taken from the mill, walked round and round a statue of William III. Gabriel has enough intelligence and distance to be able to turn this story to anecdotal account, but at a symbolic level not much has changed in three generations: he, no less than his grandfather, seems trapped by pretension and deracination in an aimless circling of alien totems.

His uneasiness continually stumbles against the gradations of social status in which his world is set, but he is no vulgar snob. Although aware of his intellectual superiority to most of those at the party, this does not give him grounds for self-congratulation: rather it multiplies the possibilities of striking the wrong note. He worries about his speech not because it may fail, or be unintelligible, but because of the way it may reflect back on him: "He would only make himself ridiculous by quoting poetry to them which they could not understand. They would think that he was airing his superior education." This precipitates an immediate and characteristically exaggerated crisis of confidence: "He would fail with them just as he had failed with the girl in the pantry. He had taken up a wrong tone. His whole speech was a mistake from first to last, an utter failure." Thus, on no evidence except his own self-doubt, he convinces himself that his audience will find him insufferable, and this prospect fuels a headlong flight into extreme and absolute self-abnegation: "His *whole* speech was a mistake *from first to last*, an *utter failure*."

Gabriel's uncertainties are accentuated by women. Behind them all is the shadow of his mother, straight-laced, intellectual, non-musical, urban, ambitious, and snobbish and thus contrasting at every point with Gretta. She opposed his marriage on social grounds and this continues to rankle; not least because Gabriel still half agrees with her: when Miss Ivors asks him if Gretta is from Connacht, he replies shortly and evasively that "Her people are."

Miss Ivors exacerbates not only his emotional and social uncertainties but also doubts about his national, cultural, and political identity. She pretends to scold him for reviewing in the Unionist *Daily Express* but, as the recent discussion about galoshes has shown, Gabriel is far too unsure of himself to be able to deal with teasing, and her needling provokes the full suite of his nervous reactions: "Gabriel coloured and was about to knit his brows, as if he did not understand ... A look of perplexity appeared on Gabriel's face ... Gabriel glanced right and left nervously and tried to keep his good humour under the ordeal which was making a blush invade his forehead." Perplexity appears, blushes invade—the syntax once again reveals Gabriel as the site rather than the author of his own sensations. Finally he cracks, overreacting with the retort that he is "Sick of my own country, sick of it!" and Miss Ivors, conscious that she has pushed him too far, makes her peace and leaves. He continues to brood upon the exchange, now detecting a malicious intent to expose him in the way he most fears ("She had tried to make him ridiculous before people"), refusing to acknowledge that it is his own outburst, an exaggerated response to his crisis of identity, which has made him act foolishly. As a consequence of this encounter he decides to use his speech to contrast the "gracious" past with the "hypereducated generation that is growing up," and the theme of past against present is caught up in the discussion between Browne and D'Arcy about singers. Gabriel's speech does indeed deal with the past, sentimentalizing it in conventional terms that by the end of the story will seem ironically hollow and misplaced. His comments on "absent faces" in particular will return to haunt him: "Our path through life is strewn with many such sad memories: and were we to brood upon them always we could not find the heart to go on bravely with our work among the living." The past as a dynamic force rather than a sentimentalized construction begins to intrude into the story when Gabriel sees Gretta listening to "The Lass of Aughrim." Characteristically he tries to transpose this immediate sensory apprehension into a verbalized equivalent. Just as he has transformed the experience of Browning's poetry into a vaguely melodramatic formula ("One feels that one is listening to a thoughttormented music."), he now aestheticizes Gretta in terms of conventional Victorian genre painting as a symbol of "Distant Music." But her reaction to the song arouses him sexually, and his feelings intensify as they return to their hotel. He wants to make his wife forget the dull years (tacitly conceded) and remember the moments of ecstasy. From a man who has difficulty in reacting directly to personal relationships this is something, but once more he oscillates between verbal sublimation and an overcompensatory physicality. Phrase-making has been one of his defenses against the rawness of experience throughout the story (part of his discomfiture with Miss Ivors is the knowledge that "he could not risk a grandiose phrase with her"), and yet he is aware that the match between language and life is elusive. He recalls an early letter to Gretta in which he asked her "*Why is it that words like these seem to me so dull and cold? Is it because there is no word tender enough to be your name?*," and now this sentiment too comes back to him from the past "like distant music." Gabriel's very metaphor shows how his process of aestheticization involves the distancing, generalizing, and taming of primary experience.

The other side of this expansive verbal evasion is an overreactive roughness. Flushed with desire as he is, he fears "that diffidence was about to conquer him" and speaks abruptly. In a "fever of rage and desire" he has to restrain himself from "brutal language" and wants "to crush her body against his, to overmaster her." He asks her what she is thinking and finds to his astonishment that it is about "The Lass of Aughrim." She tells him of Michael Furey, and Gabriel's deep insecurity surfaces as jealousy. In the exchange in which he tries to make his wife confess that she was in love with Furey, Joyce skilfully employs two registers of language. Gabriel's is denotative, urban, educated, ironic: Gretta's connotative, its country idioms resistant to his reductive analysis. The interrogation diminishes Furey's immediate threat (Gabriel discovers that he is dead and was employed in the most ludicrously unromantic of utilities, a gasworks), but paradoxically increases his emotional presence. Against the naive sincerity of his wife's recollections, Gabriel's phrase-making and superciliousness shatter; he feels "humiliated by the failure of his irony and by the evocation of this figure from the dead ... A shameful consciousness of his own person assailed him. He saw himself as a ludicrous figure, acting as a pennyboy for his aunts, a nervous wellmeaning sentimentalist, orating to vulgarians and idealizing his own clownish lusts." Many critics see this moment as a pertinent and authentic insight by Gabriel into his true position, but it seems to be a characteristic overcompensation. There is nothing clownish about his lusts; his audience at the party were not simply vulgarians; and his speech, while not without sentimentality and orotundity, was a careful attempt to fulfil an annual ritual.

The revelation about Furey forces him, however, to think not about real or imagined social representations but about absolutes, to move beyond the oscillating polarities of pompous phrase-making and self-laceration into a fuller generosity of spirit. The crucial moment of insight comes when Gabriel asks if Furey died of consumption and receives the stark reply: "I think he died for me." The absoluteness of this statement, the quality of passion and commitment that it assumes, induces terror and a sense of invasion but he manages to pass beyond these to a measured contemplation of his life and limitations. He thinks of Gretta's aging, of aunt Julia who will soon be a shade, and imagines himself trying to comfort Kate, casting about "for some words that might console her," and finding "only lame and useless ones." Language, phrase-making, is not enough. Beneath and beyond the nervous restlessness of his own existence he glimpses the larger cycle of life and death, which throws his own febrile attempts at self-assertion into relief. At last truly "generous" tears can fill his hitherto screened eyes.

Is the end positive or negative? These polarities are too crude for Joyce. In this story he moves towards the cyclical view of history that informs *Ulysses* and *Finnegans Wake*. Gabriel's epiphany is positive in that it has brought him up against the inadequacy of his own locutions and fragile sense of identity. Against the intensity of passion and the inevitability of death his own oversensitive reactions, social confusions, and intellectual pretensions shrink to their proper perspective. But how his future will be altered by this insight lies outside the story, just as much as the consequences of Stephen's meeting with Bloom lie outside the narrative of *Ulysses*. Gabriel's proposed "journey westward" is ambiguous in destination: it may refer to his passage towards death, or it may indicate the discovery of securer and more sustaining roots through an acceptance of a larger and more authentic culture. By the time we reach the end of the story these two possibilities are seen to be not alternatives but complementary.

John S. Kelly

SELECT BIBLIOGRAPHY

Books on Joyce are now so numerous that only those which are devoted mainly or exclusively to *Dubliners* can be included here. Full lists of essays and studies are to be found in Robert A. Deming's *A Bibliography of James Joyce Studies* (2nd ed., 1977), and Thomas Jackson Rice's *James Joyce: A Guide to Research* (1982).

The standard biography of Joyce is, of course, by Richard Ellmann, revised for Oxford University Press in 1982. The most easily available volume of Joyce's letters was also edited by Ellmann, under the title *Selected Letters of James Joyce*, Viking, New York, and Faber, London, 1975.

Textual materials for *Dubliners* have been published in the *James Joyce Archive*, ed. Michael Groden, Garland, New York, 1978 (*Archive* volumes [4]–[6], editors Hans Walter Gabler and Michael Groden).

Useful annotated editions of *Dubliners* for the student are the 1969 Viking Critical Library edition of text, criticism, and notes, edited by Robert Scholes and A. Walton Litz; and the 1992 (British) Penguin edition, edited by Terence Brown. Other annotations may be found in Don Gifford, *Joyce Annotated*, University of California Press, 1982. The only previous edited text is that prepared by Robert Scholes, first published in America by Viking and in England by Jonathan Cape in 1967. It is also the text of the Viking Critical Library edition of 1969, as well as of the 1992 Penguin edition.

Critical Books and Essays

Adams, Robert M., *Surface and Symbol* (1962).
—, *James Joyce: Common Sense and Beyond* (1966).
Attridge, Derek (ed.), *The Cambridge Companion to James Joyce* (1990).

Beck, Warren, *Joyce's "Dubliners"* (1969).

Beja, Morris (ed.), *James Joyce: "Dubliners" and "A Portrait of the Artist as a Young Man": A Casebook* (1973).

Blotner, Joseph L., "'Ivy Day in the Committee Room': death without resurrection," *Perspective* 9 (Summer 1957), pp. 210–17.

Brandabur, Edward, *A Scrupulous Meanness* (1971).

Brown, Homer Obed, *James Joyce's Early Fiction* (1972).

Ellmann, Richard, *James Joyce* (revised edition, 1982).

—, and Ellsworth Mason (eds.), *The Critical Writings of James Joyce* (1959).

Garrett, Peter K. (ed.), *Twentieth Century Interpretations of "Dubliners"* (1968).

Ghiselin, Brewster, "The Unity of Joyce's *Dubliners*," *Accent* 16 (1956), pp. 75–88, 196–213; in Garrett.

Gifford, Don, *Joyce Annotated: Notes for "Dubliners" and "A Portrait of the Artist as a Young Man"* (1982).

Gilbert, Stuart, and Richard Ellmann (eds.), *Letters of James Joyce* (3 Vols., 1957–1966).

Givens, Seon (ed.), *James Joyce: Two Decades of Criticism* (1948).

Goldberg, S. L., *James Joyce* (1962).

Goldman, Arnold, *The James Joyce Paradox* (1966).

Hart, Clive (ed.), *James Joyce's "Dubliners": Critical Essays* (1969).

Healey, George H., *The Complete Dublin Diary of Stanislaus Joyce* (1971).

Joyce, Stanislaus, *My Brother's Keeper* (1958).

—, "The background to *Dubliners*," *Listener*, 51 (25 March 1954), pp. 526–7.

Kelleher, John V., "Irish history and mythology in James Joyce's 'The Dead,'" *Review of Politics*, 27 (July 1965), pp. 414–33.

Kenner, Hugh, *Dublin's Joyce* (1956).

Levin, Harry, *James Joyce: A Critical Introduction* (1941).

Levin, Richard, and Charles Shattuck, "First Flight to Ithaca: A New Reading of Joyce's *Dubliners*" in Givens (1948).

Litz, A. Walton, *James Joyce* (1966).

Lyons, F. S. L., "James Joyce's Dublin," *Twentieth Century Studies* 4 (1970), pp. 6–25.

Magalaner, Marvin, *Time of Apprenticeship: The Fiction of Young James Joyce* (1959).

Ap Roberts, R. P., "'Araby' and the Palimpset of Criticism," *Antioch Review* XXVI (1966–7), pp. 469–89.

Scholes, Robert, "Some Observations on the Text of *Dubliners*: 'The Dead,'" and "Further Observations on the Text of *Dubliners*," in *Studies in Bibliography* XV (1962), pp. 191–205; XVII (1964), pp. 107–122.

—, "Grant Richards to Joyce," *Studies in Bibliography* XVI (1963), pp. 139–160.

—, and Richard Kain, *The Workshop of Daedalus* (1965).

Torchiana, Donald T., *Backgrounds for Joyce's "Dubliners"* (1986).

CHRONOLOGY

DATE	AUTHOR'S LIFE	LITERARY CONTEXT
1882	Joyce born, 2 February, Rathgar, Dublin.	Virginia Woolf born.
1884		
1886		
1888	Joyce starts at Clongowes Wood College.	
1890		Newman dies.
1891		Shaw: *Quintessence of Ibsenism.*
1893	Joyce goes to Belvedere College.	
1895		Wilde's trial and imprisonment.
1897		James: *What Maisie Knew.*
1899	Joyce goes to University College, Dublin.	
1900	Joyce's "Ibsen's New Drama" published in *Fortnightly Review.*	Conrad's *Lord Jim.*
1901	"The Day of the Rabblement."	
1902	"James Clarence Mangan." Joyce's first Paris trip and reviews.	
1903	Begins *Stephen Hero*. Mary Jane Joyce (Joyce's mother) dies.	
1904	Joyce writes *Portrait* sketch. Publishes earliest *Dubliners* stories. Elopement with Nora to Pola (Austro-Hungary).	Opening of Abbey Theatre in Dublin.
1905	Moves to Trieste. Son Giorgio born, 27 July. Suspends *Stephen Hero*.	
1906	Brief residence in Rome. First abortive attempt to publish *Dubliners.*	Samuel Beckett born. Ibsen dies.
1907	Moves back to Trieste. *Chamber Music* published. Daughter Lucia born, 26 July. Writes *The Dead.* Begins *A Portrait.* Essays on Irish politics in Trieste papers.	"Playboy" riots (Abbey Theatre).
1909	August and October–December, trips to Dublin. Letters to Nora written.	
1910	Second abortive attempt to publish *Dubliners.*	H. G. Wells: *The History of Mr. Polly.*
1911	Joyce lectures on Shakespeare in Trieste.	

First Oxford Chair of English.
Gladstone's First Home Rule Bill defeated.

Parnell dies.

Queen Victoria's Diamond Jubilee.
Second Boer War.

Founding of British Labour Party.

Queen Victoria dies.
Balfour's Education Act.

Further educational and social reform in Britain.

DATE	AUTHOR'S LIFE	LITERARY CONTEXT
1912	Last visit to Dublin.	Charlie Chaplin's first film.
1913		D. H. Lawrence: *Sons and Lovers.*
1914	*A Portrait* serialized in *The Egoist. Dubliners* published by Grant Richards. *Giacomo Joyce* written. *Exiles* composed.	*Des Imagistes: An Anthology.*
1915	Joyce moves to Zürich. Work on *Ulysses* resumed, 16 June. *Exiles* revised.	
1916	*A Portrait* published in America.	
1917	*A Portrait* published in Britain. *Ulysses* fair copy begun.	Yeats: *Wild Swans at Coole.* T. S. Eliot: *Prufrock and other Observations.*
1918	*Ulysses* serialization begins in *Little Review.* *Exiles* published.	
1920	Joyce moves to Paris. *Ulysses* serialization halted.	
1921		
1922	*Ulysses* published in Paris (February).	T. S. Eliot, *The Waste Land.*
1924	First section of *Work in Progress* ("Mamalujo") published in *Transatlantic Review* I.	
1925		G. B. Shaw awarded Nobel Prize. Yeats: *A Vision.* Eisenstein: *Battleship Potemkin.*
1926		
1927	*Pomes Penyeach* published.	Woolf: *To the Lighthouse.*
1928		
1929	*Our Examination* essays on *Work in Progress* published.	
1932	Lucia diagnosed "hebephrenic."	
1933		Leavis attacks *Work in Progress* in *Scrutiny.*
1934	*Ulysses* published in US.	
1936	*Ulysses* published in UK.	
1937		
1938		Beckett's *Murphy* published.
1939	*Finnegans Wake* published. Joyce moves to Zürich.	Brendan Behan arrested. Seamus Heaney born. W. B. Yeats dies.
1941	Joyce dies in Zürich at age fifty-nine.	Virginia Woolf dies.

World War I breaks out. Irish Home Rule passed but shelved.

Easter Rising in Dublin.

Conclusion of World War I. Partial franchise for women in Great Britain.
Irish rebel Con Markiewitz elected first British woman MP.

Irish Free State (excluding six counties) founded (December).

Baird demonstrates television picture.
Cinema "talkies."
Full suffrage for women in Great Britain.
Wall Street Crash.

De Valera's Fianna Fail takes office in Ireland.

Hitler becomes German *Führer.*
Abdication of Edward VIII.
New Irish constitution established.

Outbreak of World War II.

VINTAGE INTERNATIONAL

___	**The Fat Man in History** by Peter Carey	$10.00	0-679-74332-4
___	**The Tax Inspector** by Peter Carey	$11.00	0-679-73598-4
___	**Bullet Park** by John Cheever	$10.00	0-679-73787-1
___	**Falconer** by John Cheever	$10.00	0-679-73786-3
___	**Oh What a Paradise It Seems** by John Cheever	$8.00	0-679-73785-5
___	**The Wapshot Chronicle** by John Cheever	$11.00	0-679-73899-1
___	**The Wapshot Scandal** by John Cheever	$11.00	0-679-73900-9
___	**No Telephone to Heaven** by Michelle Cliff	$11.00	0-679-73942-4
___	**Age of Iron** by J. M. Coetzee	$10.00	0-679-73292-6
___	**Last Tales** by Isak Dinesen	$12.00	0-679-73640-9
___	**Out of Africa and Shadows on the Grass** by Isak Dinesen	$12.00	0-679-72475-3
___	**Seven Gothic Tales** by Isak Dinesen	$12.00	0-679-73641-7
___	**The Book of Daniel** by E. L. Doctorow	$10.00	0-679-73657-3
___	**Loon Lake** by E. L. Doctorow	$10.00	0-679-73625-5
___	**Ragtime** by E. L. Doctorow	$10.00	0-679-73626-3
___	**Welcome to Hard Times** by E. L. Doctorow	$10.00	0-679-73627-1
___	**World's Fair** by E. L. Doctorow	$11.00	0-679-73628-X
___	**Love, Pain, and the Whole Damn Thing** by Doris Dörrie	$9.00	0-679-72992-5
___	**The Assignment** by Friedrich Dürrenmatt	$7.95	0-679-72233-5
___	**Invisible Man** by Ralph Ellison	$10.00	0-679-72313-7
___	**Scandal** by Shusaku Endo	$10.00	0-679-72355-2
___	**Absalom, Absalom!** by William Faulkner	$9.95	0-679-73218-7
___	**As I Lay Dying** by William Faulkner	$9.00	0-679-73225-X
___	**Go Down, Moses** by William Faulkner	$10.00	0-679-73217-9
___	**The Hamlet** by William Faulkner	$10.00	0-679-73653-0
___	**Intruder in the Dust** by William Faulkner	$9.00	0-679-73651-4
___	**Light in August** by William Faulkner	$10.00	0-679-73226-8
___	**The Reivers** by William Faulkner	$10.00	0-679-74192-5
___	**The Sound and the Fury** by William Faulkner	$9.00	0-679-73224-1
___	**The Unvanquished** by William Faulkner	$9.00	0-679-73652-2
___	**The Good Soldier** by Ford Madox Ford	$10.00	0-679-72218-1
___	**Howards End** by E. M. Forster	$10.00	0-679-72255-6
___	**A Room With a View** by E. M. Forster	$9.00	0-679-72476-1
___	**Where Angels Fear to Tread** by E. M. Forster	$9.00	0-679-73634-4
___	**Christopher Unborn** by Carlos Fuentes	$12.95	0-679-73222-5
___	**The Story of My Wife** by Milán Füst	$8.95	0-679-72217-3
___	**The Story of a Shipwrecked Sailor** by Gabriel García Márquez	$9.00	0-679-72205-X
___	**The Tin Drum** by Günter Grass	$15.00	0-679-72575-X
___	**Claudius the God** by Robert Graves	$14.00	0-679-72573-3
___	**I, Claudius** by Robert Graves	$11.00	0-679-72477-X
___	**Aurora's Motive** by Erich Hackl	$7.95	0-679-72435-4
___	**Dispatches** by Michael Herr	$10.00	0-679-73525-9
___	**Walter Winchell** by Michael Herr	$9.00	0-679-73393-0
___	**The Swimming-Pool Library** by Alan Hollinghurst	$12.00	0-679-72256-4
___	**I Served the King of England** by Bohumil Hrabal	$10.95	0-679-72786-8

VINTAGE INTERNATIONAL

___ **An Artist of the Floating World** by Kazuo Ishiguro	$10.00	0-679-72266-1
___ **A Pale View of Hills** by Kazuo Ishiguro	$10.00	0-679-72267-X
___ **The Remains of the Day** by Kazuo Ishiguro	$11.00	0-679-73172-5
___ **Dubliners** by James Joyce	$10.00	0-679-73990-4
___ **A Portrait of the Artist as a Young Man** by James Joyce	$9.00	0-679-73989-0
___ **The Emperor** by Ryszard Kapuściński	$9.00	0-679-72203-3
___ **Shah of Shahs** by Ryszard Kapuściński	$9.00	0-679-73801-0
___ **The Soccer War** by Ryszard Kapuściński	$10.00	0-679-73805-3
___ **China Men** by Maxine Hong Kingston	$10.00	0-679-72328-5
___ **Tripmaster Monkey** by Maxine Hong Kingston	$11.00	0-679-72789-2
___ **The Woman Warrior** by Maxine Hong Kingston	$10.00	0-679-72188-6
___ **Barabbas** by Pär Lagerkvist	$8.00	0-679-72544-X
___ **The Plumed Serpent** by D. H. Lawrence	$12.00	0-679-73493-7
___ **The Virgin & the Gipsy** by D. H. Lawrence	$10.00	0-679-74077-5
___ **The Radiance of the King** by Camara Laye	$9.95	0-679-72200-9
___ **Canopus in Argos** by Doris Lessing	$20.00	0-679-74184-4
___ **The Fifth Child** by Doris Lessing	$9.00	0-679-72182-7
___ **The Drowned and the Saved** by Primo Levi	$10.00	0-679-72186-X
___ **The Real Life of Alejandro Mayta** by Mario Vargas Llosa	$12.00	0-679-72478-8
___ **My Traitor's Heart** by Rian Malan	$10.95	0-679-73215-2
___ **Man's Fate** by André Malraux	$11.00	0-679-72574-1
___ **Buddenbrooks** by Thomas Mann	$14.00	0-679-73646-8
___ **Confessions of Felix Krull** by Thomas Mann	$11.00	0-679-73904-1
___ **Death in Venice and Seven Other Stories** by Thomas Mann	$10.00	0-679-72206-8
___ **Doctor Faustus** by Thomas Mann	$13.00	0-679-73905-X
___ **The Magic Mountain** by Thomas Mann	$14.00	0-679-73645-X
___ **Blood Meridian** by Cormac McCarthy	$11.00	0-679-72875-9
___ **Suttree** by Cormac McCarthy	$12.00	0-679-73632-8
___ **The Captive Mind** by Czeslaw Milosz	$10.00	0-679-72856-2
___ **The Decay of the Angel** by Yukio Mishima	$12.00	0-679-72243-2
___ **Runaway Horses** by Yukio Mishima	$12.00	0-679-72240-8
___ **Spring Snow** by Yukio Mishima	$12.00	0-679-72241-6
___ **The Temple of Dawn** by Yukio Mishima	$12.00	0-679-72242-4
___ **Such a Long Journey** by Rohinton Mistry	$11.00	0-679-73871-1
___ **Hopeful Monsters** by Nicholas Mosley	$13.00	0-679-73929-7
___ **Cities of Salt** by Abdelrahman Munif	$16.00	0-394-75526-X
___ **Hard-Boiled Wonderland and the End of the World** by Haruki Murakami	$12.00	0-679-74346-4
___ **The Spyglass Tree** by Albert Murray	$10.00	0-679-73085-0
___ **Ada, or Ardor** by Vladimir Nabokov	$15.00	0-679-72522-9
___ **Bend Sinister** by Vladimir Nabokov	$11.00	0-679-72727-2
___ **The Defense** by Vladimir Nabokov	$11.00	0-679-72722-1
___ **Despair** by Vladimir Nabokov	$11.00	0-679-72343-9
___ **The Enchanter** by Vladimir Nabokov	$9.00	0-679-72886-4